IQ : Damnation

Carl Illingworth

MAPLE
PUBLISHERS

IQ: Damnation

Author: Carl Illingworth

Copyright © Carl Illingworth (2022)

The right of Carl Illingworth to be identified as author of this work has been asserted by the author in accordance with section 77 and 78 of the Copyright, Designs and Patents Act 1988.

First Published in 2022

ISBN 978-1-915492-35-7 (Paperback)
      978-1-915492-36-4 (Hardback)
      978-1-915492-37-1 (E-Book)

Book cover design and Book layout by:
    White Magic Studios
    www.whitemagicstudios.co.uk

Published by:
    Maple Publishers
    1 Brunel Way,
    Slough,
    SL1 1FQ, UK
    www.maplepublishers.com

CONTENTS

Chapter 1

A Technological Conflict

Morathos walked briskly through the smoggy streets of Doradheim. He deliberately refrained from lifting his hooded head despite the hordes of scurrying pedestrians that would frequently barge into him. The continuous booming hum of flying vehicles above and the rich oily metallic stench in the air would persist in tormenting him in ways that appeared less apparent to most civilians.

He started to quicken his pace, reluctantly peering over his shoulder and diverting his course down an alleyway where he hugged onto the corner of a wall and waited for a hovering mechanical spheroid to pass. Once he was convinced it had, he proceeded back in the opposite direction where he caught a glimpse of a parading droid with mustard shoulder plates forcing him to swiftly alter his route again.

He continued on, jostling his way through the collective swarms of mechanised and biological beings until he reached the top of a black steel stairway that descended to the dingy underbelly of the mechanical metropolis. It was relatively secluded in the slum, but he kept his pace, so as to avoid the beggars that would often tug at your ankles in passing.

He soon came to a narrow snicket that he squeezed his way through, coming out into an enclosure at the other side. He pulled on the handle of a steel plate that lay on the floor, revealing a well. He descended the ladder, closing the plate behind him. Once he reached the bottom, he placed his palm on a sophisticated holographic screen.

"Welcome back, Morathos," a digitalised voice called.

He entered his vast laboratory and lifted off his hood, flicking back his inky fringe. "I wouldn't have been back so soon. But my encounter with the DSA was a little too close for my liking."

"I am detecting increased DSA activity in the city. I have completed the programming of some updates for your laboratory's security system, just as an added measure."

Morathos squinted his hickory eyes. "This is the one place I'm safe; but you still can't be too careful."

"I strongly doubt that they will be capable of breaching your system."

"Let's hope you're right. Anyway, I'm off out to do some research for my next invention."

"Do be sure to keep your face concealed. The DSA are always updating the face recognition technology in their droids."

"Sure," he said, pulling his neck warmer over his nose and lifting his hood, before making his way to the train station.

On the back of the seat in front of him, was a holographic screen which featured a pre-recorded presentation. "Welcome to Doradheim — the world's most advanced city," the digital voice said, "Here are some fascinating facts about this marvellous city: the colossal metropolis consists of more than four thousand square miles of urban land, but thanks to self-driving mag-lev trains like this one, anywhere within the metropolis is reachable in minutes. Built on the vast open Canadian plains, it allows plenty of space for expansion..." Morathos had reached his stop and disembarked.

He entered the computer science research centre but there was nobody at the desk when he arrived. Despite ringing the bell several times, his efforts seemed to be unnoticed. He huffed loudly, then started to tap his fingers on the desk. His eyes wandered around the lobby and were led to a broadcast on a holographic projection beside him.

"Joining us on the show today, we have Doctor Lucius — an expert in human neurology. He claims technology is crippling our planet, but many oppose his views; such as Mr. Breinstalker — a technological engineer."

Breinstalker's jaw was twitching to get things underway. "You would have to be a fool to not see how our technological development has progressed over the last hundred years. We've made leaps and bounds. Man mostly works in science, engineering and research, now. Health care and emergency services are mostly machine operated; robots are capable of accurately diagnosing and offering treatment much quicker than a human would ever be able to."

The doctor looked ready to bite his hand off. "At the cost of our own ignorance to natural life. What we have created is at the expense of our very own planet, now suffocating in the toxins of our destructive means. We just can't stop to appreciate what nature provided us with, and insist on continuing to tamper with it. What use will all this be if it is to neglect our very home?"

"It's the year 2170 for crying out loud! I can't believe such lunacy still exists. There's always one straggler to spoi-"

"Machines certainly have dominated the Earth over the last century," the android presenter butted in, "and once our planet becomes uninhabitable, we will have the resources to reach *other* planets."

"Yes," said Lucius, "but a machine has no heart; not a single speck of understanding of the human sensory experience and what it stands for. Now, humanity itself is poisoned by this belief of mechanical dominance. We're just numbing everything with robotics. How ignorant and selfish of us to destroy our very home and just move somewhere else to then go and suck the life out of that planet also!"

"Mortality rates are lower than ever," said the engineer. "People have more freedom to enjoy a luxurious life whilst machines do their chores for them. Stress levels have plummeted; illness is near non-existent; people are living longer on average; robotic limbs and organs have saved thousands of lives. How can you say technology is destructive?"

"You're clearly not looking at the bigger picture and only thinking selfishly about those of us fortunate enough — or perhaps, *unfortunate*, depending on how you look at it — to afford such biomechanical upgrades, whilst neglecting all other life that needs to exist to live in harmony with humans. We may be living longer right now, but only in an artificial sense and at the cost of the inevitable destruction of nature. And you're wrong. There are still a lot of illnesses developing from the hostility of the conditions we live in, but we're just covering them up recklessly. What we're doing to humanity is essentially no different to contaminating a dead animal with emulsifiers and putting it in a tin to preserve its shelf life!"

"You tell the cyborgs that. Ha-ha. They'll laugh you out of town. Besides, this isn't the nineteenth century. I thought evolution would have done away with these deluded naturalists by now... but it seems, not quite."

"That is not what evolution wants for mankind. Why would it jeopardise nature so extremely? We'd be nothing without other life; we'd have nothing without nature..."

Morathos had heard enough and had turned towards the exit of the centre when he heard a man's voice call him. "Hey. Sorry to keep you waiting. Can I help?" There emerged a short fellow adopting a cocky stance. Several of his shirt's buttons were unfastened.

"What can you tell me about the fundamental programming of our modern machines?" asked Morathos.

"Well, it's not so different from how it has always been," he said, "Just a basic sequence of ones and zeros. Only, now we are able to create more sophisticated sequences and input more complex commands. We have pushed beyond the boundaries of quantum computing and have successfully taught an AI how to replicate simulations, with precision, of subatomic interactions. We really have developed sensationally with it. We're on the brink of being able to program a computer to learn how to regenerate its own energy consumption — something we thought never possible. It would be a very efficient procedure indeed."

"I only hope it's distributed more wisely than some of the modern technology of today."

"How so?"

"You only have to look at the dystopia around you to see what I mean."

The technician exaggerated a sigh. "Don't tell me you're on that naive wagon of Anti-machs?"

"I'm in the early stages of creating a revolutionary design; something that will put an end to these constraints we are all drowning in; something that will awaken us from our ignorance. I know there is a better way of life than this. Why everyone is so brainwashed to believe there isn't, just baffles me."

"What are you talking about? This is Doradheim — the mechanical capital of the world. The most remarkable metropolis ever built. Why did you even bother coming here?"

"That's exactly what the cyborgs want us to think. They're manipulating us with their own technology. I came here to further clarify my fears of where we're headed. And it seems my trip wasn't wasted."

"What's the matter, this city too overwhelming for you so you've got to act like the big man, chopping and changing everything? Don't like it, then what are you doing here?"

"This is my home and ever since I can remember, I've resented it. I didn't choose to be born here, but something keeps me nonetheless. I guess that resentment makes me want to make changes, but I'm becoming increasingly impatient with the ignorance of its people!" Morathos started to elevate his tone. His face flushed and he stormed off.

The technician sniggered. "So naive. Good luck with your... invention, ha!"

I know there's a way we can use computer technology more wisely without jeopardising nature so much. He tried to patronise me, Morathos convinced himself on his return journey. *I'll show him!*

He tried to contain his rage, opting to, instead, let it out in his laboratory. But it appeared that his moment of fury had distracted him and caused him to take a riskier path. He returned to find his home surrounded by drones and androids armed with stun guns. "He has to return at some point," one of them remarked.

He darted down an alley out of their sight and looked for an alternative route where all entrances except one were barricaded. But one of the droids spotted him. "Halt! I advise you to comply immediately. This is the Doradheim Security Agency. Resistance will not end favourably for you." Morathos kept running until the droid lost him in the crowds of pedestrians and he made his way back into the secret hatchway of his laboratory. The droid reunited with the others. "Send your report to the president," it said.

In the epicentre of the city stood a building which towered the rest. It was the presidential complex, comprised of various sectors and constituencies — one of which was the biology research centre. There, the head professor made his way through its many corridors on his routine commute. At the very top of the soaring high-rise stood a gangling and stocky bionic figure. He brushed his goatee whilst he awaited the professor's arrival. "Professor Horuzokh," said the distorted mechanised voice.

"President Vynzuth." The professor squirmed as his thick glasses fogged up. "We have detected the outbreak of a new pathogen, but I'm confident my team has the resources to exterminate it."

The president rubbed his shaven dome. "What exactly are we dealing with? We've effectively dealt with a whole scope of infection and disease now. I'm sure this won't be an exception."

The scientist removed his spectacles and gave them a wipe before placing them back over his pointy nose and dusted off his lab coat. "This looks like a new strain of parasite that can infect the digestive tract. We have already begun to build mechanisms to counteract it. Our computers are currently generating genetic modification protocols, as well as integrated bionics. Soon we will have developed a way to completely remove the entire human digestive system."

"Excellent." The president placed his hand over his metallic abdomen. "It never served me any good and I certainly don't need it now."

"Precisely." The professor's voice squeaked a little. "Machinery will always outlive a cellular structure and I am determined to keep all pathogens at bay with this technology, even if it kills me! After all, that is entirely how we stopped cancer."

"Indeed."

"There will always be outbreaks as we drift farther away from nature. But I am confident we will have the technology at our disposal to keep ahead of the game."

Vynzuth gestured for Horuzokh to leave, then folded his arms. "I'm getting a report back from the DSA droids. We will discuss more later." The professor nodded and strolled out.

An android hologram then appeared before the president. "We're getting closer to finding the whereabouts of Morathos Reina."

"Excellent news. I'm aware that he resides somewhere in the slum of the Lower Eastern Quarters," said Vynzuth, pressing his palm on his rugged chin.

For the next few days, Morathos continued to study and monitor his system's protocols until he could establish some sort of pattern. But he became so fixated that he abandoned his physical needs and could no longer concentrate. Frustration overcame him that disrupted his advances. Unable to make more progress, he proceeded to examine what he had so far constructed. It was a fine, but long antenna that pulsated. He picked it up and gripped it firmly in his left hand, widening his eyes and clenching his jaw. He grabbed the other end of it, feeling an urge to snap the device in half but managed to discipline himself and put it down. "What is happening to me?" He paused for a moment, took several breaths and allowed himself time to decompress.

"Perhaps you should take a break, Morathos," said the mechanised voice.

"There's no time. I need to concentrate." He resisted the urge to push the computer's deactivation switch.

"I'm detecting vast numbers of DSA droids in the vicinity," it said.

"As long as they can't bypass the system, all should be fine. ...Perhaps I *should* take that break." He made his way upstairs into his apartment but was soon met with a firm knock on the door. "This is the Doradheim Security Agency. Open up!"

It was only a matter of time before they'd find me. His mind dictated that he made his way back into his laboratory.

"They're probably going to ransack your home," said the computer.

"They won't be able to find me as long as I stay down here."

The DSA droids burst their way in and began to raid the property in search of any information but were left disappointed. Morathos had been cautious and was sure to not leave any traces in their access. "Nothing here," one of them said. "What now?"

"Let's report to Mr. Bane and just continue to survey the area," said the commander. "He has to come back sooner or later."

Chapter 2

Part-Exchange

Outside, acidic raindrops plummeted from the darkened Doradheian skies, punishing those who weren't protected. In the slums, men and women scarpered through the streets, many in soaked and worn clothing, trying to shield themselves from the bitter sting.

"Beat it, scavengers!" one of the shopkeepers yelled at a group of people who were trying to take shelter. He pushed them out of his shop. "You're disrupting my business! Can't you take your sorry selves elsewhere?"

One of them looked at him, clasping his hands. "Please. It's torturous out there. I have no home, no shelter."

"I don't care. If you're not buying anything, then beat it."

"I beg you to spare me some food," another cried. "My children are starving and I have no job."

"Not my problem, lady."

Another man piped up. "Technology took *my* job. And it's taking away our resources."

"Too bad," said the shopkeeper. "That's just the way it is. Now get out of my shop." He shoved him forcefully out of the door, simultaneously giving a friendly greet to a paying customer.

"It's alright for those filthy rich cyborgs," said a woman trying to barge her way into a shop. "They've got all this fancy anti-acid shielding technology and barely any exposed human flesh, while we're all down here dying."

"Yeah. Survival of the richest. That's all this forsaken city is about," said another man. "They think just because they're incorporating ways to avoid needing food, *we* don't need to eat either."

"I can't remember the last time I saw sunlight," said the woman, "And all this artificial light is by no means a healthy compensation."

"Not to mention all the radiation leaks from a severely compromised magnetic field."

"Yeah. But they never tell you about these things. They only brag about their technological progress and cover up their issues with bionics."

"Probably because they'd *rather* ignore it."

"Would you mind? I'm trying to run a business here, not a gossip house," the shopkeeper yelled, shoving more of them out.

Morathos continued with his calculations and experiments, desperately trying to get his design to work. But it seemed every time he thought he had cracked the code, he was knocked back to the drawing board when his final calculations didn't add up.

Several months went by. He did not leave his laboratory. DSA androids remained on the premises. Sooner or later, he would have to surface for food, as he was very much against using the services of machinery. He strained, unable to fight his urge to hammer his fists into his desk. *I'm so... exhausted*, he thought. *But I mustn't stop. I mustn't lose momentum. The DSA are ruthless.* The more he tried to reason, the more he couldn't fend off the inevitable. *Perhaps I ought to sneak out.*

He reluctantly got into his disguise and opened the hatchway, following it out to his secret exit. He tried to blend in and stay hidden under his hood, quickly darting down the one alleyway that seemed clear. As he got to the end of the alley, an android had made its way to the opening and noticed him. It raised its gun. "Halt!" it commanded.

Morathos quickly darted behind a building and reached for the secret hatchway cover, making his way inside. He slammed it shut just as the android made its way around the corner and attempted to fire at him. The bullets pelted into the reinforced iron covering and ricocheted off it as Morathos continued on through the passageway. The machine tried to barge through the metal, but soon realised it could not remove it and jolted off to regroup with the others and report to its commander.

Soon after, multiple bots and spherical drones made their way down to the iron covering to inspect it, but neither could find any way in. Morathos made his way safely inside his laboratory and slumped himself down uttering a deep exhalation.

A gruesome looking cyborg stood before Horuzokh, his left eyebrow twitching as sparks flickered inside his empty eye socket.

The professor grinned at him. "If it isn't Magnetus Bane himself. Chief executive of the Doradheim Security Agency. It's been a while."

"Am I going to have to go and fetch him myself?! He's really testing my patience!"

"Mine also," said Horuzokh. "For too long he has been an irritation to us. I don't doubt that a specimen of his DNA will be most useful."

"He's playing a dangerous game indeed."

"Oh, by the way, the president said he would be most delighted if you could stop by his office for a catch up."

The cyborg straightened his dull jacket. "There's no time. I must proceed to my engineering team. It seems my androids are looking a little rusty." He fled off to his headquarters to confront his lead engineer. "Reginald Forathorn!" he called. "Why are my androids lagging?"

A slim cyborg with mousy blonde hair, shaven like a military cadet emerged. He was wearing a dark body suit, his icy blue gaze fixed on Magnetus. "I'll get right to work on their upgrades, boss. But we'll have to call them all back from duty and place them in their charging stations."

"Very well. We will deal with Morathos soon enough: but without the proper upgrades, they won't be as effective. See to it that these upgrades are executed swiftly and precisely."

"It will only take seconds to upload, just as long as we have them in their vaults. We could upload wirelessly but many of them are out of range and it may take longer or cause more complications."

"Well, let's not waste another minute. Call them back!"

Reginald promptly pressed a grey button on the panel in front of him as the colossal vaults opened, stretching for acres. Large flying cargo carriers landed across multiple locations of the city as hordes of androids entered them before they all collectively touched down at the headquarters. They slotted into tracks that swiftly transported them directly to their stations and locked them in place. He then headed off to another room and began inputting some commands on a large device that started the uploading process.

"Upload commencing," a feminine computerised voice announced. Within seconds, the voice called out again. "Upload complete. All units are now at optimal level." With that, the androids were soon shipped back out and deployed at various locations as they continued their scouting objectives.

Morathos was so deeply lost in his experimentations that he had no idea what was unfolding. He continued trying to wrap his head around where he could be going wrong and started to feel more strain. A shower of doubt began to flood his mind that he hadn't experienced in a long time. *To fail at the last hurdle, after coming so close...* But he continued to deny his doubts, pushing himself beyond his limitations. "There's no way I could have got this wrong!" he cried. "All my prior calculations are making sense; everything looks in perfect order and yet the final piece of the puzzle just doesn't seem to be fitting somehow."

On the upper levels meanwhile, a large group of protesters had gathered outside the president's headquarters all marching around, chanting, with banners that read:

Robots Robbed Us of Our Rights!

The chanting got louder as the group stormed towards the entrances of the building. "Robots robbed us of our rights, give us back our own lives!" The group were well known across Doradheim and went by the name of the Anti-machs, a minority group — mostly middle class — that strongly opposed the city's technological advancement.

They stomped into the headquarters, chanting and protesting and vandalising the interior like hooligans. Every time, it would end miserably for them, but they persisted in returning. The leader of the mob shouted, "Who wants to live like a fraud? Who wants to reject their humanity in exchange for a lifeless machine? That's right, those who are poisoned and deluded; those fakes with too much wealth and status; those greedy, power-hungry cyborgs!"

"Deal with those pesky insects," said Vynzuth to his guard droids.

"They think they can just suffocate us in this inhospitable city. But they're forgetting we have fight in us. Our urge to make a stand for freedom and putting them in their places, the adrenaline, the determination. That's what keeps us standing," said the leader of the mob.

They charged to the stairway and proceeded on up, despite knowing that that was going to be as far as they would get before a jolt of electricity surged through them, sending them all flying backwards. Stunned and shaken, they were escorted out of the premises as androids swooped in and had them shipped off to their homes. Bots came to clean up the mess and put everything back in order. Some Doradheians believed the president got some sort of entertainment out of the whole ordeal and would often speculate, *"Why would he keep letting them get so far inside in the first place?"*

More cargo holds touched down around the metropolis as the machinery that manufactured them drastically increased in its productivity daily. Wave upon wave of the mechanical constructs poured out into the city streets, scouting and capturing the panel's next research project. Some were even programmed with enhanced curiosity that would make them that much more effective in their role.

Some people were so far swayed by this movement that they welcomed the droids and willingly allowed them to take them away from their suffering. Some screamed out to be the guinea pig for Horuzokh's tests just to escape the strain of watching the misery unfold around them. Deep down, they probably wanted to be free, but they couldn't see a way out. So, they opted to be cut from their ties and submit to the cyborgs.

Bots fled into the laboratories with hordes of the public under their command; some writhing in unbearable pain from the intoxication. Professor Horuzokh looked on in sheer delight, his eyes widening. "Yes," he screeched. "Come, my specimens. Come!"

He was consulted by one of his head biologists. "Good news, boss," he said. "We have just this moment, placed the final piece of the puzzle. After countless testing, research and dedication, I bring you the answer to all these people's pain." He pulled out a prototype of a complex system of wires.

Just then a man, clenched up in agony, came into the biologist's work station, escorted by several droids who hoisted him onto the table. He let out a vicious scream as his brittle bones cracked from the impact. "The radiation in the air has made its way into his bone marrow and has started to corrode it," the biologist explained.

"Don't worry," said Horuzokh, "all your pain will soon end." He swiftly drove a needle into the man's ribs to sedate him.

The biologist began making deep incisions all over his body before presenting him with a machine that had a fine nozzle and a mechanical arm; it had very sophisticated and precise programming. The arm moved in on him as the nozzle fired tiny lasers into his incisions, completely scorching his nerve cells. The biologist then began inputting some commands on his computer and started to thread his complex design of wires through a small opening in the nozzle head. It then started a series of intricate actions that weaved the wiring into his muscle fibres and the rest of his anatomy. The man lying unconscious on the table, would be the first human to have a synthetic nervous system implanted into him. He would never feel an ounce of pain again. Of course, he would never really feel *anything* else again either.

Horuzokh thought it was genius, as did the majority of the panel and the governors, as they all stroked their egos. Had the man still been able to experience gratitude, he too would have been grateful for no longer having to endure such continuous torture. His brain would now be nothing more than a CPU inputting commands to its network of wires.

The man awoke, no longer in pain. But now he expressed no emotion at all. He simply got up and made his way home as if nothing had ever happened. He had no conscious awareness that his brain had been reprogrammed to serve the president's schemes.

The biologist gave Horuzokh a nod and the professor could not contain his joy as a twisted smile exhibited itself across his face. "Success!" he cried. "Proceed with the rest."

More droids flooded in. "Right away, sir!"

"There is one other problem." Horuzokh acknowledged. "It is beginning to become quite the thorn in my side." He wanted to establish a way to remove the need for blood and exchange the entire human circulatory system for an artificial substitute. Of course, with the removal of most organs, blood wasn't *as* important, but it was still something that was required to function and this irked him. He would be on his panel's backs daily. "Get me those updates! It's make-or-break time. This progression is a must and I will not settle for failure," he repeatedly stressed. But for now, he would have to wait as he obtained his pleasure elsewhere.

"Professor," said one of Horuzokh's biologists.

"Yes?"

"Whilst these biomechanical advancements are truly sensational, don't we risk missing out on so much that we can only otherwise experience as humans?"

"Hmm. I'm glad you brought that up. There is a way we can have both." And so, began the development of the creation of complex programming that would still allow man to experience a simulation of some of the sensations they would otherwise abandon.

"Thanks to the technology at our disposal, those rich enough can ensure such pleasures as taste, and sexual and romantic experiences will not be extinguished — albeit only in a synthetic sense," the biologist said. "But of course, they don't really care about that, as long as they have some sort of way to not part with *all* of their humanity, right?"

Horuzokh was eager to get things underway and deliver a presentation to his panel. "Simulations are nothing too sophisticated." He sneered, holding a tiny electronic chip between his right index finger and thumb. "We can simply give our brain the illusion that we are still experiencing something, with or without a nervous system. We have monitored brain activity enough to know what chemical reactions occur during such experiences. So, we can simply recreate that chemistry and program it into this chip. Then, we just insert it and wire it up to the brain.

"This way, we can get rid of the unwanted and unpleasant experiences of being human with mechanical substitutes, but still enjoy those pleasures we all crave. You could regard it as an interface upgrade. It's perfectly genius! I don't know why I didn't think of it sooner!"

The entire panel undoubtedly agreed. And so, procedures would commence immediately.

Chapter 3

Counter-Attack

Morathos sat day dreaming, holding his invention in his palm. He had started to clench his fist for a moment before loosening up again. The antenna he had built was pulsating more vigorously than it had been before. A sharp jolt of electricity shot from its tip causing him to spasm and tense up, dropping the device. He watched as it started spinning on the ground, a bright light blinkering from it. In that moment, the genius jumped out of his seat as the penny had finally dropped. He had suddenly realised where his equations had faltered and immediately began to dismantle the antenna, restructuring it.

Concealing his identity once more, he fled across the city to visit one of his regular customers. He wanted to lay low (he had refrained from making any phone calls or electronic communications long ago) and headed straight to the man's house. A small but well-built fellow with spikey bleached hair answered the door in a slouched manner. His notorious vibrant shirt and three-quarter length pants certainly wouldn't go unnoticed. "Morathos," he said. "Long time, no see."

"I have what you've been waiting for, Zeoc."

The two of them headed inside.

Zeoc admired the small device as Morathos placed it down on the table in front of him. "With the single press of a button, this device will emit a powerful electromagnetic wave that could alter the entire programming of the cyborgs. It might just open their eyes to the bigger picture."

"What?! Are you out of your mind?"

"I'm running thin on better ideas. Especially when so many people don't seem cooperate with me."

"This could work... or this could be an absolute disaster."

"We don't have much time. We should launch it soon."

"I'm surprised you didn't just launch it yourself."

Morathos picked the antenna up. "If this backfires, I'm going to need as many people in my corner as possible and I'm not exactly a fan favourite in this city."

"Fair point... So, when are we doing this?"

"We commence tonight! Perhaps you ought to head back to my lab with me. We'll be much safer there. We should board separate trains and rendezvous outside the station. You'll have to follow me through the secret entrance, but keep your distance."

Zeoc gave a firm nod and gulped as they ventured across the mechanised city, back to the slums of the Lower Eastern Quarters and crept their way past the droids into the safety of Morathos' laboratory.

Dusk soon rolled in. It didn't make much difference to the sky — what with the already clouded murk above. Morathos picked up his device and hovered his thumb over the button. "Three, two, one." He swiftly pushed it and a blinding flash ensued. The beam swept across the skyline and within a mere blink had vanished again. There wasn't an awful lot to observe after that. Everything seemed to continue as it had, at least until Morathos stepped outside.

The waves of droids in the vicinity had started to retreat. Some of them lost their cohesion and awareness and just darted off in random directions; some of them were spinning around aimlessly; several of them had even short-circuited. But the majority appeared to be heading back to headquarters.

Shortly after, a silence that seemed so alien projected across Doradheim. The Machine City had come to a halt as all its mechanics stopped dead. Morathos took a moment to appreciate the stillness. "Can you hear that?" he said.

"Sure, is nice to have some peace and quiet for a change," said Zeoc. "So, did it work?"

"I'm not sure yet. We should probably wait until morning. I had to program it to first shut down the systems before I could alter them."

Professor Horuzokh was quickly disrupted by the events and stormed out to see what was happening. He found Magnetus Bane in a state of confusion. His head was rocking from side to side in a rhythmic motion; his body projecting a repetitive electronic sound. "What is the meaning of this?" The professor's concerns led him to the presidential headquarters where he found President Vynzuth lamenting.

"Oh, rotten world! What has become of humanity? We're nothing but destructive monsters. We think we can just exploit the resources we have because we are capable of just creating new ones or vacating when it gets uninhabitable. Everything is disposable or replaceable to us — so we never appreciate it enough."

"Have you gone mad, Mr. President?" Horuzokh grabbed Vynzuth by the shoulders and shook him vigorously. "Something loosened in there?" The lamenting continued. The professor became infuriated and stomped out of the presidency. His rage carried him to the engineering quarters. "Reginald!"

"Do not fret, Professor. I'm already dealing with everything. All is under control."

"Thank goodness *you're* still sane. The President has lost his marbles!"

"Thanks to my unique advanced mechanisms, I have programmed some immunity protocols for such interferences. I am in the process of rolling this technology out, but right now we've got bigger issues to resolve."

"So, you think this is some sort of tampering with our machinery?"

"I don't *think*. I know. But I will have it reversed soon enough."

"That's what I want to hear."

President Vynzuth was lying on the floor in a pool of his own sorrows. He started to resent all machinery and began ripping out parts of his bio-mechanics, screaming in agony. "All this just from a rotten polluted meal!" He started tearing at his abdomen, shredding away at the very mechanics that had once saved his life.

Horuzokh charged in to intervene. "Mr. President, what on earth are you doing?"

"I can't live like this," he confessed. "Humanity is the most creative and, yet simultaneously, the most ignorant and destructive species. Bionics may have saved my life but it is our very own carelessness as men that first intoxicated the food that forced me to resort to such acts. If to continue living should cost me my authenticity, then I will not preserve myself one moment longer." He tugged harder as metal and flesh tore away from one another, sparks jolting violently.

Horuzokh was forced backwards as he caught a shock. He quickly got to his feet and shook himself off before witnessing the president destroy himself, leaving nothing but a complex mess of mechanical and human remains in his wake. The professor turned his head in distaste and slowly proceeded out. "I hope Reginald hurries up!"

Several hours had passed and many of the bots and droids of the city were manoeuvring once more. But Morathos had hoped the cyborgs would be the ones most affected, as these had human components; a consciousness that he had envisioned their hosts would reconnect with in his attempt to awaken their awareness.

A small proportion of the droids and bots resumed their duties as if nothing had happened, whereas some of them remained in shutdown. But what Morathos was not expecting was that some of them had begun to destroy each other. Their entire programming was tampered with, in such a way, that they could no longer compute the functions they were originally designed for. But that wasn't the worst of it.

Magnetus Bane had snapped out of his trance. He stormed through the city remorselessly, hacking at anything that stood in his way, his empty eye socket surging with electrical activity. The cyborgs had certainly been affected by Morathos' invention, but not quite in the way he had imagined. They began slaughtering not only each other, but other humans and bots alike.

Morathos and Zeoc raced back into the laboratory as they tried to assess what was happening. "It seems I had failed to account for something," Morathos admitted.

"What do you mean?"

"Well, the purpose of this device was to reconnect the cyborgs with their humanity and awaken their conscience to the horror they have created. It seems it has reunited them with their humanity, alright. But it has sparked their resentment and bitterness. All the problems they had concealed within their bionics have come flooding back into their consciousness and they can't control them.

"Whilst some have been reminded of their hatred for machines and their destructive creations, others have been reminded of their torturous humanity. Now they're either against humanity and want to destroy it, or they want to destroy all machinery. Either way, onslaught is inevitable."

"How do you keep doing that?"

"What?"

"Immediately recognising what you have done after the fact. Most people would not realise something so quickly or at least avoid responsibility for it."

"Well, I guess I'm not most people. But maybe I should have taken more care to think of that first."

"At least now you know the problem, we can work to rectify it."

"Thanks for the encouragement, Zeoc. It doesn't come without its challenges though."

"What?"

"Living in this brain of mine. It feels like I just have an increased attention to detail and insistence on solving problems that nobody else seems to notice. It sure is exhausting at times. Oh well. Back to the drawing board it is!"

Reginald wasted no time in completing the procedures necessary to undo the wreckage, and soon had repair bots out to patch things up. He quickly placed the final chip into the handheld device that he had been developing — it resembled the antenna that Morathos had created. With the quick press of a button, a shockwave rippled through the city as countless machines began to re-configure and conform as they had been designed. Cyborgs quickly detached from their inner-humanity and resumed their duties, as their protocols soon became their primary function once again.

The head engineer proceeded to the presidency with his droids to clean up the remains of the president. He then, without any hesitation, perched himself high above the city from the president's observatory and projected a hologram of himself for all to see.

"Beings of Doradheim, I am Reginald Forathorn, chief in command of DSA computer technology. I hereby deliver the news of the president's death. This man is responsible." He reached for a device that projected an image of Morathos. Morathos and Zeoc watched on as Reginald made his intentions known. "Anyone who finds this man alive and brings him to me shall be rewarded generously. This man is a destructive monster and should not be trusted. I am the one who restored order to this city in the blink of an eye. If not for me, this city would have crumbled at the hands of its very own kind, thanks to him. I therefore declare myself the new president of Doradheim."

There was an almighty roar as civilians obviously cheered on for their new president. Little did they know what influence their robotics had already programmed them with. Magnetus Bane then surfaced and stood beside Reginald as the president continued, "With the help of this man, we will make this city even greater than it is already." The president placed a hand on the cyborg's shoulder. "We will dominate and finally eliminate all who oppose our principles."

A grimacing Professor Horuzokh made his presence known also. "We have made extraordinary advances both biologically and technologically. Soon every essence of humanity will be no more, and machines will be our way of life entirely. But fear not, we have ways of making the pleasures of being alive still possible. It is a very exciting time to be alive indeed."

Morathos had heard enough. "You must leave. I have to concentrate and get this right."

"Can I not help?" asked Zeoc.

"I said leave!"

"Very well. But if you need me, you know where I am."

Chapter 4

A Different Approach

Morathos began to dissect his antenna and analyse it further. It wasn't long until droids were surrounding his apartment again, should he surface at any point. But he knew better and was far too engrossed in his work to even contemplate it now. Despite his efforts, he didn't seem to be making much progress and he was becoming impatient. "I'm tired of this city! I'm tired of these cyborgs!" he said. An unfamiliar energy soon came over him. "Perhaps it's long past the time that people started thinking like me. What if I were to somehow wash them of their impurities? I'm tired of being held back by the ignorance of this civilisation. Perhaps intelligence can be so dangerous because it figures things out too quickly and gets bored, causing it to deliberately make things more complicated than they ought to be. Perhaps intelligence can sometimes get caught up with problems that don't need solving, and even end up creating new ones. Maybe it's something else that seems to be short in supply around here... Wisdom. What if I could create it?"

It seemed that attempting to awaken the cyborgs to their conscience was not going to work because Morathos still had to rely on them making the next move. So why not go one better? He knew Reginald would likely have a counter sooner rather than later — if not already. But Morathos couldn't help but notice that he had an edge over Reginald. He was still completely human; Reginald was already swayed to the ways of robotics and very far advanced in them too.

He quickly got to work whilst President Forathorn continued to sweep his electronic broom across the metropolis, brushing aside any disturbances in his plans and implementing his adaptations. "As your new president, I offer an approach to the people of this city that Vynzuth did not. I offer lifesaving technologies to all of my people. One reason we aren't where we want to be is because we were too foolish and selfish with our funding. We should offer more of this technology to those less financially fortunate too."

"But sir, how can we afford such expenditure?" asked Horuzokh.

"Oh Horuzokh, you are a clever scientist, but you really are missing some intellectual properties. Your human error holds back your ability. With some components of your own, you might better be able to think on my level and not keep falling behind the times. The remaining pure humans are exactly what is holding this city back. Think of how much more we could achieve if they were all brought up to speed with us. Humans are prone to errors that machines simply are not."

"I never disregarded you, Mr. President. I merely questioned our resources to fund such an act."

"Yes, but nonetheless, my point still stands. What you need to learn, Professor, is that I am very different from Vynzuth. He was weak and feeble. That was his greatest shortcoming. I can simply program my machines to fund themselves. Money will no longer be an issue if we're able to keep producing it faster than we're spending. In fact, money is nothing more than a digital trading procedure anyway. Think of it as a metropolitan loan. We debt ourselves to make this happen and just wipe the slate clean by producing more funds.

"Not only that, it wins me more popularity, which in turn convinces more people to jump on board. And I certainly won't hesitate to remind the people of Doradheim what a reckless, sorry excuse of a man Morathos Reina is. He's a perfect example of how destructive and ignorant man is without the influence of state-of-the-art machinery incorporated into us — something you, Professor, are well overdue of."

Magnetus Bane lifted his head in delight at the president's words. "Let us commence," he said.

The Anti-machs were soon on the march again trying to convince those more vulnerable not to buy into this brainwashing. But the poor were so sick and desperate that many of them could not see the sense behind the protests; many of them were lining up outside the facilities.

President Forathorn didn't have the same patience for protesters that his predecessor had; he would deal with them more assertively. But of course, these people were driven by sheer will and determination and would persist anyway.

Bots and droids swelled the streets of the slums as they began tending to the city residents. A great majority of them had developed breathing dysfunctions as more and more plant life deceased and the oxygen levels in the air plummeted. Others had difficulty with temperature regulation as the Earth's atmosphere was thinning and its rotation was slowing, causing chaotic heat distribution leading to longer, hotter days and colder nights. But these problems were not to persist; certainly not for the more financially fortunate at least.

The biological research centre was revelling in its latest development. "At long last, we have successfully tested an internal heating system that will serve to keep the human body warm in these treacherous times! Hyperthermia will no longer be." Professor Horuzokh's eyes were almost popping out of his sockets as groups of droids actively installed breathing and temperature control gadgets into the torsos of the suffering.

Morathos had to pick up the pace and he knew it. If Forathorn had his way, he would no doubt overcome the minority of resistance as the pool grew smaller and smaller. He toyed with the idea of extinguishing ignorance and ego. "If such destructive characteristics were created by humanity in the first place, then why can't they be destroyed again?" He believed he could 'see' the ego as actual material matter. "*Its darkness clouds your judgment and consumes your ability to reason,*" he often expressed. "*I see it as its true form. A substance of a sort. Viscous. It latches on and weaves its way into the complex biological constructs of man like poison. I'm not sure if I'm blessed or cursed with such observations. But I know I do not crave such poison, at the expense of my humanity... So perhaps I'm not cursed in that regard.*"

Of course, most people took what he said to be a metaphor but Morathos claimed to actually be able to physically see what he was describing. Then again, most people were so far intoxicated that they barely took a word of his seriously anyway.

He questioned why — if he could see ego and ignorance as such substances — he could not see wisdom or intelligence in such form. But the possibility perplexed him nonetheless. He dug deeper into his mind. Being so detached from such societal influences, his imagination was left to run wild. This only allowed him to explore even more ideas and dig even further. But his frustrations were stirring some unsettling emotions that he would often opt to not confront.

Meanwhile, Zeoc was trying to formulate a way to distract the DSA and divert their attention away from Morathos. Even though he was perfectly safe in his laboratory, Zeoc couldn't help but feel a need to help in some way despite Morathos making it clear that he didn't need him. But realistically, there were far too many bots and droids at the president's disposal for any practical solution to really come of it.

Zeoc began trying to find any information he could that may have aided Morathos but he had soon encountered a glitch in his computer and pondered for a short while over it. "What's this?" he asked. It appeared he had found some kind of access code into a server he had not seen before. He promptly clicked on the server and attempted to input the code. As soon as he did, he realised he had managed to access a data bank belonging to the DSA. He became highly intrigued and deeply tempted to explore it but he knew he wouldn't get far. The DSA always had ways of stopping you in your tracks. Sometimes they deliberately set such traps, just to have an excuse to take you in. However, it seemed he had inadvertently obtained the attention of the DSA anyway and his withdrawal came too late. His home became surrounded by bots and droids.

"Zeoc Bleadbury!" a mechanical voice called. "We have you contained. Your only option is to vacate the premises." Zeoc ignored the voice, but the sheer number of machines began to use force to enter his home.

"What do you want from me?" he quizzed.

"You have breached legislation. You are being detained for the execution of code 409. Should you conform, your punishment will be lighter. Resistance, however, will not end favourably."

"409?!"

"Attempting to make a fool of us will not rescue you. We have witnessed evidence via surveillance."

"What on earth are you talking about?"

"Attempting to intercept DSA procedures in a deliberate manner is an offence deemed worthy of detainment," the android explained.

Zeoc knew they had him pinned in the corner and he could not resist the inevitable. He didn't even have time to explain his honest mistake and before he knew it, he was locked in a cell, helpless.

"Well, Mr. Bleadbury," an electronic voice called. It had a tint of wryness in its tone. It was none other than Magnetus Bane himself. "It would seem you have connections with a Morathos Reina. We know his location, but his sophisticated system is frustratingly preventing us from reaching him. Perhaps you would like to share with us what you know."

"So that's what this is all about?! If you're expecting me to tell you how to override his security systems, I have no idea." Zeoc rolled his eyes. "Even if I did, I wouldn't tell you!"

"I don't doubt for a second that it is only a matter of time before we hack our way into his system. But I'm growing impatient." Magnetus started pacing before returning back to Zeoc's cell and glaring at him. "I actually trust your word. But nonetheless, having you here could prove useful some other way. A 409 is a serious offence, you know?"

Zeoc glared back at the cyborg distastefully, but said nothing at first. "I found an access code that was unfamiliar on my system. I had to check it out to ensure it wasn't a threat. You set me up!"

Magnetus grunted and proceeded to leave the cell as a host of guard droids swarmed in. "See to it that this man delivers anything of the sort regarding Morathos Reina," he commanded his droids as several of them marched into Zeoc's cell and threatened him with electrical equipment. Zeoc pleaded with them, expressing that nobody knew how to bypass Morathos' security systems except Morathos himself. But the droids persisted in demanding information.

"What is he up to in that laboratory?" one of them asked.

"I don't know, he's an experimentalist. He's always inventing."

"According to our records, you have done business with him before."

"Well, what can I say? The man's a genius. He's never going to conform to this biomechanical movement. He's always looking for more efficient and innovative solutions."

"That is why we must detain him. He is tampering with our project." The droid spoke in a screechy tone. "He must be dealt with."

"Tampering — or actually *fixing*?" Zeoc quizzed in a slightly sarcastic tone. He went on to share some of the inventions and gadgets he purchased from Morathos. "I could tell all I know. I could sit here all day and talk about anything else. But I cannot tell you how to break through his genius system. That is a system far beyond any yet known. You're going to have to figure that out for yourself, if you even can."

"We ought to report to Francesca," said one of the droids. "I'm sure she will research the rest of the information we require." With that, several of the droids scurried off, whilst a few of them remained on watch. Zeoc let out a loud sigh and sat himself down on the floor in anticipation as the droids outside his cell paced around.

Magnetus Bane awaited his androids' return. "Well?" he pressed.

"He said we were wasting our time. He knows no way of obtaining Morathos as long as he's inside his laboratory. He gave us all the information he knew. So, we ought to make use of Francesca."

"Hmm, Francesca, eh?" The cyborg tilted his head in a bemused manner.

"Francesca Tritus works for Professor Horuzokh's research team. She is an exceptional analyst and has been invaluable to the professor on countless occasions."

"Why have I never heard of her?"

"Well, you haven't needed her services before," the droid said. "She usually works in biological research. The DSA have only recently more tightly coalesced with the presidency in a bid to achieve its ambition more efficiently."

"Indeed. Very well, I shall contact the professor." He swiftly gestured for his droids to leave.

Professor Horuzokh was pondering in his office when a hologram projection of Magnetus Bane emerged. "Ah, Magnetus. What a pleasant surprise!"

"Professor, I am going to need the expert services of Francesca Tritus. What information can she obtain about Morathos?"

"It seems great minds *indeed* think alike. I have already had her do some research. But I will stress to her that it now be a priority and to gather more information."

"Very well."

The professor could not contain his devious laughter and delight.

Chapter 5

A Discovery Like No Other

Francesca Tritus was deep in her studies, absorbing streams of information like a sponge. Emotion swept over her that she hadn't experienced in quite some time. She suddenly paused. "What an interesting character!" she expressed as she encountered some of Morathos' inventions.

Professor Horuzokh's hologram appeared before her. "My dear, Francesca. I bring word from the president. He has requested that you make your continuing research on Morathos Reina a priority above your other duties."

"Yes, Professor," she responded, trying to stay composed, her aquatic green eyes sparkling. Little did the professor know that she was several steps ahead and had already made this her priority. The inner excitement around the act was barely containable.

"Ah-ha!" Reginald grinned to himself as a realisation came over him. "I've got you this time, Morathos!" He inputted a series of commands into his computerised forearm. There, a digital display projected a sequence of numbers. "It looks like your little game of hide and seek is over!!" He immediately called upon Magnetus.

"Mr. President," the cyborg responded.

"Prepare your droids for a raid. It seems I had the components at my disposal all along. They were staring right at me the whole time. How could I have been so foolish?"

"Sire?"

"If my calculations are correct, it's only a matter of hours before a construct capable of breaching the security constraints of Morathos Reina shall be born." The president exhibited a wry smile. "Everything had been in place all along. I just didn't see the weak link in the chain. Ha-ha-ha!"

"Excellent. I shall get right to work." Magnetus proceeded to leave.

"One moment, Magnetus," Forathorn intervened. "There's *one* more thing that has been burdening me lately."

"Yes?"

"Professor Horuzokh," the president paused, "he's always being a little strange — that I can accept. But haven't you noticed something awfully peculiar lately?"

"I'm not so sure. What exactly did you have in mind?"

"Well, to cut to the chase, his reluctance to have any technological integrations is beginning to test my patience. Fetch him to me, would you?"

"... Err...Certainly."

"You have a problem?" Reginald snapped in a patronising tone.

"No, Mr. President."

*****

"Mr. President." The professor presented himself. His back was slightly hunched over, his hands clasped tightly. "You requested my presence?" The moment the professor's last syllable had left his voice box Magnetus tramped in with several droids. He was left helplessly paralysed by a surge of electrical current and immediately cuffed.

"Hypocrite!" the president spat. He strolled closer to Horuzokh, gripping his hair and pulling his head back so that their eyes met. "You could be such a remarkable professor without the hindrances of human error. Your unwillingness to upgrade and keep up with the rest of us is foolish. I can no longer trust you. Your services are surplus to my requirements. I will have Magnetus supply a worthy replacement."

The professor stared at him in horror, attempting to open his mouth. But it was no use. The president walked away as the professor was consumed by more electricity. Magnetus Bane then delivered a sharp blade into his abdomen before swiftly and mercilessly slicing his throat. With that, he ordered his droids to dispose of his remains down the waste hatch.

Morathos had been in the process of developing a microscope far more powerful than any. He had been deep in thought and experimentation for months and wondered just how much further one could see into the quantum world. Most microscopes were capable of observing the most fundamental elementary particles known to exist, but he never wanted to stop there. "What if there were a way to make raw energy visible?" he anticipated. He envisioned an apparatus that could visually monitor raw data. "Perhaps I could manipulate matter or even data itself!"

He wasted no time to get the finishing touches complete and attempted to clutch his excitement as he prepared to test his new device. He placed a small computerised component under the scope and as he peered into the lens, became mesmerised by a substance he couldn't identify that appeared to be moving in a trickling motion. "Could that be data?!" he cried. "I have to find Zeoc." But just as he prepared to leave, he noticed something else. Some of the subatomic particles he observed were behaving in an unusual way. This made him more curious about matter and the elements, and he proceeded with a new experiment.

He decided to observe hydrogen atoms and he noticed that some of them were emitting energy in a way he had never known possible. After a few moments, the hydrogen atoms reformed into helium. "Hmm, it seems some of these hydrogen atoms are fusing into heavier elements. It's the very same process as what occurs in stars, but without the extreme temperatures. How could this be happening?"

He then proceeded to experiment with different heavier elements, and he witnessed time and time again that a select few were fusing in the very same way. The more he experimented, the higher the ratio of fusion became, until he eventually witnessed various liquid and solid matter convert into new substances entirely. He continued to toy around with this new discovery —unclear how it had unfolded. He contemplated whether or not it would be possible for a potential new element to be created — or perhaps, even discovered — due to a lack of technology to find it previously. He immersed deeper into unimaginable realms, proposing unthinkable possibilities. *What if the very laws of physics themselves — with the right tools and advanced calculations — could be manipulated in such a way, that all materials capable of transferring data could mould into matter incapable or even destroy itself?*

Days ticked by like seconds as Morathos was consumed by his work. He started to combine different compounds and fusing various elements together until his attention was quickly grabbed by a phenomenon he could barely believe. The atoms and molecules he observed were behaving like no other, seemingly existing in all states without any influence of energy. Soon, enough molecules combined to form a visible substance that he had never witnessed before. It was colourless; but an occasional silver tint would glow from it. It seemed to behave like a solid, liquid and a gas simultaneously. He took a closer look as he placed some onto a small computer chip and inserted it under his microscope. The substance began to weave its way into the intricate circuits, branching out like dendrites. As he watched on, the substance showed indications of manipulating the very atoms in the chip, reforming them and destroying them. He even witnessed raw data being completely erased or rearranged into new coding all together. "This is it!" he cried. "Behold, the element that will undoubtedly save this city and our planet — plasmantium!"

He promptly conjured a genius disguise, darting out of his laboratory. He convincingly camouflaged himself as an oil pod repair droid — depositing small amounts of plasmantium into the many pods of oil that were darted around the city as he pretended to restock them. As soon as any droids or bots should need to replenish their oil, the plasmantium would get straight to work on their circuitry. As long as he kept it under his manipulation, no humans would be harmed. And as for cyborgs, his intentions would depend.

He was confronted by a couple of androids during one particular instance. "State your business," one of them said.

"I am changing this oil pod. Can't you see?"

"That won't be necessary; this one was only changed last night."

Morathos had to be quick. "I have detected inconsistencies in this one, so I'm going to sterilise them all to be safe."

"I haven't noticed anything," one of the droids replied.

Morathos smiled. "You aren't programmed to. There are an awful lot of pods in this city. I'm going to need a hand." He passed over a couple of thimble-sized bottles of plasmantium. "This is highly potent. One drop per pod should be more than sufficient." The droid didn't question him and obeyed his wish, gathering more droids to complete the task.

With that, he scurried to Zeoc's house. Upon arrival, he spared himself the headache of where he might be and decided to get himself back to the safety of his laboratory before anyone started to suspect anything. He prayed that by the time anyone of authority had noticed anything, it would already be too late.

Within hours, androids and robots across the city were starting to behave abnormally; some short circuiting, morphing into completely lifeless objects, shutting down, or even reprogramming themselves.

"Mr. President," Magnetus Bane cried. "Something terrible is happening."

"I'm well aware of what is happening, Magnetus. I wouldn't fret, for this is only the beginning."

"What are you talking about?!"

"I know exactly what is happening. Now, remember my orders to gather your droids?"

"Yes, of course."

"Execute it now. Here is all you need to breach the security system of the laboratory." He handed Magnetus a small electronic card. "Bring him to me alive; sedate him if you have to!"

"Affirmative, Mr. President." The cyborg slotted the card through a small mechanical hatch in his side and gathered his droids as they transported a large capsule that hovered, using magnetic power, to Morathos' laboratory.

Magnetus Bane took out the electronic card and inserted it into a key card slot located on the side of the laboratory door that the DSA bots had tried to assault earlier. Within a blink there was a beeping sound as the doors opened. The androids flooded in immediately, firing tranquillisers before Morathos even had a moment to process what was happening. He managed to dodge several shots, but was soon overwhelmed by the volume of droids as a dart penetrated his Adam's apple, immediately dropping him to the floor. Magnetus ordered his droids to pick him up and place him inside the capsule where mechanical restraints would wrap around his limbs and he would soon be at the mercy of the president.

"All too easy," the cyborg boasted.

Without Morathos at the helm of his elemental creation, there would be no assurance of its path.

"Excellent work," praised Reginald. "Now destroy all oil pods in the city."

"Are you mad?" Magnetus cried.

"You need not worry. I know Morathos inside out and I'm streets ahead of him. We will be perfectly protected here. Now, just do it!"

Magnetus hesitantly ordered his androids to obey the president's wish. "You heard the president!"

"Oh, and Magnetus."

"Mr. President?"

"Save a fraction of that oil, will you? I want you to extract it and bring it to my research team."

The cyborg nodded. "Very well."

With all the oil pods demolished, plasmantium began leaking onto the city streets, shape-shifting, evaporating and demolishing all in its path. Now not only mechanical beings would be affected, but innocent humans too.

The president wasted no time to project a hologram over the city. "People of Doradheim. I urge you not to panic at this moment. The man responsible for this has been detained. The very man I despise has demonstrated what a monstrosity he is. I will save you all from this destruction. I am already well ahead technologically and any mechanical damage will be undone. For those of you without mechanical parts, I urge you to seize this opportunity to abandon your trust in nature and biology, and join the cult of robotics. It is the only way you will be saved."

Morathos awoke; he felt nauseous and disoriented. He soon acknowledged the enclosure he was in — an empty room, with bright white walls and one small window to his left. As he made his way to it, all he could see was darkness. He felt helpless and plonked himself in the corner with his head in his hands.

"Finally, Morathos Reina, I have the last laugh." The president's voice resonated through the walls of the enclosure. "Oh, how long I have waited for this day. This is the end for you."

"You won't get away with this, Reginald," Morathos yelled.

A pompous laugh followed. "It's too late, I already have. There was only you standing in my way. I told you technology would prevail."

"You've always only been about yourself with no regard for anyone! You'd rather destroy your own city than relinquish your ego. All you've proven is how selfish and power-hungry technology has made you by neglecting the natural world. But you're too brainwashed to admit it!"

"Oh, you're quite a fool for a so-called *genius*. Your lack of integrated technology is probably the cause of that. Don't you see? You're the one destroying this city. You're cornered now and there's nothing left for you but to join the cult and let technology reign supreme over nature, once and for all."

"I'd rather die!"

"Well, it seems your stubbornness will kill you anyway. Goodbye, Morathos. There's no escape for you. You're clever, but I am the ultimate genius where technology is concerned; you'll never surpass me. My research analysts are already dissecting your little experiment and I must say I'm quite impressed. I didn't think you had such capability. But you have failed. I know you all too well and I know how to manipulate your creation to my advantage." There was an abrupt silence as the last syllable of the president's words phased out and Morathos resumed his head-in-hand position.

Reginald had already ordered his research panel to start duplicating the extracted plasmantium and begin manipulating it with his technology. "As promised, all those with mechanical components will be spared and the initial destruction will be undone. And for all those who refuse to partake... unlucky for you! Ha-ha-ha!"

The energy that plasmantium carried made it highly radioactive and more disease would soon spread to those affected. Reginald had the ability to program highly advanced mechanics to tamper with the nature of the substance, but still keep its radioactive properties. He quickly rolled out the upgrades required and had them installed into the majority of bots, droids and cyborgs throughout the city. This upgrade would make them immune to the effects of this phenomenal substance and any robots that weren't already too damaged, could easily rebuild their systems.

But Morathos would never give up. He knew that Reginald knew him inside out, which only meant that he knew *him* equally as well. *Everyone has a weakness,* he told himself. It would take time to chip away for sure — something that was sparse — but it was the only option left at this point.

Just then, the door of the enclosure swung open and a man was thrown across the room, landing face down. He looked pale, stunned and vacant. The door slammed shut immediately after and a voice resonated throughout the enclosure once again. This time it was Magnetus Bane. "Enjoy your last moments together," he said.

The man tried to pick himself up; but failing to do so, he attempted to roll over. He was too shaken and could barely get a word out. "The... electricity..." was all he could conjure.

"Electrical paralysis!" Morathos remarked. "There's only one thing for that, but I have to get it right." Morathos was always prepared and just so happened to have a small Taser at hand. But this was a specialised design of his own and was well disguised as a pen-drive that would fit snuggly inside his hidden pocket. "Your body is trying to shut down from the shock. This will reboot your system." He firmly pressed the device against his neck and released a short, sharp current through him. He jolted and stuttered for a couple of seconds then took a deep breath before picking himself up.

"Thanks," he said. Morathos quickly realised who the man was, as did he, him.

"Zeoc!"

"Morathos!" They both cried simultaneously.

"What happened to you?" Morathos quizzed. "I stopped by your place and didn't find you there, but I didn't think anything of it."

"They just came barging in. I had no chance. They tried to get to you through me. But I gave them nothing, I promise."

"I believe you. Reginald has an ego like no other, and that's why he never knows when to give up."

"What did they do to you?" asked Zeoc.

"They put me in some kind of capsule, it was awful. I was sedated, but it's as if I could still consciously feel everything; I just couldn't move."

"Do you think the damage is repairable?"

"I'm not sure. I mean, my Taser should help things continue ticking. Technology has some use I suppose. It's just the way we use it that I despise."

"Yeah, I agree. So now what?"

"I honestly have no idea right now. Reginald is so good at concealing and compensating for his weaknesses. That's what an inflated ego does to you. It makes you deny your own flaws so much, that you learn to hide them or at least manipulate others into thinking you don't have any. I know time isn't exactly on our side, but all we can do is wait for a crack to open."

"What if we don't make it? We can't survive in here for long."

"We're going to have to avoid thinking like that and just hope."

A citizen paused in the street and huffed to himself. "Morathos Reina, responsible for this?! I never suspected that.

I have purchased many of his inventions. He seems like such a good man."

"Well, you better believe it!" exclaimed a passer-by. "That man has done nothing but meddle and tamper with our plans. Even those that adored him have soon altered their opinion."

"I just don't see it. There's something more going on than meets the eye here."

"The majority of this city would laugh at you. You would have to be a fool to not see the truth. President Forathorn is exactly the breath of air this city needs. I waited so long for his bionics to rid me of my suffering, but I could never afford them. Now that won't be a problem."

"I've heard of many people that regret having those upgrades. They are only causing more problems and giving us an ignorant, 'why worry about my health and fitness, when I can just replace my biology with mechanical parts?' attitude."

"Why don't you come back to me when I'm disease free and you're suffering because you didn't listen to the president? We'll see who's right then, shall we?"

The man rolled his eyes and started to walk away. "The real disease here is ignorance," he said under his breath.

"Just as I thought. Off you scurry now," the passer by continued. "I don't have time for arguing anyway, I've got a city to repair."

Repairs were under way in rapid succession and Reginald had stuck to his word. But at the expense of those who opposed him. More and more humans queued up obliviously for mechanical transformations. A select few made a conscious preference to die than to resort to such desperate approaches. "I'd rather die authentically than live artificially," one woman stressed. The Anti-machs would of course continue their protests. Even in such small numbers, their undying passion would continue to carry them.

"Everything is going just perfectly," the president said. "Those who dare to challenge me, will soon meet their end. Bots, droids and cyborgs are repairing; damages are being undone swiftly; more and more humans are joining the cult; Morathos' pathetic attempts have been sideswiped and his little *substance* is my hands now. It is only a matter of time before this metropolis can truly live up to its name as the Machine City!"

Within just a couple of days, the plasmantium that had swept across Doradheim was contained and the city looked almost fully reconditioned.

*****

Zeoc was having difficulty concentrating. "I'm so hungry! How long have we been in here?"

"Almost two days," Morathos stressed. "Thinking about food is no use right now. We have to find a way out of here. Dehydration is starting to affect us cognitively. That is what I am more concerned about."

"Yeah, I know. The mind certainly can play tricks when you're in such a vulnerable state."

"Hence the flaw of humanity; and why robotics prevails." The president's voice could be heard once more. "There is a way out for you; I have the technology to save your lives right now."

"Forget it!" Morathos snapped.

"Suit yourself. Enjoy your last twenty-four hours! Ha-ha!"

In their weak and weary states, Morathos and Zeoc lost consciousness and drifted off.

Within hours, the city of Doradheim had been completely overhauled with robotics. The only surviving humans were dwindling out of existence and not much natural life remained. "There's no time to waste," Reginald grinned. "It's time for phase two!"

Magnetus Bane anticipated. "Awaiting instructions, Mr. President."

"Now that this city is almost completely operated by robotics, I aim to do one better than any ever have. The rest of the planet is not my concern right now; that will fall into place soon enough. I have my eyes set on something far greater — the very universe itself."

"What are you saying?"

"I'm saying your next mission is to make use of my laser powered probe, at long last. I developed light speed technology a few years ago, but since, have had no real use for it. I want you to send my probe beyond the boundaries of our solar system and release the rest of the plasmantium I have extracted. By releasing it beyond the solar system, in interstellar space, it should be less affected by any gravitational influences and grow more rapidly."

"What do you propose will happen?"

"It's not even a matter of postulation. It will reshape the universe in such a way that technology and robotics will be eternal, and nature will matter no more! Any problems that should arise, I am certain I have the technology capable of dealing with them."

"Sounds risky."

The president ignored him and eagerly ordered him to get his droids prepared for the launch, taking him to the control panel. "You simply need to press this button as soon as the probe leaves the atmosphere." He pointed to a large switch through the window before tapping the side of the probe. "She will do the rest herself."

"An unfamiliar substance in space?" Magnetus pondered.

They got themselves prepared for the launch. "Three, two, one," the probe's computerised voice counted down and was soon airborne. Within just a few seconds it had escaped the Earth's atmosphere and careered off into the depths of space.

Morathos had been awake most of the night. He kept pondering and hoping for a breakthrough of some sort. He observed Zeoc lying helplessly in the other corner of the room but waited until the early hours of the morning. "Zeoc! We've got to think of something."

"What's the use?" he grunted. "There's no way out of here. We might as well just rest while we wait to die."

"Get over yourself!"

Several hours passed, yet nothing struck either of them. They were feeling more and more fatigue as hunger and thirst intensified. Even Morathos had started to come to terms with what was happening and that he might just have to accept what was laid out. But the thought that Reginald would have his way made his stomach turn and, the bitter taste that circulated, left him restless and resentful.

The president had already consumed several bottles of plasmantium by now. He had very quickly developed an insatiable thirst for it and would frequently knock them back in the same manner that a distraught man might guzzle shots of whiskey one after the other. As his cravings intensified, something that had initially been created in such scarce quantities, soon began to multiply thanks to his instinctual thirst and the technologies it motivated him to develop. Each swig coursed through his remaining human cells, as the substance slowly but surely re-engineered more of them into bionics. It would only be a matter of hours before no biological traces of his existence would remain, except for his own thoughts, memories, ideas and imagination.

As the last of the most desperate humans barged their way through the queues to get their biomechanical upgrades, others had given up on their battles and took their own lives. Only a few hundred pure humans were left in the city and the numbers were plummeting ever more. Some of them knew they wouldn't make it through the wait and aborted the queues on their own accord. The Anti-machs were now nothing but a little hiccup to Reginald. He knew it would only be another couple of days before he had weeded the rest of them out.

"People of Doradheim," he announced via a holographic projection. He was holding a bottle of his ravishing substance and could not resist the urge to take several swigs. "Today marks the dawn of a new era. Today all suffering shall be no more. Today is the beginning of the true age of machines. There shall be no more biological inconveniences. You're either with me, or against me. But I assure you, should you jump on board, your deepest desires will only be a download away. For those who oppose, your fate is sealed, for the inevitable will follow. Those who have deceived me, tried to tamper with my dream, or intervened in any other way, I'm afraid it's game over for you." The acclamation below increased in volume. "From here on we are one city, one unity. We're all going in the same direction and nobody is going to stop us!"

With the exception of a few who still tried to resist and protest, all those who hadn't been bio-engineered, were too fearful to retaliate. One man tried to be heroic and charged toward a group of androids in fury at what was unfolding. He was shot dead before he even got close enough to them. "All those who oppose the president shall perish," one of them remarked.

"My ambition is to transform this planet into a technologically dominant body and begin to expand the race of machines across multiple star systems," the president continued. "I aim to use this planet as a hub for technology far more complex and advanced than you could ever imagine. The possibilities will be endless. I'm going to create an eternal race that will outlive time itself and be the ultimate superior of all to have ever existed, or will exist in the universe!" As he finished his last few words, he was confronted by Magnetus and the rest of his droids. "Excellent timing."

"All of your commands have been followed exactly as instructed and everything is in order, Mr. President," the cyborg reported. "According to our monitoring, the drone reached its destination around ten minutes ago and the substance has been deposited around three billion miles beyond the orbit of Pluto."

"Perfect!" Reginald turned to the city. "Our journey begins here. All shall be revealed in the coming days, my people."

As dusk soon loomed over the city skies, Morathos and Zeoc were fighting with every last ounce of energy they could, but their bodies could not sustain much longer. Their cognitive ability was significantly compromised by this point and they just couldn't see any potential escape. They were gradually becoming less and less functional as the sky darkened, and their words began to slur and become even more challenging to form. They were becoming short of breath, their voices coarser, their level of alertness dissipating. The room appeared brighter for a moment before everything became contrastingly darker and visibility lessened substantially. It was only a few more minutes before Zeoc could no longer keep his eyes open in his fragile state, and he collapsed.

Morathos dragged himself over to him with all he had left in him, and could still detect a pulse, but he knew he was in a critical state. He couldn't muster any more energy and had very little in terms of resources to work with, but in that very moment, his fatigued body went numb as he fought one last strain before he could no longer resist his eyelids from closing. The two of them lay in an unconscious and depleted state, appearing lifeless.

Chapter 6

In the Brink of Time

Francesca Tritus suddenly gasped as her awareness of her surroundings returned to her. She could often get so lost in her research that she detached from all concept of time and her environment would just seem to merge and combine into nothing around her. It was as if she was living in a different world sometimes, diving deep into the depths below and resurfacing for air now and again. She looked at the clock on her office wall then raised her right hand, pressing it gently against the metallic plate at the back of her neck. "Oh my, is it really that late?!" It was almost three a.m. and there was nobody else around. Reginald had left hours ago and she began to process some feelings she had seemingly been suppressing for some time. "What am I doing here?" she asked herself. It was as if it was an existential question, as opposed to any attempt to grasp anything in particular.

There were still a few droids around the premises for security and cleaning purposes, but the research centre was mostly empty. She gathered her few belongings and fastened her maroon trench coat all the way up. As she made her way past the various rooms of the presidential complex on her way out, she came across a room with the door ajar and the light on. She brushed back her silky amber hair and peered inside. There was nobody in the room, but the computer monitor was illuminated. As she inspected it, she noticed some blueprints for some kind of spacecraft of which she had a sense of familiarity, despite never seeing anything quite like it before.

It offered a distraction — albeit momentarily — from her internal philosophical search.

Nonetheless, she rushed downstairs where a large hangar was located. She had never had access but had always been curious about it. She peered through a small crack in the wall structure and her eyes met with what resembled a large canopy of some kind. It appeared to be concealing something, but she had no way of getting inside to observe it, so, proceeded to leave.

Just then, a droid approached. "Francesca, what keeps you here at this hour?"

"I just got my head wrapped in research. You know..." The droid continued about its duties and as it passed, Francesca immediately felt an urge to follow it.

It headed into a small room where another droid was observing something through a window. "How much longer?" the droid asked upon arriving.

"Take a look for yourself," it responded.

"Release the hatch. They're not dead yet, but they won't make it. President Forathorn will want them out of here," it replied. And with that, a lever was sprung and the floor of the room they were observing opened up.

During the commotion, Francesca had quickly processed what was happening and proceeded to insert a small chip into the side of one of the droids, causing it to shut down instantly. The second droid swiftly turned and attempted to charge at her, but she was quick on the mark and already had a second chip at the ready which she slotted into the droid just as rapidly.

In some respects, androids were more trusted than cyborgs when it came to accessing certain areas of the presidential complex because they were programmed to obey their very protocol only and weren't swayed by any kind of consciousness. This meant that most androids and other bots were equipped with electronic security tags that granted them access to specific areas where even cyborgs might not be permitted.

Knowing this, Francesca removed a tag from one of the androids and scurried down to the lower levels of the complex. This is where anything — or anyone for that matter — that should end up being disposed of down a waste hatch, would end up. She attempted to filter out the foul concoction of odours and with the aid of a handy portable artificial light, she quickly waded through endless debris where she climbed her way across the carnage until she encountered two figures that appeared utterly defunct. The sensor technology in the vicinity was amongst the most optimal known and highly accurate in its judgments, so she didn't doubt the droid's verdict regarding their states of being. She didn't know how she was going to do it, but she knew she had to get them out of there and dragged them one by one.

Most droids operated by sensors and used them to process their environment. Although they had face recognition components, Francesca with all her research, knew of a glitch that nobody else — even Reginald — was ever aware of. If a droid detected another electronic security tag in their vicinity, their programming would immediately process it as another droid and override the face recognition technology. As long as she had that tag and stayed out of cyborg territory, she would not be stopped.

Now, I can use this same tag to gain access to the hangar, she calculated. She swiftly removed the canopy to reveal the very craft that she had suspected from her research and recent observations of blueprints. Without hesitation, she got herself and her rescuees on board. *I had my doubts*, she thought. *But one must keep an open mind when researching. The idea of this craft seemed a little out there when I first read about it. But here it is!*

She hooked them both up to some machinery and inputted some commands. Once she felt assured that she had done what was required, nothing more could distract her from the realisation of her exhaustion, and she took herself to one of the ship's many dormitories to rest for what few hours of darkness remained.

A consistent and unpleasant pressure rested on Morathos' skin. He awoke disoriented and soon realised he couldn't move his limbs. He took a moment to process his environment and immediately comprehended that it was unfamiliar. "Where am I? Where's Zeoc?" He had become alert and more energised than the night before, but he was far from recovery.

"Ah, good morning, Morathos." He was greeted by a beaming grin belonging to a woman with rather attractive features. "I've waited so long for this moment. What an inspiration of a man you are. I could just kiss you right now!"

"What is going on? How do you know my name?"

"Oh, don't worry, you're safe now. If I'd have gotten there any later, you might not have made it. A little while longer and you should be right as rain...Then I'll be privileged enough to see you smile."

"Who are you? What have you done with Zeoc?"

"Relax. Your friend is in that incubator over there. He was in a bad way; he might need a little longer."

"So... you saved our lives?! I guess I should say thanks... You still didn't tell me who you are though."

"I can't tell you right now. If they catch me, I'm done for. Once you and your friend have recovered, we can take off out of here and I can tell you everything. But as it is, I need this ship to remain stationary and concentrate solely on getting you two stable."

"How can I trust you?"

"Well, I hate to break it to you sweetie, but you're not exactly in a position *not* to."

Morathos huffed. "Fair point. But right now, I can't tell if I'm a hostage or a patient."

"Now, all I can tell you is this machinery is restoring your fluids, replenishing lost nutrients and getting everything ticking as it should, but your friend was in a much more critical state. This truly is a remarkable piece of kit though and you should be back to your old beautiful self in no time."

"And what if they come for you before this ship is ready to launch?"

She hesitated for a moment and walked over to him, then placed her index finger softly over his lips. "Shh!" She then grabbed his hand, moving her lips closer to his neck. Morathos gulped before she whispered in his ear. "Trust me... Now please rest."

Morathos sighed softly as the woman steadily walked away. He tried to look over in the direction where she had claimed Zeoc was. But the way he was positioned and fastened to the machinery made it difficult for him to move his head far enough. All he could hear was a continuous buzzing noise from what he perceived to be the machinery, but it seemed to be gradually amplifying in volume. It then became more apparent that the engines were kicking in.

An energetic voice illuminated the craft. "Alrighty! Let's warm her up! We're going to have to launch in the next twenty minutes maximum. Otherwise, we're all busted! You won't be quite stable by then, but still, a steady enough state to proceed with our journey — at least until we can find somewhere safer."

Morathos tried to refrain from asking any more of the burning questions that were circulating through his brain. After all, he often liked to think that it was his very inquisitiveness and curiosity that aided his genius. But all he could do for now was let his mind rest and store those questions away.

After a few minutes, the engine seemed to quieten. Morathos wasn't sure if it was just a feature of the technology of the craft to preserve energy or if his senses had become accustomed to the sound. He didn't doubt the latter to any degree but given the technological advancements, he concluded that it would likely be the former. He had been stationary for many hours by now. So much so, that despite the minimal influence felt when the ship began to gradually accelerate and leave the hangar, he experienced a significant g-force for a brief moment. The ship hadn't even left the ground yet.

In that very instant, a familiar and domineering voice could be heard. "My craft! Stop them!" Reginald had already interrogated his droids the instant he arrived. "What on earth possessed you to release the hatch without my authorisation?"

"A mutual observation of their vitals indicated that they were all but dead, Mr. President," one tried to justify. "After that, some phenomenon we don't recall occurred. Our systems were temporarily immobilised."

"Impossible!" the president snapped. "My technological expertise would never have caused such faltering."

Droids came hurtling into the airbase in vast numbers, charging towards the ship just as it had lifted from the ground. They opened fire but none of their ammunition was effective; each laser shot simply ricocheted an inch away from impact. Reginald became increasingly animated. "There's no way anyone could know how to operate my sophisticated force-field protocols like that! Cease firing!" The droids immediately halted as the president angrily watched his ship take to the skies, surpassing the range of his vision in seconds.

Magnetus Bane awaited Reginald's return to his office. "Mr. President."

"What is it, Magnetus?" he snapped.

"Shall I have my droids track your ship? I should be able to disable it."

"It's no use. Whoever stole this craft knows far too much about it for my liking. I'm inclined to believe we have a spy or traitor amongst us. They've enabled its stealth protocol and navigated its sophisticated systems far too quickly. These skills require years of training, even for a cyborg of complex upgrade. I deliberately ensured that no such knowledge could be available for upload. Just let them have the ship for now. Keep your eye on everyone in this building. Interrogate them to death if you must and report to me all of your findings."

Magnetus nodded, "Affirmative."

As the colossal ship came to a halt several hundred miles into its rapid journey, it descended into a desolate plot of land and the engines slowly powered down before switching off. "Isn't she beautiful?" their rescuer expressed as she paraded past Zeoc's incubator. He stirred and opened his eyes.

"Whoa!" he gasped, staring at her in awe. "She certainly is! ...I must be dreaming."

"Oh please." She rolled her eyes at him. "Save the cheesy pick-up lines for someone else."

Zeoc laughed to conceal his embarrassment. "You could at least tell me your name."

"Well, I am a woman of my word. I suppose I could now." She walked towards Morathos and released him from the equipment he was attached to. "My name is Francesca Tritus. I work for the president."

Zeoc couldn't resist the urge to introduce himself. "I'm Ze-."

"Zeoc Bleadbury, I know," she interrupted. "I'm a researcher. I know all about you and Morathos. That's the reason you're here, still alive."

"No wonder you know so much about this ship," said Morathos. "You work for Reginald, but you rescued us. What gives?"

"I learnt a lot about this ship in my research. I didn't believe it existed because of how long I've worked there and never seen it. But Reginald is a very devious and secretive man."

Morathos' questions could no longer be suppressed. "So, whose side are you on exactly?"

"It's complicated. But rest assured, you're safe. Especially you." She ran her fingers through his hair.

"Oh, I get it," Zeoc piped up.

Francesca laughed to herself slightly. "*You're* not shy or subtle, are you?"

Zeoc was resilient and persistent in many aspects. As great as these qualities are, he didn't always seem to utilise them in the most intelligent ways. "If you don't ask, you don't get," he said, with a smirk on his face.

"Ask all you like, darling. But you're not my type."

"We're not here to play silly games," Morathos remarked. "I want to know why you saved us."

"Oh, you know. Ever since I first heard of you, I was fascinated with your genius, your inventions and determination. I was instructed to conduct research on you long after I already had begun. You're an inspiration and you made me realise how much time I've wasted. There was never much in the way of a career for me." She opened Zeoc's incubator and assisted him to his feet. "I was naive and wanted to express myself in the arts. I had big dreams as a child. But then I woke up to the world we *really* live in. Everything artistic has lost its meaning, what with how digitised things are now — quite a recurrent story these days."

"There's something more. I know it," said Morathos.

"The president has completely lost it. His latest actions were the last straw for me and what led me to rescue you and flee from his presidency."

"Reginald was *never* with it. He's an egomaniac," Morathos remarked.

"Whilst you were locked up, he conducted something far more dangerous than you could imagine. He launched a probe into space and released your plasmantium into the vacuum. He has tampered with it in a way that aims to manipulate it into recoding the very fabric of space-time itself. There must be a way we can intervene and reverse it before all biological life is eliminated in exchange for nothing more than data and robotics."

"It was a fluke," Morathos confessed. "I have no idea how I created plasmantium... And I lost control of it."

"If only there were a way to undo the past," Zeoc stressed.

"That's exactly it!" said Morathos. "Undoing the past, will undo the substance even being created in the first place. Or better still, give me more understanding of how I was able to create it. Then I might be able to gain control of it again."

"You really think we have a shot?" asked Zeoc.

"Well, only hypothetically at the moment. But there must be a way. How much plasmantium was sent?"

"I don't know exactly," Francesca informed. "But Reginald insisted that it was to be released in a particular location, far enough out from any significant gravitational influences, but still reachable in sufficient time. He had already developed a method for propelling probes at light speed using a laser thrust. His technology uses power from the sun to activate countless powerful lasers. By concentrating the lasers into a single point for several months, it generated enough energy to propel a small probe at light speed. The energy was contained in an electromagnetic cylinder."

"So how far exactly?"

"About seven billion miles."

"I'm not sure how this substance is going to behave out there. But it's a very heavy and radioactive substance. It's likely highly unstable. I just don't know what tampering Reginald has done with it."

"Perhaps we ought to hang around here for a few days, at least until we can conjure up something. Looks like there's enough supplies on here to feed a whole city for a month!" cried Zeoc.

"Luckily we have this on board." Francesca directed Morathos to a large telescope. He peered through the lens.

"I think I have just the thing for this." He pulled a small device out of his pocket and held it up to the light.

Francesca glared at him with glowing eyes. "Oh, aren't you just remarkable?"

"Here's a little something I invented a few years ago. I almost threw it away as I never thought I'd find use for it," said Morathos. "This lens contains a small but powerful micro-magnet. Because of tiny ionised particles that I fused into the lens, the magnetic field is strong enough to influence light rays just enough to increase its magnification considerably without causing any destruction."

"Why did you never tell me about this?!" cried Zeoc.

"A good inventor never reveals all his creations, or else they're left vulnerable to too much competition." He inserted the lens over the eyepiece of the telescope and peered through again. "That's more like it."

Zeoc and Francesca were left in awe at both his genius and what they observed in the sky.

Morathos spent several days observing the stars with his new modified apparatus and there didn't appear to be anything noticeably unusual occurring at first; but then something caught his eye. "This may be even more disastrous than I had first thought," he said, concerned.

"How so?" asked Zeoc.

"It's taken several days of careful observations and pattern recognition, but I fear the plasmantium might be behaving in far more destructive ways than Reginald may have intended."

"What is happening?" Francesca inquired.

"I can't say for certain yet. I'll need another few days of monitoring and examining to truly establish some sort of pattern. Then I should be able to predict — to a reasonable extent — what this means."

"Is there anything we can do in the meantime?" asked Zeoc as he began rummaging through the refrigerator. "Oh man, I've missed food so much!"

"The only other thing I'm worried about, is Reginald finding us. But I'm sure you've got that covered, Francesca."

"Yes, I've encountered many blueprints and design models in my time at the complex regarding this ship. And I downloaded a great deal of the rest from various systems. The craft's stealth system is of sheer optimal quality, so take as much time as you need."

"I'm afraid time is not something we can take for granted here," said Morathos. "But I acknowledge your point."

Francesca nodded. "No, of course."

*****

"Any news?" The president confronted Magnetus, anxious for any progress.

"I'm afraid not, Mr. President."

"There must be something around here. Fetch me those two droids, would you?"

"Yes, certainly."

As he returned with the droids, the president disabled them then inspected them closely and observed a small slit. "What is this for?"

"Sometimes when you power off an android, it has residual current to disperse before it completely shuts down its systems, meaning there can be a slight delay."

"Yes, yes. I know."

"I added a feature, as a safety precaution, should anything drastic occur. Inserting a specific chip in here will ensure that the android shuts down immediately."

"Hmm. Seems a bit odd to me. I wouldn't have resorted to such methods, but anyway... I presume your own droids won't have any programming to make them aware of this? That would be rather counterproductive."

"Absolutely. No awareness whatsoever," the cyborg confessed. "Any suggestions on how to improve?"

"Never mind. We'll discuss that later. Where exactly are these specific chips?"

"I only made three in total. I keep them locked away amongst my spare components. I found one in each droid, but the other was still where it should be."

"These droids claimed to have detected another droid in their presence before this occurred. But if they are incapable of using these, someone else must be responsible."

"I agree," Magnetus cried. "But they should have been able to identify the culprit. I cannot explain what happened."

"Someone must have followed you or eavesdropped when you weren't aware, to know the location of these chips. But even so, how did they get in?"

"Wait!" exclaimed Magnetus as he examined one of the androids more closely. He noticed its security tag was missing. "These tags are very well hidden deliberately. The droid likely hasn't had to depend on it today."

The president's tone had risen in volume. "So, someone, somehow, knew how these tags operate, where they're subtly located, and successfully removed one to gain access to unauthorised areas!"

"Even so, they still couldn't access my component room with one of these tags."

Reginald tried to contain his rage. "Let's be patient. I don't think this is something we can solve right now. Whoever is responsible has put an awful lot of careful calculation into this; probably years of preparation. It didn't just happen overnight."

"I don't believe it did, Mr. President... I don't believe it did."

Morathos had been so deep in his observations for several more days, that it only just struck him. "How did you possibly manage to obtain this ship?" he asked Francesca.

She smirked at him. "Pretty easy really. Thanks to you at least."

"What on earth are you saying?"

"I'm saying I didn't hijack it. Technically, you did."

"You're talking nonsense again."

"Don't you remember your genius invention?"

"Which one?" he laughed.

"Oh, *sorry*. Ha-ha. I guess I should be more specific. Quite a few years ago, you needed to enhance your laboratory's security system to ensure the DSA wouldn't snatch you."

"Are you some kind of obsessive stalker or something?" Morathos gave her a look of concern. "I wouldn't believe everything you read you know. Besides, what *don't* you know about me?"

"Like I said, I start researching and I just can't stop. I'm a pro; I know which sources to trust." She flashed her eyebrows, her left raised slightly higher than her right. "You ignited a flame inside me that I thought had long blown out."

"So, the invention? I'm intrigued now."

"Oh yeah. You developed a device that could scan their electronics and use that data to create a counter lock against their own technology. I was so amazed by it, I tried to replicate it. It took a lot of attempts and still, not a wink on your design. But nonetheless, I was keen to test it out. I scanned Magnetus Bane and manipulated the technology into replicating the same coding as some of his sensors, allowing me access to his spare components. To cut a long story short, that's when I found the shutdown chips for the droids and removed one of their sensor tags that granted me access to this ship."

"That's impressive."

"It was all thanks to you, sweetie."

"Perhaps. But all that precise calculating for all these years. They might be able to figure some of it out, but I doubt they'll ever crack you. Especially since not even Reginald is aware of the flaw in the droid's sensor tags and his ego will probably cloud him even more."

"Oh, it was nothing. I've worked for them since I was seventeen. Despite their deeds and the damage my decisions have cost me, both mentally and biologically, they saved me from ending my life..."

Opting to avoid confronting the uneasiness, Morathos changed the subject. "Take a look at this," he said, directing her to the telescope. She gazed into the lens in complete wonder, unable to form any words. "Sometimes I like to just look at the night sky. It helps me think clearer. It opens our eyes to the beauty of nature that we so often take for granted."

"Aren't you so romantic?!" A tear streamed down her face and he thought about wiping it away, but something stopped him. Something in her eye told him that she'd hoped he did too. But her mood soon switched as something horrific caught her gaze. "W-what is that?!" she screamed. Morathos took a look through the lens.

"It's exactly as I suspected and what I feared most." He gulped hard. "It seems Reginald's and my calculations were both inaccurate. Plasmantium in the vacuum, even with his tampering is not just *altering* the fabric of space-time. The substance appears more stable than I predicted in terms of how it has bonded without air pressure. But I'm afraid the reason for that is because of how dense it has become. It is eating the very fabric itself and may even rupture it. We're about to be its next meal."

Zeoc piped up. "Did someone say *meal?* Man, I'm hungry."

"This is not the time," Francesca stressed.

"Where have you been, anyway?" Morathos asked.

"Oh, you know, just checking the place out. It's some ship this!"

"This is my mess to clean up," said Morathos. "That substance has ruined everything. And now it's forming into a black hole powerful enough to end all of life... I suppose Reginald gets half of what he wants."

"Hey! We're in this together," said Zeoc.

"Yes, I'm afraid you're stuck with us, whether you like it or not," Francesca asserted.

"I'm sorry. I'm just trying to not get distracted," said Morathos.

"Yes, and that's what's exhausting you so much. Your mind never stops," said Francesca.

He tried to digest her words and took a deep breath. "Maybe you're right. I should rest and hopefully I can draw up some solution in the morning."

"Don't forget, we're here too," said Zeoc.

Morathos nodded softly. "Perhaps we should *all* get some rest."

Francesca smiled. "That might just be the wisest thing I've heard you say."

Chapter 7

Slingshot

Morathos charged into Zeoc's dorm. "Guys, wake up!"

"It's six a.m. man."

Francesca overheard and made her way to the two of them. "What is it?"

"Sorry to wake you at this hour, but I have a potential solution. It was staring at me the whole time, I just needed to quieten everything else. We really should get cracking."

"Let's hear it," Francesca anticipated.

"First of all, just how advanced is this ship?"

"Probably more so than any," said Francesca.

"Do you think it's capable of getting us into interstellar space quickly?"

"Well, nobody's ever gone that far before. We achieved forty percent the speed of light a few years ago and reached as far as Saturn's moon, Titan's orbit. But the mission was a failure because nobody made it home."

"Yes, I remember that mission. I know nobody has ever gone beyond that point. But do you think we have the capability with what we have at our disposal?"

Francesca hesitated. "I'm not so sure. I mean, the Mars missions were a success if you base them on the fact that we actually landed man there. But even they didn't come without their reported problems in becoming accustomed to the hostility. And the overall objective of the missions was not accomplished. Where we aim to go is obviously much farther."

Morathos reminisced. "Yes, all the drawbacks with terraforming and the impact it's had on our resources on Earth. But this ship looks as if it was designed for the long-haul."

"What exactly are you intending to do?" asked Zeoc.

"It's quite a simple concept really. It's actually accomplishing it that is the challenging part. The way plasmantium is behaving in space — whether or not it has anything to do with Reginald — is causing it to become incredibly dense. It was already a heavy substance, but now it is developing properties of a black hole. If we can reach just outside its gravitational field, we may be able to accelerate faster than light by using the warped space-time it will create. This will enable us to travel backwards in time and, hopefully, interrupt the creation of the element."

Zeoc gaped his jaw in sheer shock at what he had heard.

"That sounds plausible in theory," said Francesca.

"But space is unbelievably vast. We have to be so precise with our coordinates," stressed Morathos. "We also need to time our trip perfectly. Too early, and it won't have compacted enough to warp space-time in a way that would generate the energy we need to propel at such speeds. Too late, and it will become even more powerful than any black hole in space and essentially reverse time by contracting the universe back into its hot, dense state."

"Can't we just use that contraction of space to our advantage and let time flow backwards anyway?" Zeoc quizzed.

"That's a great question. But the problem with that is it doesn't give us any control and it makes it harder to predict what window of time we'll end up in. If we overshoot our window, time will keep reversing and we'll never reach the point which we are aiming for. At least with my method, we have some hope and control of where in time we will end up and it gives us more margin for error."

"Ah, I see," said Zeoc.

"So now it's just a matter of doing some calculations and ensuring we have everything," said Morathos.

"I know someone that might be able to help," said Francesca.

"Who?" Morathos asked.

"During my research I found out some information about a certain someone; a woman by the name of Sequititah Steeple. Her parents were Archquar and Ignerenous."

Morathos seemed taken aback. "Wait! Say that again."

"Sequititah's parents were called Archquar and Ignerenous."

"That's impossible. Archquar and Ignerenous were my parents. I have no siblings."

"Maybe not to your knowledge," said Francesca. "I don't know much more about her, or where she might be. I only know of her from researching you. I found nothing of your history or childhood but there's plenty of sources with information of who your parents were and that they also had a daughter together. Perhaps your only memories together were from an early age and you've forgotten."

"Maybe," said Morathos.

"If we can find her, she might be able to give you some information about your childhood and guide us towards the right time."

"Why is there so much information about me loosely hanging around anyway?" Morathos questioned. "I keep to myself mostly."

"A genius like you could never go unnoticed," Francesca complimented. "You might not feel like many people appreciate you, and some won't. But most either idolise you or envy you. Either brings merit to broadcast who you are."

Morathos had heard enough and changed the subject. "Let's look for her. I have no idea where to start and we don't exactly have much time. But we stand a far greater chance of pulling this off successfully with extra information."

"Wait, what's this?" Zeoc had obtained some kind of disc that displayed an abbreviated message. "N.O.D.R.O.G, huh?"

"Where did you find that?" asked Francesca.

"For some reason, it was hidden among the food supplies." He passed it to her and she inserted it into the ship's main disc drive. It projected holographic images of the different compartments of the craft and a mission briefing presentation began.

"On behalf of President Vynzuth, thank you for your dedication to this N.O.D.R.O.G. mission. We aim to launch this craft into the far reaches of the solar system and go beyond where any man has ever been. Our advanced teams have developed a state-of-the-art technology, and this space programme guarantees to break the boundaries of what man is capable of..."

"An aborted space programme!" Francesca cried. "This must be at least a few decades old now. They sure kept this quiet!"

The hologram continued to display visuals of how the ship intended to break apart and reshape, and at what intervals. "Using cylinders containing antimatter, we're able to create enough thrust to reach ninety-nine percent the speed of light in a manned craft for the first time ever..."

"So, a spacecraft capable of reaching light speed has existed all this time!" Morathos remarked. "But why was the programme aborted?"

"That's a good question," Francesca pondered. "But everything looks intact. This disc should give us all the information we need to reach plasmantium."

Morathos nodded. "Yes. Now we just need to time everything else perfectly and find out just where we're going."

"How are we supposed to find Sequititah?" asked Zeoc.

"I'll see if I can find any more information." Francesca quickly browsed her system. "All I've got is that she was born in a city called Karahdor. But no such place is showing on my map."

"It's no use," Morathos sighed.

Francesca froze for a moment. "Hang on. I've found some data I didn't know about. I've somehow ended up with an e-letter stored in my system. I don't remember seeing that there before."

"What does it say?" asked Zeoc.

"It looks like some kind of love letter." She projected it for everyone to read:

My Dear Sequititah,

How long I have ached for your return. That day you left was like a dagger in my heart. I fled to Doradheim after the disaster and I had hopes of reuniting with you. But still I await your presence.

Word has it that you left Doradheim for a quieter life in the village; it was all too much for you, they said. But I was so afraid of not finding you there or being pushed away, that I didn't look for you; I didn't want to impose or seem intrusive.

I'm not the same man without you. I didn't become what you envisioned and I feel so ashamed for letting you down. But wherever you are, I will hold you dear in my heart and I will never forget you.

All my love, Magnetus.

"Magnetus?!" Morathos spat. "That good for nothing heartless machine? And *my* sister?!"

"It does sound outlandish," said Zeoc.

"Disaster...?" Francesca pondered. "I must have accidentally downloaded a copy of this when I scanned his technology. I wonder if he ever sent it."

"I find this hard to believe," said Morathos. "But nonetheless, he said something about a village."

"The only nearby village to Doradheim is Staistreim," said Francesca. But it is awfully close to the city, so we should be careful. Stealth will aid us there but disembarking..."

"Let's go. We don't have much time," stressed Morathos, and they fired up the engine.

The Machine City lay just a few miles on the eastern horizon. Most of its skyline was visible from ground level but as they hovered nearby, the city seemed even smoggier than they had remembered it. They had only been gone a few days, but the feel and the overall intimidating, unwelcoming scope of the place seemed to have amplified significantly.

"Usually, it's only when you step outside of something so sinister, you realise its true toxicity," said Zeoc bitterly.

"That was quite profound coming from you," said Morathos.

"I might look like just a pretty face but I'm quite capable of being philosophical, you know." Morathos and Francesca let out a chuckle and Zeoc quickly turned his head away in despair.

Staistreim was a small, delightful village; a striking contrast to its neighbouring city. There was an immediate sense of unity and togetherness about the place; a profound humility in its people. The houses and architecture looked old-fashioned for its period, almost Tudoresque, the white exterior walls contrasting their thatched caramel roofs.

As the three of them entered, they were immediately greeted by a friendly face. "Welcome to Staistreim. Please state the purpose of your visit so that we may assist you accordingly."

"We're looking for someone," said Francesca.

"Who might that be?"

"Do you know a woman by the name of Sequititah Steeple?" asked Morathos.

The man paused and turned away from them. "Yes, but she is not here. She is sick and in quarantine at a nearby hospital. I'm afraid I cannot grant your request."

"What is wrong with her?" Zeoc concerned.

"That information is classified."

"Well, is she going to be okay? How long is she expected to be in quarantine?" Francesca asked.

"I'm no doctor, I cannot say. But she is old and her immunity is compromised; she may not recover."

"Old?!" Morathos puzzled. "She's my sister. She can't be *that* much older than me. You must be mistaken."

"I'm terribly sorry," the man said. "Perhaps you have the wrong person. Please feel free to explore the village and if you should require anything else, we will be happy to assist."

"That's very kind of you," said Francesca. "But I think our business here is done. We should get moving."

"Very well. Have a safe journey."

"Wait!" cried Morathos. "Maybe we should stay here for a little while longer."

Francesca and Zeoc looked at him with confusion.

"Yes, of course. Be my guest," the man said.

"Are you sure about this?" Francesca asked Morathos on their trek into the village.

"No, not really. But we could really use her help. Perhaps we can find out some information, or an alternative way to contact her."

The other two nodded and continued their stroll.

"This place is beautiful," cried Francesca. "It's like a whole different world here. How could a place of such splendour reside so close to Doradheim?"

"Sure, is fetching," said Zeoc.

They had only walked a few paces before encountering a warm but quiet shop that appeared to sell a variety of miscellaneous items. It looked well stocked and neatly presented, and had a welcoming demeanour about it. "Well, hello there," the shopkeeper greeted them. "How can I help?"

"We're actually here for someone," said Francesca. "But we're forbidden from seeing her due to quarantine reasons. Is there any other way of reaching her?"

"The nearby hospital is very strict with whom it allows entry. I can make an enquiry if you like."

"That would be awfully kind," said Morathos.

The shopkeeper dialled a number and a hologram of a secretary projected before them. "Good day," she said. "How may I be of assistance?"

"I'd like to enquire about Sequititah Steeple," said Morathos.

"Do you have a patient ID?" she asked.

"No," said Morathos.

"One moment." She brought her details up. "It seems she is showing signs of recovery, but we cannot grant visitors at this time. If her condition improves in the coming days, we will allow *one* visitor for a half hour. But they must be a relative and wear the protective clothing required."

"I'm her brother," said Morathos. "Thank you so much for your help."

"So, I guess we just keep our fingers crossed and hang around here for a few days," said Zeoc.

"Well, you guys can do that if you like," said Morathos. "I'm going to head back to the ship and make some final calculations. It will save us time later."

Francesca showed a look of concern. "Just be sure to take a break."

"Alright," Zeoc chirped, directing his words towards Francesca. "What do you say we spend some time getting to know each other a little better?"

"Sure." She expressed an ironic smile. "In your dreams."

"Whoa! Feisty. I like it," he grinned. "If you get lonely and change your mind, I'll be in that bar over there." He pointed to a building that looked similar to the rest, only a little larger in area. Its straw roof was slightly darker in comparison and there was a swinging brass sign hanging from its upper storey that whistled every now and then when the gentle breeze caught it.

"You're really gonna leave me with *him?*" Francesca stressed to Morathos as Zeoc scurried off.

"You'll get used to him."

Francesca decided to explore the village. Although it was small and would only occupy a few hours of her time, she found an art gallery where she froze in awe at the majesty of the paintings and sculptures she observed. Hand crafted creations of some of nature's lost treasures; animals that had been extinct for decades; scenic greenery and rivers... It was as if her soul had spoken to her for the first time and she could rekindle some of her most freeing and magical times as a child.

Meanwhile, Zeoc lost himself amongst the village locals, washed under the influence of alcoholic beverages. "I'm telling you, she's the most beautiful thing your eyes could ever behold. She'll be here any minute now, just wait." But as more pints flowed and the hours passed, the seat he had been saving remained empty. Nevertheless, he nattered into the night, reluctant to leave as they called for last orders.

Morathos was so wrapped up in his thoughts and calculations, that he hadn't even noticed dusk convert to dawn. He was solely dedicated to what awaited and the precision it would require. But after two days, he had stalled in his thinking and made his way into the surrounding unfrequented land to gaze at the night sky. He tried to clear his head in the hope that the final piece of the enigma would beckon.

Lost in the moment, he hadn't even acknowledged Francesca's presence until she spoke, for she too was lying in the grass, gazing at the sky. "I'm so glad to see you out here," she said. "You could do with the break."

Morathos sat beside her. "I'm almost there," he said softly.

"It will come," she reassured him. "It always does."

"Yeah."

"I want to thank you. You've shown me what it's like to really feel alive again."

"But I didn't do anything."

"You've done more for me than you could ever know. I was so afraid; I hid away from reality. I was so ashamed of myself, but I buried that shame deep amongst a toxic desire to be one of *them*; one that they wouldn't ridicule. But now I think I've found the source of what I yearned and what it means to be fulfilled; to express myself the way I always did when I was younger; to embrace and accept my authentic self."

"Wisdom does not grow with maturity," said Morathos. "It is ever present in the spirit. It's how well we keep in touch with it that dictates how wise we really are."

"Your words are truly magical." Francesca sat up and reached her arms out, wrapping them around Morathos. He turned his head away and swiftly got to his feet, pushing her off him quite vigorously.

"I have to get to work; we don't have much time," he said.

"Why are you so uptight?!" Francesca hissed. "You know what? This trip might just actually help you offload some of that baggage!" She got to her feet and stormed off, ensuring to keep her tears concealed. Morathos sighed and put his head in his hands, then made his way to his dorm.

As dawn approached, Zeoc awoke in a fragile state. "Oh man! I got carried away again." He just didn't seem to learn. When it came to work, he was capable of getting his hands dirty, but he always played twice as hard.

Francesca had a rough sleep. She summoned her weary panda-eyed self into the lobby. Morathos charged past her and she turned her head away, hoping to avoid him seeing her like that. "Alright guys," he said. "The hospital called. I'm going to visit my sister. You guys may as well wait here."

"Don't try anything fancy," Francesca barked at Zeoc.

"All I want right now is coffee and a fat fry up!" he stressed as Morathos wasted no time to get himself to his escort. Francesca watched him on his way into the village, angst in her heart. Whilst Zeoc — in spite of his cravings — felt conflicted and reluctant to indulge, should his tender state reject whatever he might care to consume.

Morathos made his way to the helicopter that would escort him to the hospital. He sat in silence in the company of the crew, gazing out of the window at the vast stillness around him before disembarking on the roof where he was greeted by numerous site staff. They layered him with a hazmat suit and led him to Sequititah's room. There she lay almost motionless, but conscious, her shoulder-length silvery hair reflecting the artificial lighting. She looked incapable of speech but startled

Morathos when she suddenly called him to her side and the door was closed behind them.

"Sequititah," he said gingerly. "I'm not very good at these things. This may sound crazy, so buckle up..."

"So, you're my brother, eh? Cut yourself some slack, will you? I mean it's not exactly a common occurrence."

"It would seem I am. But I can't quite understand something." He hesitated. "I don't mean to offend you, but...."

Her hazel eyes fixed on him. "I know what you're going to say; I'm only thirty. I was born with a rare rapid ageing condition."

"I can't believe mum or father never told me about you."

"Why would they?" Sequititah said in a cynical tone. "They didn't love me; they weren't proud enough of me."

"What makes you say that?"

"Mum seemed all sweet and kind on the surface, but maybe she treated you better. I was shipped off like an unwanted parcel before I even had a voice to stand my ground." Her eyes began to well up. "Father was a goody-two-shoes and overly submissive to her. I might have only been a kid, but I was bright and intuitive."

"My memories of mum are fuzzy. I'm sure she wanted the best for us. But I aim to seek the truth." He grabbed her hand. "I'm going on a mission through time. I created something in the hope of saving the planet, but it's ended up in the wrong hands. The only way I can stop it, is to travel into the past."

"You came all this way to tell me that. What exactly do you expect *me* to do?"

Morathos took a deep breath and released his grip. "Time travel requires precision and you're the only one left who can take us to the right moment. If I get it wrong, you can guide me closer. It gives us a little more breathing room."

"I don't even know you." Sequititah rolled over to face away from him. "Only you know what the right moment is. Besides, I'm still finding this hard to believe — that we're even siblings."

"You think I'm doing this just for me? We could find out for certain," said Morathos. He tried not to sound too pleading. "This could answer a lot of questions for both of us, *and* save the universe."

Sequititah rolled back over and looked Morathos deep in the eye. She paused and saw something twinkle. "You know what. I'm itching for an adventure... It's a pleasure to have finally met."

Morathos tried to make sense of the moment but saved himself the headache and smiled. "Pleasure to meet you. Why exactly are you here?"

"No reason." She twitched her mouth to one side and swallowed slowly. "They think I'm too fragile because of my age. They don't get that I'm still young inside. But I just accepted it at the time because I felt helpless. I'll show them who's fragile!"

There was a knock at the door and a nurse appeared. "Just to inform you that you have two more minutes of visiting time remaining."

"Thanks." Morathos nodded as the door closed again.

"Get me out of here. I can't cope anymore," Sequititah whispered, pulling herself out of the equipment she was hooked up to.

"How do you propose I do that? I mean, I could probably think of something, but not in two minutes." He looked around the room, but to no avail.

"Time's up." The door swung open before long, and the nurse gently guided Morathos toward it. Sequititah looked at him longingly. He started miming to her and she paid attention to his lips as he mimicked the words, "*I will get you out.*"

Following his escort out of the hospital, Morathos sought after a figure of authority in the settlement. He moseyed around, asking various residents about who governed the village. He soon ascertained that the village was ruled by a mayor and he even found out where his house was. But of course, it wouldn't be that simple.

"I'm afraid the mayor is too busy for drop-ins," one of the guardsmen at his front door said. "If you wish to speak with him, you must make an appointment which is subject to his discretion. If you really insist on speaking with him, his secretary may be able to help." He pointed to a small outhouse a few yards away.

"Thank you." Morathos nodded politely and made his way over to reception.

"Let me see." The secretary scurried through piles of documents. "I'm not sure we can fit you in anytime soon. May I ask what it is regarding?"

"I believe you have someone wrongfully quarantined who should be released."

"No disrespect sir, but our doctors are highly skilled. I'm sure their judgement is worth trusting." The secretary looked down at her desk for a moment and started tapping her pen on it. She then raised her head and firmly pushed her glasses up to the bridge of her nose. "Would you like me to type up an e-letter and send it to him?"

"That depends on if he'll actually read it."

"You genuinely seem very concerned. I will speak with him and try to make it a priority."

Morathos exhaled. "Oh, thank you so much."

She smiled. "No problem. Expect to hear from the mayor or myself shortly."

Morathos couldn't feel completely convinced, but it was the best he could do, and so he returned to the ship.

Francesca was waiting eagerly in the lobby and raced toward him. "Well?"

"I promised I'd get her out of there," he said solemnly.

"And you wouldn't make a promise if you couldn't keep it, right?"

"Of course not. But it's out of my hands now."

Zeoc placed his hand on his shoulder. "Don't fret. You've accomplished far more difficult things than this."

"I know. But it's hard to trust when you have such precise expectations. Besides, we don't have much time. We've probably got one more day before we're going to have to just go for it and risk everything."

"She'll be here," Francesca reassured. "Listen, I know this is probably not the best time. But I owe you an apology. I shouldn't have reacted the way I did."

Morathos had already forgotten about it and attempted to distract himself while he awaited more news. "I never let conflict get in the way of my work," he said. "Logic surpasses emotion." He decided to check over his calculations and preparations one more time, scanning over the briefing blueprints.

"I still worry that you don't give yourself enough rest and actually let yourself feel things. Emotion is important too," said Francesca.

"I'll rest once this is over. I can't be at ease until then. I can't get complacent or take my foot off the gas yet."

"Hey, Francesca," Zeoc yelled across the lobby. "I think I heard something going on in the cockpit."

She raced over and observed the main screen.

"What is it?" Morathos quizzed.

"It's an e-letter from the mayor. He wants to discuss things with you. He says to head to his house."

Morathos immediately jolted up and made his way there.

"You again!" the guardsman howled.

The secretary had seen him arrive and came out to him. "It's okay, let him in."

"Very well." The guardsman nodded and opened the door.

Morathos was astounded when he walked into the hallway. The house was pristine. The staircase and flooring were a beautifully varnished pine. There really weren't many like it anymore.

"Right this way," said a well-presented young man. He led Morathos to the mayor's office and knocked on the door.

"Come in!" a chirpy voice called. "Ah, Morathos. What a pleasure!" The mayor was short and slightly chubby. His hair looked to be in the early stages of receding. But he was a jolly fellow.

"Pleasure to meet you, Mr. Mayor," Morathos politely greeted.

"Please, call me Rupert," the mayor insisted, neatening up his umber tie. "Now, I'm concerned that you feel strongly against your sister's quarantine and my secretary has told me that you genuinely feel worried. I mean, she is your sister, so I can imagine you would be. I just want to be sure there is no cognitive bias at play, if you know what I mean."

"I didn't even know I had a sister until a few days ago, so I've had no time to bond in that way. I need her help and we don't have much time." Morathos gave him a quick briefing of plasmantium and what was at stake.

"Oh my!" he gasped. "Well why didn't you say so earlier?"

"You're not exactly easy to get a hold of," Morathos sighed.

"Very well, I shall grant her release. But you must promise me you will try to maintain a distance from my people and take extra safety precautions. And you agree to your sister being escorted to your ship, to only remove her suit when we send instruction to."

"Yes, of course. I agree. Thank you, Mr. Mayor."

"Please, it's Rupert... Best of luck to you all and I hope you make it back safely."

Morathos nodded firmly and made his way to the others. Zeoc saw him walk aboard alone and jumped to assumptions. "Those selfish rotten scoundrels! How could they?"

"Relax!" Francesca cried. She looked at Morathos deeply and he didn't need to say a word.

Sequititah lay in her bed feeling distraught. She knew Morathos was still around but she couldn't help but doubt his promise. It was hours since he left her. Deep in her doubts, she was stunned when several hospital staff arrived. "We have authorised instructions from the mayor to escort you out of the premises. Please put these on." One of them handed her a protective suit which she promptly put on. She was still struggling to process exactly what was happening but didn't hesitate to embark upon the ship as her jaw gaped at the sheer magnificence of the craft in front of her.

"Now you must fly at least two hundred miles," said one of the doctors. "Then we will send confirmation for Sequititah to remove her suit." Morathos nodded and Francesca gave the command for the engine to start.

To their word, the authorisation was delivered the moment they had covered the distance required and the craft landed once more. Sequititah removed her suit and Morathos could now properly introduce her to Zeoc and Francesca.

"So how did you meet?" she asked Zeoc first.

"This guy's inventions kept me from needing mechanical integrated technology," he said.

"Remarkable," she replied before turning to Francesca. "And you?"

"I'm a researcher and despite his preferences not to be in the spotlight, your brother's accomplishments are not exactly kept in the dark."

"This is all well and good, but we must keep it brief for now. Time is of the essence," Morathos stressed. "Let's begin the final briefing. Without any kind of ground control to assist us, we've had to make additional preparations.

"First, we launch as we would, normally. Then, we increase the thrust by twenty percent to reach the Earth's escape velocity. Once we're out of the atmosphere, we will bypass the moon and Mars. During this time, I can assess my calculations and determine the exact time in which to deposit the rear components of the ship and then use the gas giant's own monumental gravity against them to gain more momentum. Then we propel at light speed using the magnetic anti-matter engines, to take us within the orbit of plasmantium.

"Once there, I'll make my final distance calculations to nearby stars and we will slingshot at faster than light speed. Travelling faster than a photon, we will catch up with photons that we previously encountered; thus, experiencing a past event. Since staring into space is essentially looking into the past, I will use the distance of the stars in light-years to calculate how far we need to travel. As we'll be travelling at just over a thousand times faster than light, I'll shave that percentage off."

"Incredible!" cried Sequititah before she changed into a leather redwood suit.

"Let's do this!" said Zeoc.

"Say the word and I'll get us going," said Francesca.

"Just one more thing," said Morathos. "I have integrated specific technologies in each of the escape capsules on board. Once we reach our destination, the ship won't be able to sustain itself much longer. We're going to each get propelled on our own journey into our respective pasts where time will stop from our own conscious frame of reference and, once we reunite, all our data will amalgamate."

"What!? Are you mad?" cried Sequititah. "What if we don't reunite and end up drifting off into outer space forever?"

"Yeah, how we getting back?" Zeoc puzzled.

"Relax guys," said Morathos. "We will still be in close enough proximity of each other and able to communicate through electromagnetic signals. I have programmed the capsules with a clever technology that — once we're ready — will create their own increased gravitational fields on our command that will be powerful enough to cause each capsule to gravitate towards one another and they will merge into a small, sustainable craft. Its complex programming will then fire us home. But I'll explain more about that later."

"What if we don't make our required window?" asked Francesca.

"I've run over these calculations ample times. I have every faith we will. But if we don't it'll only be by a small margin. The capsules will be able to compensate for that." Morathos looked up at the sky eagerly. "Are we ready?"

"Yeah!" Zeoc chirped.

Sequititah nodded as a cocktail of fear and excitement flooded her senses for the first time in as long as she could remember. "I can't believe I'm doing this!"

Francesca instructed the ship's computer to launch the craft and they lifted off once again — Morathos gave the nod several moments later. "Increase thrust by twenty percent," she commanded.

"Fifty thousand feet," the computer communicated. "Eighty thousand... Two hundred and fifty thousand... Four hundred and eighty thousand..." Despite the insane speeds, everything looked calm and slow-moving outside. The vast distances of anything considered remotely nearby in space, made even the fastest spacecraft ever built seem slow in comparison. The four of them looked out in mesmerisation as the Earth became increasingly smaller. But they wouldn't get long to enjoy the scenery. Before they knew it, they had surpassed the orbit of Mars.

"Proceed with phase one of the programme," ordered Francesca. The ship began to detach its rear components and morph its shape into something more circular.

"Launch the anti-matter propulsion engines," cried Morathos. The nuclear reaction that took place inside these engines generated unimaginable amounts of energy, contained inside a strong magnetic field. The engines swiftly boosted up to full throttle. "On my word, propel the thrusters. Three, two, one... NOW!" The now much smaller modified craft was on its ten-hour journey to beyond the far edges of the solar system. Although relative to the time that would pass back on Earth, they would reach their destination in a mere sub second.

Morathos stared in horror at the space in front of him. The thought that he was partly responsible for what he was witnessing made him feel nauseous, but he knew he couldn't lose focus now. He had to be more cautious and precise at this point, than any other. He looked on as the spacecraft slowly drifted closer to the deadly substance, waiting anxiously for the right moment. Whilst everyone else's minds were ruminating worries of what might happen next, Morathos watched his equations looping endlessly around his head. The ship was accelerating at an eye watering rate, but he kept his composure and as they gravitated closer to the plasmantium pool, he fixated on the precise moment. "Now!" he bellowed.

Francesca commanded the ship to accelerate in the opposite direction but it was struggling to escape the powerful gravity of their encounter and even Morathos began to fear that he had made an error. The ship seemed locked in a stalemate; enough thrust not to be swallowed up, but not quite enough to escape either. It teetered on the edge of the event horizon for several more minutes.

Morathos ordered for more acceleration. "Be gentle," he stressed. "We don't want to escape its orbit." Just a notch or two seemed enough as it slowly began moving in the opposite direction of the gravitational pull and hit the precise spot required to send it into orbit around the destructive substance. The four of them cheered on in delight and took advantage of the opportunity to take a short breather.

"Phew! Close call," said Francesca.

"Alright guys," said Morathos. "The next phases from here on were never part of the original programme so none of this has been previously coded into the ship's computer. It's utterly in our hands now. You all remember what to do?"

The three nodded in perfect synchrony and Morathos proceeded to look into the telescope. "The nearest star to us is four light-years away. When I stared into the void of space-time that the plasmantium has created, I realised its true power. There's no way I can stop this by simply travelling to the moment before I created it. I need to study its source if I have any hope of destroying it. I need to dissect and understand its origins. These capsules should contain enough energy to carry us about twenty-four years into the past. Any further could be too much of an ask. That would take me to my first birthday."

"That would be my birth year," said Francesca.

"I wasn't even alive then," said Zeoc. "Is that going to be a problem?"

"No. Your capsule will only travel as far back as your birth unless you're being accompanied by an elder," said Morathos.

Sequititah stared solemnly ahead. "I was three years old when I was shipped out of Karahdor. Although I could probably pass as an adult even then. Don't worry about me guys, honestly. My earliest memories are as vivid now as they were then and I doubt that will ever change. But it's a long story that I hope will all make sense later, once we get home. If I can only go twenty-four years back, that would make me chronologically six years old. If it's what must be done for the sake of the universe, then so be it."

"Wow, that's very bold of you," said Francesca. She looked as if she was welling up.

"The most important journey here is yours, Morathos," said Sequititah. "I'm sure we'll still learn a lot about each other along the way."

Morathos nodded. "Indeed."

"Let's do this!" Zeoc exclaimed as he and Sequititah climbed into their capsules.

"Don't worry, I've got it from here," Francesca reassured Morathos. "Besides the ship will only respond to my instructions."

"Just be sure to enter your capsule the moment you give the command," he warned.

She nudged him. "Relax. Now get in your capsule."

"Initiate escape velocity and slingshot us into the warped space-time," she commanded. And the ship accelerated immediately into the clutches of the gravitational ripples of space as she darted for her capsule and closed it abruptly. There, the craft shimmied and shook, spun and jolted before — as Morathos' calculations had predicted — shooting them off on a tangent at unimaginable velocity. They would catapult to a star twenty-four light years away in just over seven days. But from their subjective experience, time duration would mean nothing to them.

⸺⋇⟨◈⟩⋇⸺

Chapter 8

The Great Hatch

Magnetus Bane came storming into the president's office. "Mr. President, do you have a moment?"

"What is it?" he grunted.

"We may need to prepare our military forces."

"What is this nonsense? Who dares to even think they can wage war on me?"

"I have reports that some unidentified species is roaming the Earth, destroying everything in its path."

"That's ludicrous. Did they just magically appear from thin air or something?"

"I don't think my sources would attempt a hoax of any kind."

"Very well, I'll call the general," Reginald said in a hesitant tone.

A hologram of a part-mechanical man in an orderly-looking olive suit, abundant with medals arose. "I wondered how long after you took the reins we would speak, Mr. President." He placed his hands behind his back, parting his legs and broadening his shoulders.

"With all due respect, General Ribery, I'm too wrapped up in technological projects to care about military affairs; that's your job. In fact, I'm surprised it isn't you calling me first considering what's supposedly happening."

"Forgive me, Mr. President," the unrelenting voice replied. "I am in the process of preparing units as we speak. All my forces are engineered with the best technology available and are virtually indestructible. Their plasma and electromagnetic weaponry will tear through any who dare to contend with them."

The president projected a grin of delight. "Excellent. Keep me posted."

"Yes, Mr. President."

The city was advancing at an even more rapid rate than it previously had. Humans were virtually non-existent in Doradheim by now. There was only room for the mechanical. The president was gradually squeezing out even more of what little biology was left of him and artificial intelligence had plagued the minds of many others too. Soon, AI would be capable of becoming intelligent enough to question its own origins and programme its own upgrades — a dangerous concept, but just another demonstration of the man's apparent ignorance. He felt invincible. No fear of any attack on the fortress of a metropolis he had helped develop and no news of any invasion, would faze him in the slightest.

It was only a matter of hours before the skies of the Machine City were darkened — more so than usual — by a blanket of unfamiliar aircraft that began to open fire. The unpigmented ships were small, only holding a pilot and shaped like a crescent. General Ribery's forces were soon to follow, but the city already had its stronghold prepared with an onslaught of electromagnetic shockwaves that would effortlessly tear the flying machines right out of the sky.

"Who needs a military with me as president?" Reginald gloated.

As the craft came hurtling, rapid self-piloted jets screeched across the city and intercepted their descent, disintegrating them into shards that could easily be swept by the thousands of robots parading the streets below. Many of the pilots of the foreign aircraft had ejected before impact, parachuting into the unforgiving metropolis where they would be hacked down by overwhelming numbers of droids.

The invaders were heavily armoured and appeared to possess an extra pair of limbs. Their ivory faces were long and their eyes narrow. They seemed to carry quite sophisticated plasma rifles and those that were quick enough to hit a target would easily blast their adversaries apart. But despite their armour and agility, they were heavily outnumbered by Doradheian forces and so didn't pose all that much of a threat. They appeared to just dissolve and vanish once they were struck down.

A frantic array of electromagnetic impulse and plasma fired, as chaos unfolded. The city had become increasingly more hostile as civilians were anxious to turn a corner through fear of being obliterated. Robots, androids and cyborgs all exchanged blows with the mysterious invaders, leaving little breathing room in any corner of the metropolis in a free-for-all frenzy of mayhem and decimation. One of the unidentified creatures was much stronger, more agile and resilient than the rest. All the Doradheian attempts to take it down seemed useless as it sliced through numerous droids ferociously.

Magnetus Bane charged into the heart of the city with hordes of his droids. Using his enhanced tracking and scope technology, he located this seemingly unstoppable being and sniped it down in a flicker. The entity exploded violently and ejected some sort of mucus-like fluid in the process which appeared to evaporate in rapid succession. "It has begun." What looked sure to become a war-zone, was soon relaxed by the myriad of machines that eliminated the intruders in just a little more than a blink.

"What were they?" the president pondered to himself. "Where did they come from? Whoever or whatever they are, I'll make damn sure they don't interfere in my affairs again!"

Magnetus Bane had also begun to contemplate who the intruders might have been and although he had suspicions, he thought he ought to keep quiet for now, at least until he was assured. He decided to confront the president with some other news. "Mr. President, I believe I may have established who stole your ship. You were right about there being a traitor. It seems one of Professor Horuzokh's very own researchers, Francesca Tritus, was the mastermind behind it all. She made a minor error yesterday by disabling the ship's detection barrier. But she must have realised immediately, as I was unable to locate it after."

"Why bother to tell me then?" the president barked. "Unless you're going to do something about it or you've got some better news to report, don't waste my time. Besides, I don't care about them anymore. They're finally out of my face. Nobody is a threat to my power now. I've already begun designing technology for an impervious force-field around the city boundaries. No more unexpected, pathetic invasions."

"I was actually thinking of something similar myself. But of course, there's no doubt that your technology will surpass what I had in mind."

"Hmm. I'm glad you're finally thinking a little more pragmatically. But, as you say, I'd leave that part to me." The president's eyes widened. "Perhaps you should scout for damages and have all casualties rebuilt. Then when you're done, look at implementing any self-repair software updates that might have surfaced... Oh, and although it's doubtful, whilst you're out there, find any traces of the offenders for research. Then maybe integrate some offence and defence upgrades for more of my citizens."

Magnetus grinned. "Excellent idea, Mr. President." He didn't hesitate to collect his droids and have them sweep up the debris in the streets. He had all the components shipped for repair and got his builder bots to begin reconstruction. Software upgrades were rolling out for fun as each reconstructed bot received several uploads for resilience and combat abilities. The software was even available for the general population which only helped to conceal the minds of many more of his people, whilst enticing more in. They believed they were highly privileged to be a citizen of Reginald's city.

Meanwhile, Reginald had cyborgs of his own scurrying around the city boundary fitting large metallic plates at certain intervals of the ground. "Citizens of Doradheim." He could not wait to share his genius with his people. "I bring you my latest technological upheaval. As I speak, thousands of my machines are working hard at a mass under-city wiring that will hook metallic plates up to an enormous generator. The very power of the city of Doradheim itself will charge up jolts of magnetic power that will fire out of huge cylinders attached to the plates. Each cylinder shall emit waves of magnetic power that will form a dome blanket over the metropolis. They're integrated with an intelligence capable of mimicking the charge of whatever should assault them. Thus, causing a repulsion and making the city indestructible. Any unauthorised personnel that attempt to pass this point, will be locked out thanks to the clever security sensors."

The city erupted in rapture as Reginald once again absorbed the adoration of his citizens. With Doradheim protected from intruders, he could now concentrate on his unquenchable need for universal dominance. He had already manipulated plasmantium, reproducing it in liquid form by the gallons. Unbeknownst to him, in the Earth's atmosphere, it would behave very differently than in the vacuum. He would devour the stuff, ingesting it like it was his first meal since fasting.

He envisioned the world in the near future, under his influence. He imagined how the substance would consume the remnants of Earth's nature, thick and fast, and large quantities of it would begin to evaporate into the upper-atmosphere where it would expand across the skies and slowly choke the planet's biological life out of existence. He had calculated that at this stage, the substance would then collapse in on itself and scorch the surface of the Earth. Raw data would rain as the substance embedded itself into the planet's core, completely suffocating and recoding it. Electro-mechanical components would emerge and the once natural habitat for complex life, would be converted into a formidable gargantuan super computer that would soar through the cosmic abyss.

He visualised how plasmantium would suffocate other bodies in space in a similar way and he'd hope to start seeing some progress at this point, but his telescopes gave him nothing. Although the substance was unimaginably powerful, its gravitational influence on the sheer vastness of the universe would take far longer for an untrained eye to acknowledge.

The president turned his eye back to the metropolis before him as it presently stood, and mellowed in the perceived order that his ego had exacted. His comfort was forthwith disrupted as a glimmering, brisk movement traversed through the city. He watched it dauntingly as it accelerated. It seemed to possess no distinguishable form other than a flicker and, as fast as it had appeared, it vanished once more.

Magnetus Bane had sensed something suspicious before word of Reginald's experience had reached him. But the entity was too agile for his tracking software. He had thousands of search bots scanning the streets for any traces, but not one successfully reported anything back.

Something suddenly came over him. His body stiffened and he felt as if he was being constricted. The more he tried to resist, the tighter it seemed to get, until he was completely paralysed and dropped to the floor. There he noticed a small puddle of transparent liquid which appeared gloopy in consistency. It started to manoeuvre into various shapes and levitated off the ground. Magnetus could only watch in angst as the substance quickly became more solidified and started to form the shape of a man. It was still colourless at this point, but the facial features could vaguely be made out and appeared recognisable. Then, in a swift motion, the entity projected itself fully, as a familiar, sinister smile exhibited, his thick-framed spectacles so easily distinguishable.

"P-Professor H-Horuzokh!" Magnetus panted. "Impossible!"

"Where is he?" The professor's voice seemed much more resounding than it had previously.

"Who?"

"Morathos Reina."

"I don't know," the cyborg gasped. "Your so-called *researcher* betrayed us and rescued him. They took the ship."

"Is that so?" The professor realigned his glasses. "Today is your lucky day, Magnetus. I haven't forgotten about our previous engagement. But I've got more important matters to address right now. Don't worry, I'll be back for you soon enough."

Magnetus felt even more hindered as the force that smothered him seemed to increase in intensity. He was left astounded as the professor morphed into an exact replica of him and left him lying helplessly immobile.

"Mr. President," Horuzokh stomped into Reginald's office and convincingly assimilated his identity, "I'm picking up the whereabouts of your ship on my tracking system. I know you're a busy man, so I will go and take a look. I might be gone a few days," he lied.

"I presume all your other duties have been completed."

"Yes, of course."

"Very well then. Report back to me."

"Certainly." He expressed a cunning smile to himself as he turned away from the president on his departure and proceeded to return to Magnetus Bane.

The cyborg got to his feet as he felt the asphyxiation relax and Horuzokh morphed back into his former state. "I told you I'd be back," he remarked. Magnetus attempted to charge at the professor with his bionic fist. But just before his blow connected, Horuzokh shapeshifted his form to avoid the strike.

"What the hell are you?" he asked, puzzled.

"I'm your puppet master. I've told the president you're leaving Doradheim for a few days, to avoid suspicion. You're coming with me."

"I'm not going anywhere," he squirmed. "You better not have done anything to the president!"

"Ah, but you don't have a choice. You're under my manipulation." The professor squeezed his right palm into a fist and Magnetus immediately fell to his knees at the unbearably tight sensation that coursed through him. "And for the record, the president was unharmed. I'll settle my business with him in due course." Horuzokh dispersed into a gloopy substance once again and subsequently vanished.

"You'll never get back in this city!" Magnetus yelled before he made his way out of the complex feeling an intolerable strain whenever he tried to resist. The professor manipulated his path to the outer boundaries of the Machine City. There, he awaited the landing of a small craft that slightly resembled those from the recent invasion. Magnetus tried to fight with all his strength and resist boarding, but that only made it harder for him.

"Pleasure, seeing you again." Horuzokh's twisted tone resonated as Magnetus embarked upon the craft. "Now, let's go on a little adventure."

An unsettling familiarity soon struck Magnetus as the ship approached a dreary, rundown plot of land, stretching for tens of miles. Just ahead of their horizon lay, what resembled the derelict ruins of a once vibrant city. "Karahdor!" he gasped. "Why did you bring me here?"

"The brain is nothing more than a biological computer. It can be replicated without biology, into something mechanical. Reginald's desires of bio-engineering the planet from its natural state, into one of mechanics is essentially no different.

"But you see, there's a flaw in his design; something he failed to account for; a resistance he had not anticipated."

As the ship drew closer, Magnetus became horrified at what he witnessed. The ground where the ancient remains lay showed signs of rupture. What appeared to be large openings like burrows, could be observed at various locations. Some of them were spewing a gloopy substance very similar to what he had just encountered in Doradheim. Others emitted occasional sparks and flickers, or began to eject a potent fountain of emerald luminosity.

Horuzokh led him towards the hostility of one of the burrows; which, once they eventually reached a certain depth, began to broaden out into an all-encompassing hive-like structure. There he observed what looked like enormous eggs, each deeply embedded into some sort of system of arteries as thick as tree roots. They were structurally lodged into the very crust of the Earth itself.

"Behold the forthcoming, Great Hatch!" he yelled.

"It's just as I feared." Magnetus was left trying to untangle a complex web of memories. Despite his words suggesting he knew what was happening, he wasn't so certain. He tried to rationalise. "You honestly believe you can withstand the power of plasmantium?"

"Oh, you foolish outdated pile of rust!" Horuzokh spat. "You have no idea of what lurks inside these eggs and it is only a matter of days before the Great Hatch shall commence. Better strap in tightly as you shall be granted the privilege of being the first to lay eyes on the spectacle! Ha-ha!" He closely observed the cyborg's empty eye socket. "Or should I say, *eye!* And to think that such an event should occur in the very location that left you in that state."

Bane was left speechless. He pondered about how Horuzokh could possibly know about his origins but was too paralysed to verbalise anything as the Earth around him began to crack, weaving vines engulfing him, wrapping around him like a serpent. The professor squinted callously as he came to within an inch of Magnetus. "Now, I shall resume my business with the president." And he immediately abandoned the vicinity, making haste back to Doradheim.

There, he observed the magnetic force-field system that now surrounded the city and simply transformed into a mucus state that would effortlessly pass through it, traversing the streets. Once he had reached the epicentre of the metropolis, he resumed the form of Magnetus Bane, and charged into the presidential complex.

"Magnetus. A rapid return," Forathorn greeted.

"Bear with me, Mr. President. I have located your ship as promised," he lied.

"But?"

"But I'm afraid, unless we develop software to hack into its systems, I cannot relinquish it."

"Very well. It is not a priority right now. But if you insist, I will have my researchers and engineers look into it."

"Excellent."

Several days had passed; the city grew and developed ever more exponentially and became increasingly overpowering and intimidating. They had also paved way for Horuzokh to keep close tabs on the president's plans and progress, digging and fishing out all he could whilst he bided his time to seize his opportune moment. "It's inevitable," he remarked.

"What are you talking about?" the president queried.

"Your end!" Like a shot, the professor had vanished and re-emerged in his true state. "It's simply a matter of when, not how. But I'll leave that in your hands."

"Horuzokh! I thought I did away with you."

"You fool. Your ignorance blinds you."

Forathorn tried to take a swing for him and yell for security, but he agilely dodged his blow. "Your cries for help are useless. This room has been encased in a substance that sound waves cannot permeate. Ha-ha!"

"Impossible!" Reginald gasped, failing all attempts to strike him again on several occasions. "What have you done with Magnetus?"

"Your plan is over," the professor hissed. "Magnetus is safe for now, but your beloved computerisation mission isn't. That first invasion was a mere warning. Your city will be obliterated."

"Nothing can break my magnetic force-field. Nothing can stop my technological power. Nothing will stop plasmantium!"

Horuzokh smiled derisively. "Oh, but it can. You see, I'm a biological being. I've been busy developing something very damaging to your cyber-kind. You will surrender to me if you have any amount of sense."

"Nonsense! If it's a war you want, then a war you shall have! You're foolish to think you can break my technology. No one shall stand in the way of my project!"

"Very well. Be prepared for a failure you are only delaying anyway. Your sacred digitalised components will perish under my newly developed threat."

"I beg to differ, Professor." The president gritted his teeth. "Bring me your best shot!"

Horuzokh morphed himself again and let out a screeching guffaw as he fled the presidency. The president was sceptical and certainly didn't see his city to be under any threat. Nonetheless, he ordered General Ribery to gather his forces, sending a portion of his own machines to join the convocation of incalculable flanks that would circumnavigate the city's surrounding plains.

Meanwhile, in the depths of the Karahdoran remains, Magnetus Bane helplessly watched on as a multitude of giant eggs, each about the size of a spacecraft escape pod, began to quiver and crack. From them emerged creatures similar to those he had encountered in Doradheim, only much larger. They looked sharper, more daunting. A great deal of them let out almost unendurably deafening screeches that punctured the atmosphere. The hive stretched for many more acres and what was observable to Magnetus would only be a fraction of the true magnitude of hatchlings that would emerge. They sure wouldn't be outnumbered this time, by any stretch of the imagination. Much to the cyborg's relief, he was spared as the species had their hungry eyes set solely on war.

Many of the lifeforms were identical and travelled on foot but some were capable of flight, whilst others would rely on technology of their own to get airborne. They soared the skies before meeting their waiting adversaries in the unfrequented earth, as phalanxes of the beasts marched behind them, each stomp punishing the soil below it.

Without hesitation the two combatant forces charged forth opening deadly beams of electromagnetic and plasma energy at one another; each hit almost certainly eradicating its target. The foreign species were equally as brutal in melee, too, for any who got close enough, would suffer at the being's merciless talons. They seemed to transfix their foe with unimaginable ease. The mechanical automata would not fall short though, as they would have some equally capable and formidable blade weaponry themselves.

Fleets of ships soared through the clouds as both races took combat into the air. Mechanical warriors hurled towards their foe, slashing and slicing the biological beings. But they were met by surprise upon witnessing severed limbs growing back and those that had been detached morphed into entirely new entities. Many of Reginald's machines had sophisticated repair programming and could swiftly reassemble themselves to counter the piercing talons of their enemies. But it would seem the mysterious creatures would be capable of regenerating much faster than their opposition. It would be no easy conquest for either competitor.

Some of the beasts made their way to the city boundary and attempted to break through the president's magnetic force-field system. The repulsion would send them firing off for hundreds of metres, stunning them sufficiently enough to make them reluctant to attempt any further assaults.

Horuzokh hacked his way through robots as if they were toy soldiers, slashing through their complex mechanics. It appeared that his shape-shifting and regeneration abilities were far superior to those of his allies. The droids would soon recover and rebuild their components before attempting to bring the professor down. Each attempt was wasteful though and only fuelled his rage further. It seemed that nothing could stop him and this war would be a vicious cycle of brutal combat.

One of the droids became constricted by its adversary. It quickly raised its talons up and would have pierced the robot straight through the head if not for an intervening electromagnetic jolt from across the plain that forced it to release its grip. The droid then shot it again at point-blank range and it squirmed and screeched as it appeared to meet its demise. Reginald could only watch on in angst from his office observatory. Deep down, he was uncertain of the fate of his city, but his ego clouded his worries, smothering him with a false confidence.

Chapter 9

A Bitter Unveiling

Sequititah didn't need to time travel. Everything was as evocative to her now, as it would have been in the moment — the torment, the neglect, the discrimination; even the transition from Karahdor to Doradheim, the noise, the distinct metallic odour of the mechanics. She was only here for her brother, but she presumed that her story wouldn't really clear anything up for him. Despite that, she felt she had some regrets to process and accept, which this journey may well have succoured her with. Her desire to resort to machinery to help her to self-preserve and combat her condition, was still something she needed to come to terms with. Much of the damage could not be undone in the physical sense — as a significant proportion of her body was no longer biological — but she still had a conscious desire to move on from her toxic addiction and release her inner resentments towards herself...

"What's wrong with her?!"

"I don't know. But we ought to love her all the same."

"What do you think I've been trying to do for the last three years? She's hideous, we have to ship her out..."

"It seems your daughter has an unnamed condition. It's apparent she is ageing too quickly, but it's unlike any other condition of its kind that we have any recognition of..."

She felt even more lost than a typical outsider. Not only was she outcast, but she had no label of any kind, no tribe to belong to. She had a condition that no other known being on the planet had to endure, and that was awfully lonely. All she could do was long to be accepted and resort to the habits that were indoctrinated upon her from a young age — the technological transformations that would 'fix' her. She started to reflect.

When you're told you're broken at such an age, it soon becomes all you've known; when you're taken away from your family and tested on to see what's 'wrong' with you; when your very biology is tampered with in exchange for artificial parts, right from the earliest moments of life, it bears a heavy influence on your identity. Your environment shapes your existence, and everything you're led to pursue, leads you into a toxic cyclone. It's harder to break habits when they're all you've been conditioned to, and the role models around you were undesirable in the first place. It's harder to accept your truth when everyone else has left you behind and made you feel so dysfunctional. She started to sob deeply. It was as if — suddenly — something inside of her had awakened. The burden in her heart that she had carried for so long, had suddenly lifted and she could turn her attention to her brother's needs now. She wiped her tears and composed herself. "Morathos, can you hear me?" There was some disturbance, but no clear words at first. She tried again.

"Yes! Yes, loud and clear. Everything okay?"

"Just a check-up."

"Very well. I'll report back once I gather everything I need," he said. "You heard from the others?"

"No. I'll try them now... Francesca, are you there?"

"Yes," she responded immediately. "This is Morathos' journey, right? I may as well just hang around here. Ain't much I need to know about my own past, right?"

"Yeah, me neither. I can tell Morathos all about me later; I think he was just trying to make us all feel involved. I might not know him well, but it didn't take me long to realise that he has a strange way of showing how he feels."

"You can say that again!" Francesca cried.

"Zeoc?" Sequititah called. "Zeoc?"

"Zeoc, respond!" Francesca bellowed. But there was nothing. "He's probably fallen asleep or something knowing him."

"I hope it's nothing serious."

"I'm sure he's alright. I wouldn't worry just yet."

"Yeah. Maybe you're right."

Sequititah often had strong intuitive feelings that were rarely wrong, but she had been conditioned to ignore them and tune them out. Her gut was telling her that something wasn't right, but she felt so conflicted at such times (something that perhaps stemmed from her experiences with those around her and how they often dismissed her) that she thought it best to try and relax for now.

"So, what do you think Morathos will find?" Francesca pondered.

"I can't really say. I just hope that it serves him more than just discovering the origins of plasmantium. I get the sense he's a lost man."

"Me too. I think you and I are going to get along great."

Zeoc's head was in a whirlwind. He tried to discipline himself and gather his bearings. It was dark. *I must have lost consciousness*, his mind echoed to him. *What happened? It all unfolded so fast!* He tried to make contact with the others. "Morathos... Sequititah... Francesca. Do you read me?" but there wasn't even a murmur. An unnerving emotion washed over him as he stared at the various dials, buttons and screens in front of him, trying to contemplate their functions. He tried to stay calm and began talking to himself softly. "It's okay. Let's just try this one." But there was nothing; not a single sound, light or any sign of functional operation. He started to lose his rationale, his heart rate increasing substantially. He had begun to respire more heavily for a moment, before the realisation of how scarce his oxygen supply was had forced him back into relaxation. He knew there wasn't much he could do but hope that the others were fine, and they might acknowledge his whereabouts.

Morathos was too far gone to worry about anything else at this point. He had designed his capsule to take his subconscious directly to his past. It was like a dream, except for the fact that the events that would unfold actually happened. His unconscious body would remain in his capsule whilst his subconscious would paint a mental picture of everything...

"I don't think I can bear this again." Ignerenous sobbed as she observed her son who seemed completely disassociated. She ran her fingers through her short greying hair and observed some of it fall into her hand.

Archquar couldn't keep up with his wife and he had been suppressing his frustration towards her uncharacteristic restlessness and indecisiveness for a long while. He firmly massaged his shiny scalp. "You wanted Sequititah gone. Then you wanted to move to Doradheim because you missed her. Now you're wishing you never did and don't want to see her. And to top it all off, you stressed that you never wanted another child, but then you begged me to have one with you. Yet, now you wish you never did. What is going on with you lately?"

"I thought it would be different this time. Sequititah was broken. I sent her here to get fixed... and they didn't fix her."

"And what about Morathos? You think he's broken too?!"

"Just look at him. He hasn't got a clue where he is. He looks so distant." She waved her hand in front of his face and there was nothing. "See. You keep telling me we shouldn't talk about him in his presence like that, but he's not even with us. I've given birth to a defective child who is ageing too quickly and now I've given birth to a vegetable too. It's your fault."

"What are you talking about?"

"You must carry some kind of genetic defect that you've passed on to my children."

"That's nonsense." His wife's words invited a deep sting that punctured him. "Besides he's one year old!"

"A mother's instinct is never wrong."

"That's no instinct. You're jumping to conclusions..."

Morathos' subconscious experience was projecting what it thought was most important. He had designed his capsule to do so out of efficiency and so he found himself skipping several years at a time on his journey. But he would still be restricted by energy limitations that were required and so he'd hoped there would be sufficient resources to get just what he needed and nothing more.

Ignerenous heard a knock. There stood a mechanical body that had a tight hold of Morathos and it threw him at her as she opened the door. "I have been ordered to send your child home," it said.

"What?! Again?!" she bellowed. "I'm getting tired of you, Morathos!"

"I'm afraid if he doesn't pick up pace and start actually learning what he is taught, he can no longer attend our school."

Ignerenous snarled at the machine, glaring at it with her serene eyes and slammed the door after dragging her son inside.

"You used to be such a patient woman. That's one reason I fell in love with you." Archquar said. "He's proven he's not a vegetable. It's just taken a few years."

"There's still something wrong with him. He isn't mingling with anyone at school. He daydreams all the time and hardly ever pays attention. You ought to be concerned."

"Yes, I am concerned. Perhaps he needs a different environment. That school is no good for him, but you insist the problem is with him."

"That school is the best in the city!" Ignerenous snapped. "If they can't educate my son, nobody can."

"You just don't get it. *Our* son is different."

"He's different alright!" Ignerenous stormed off and Archquar sighed deeply. He pressed his chin onto his palm which allowed for his thumb and index finger to slot into his sunken cheeks.

The next day Ignerenous and Archquar both sat in silence frequently watching the clock tick by. They were both anticipating whether or not their son would make it through the whole day or be sent home again. Archquar was sure it would only be a matter of time before there was another knock at the door. But there wasn't. He was transported home right when he ought to have been. He raced through the front door as his father came to greet him. "Whatever you did, it worked," the transportation droid said.

"What do you mean?"

"Your son has shown his potential today. There's still work to do, but there was something different in him."

"Oh, that's remarkable," Archquar beamed.

Ignerenous piped up. "What happened?"

"I think he made a new friend."

Ignerenous raised her brow.

"See I told you," said Archquar.

Morathos raced up to his room. "Aren't you going to tell us about your new friend?" Ignerenous asked him on his way upstairs.

"Not now, Ignerenous," Archquar cried. "Give him some time to unwind."

Ignerenous became exasperated. "Who do you think you are? You think you know my son better than me?"

"Stop being so possessive and controlling," he snapped. "What is wrong with you?"

"You're the problem!"

"Just stop! He will talk to us when he's ready. I don't understand you anymore. You're not the woman I fell in love with..."

The arguments would escalate endlessly. Archquar had no idea who his wife was anymore. He felt like leaving her, but for the sake of his son he knew the timing would not bode well. He often kept things inside because anytime he tried to express himself, that tended to make him feel even more alienated. He had been suffering with abdominal discomfort for quite some time and it was affecting his energy. But he knew he had to stay strong for Morathos. Despite Ignerenous' several attempts to disown their child, Archquar would persist with her and try to find solutions.

"Reginald!" Morathos yelled.

"What d'you say, son?"

"That's his name."

"Whose name?"

"My friend." Morathos paused for a moment. "Look at this." He pulled out a handheld device from under his bed.

"What is it?"

"It's the beginning of humanity."

Morathos would often say some perplexing things that neither of his parents could quite grasp. He might have daydreamed a lot, but when he did speak, it would often be something mind-bending.

"What are you saying?"

"It's a technology decomposing device. Or as I like to call it, a nature accelerator."

"If you say so son." Archquar tried to contemplate what he was talking about but his mind could not fathom it. "Where did you get it from?"

"I invented it, silly. Reginald taught me a lot."

Archquar froze in disbelief, unable to respond.

"Technology decomposing device?!" Ignerenous cried. "Sounds awfully concerning to me."

"Yes, but he invented it himself. Don't you see, our son is special!"

"There's still something not quite right. A technology that destroys technology."

It seemed that no matter what, Ignerenous could not accept her son as he was and all that he was accomplishing.

"There's just no winning with you, is there? You get an unrealistic image of what you expect and refuse to accept anything that even remotely deviates from your selfish projection."

"I've seen it before — a reclusive child that stays in his room all the time and goes insane with inventions. He grows up with hate and seeks a way to destroy and control everything."

"I think you've been watching too many movies. Why don't we find out how his invention works before assuming it's something bad?"

"Again, you insist on invalidating a mother's instincts!"

"Oh, cut it out!" Archquar had heard enough and he went to see his son. "Morathos, can I come in?" There was no answer so he slowly opened the door a fraction and peered in to find him in deep concentration. "I wanna know more about your invention. How does it work?"

"Look around you, father. We basically worship technology, but it's making us so lazy and unappreciative. Only an ignorant fool could deny the fate of our species. It might already be too late, but we have to try at least."

Archquar cleared his throat. "I think I understand. But we depend on technology so much now."

"This device is capable of downgrading dysfunctional technology that will give nature a chance to breathe again."

"And Reginald taught you how to build it?"

"He's the only person that has ever understood me; I don't talk to anyone else. They bore me with their insistence on learning mind-numbing, uncreative stuff."

"I tried to tell your mother that school wouldn't be right for you."

"It wasn't... until I met Reginald, that is. He has such a unique way of looking at things and he applies it to technology in a way I haven't seen before. We make a good team."

"Well as long as you know that not fitting is a good thing."

"Nobody else makes much sense to me." Morathos gave his father an earnest look and nodded at him. "But nobody else is my responsibility. I cannot afford to be inauthentic."

"That's my boy..."

With the aid of his newfound knowledge, Morathos had built himself a reputation amongst his fellow students. The quiet reclusive child that was once the laughing stock and prime target for bullies, was now the talk of the school. Many of his inventions weren't particularly desirable amongst them, but that's because his creative ability and wild imagination were so far beyond what most his age could comprehend. Nonetheless, he had unintentionally made a name for himself and — much to his distaste — attracted a great deal of attention.

Morathos' parents went to attend a consultation with his tutors to discuss his progress. It would be the last one before a long summer break. "Your son's creativity is astounding," one said, "but he is falling behind with his curriculum."

"Who cares about curriculum?!" said Archquar. He had been holding back for too long by this point. "It's all useless. All you're teaching him to do is memorise information that he really doesn't care about. Information that is just distracting him from his creative authenticity."

Ignerenous looked concerned; she didn't say anything. But after a moment, her facial expression had changed. It expressed a look of realisation that Archquar seemed convinced with.

But upon returning home, it wasn't so long before Archquar had established that perhaps she hadn't. "Let's advertise our son's inventions. We could make a fortune!" she exclaimed.

"Just when I thought you were starting to actually show some sanity and compassion, you say this!" He exhibited a sour expression at his wife. "Do you realise how monstrous you sound right now?"

"His inventions are unorthodox, I'll admit, but even if they aren't popular, we could make headlines!"

Archquar rolled his eyes at her in a huff. "I can't deal with this anymore. I'm going for a walk," he said dully. "I don't know what time I'll be back."

Morathos spent the majority of the summer in his own mind. He continued to create inventions that not many could understand the purpose of. But to him, they were something meaningful. His father did his best to appreciate that. But his mother was monitoring everything he did. She tried to wrap her head around his creations and how they functioned but only for means of trying to make money. Nonetheless, their complexity would be too great a challenge for her to come to grips with.

Archquar still hadn't returned home. Ignerenous looked at the time. Her clock displayed 7:52pm. That was unusual for him. Sometimes he worked long hours as an engineer, but he had been on long-term leave for a few months and would usually be home for dinner. As much as Ignerenous enjoyed the peace, she had started to worry a little.

Just then, the door rattled and she opened it to find a boy standing there. "Is Morathos home?" he asked.

"He's upstairs. Who might you be?"

"I'm Reginald. Has he ever mentioned me?"

"Oh, yes, he has! I wondered when we would actually meet." She sidestepped and opened the door wider. "Come in."

He made his way into the lounge where he stood anxiously.

"It's alright, take a seat. I'll let him know you're here."

Reginald sat admiring the room whilst he waited.

"What are you doing out in the city at this hour?" Ignerenous asked on her way back downstairs.

"It's just..."

"Go on."

"I'm locked out."

"Well how about we march you home and make your parents open the door?!"

"It's not that simple." Reginald bowed his head in a gesture that expressed shame.

"Where are your parents?"

"Oh, they're home."

"But?"

"I don't want to say."

"That's alright. You talk when you're ready. Can I get you a drink?"

"That's very kind of you."

Morathos came stomping down the stairs. "Mum, can he stay here tonight?"

"Wait 'til your father gets home. I'm sure he'll be here soon. He must've gotten held up. Besides, it depends if he even *wants* to stay." She turned to face him and he looked at her longingly, unable to stop his head from gently nodding.

Ignerenous was good at being hospitable. She always went the extra mile to make her guests feel welcome. Archquar had pondered about her seemingly striking contrasts of character at times. But this was all quite recent in the grand scheme of things.

As Reginald and Morathos exchanged words, she excused herself and resumed her business. She let herself into her son's bedroom and took photographs and video clips of all his creations. She had even been recording the conversations she had had with him, as well as those her husband had exchanged. She wanted to advertise her son's ability and, despite Archquar's distaste towards the ordeal, she persisted in doing so covertly.

It was getting late. Just when everyone was starting to wonder whether Archquar would even be coming home, the door swung open, and there he stood, completely drenched from the torrential downpour outside. Morathos raced to him with no concerns of getting soaked from his father's attire. "Where on earth have you been?"

"It's a long story." He made his way inside, hung up his waistcoat then approached Ignerenous. "I need to speak with you in private."

"Father, this is Reginald," Morathos eagerly introduced. "Can he stay tonight?"

"It's nice to finally meet you. Sure, why not? It's too late to be going home now." He turned to his wife and gestured for her to head out into the hall. "Shall we?" They both headed out and made their way toward the rear of the house.

"What is it?"

"I've seen Sequititah. She's in a bad way."

"What?!"

"She's become hooked on robotic implants and upgrades and it's destroying her." Ignerenous turned her face away. "Don't you even care about our daughter?"

"Why else do you think I don't want Morathos to know about her?" she said coldly. "She was already damaged from day one."

"How can you be so heartless? Why suggest moving here to find her then? Can you not see what Vynzuth is doing to our humanity? Sequititah is in grave danger of losing her battle and all you can do is sit and shrug." He paused in deep thought for a second. "Wait a minute! Morathos' invention. It could save her."

"Hmm." Ignerenous seemed to display a swift change of heart.

"The other thing I wanted to say was there is a minority resistance being formed called the Anti-machs. They aim to overthrow Vynzuth and his wicked schemes. If you insist on making money from our son, then we should use it to help fund their ambition."

"I'm not a charity. Besides, they'll only fail so why bother?"

"You never used to be such a defeatist either," said Archquar in a tone of disappointment.

"They hold the power to stop Morathos' invention being a success."

"I've kept this quiet for long enough. The real reason why I've been taking such long breaks from work is because it makes me sick to my stomach working for this heinous government. I'm dying, Ignerenous."

"What are you talking about?"

"I've been suffering for years with this abdominal pain. Something inside isn't working properly. But, even if I could afford it, I refuse to take their poisonous medicine. I've become reluctant to express my pain because nobody cares. Nobody listens to the true problem. They just want you to jump on board their artificial bandwagon."

"But they can save your life."

"I want no part of their schemes. I would rather die a pure man. And I had wished that of our daughter too."

"You're telling me that you would rather risk dying and hold out for a very slim hope to overthrow a government, to then have our son save our daughter's and your own life, when you could just get the mechanical transplant now and end your pain?"

"Yes. That's exactly what I'm saying. Think about it. I know deep down you want the same, but something is influencing you."

"I don't know who you are anymore, Archquar."

"I haven't changed! I'm still the same man you fell for ten years ago. But something is definitely different in you!"

"You've lost your mind!" Ignerenous cried. "We have guests anyway, so if you'll excuse me..." She stormed off to the lounge to find Reginald and Morathos both asleep in their respective chairs, then placed a cover over each of them before she headed up to bed herself. Archquar peered his head into the lounge for a brief second and proceeded out of the front door, into the cacophonous, bustling street. He didn't know where he was going, but he just kept walking in the hope that something would inspire him along the way.

Ignerenous lay wide awake right into the small hours. Her husband had not returned, although she'd rather he didn't at this particular time. She sat with her thoughts, none of which reflected on their conversation or any of what Archquar had tried to convey to her. She continued to gather more and more of her recordings and started to edit them together. She tried to reconstruct what she had, to make it more professional and appealing, in the hope of making a comfortable sum of money at her son's expense and with Morathos so deeply engrossed in his experiments and inventions, she could be even more discreet about it.

The next morning, Morathos and Reginald engaged in discussions about various ideas. Although Morathos could put ideas together and make connections in ways that Reginald — or anyone for that matter — was simply not capable of, Reginald had explored technological avenues that Morathos would not even consider. "I'm sure they think the same of me, but all the other kids seem so peculiar," Reginald remarked. "They all just sit there and absorb everything they're told. They don't seem to question any of it. I just can't relate to any of them and that's why I think we gel like we do."

"I agree," Morathos admitted. "We're both so distinctly different from the rest, but also have such individual strengths, that we just bounce off of each other. It's like father said: school is a distraction for people like you and me."

"I wish my parents would see it that way." Reginald bowed his head sorrowfully. "I think they locked me out because they're ashamed of me; because I'm not like the other kids."

"Well, stick with me," Morathos smiled. "We can be outsiders together..."

"What are you doing back here?" a distressed voice cried from the other side of the door that Archquar was standing at.

"I've come to help you. I'm suffering too, you know. But it doesn't have to be that way. There just might be an alternative."

"It's too late!"

"Sequititah, your mother has lost it." The door swung open.

"Mum never wanted me in the first place. That's how I ended up here, in this hell hole of a city. The only thing that can save me now is to carry on as I am — it's irreversible. Why did you even come to Doradheim anyway?"

"I'm trying to understand that myself. Your mother claimed to want to see you again. But she isn't the same woman she used to be. I didn't get her motives or reasoning for her change of heart, but I came here in the hope of finding you again myself."

"And look what you found instead," she sobbed. "I can't see you. You must leave."

"I'm trying to help you."

"Well, don't!" She slammed the door in her father's face. He turned away in despair and slowly went on his way.

"Perhaps I should do some further research on the Anti-machs," he said to himself. "I might be able to establish where they might be based." But he found no information regarding their location and presumed it was deliberately located somewhere elusive. After all, it would make sense that it was a private organisation that didn't want to be tracked by the government. But Archquar was a persistent man.

He never saw his daughter again. He spent many a night curled up in discomfort and his health was deteriorating with the years, but he kept himself occupied, grinding out through just enough working hours to get by and provide for his son. The rest of the time, he spent researching the Anti-machs. Things would gradually get easier for him as the organisation became more known, but he still couldn't construct a plan to go forward and despite his continued attempts to persuade Ignerenous to aid with funding, she would continue to refuse whilst keeping her actions from his awareness. His worries were projected in a manner of panic that he was going to run out of time.

Reginald had attempted to go back home on several occasions, but each time ended in no success, until eventually, he discovered that his parents had fled from their place of residence. They would refuse to speak with him every time earlier and whilst Archquar had no qualms about him staying,

Ignerenous wasn't as relaxed in the matter. "He's been staying here for six years now!" she cried.

"If anything, I thought you were the more hospitable one of us," sighed Archquar.

"There's being hospitable, then there's being a pushover."

"I shall leave in the morning," said Reginald.

"No, that won't be necessary," said Archquar.

"Yes, it will!" Ignerenous cried. "Six years of inventions, experiments and discoveries and nothing to show for it except more inventions and discoveries. When will our son actually contribute to society?"

"You have to be more patient," Archquar stressed. "He's an innovator. His inventions aren't for the convenience of our conventional society. They are designed to change the paradigm and so the majority that are stuck in its algorithms cannot see their usefulness."

"I'm tired of hearing you say that!" Ignerenous hissed. She pointed at Reginald. "He is holding our son back! That's why he has to go."

"Nonsense!" Archquar retaliated. "Don't you remember the influence he had? If not for him, our son may not be at the stage he's at now. They're both going to make remarkable leaps one day because they dare to venture and challenge the norm."

Ignerenous rolled her eyes and stormed off in a huff.

Morathos had already retreated by this point. He tended to stay out of the way of such conflicts to avoid the discomfort it would bring him and how it would distract his focus.

Reginald gave Archquar a look of concern. "Don't worry. I will make sure you're not out on the streets," he reassured.

Archquar watched the days pass by ever more quickly before him. The city of Doradheim became even more intimidating, yet alluring, and soon the days would roll into months, and months into years. He grinded through the agony of his physical vulnerability and kept the bitter sting of his debilitating, stagnant marriage numbed by witnessing his son's transition from a boy into a young adolescent — the pride was all he had to keep him afloat.

Then the day came when he had to make the most soul-defining decision. He felt he could take his son no further, there was nothing more for him than to flee the city and let nature run its course. His only regret, was the time he had wasted, and he knew he didn't have much longer.

Morathos awoke that morning. He stared blankly into the space in front of him. It was as if a part of him was missing. But there was some other sense that subsequently seemed to fill the void. His hard work had started to pay off in the months leading up to this day; a small audience would start to utilise some of his inventions. His first invention was still the ultimate one; yet, that had seemed to falter. He had been so busy in his work and it had been so long. It had been stored away for all those years and it had just so happened to cross his mind again now. He rummaged through all his experiments, prototypes and components. But it was nowhere to be seen. He contemplated what could have happened. *Did I make a mistake?* he thought, given how long ago it was built. But he couldn't seem to stay focussed. Not only had his father's sudden disappearance bewildered him, but his only friend Reginald had vanished just a few days earlier also.

Meanwhile, Ignerenous was busy revelling in the income she was receiving from advertising businesses and the media. Although her son's inventions weren't reaching large audiences, they still made headlines, and that would bring a surprisingly substantial amount of earnings. But Morathos would know nothing of it, only receiving a small proportion for himself. He didn't question it though and presumed his inventions just weren't reaching enough people. So, he ventured out into the sprawling metropolis in an attempt to self-promote his products. Most people he tried to approach ignored him, barged into him in their scurrying commutes or just laughed at him. Just then, his attention was clutched by an advertisement for the Doradheim Security Agency glimmering before him:

"We aim to make this city more safe and secure for all residents and inhabitants."

Doradheim Security Agency, huh? he quizzed. *It can't be much worse than the government's current policing and law enforcement systems, surely.*

After contending with much disparity, Morathos headed home to find it empty. "Mum?" he called several times to no response. He made his way to his room where he descried the absence of all of his inventions. Now he had so much emotion coursing through him that there was little more he could conjure. He tried to turn his attention back to his recent works, but he couldn't detach from his wandering mind's burning questions. Reginald had been by his side all those years; he was the very inspiration that unleashed all of his contained potential and now he had to go on alone.

Dawn brought a glimmer of hope to him though, as he made his way downstairs to find an envelope lying by the front door. Written letters were a rarity in such an electronic and digitalised era, but he opened it nonetheless:

Dear Morathos Reina,

I know you're somewhat an old-fashioned kind of person and don't particularly care for technology all that much, so I thought it best I wrote to you in this manner.

You've been a good friend to me, but I think it is time we went our separate ways. I've just successfully completed my dream of becoming a head engineer of computer technology for a new organisation known as the Doradheim Security Agency. I always felt that you were more attuned to nature and despite our formidable coalition, I think we might be much more different than I had first realised and that may cause complications somewhere down the road.

I hope you can forgive me, but I took your inventions with me. Technology has consumed me like a drug. It would appear that you seem to loathe something that I bleed so ritualistically so much, that I couldn't have anything that might jeopardise our advancements as a civilisation intervene with it.

To demonstrate my admiration and respect for you, I thought it only fair to write to you and warn you that this organisation will not tolerate any sort of resistance or incompliance with the government's schemes and what it has set out for the future of this city. Therefore, you have been enlisted under the agency's surveillance and DSA droids will be monitoring your actions. Should you continue to intervene or protest in any way against the movement of President Vynzuth's desires to bioengineer the inhabitants of this city, you shall be tracked down and detained, and may even be executed depending on the scope of your conviction.

I wish you well in life.

Kindest regards,

Reginald Forathorn, Head Engineer of Computational Systems, Doradheim Security Agency Ltd.

Morathos couldn't believe what he had just read. The feelings of hope, shattered in an instant. The bitter injustice in his words; deceitful, yet, constructed in a way that attempted to conceal his true intentions. He tried to reason with his frustration and tell himself that it was nothing personal and strictly professional. But the manner in which it was conducted, the cunning demeanour struck him so harshly, like a blade in the chest. All he could do, was escape the turmoil inside of him and strive even harder to pursue his own dreams.

Ignerenous, on the other hand, appeared to be elated. "I finally have enough!" She stormed into the DSA office.

"Welcome to the Doradheim Security Agency. Can I help you?" a robotic voice greeted her.

"I would like you to track down a man for me. If he finds my fortunes..."

"One moment." The droid began scanning through a system. "If you would just like to take a seat, someone will be with you in a few minutes." She witnessed a distinct familiar face walk by her. Where his left eye ought to have been, there was only an empty socket and he was being accompanied by some important looking individuals. "Magnetus?" she called. He had acknowledged her voice, but refrained from responding and continued his discussion with his corporates. Within a minute she was confronted and taken to an office.

"So, this man is dying and you want us to put a stop to him through fears that he will steal your money to save his own life?"

"Yes," Ignerenous lied. "This man is a danger to this city. His desperation could lead to disastrous consequences."

"I see," said the consultant. "And what relationship do you have with this man?"

"He's my husband. But we're separated." She knew lying about his identity could cause upheaval. "Even though we aren't together anymore, I still wouldn't want him to continue suffering. Besides, it's too risky."

The consultant rubbed his chin. Yes, I see. Very well. We shall look into it." And with that, Archquar's last moment would ensue in the coming days, as a specialised artificial intelligence would be promptly programmed into one of the agency's most notorious cyborgs. The AI would essentially make him an even more advanced and precise cyborg assassin. The intricate design of Reginald's own software, would ensure the assassination would be accurately executed, expeditiously and stealthily.

Once the news had reached Ignerenous, it was as if she had become completely conscious of her identity all of a sudden. It was as if — for a brief moment — she had come to her senses and whatever had been influencing her peculiar behaviour was no more. She sat and sobbed to herself in sorrowful regret. But her tears would not flow for long as she collapsed to the floor without warning, emitting a thick, transparent substance from her mouth, before her remains dissolved into nothing.

Chapter 10

Dimensional Transcendence

An artificial light dispersed, penetrating Morathos' closed eyelids and reaching his retinas. Then his eyes slowly opened as they met the surrounding contents of his capsule and he was reunited with his consciousness again. *Mother... Father... Reginald.* His thoughts were processing slowly as he tried to comprehend what he had witnessed. He felt some sense of understanding but was still somewhat disoriented. He couldn't yet bring himself to understand how he had no prior recollection of the events he had re-experienced, but gaining the knowledge — albeit unpleasant — of those that he wasn't present to, had invited a wave of clarity.

But there were still so many unanswered questions. Plasmantium remained a mystery to him. He knew there was really only one other thing he could do. "Sequititah," he called. There was a brief delay.

"Morathos," she responded.

"I have some clarity, but there's still more I must uncover. I need you." He gulped and took a deep breath. "As I mentioned, travel into the past by means of my design forbid me to travel into past events that have occurred before my existence, unless I am accompanied by another who has existed in that time. It appears that I made a slight miscalculation earlier and failed to compensate for the stopping of time. We should have just enough energy stored from the slingshot to take us where we need to go."

"Francesca," Sequititah called. "Did you get that?"

"Yes," she responded.

"Zeoc," Morathos called. But there was no response.

"Zeoc, do you read?" cried Francesca.

"Zeoc!" Sequititah called.

"Even Zeoc surely wouldn't sleep for *that* long!" Francesca remarked.

"Something isn't right," said Morathos. "I fear we may have lost him."

"His capsule must have malfunctioned," said Francesca.

"There is a way we can get him back," said Morathos. "But we only have enough energy to propel in one direction. We either travel back with the hope of saving the universe or we travel to a moment before we lost Zeoc and bring him back into the present."

"There is a way we can do both," said Francesca. "What if you and Sequititah go back and I'll go get Zeoc? We can split the energy we have between the capsules."

"Yes. That should work," said Sequititah.

"It should." Morathos hesitated a little. "It's going to be risky though and we will need to get it precisely right for both journeys. Not only that, reuniting and getting back to the present might be more of a challenge."

"Do we have any other options?" Sequititah queried.

"Not really," said Morathos. "I guess we're just going to have to go for it."

"Alright, here goes nothing," said Francesca. "Commence gravitational merging of Morathos' and Sequititah's capsules." On her command, the two capsules merged and the residual energy from the slingshot fired them off into the cosmos. She then activated her own capsule using Morathos' carefully conducted calculations and projected herself into a moment in space and time before Zeoc was captured by the DSA. There she surrendered to the capsule's configuration to temporarily relinquish her consciousness, as a physical manifestation of her subconscious would roam the streets of Doradheim.

Zeoc's research was promptly interrupted by a knock on his door that he was reluctant to answer. "Zeoc Bleadbury!" Francesca cried. "You are in great danger; you must come with me right away. There's no time to explain." He approached the door but refrained from opening it, peering through the spy hole.

"Who on earth are you? How can I trust you?"

"If you don't, the consequences will be devastating." He looked more closely at her and could not resist the temptation of her beauty.

"Oh...," he smiled. "A pretty woman has come to take me away. This must be my lucky night!"

"Don't be getting any ideas!" Francesca rolled her eyes as the door opened and she grabbed him by the collar dragging him ferociously through the bustling avenues of the mechanical metropolis. Zeoc tried to process what she had explained to him.

"So, you've travelled from the future to prevent me from getting stranded in space but because you have interfered with my kidnapping, you never rescued me from the presidential complex or hijacked the president's ship, meaning we never travelled into the past to save the universe?"

She nodded. "Yep. It's known as the bootstrap paradox — a causal loop in space-time." Zeoc gave her a vacant stare and was left unable to do anything more than to follow her instructions as they made their way into the hangar and history repeated itself. "Put this on. It might be a little tight." Francesca passed him a uniform and they pursued onwards through the complex. She used the same calculations that Morathos had conjured, to fire them towards the body of plasmantium and use its unfathomable gravitational force to catapult them into the past once again.

"So, if the bootstrap paradox is a casual loop and Morathos has travelled into the past to discover its origins, then he never created the substance?"

"That's correct," said Francesca, expressing a look of surprise following her preconceived judgement of his intellectuality.

"So, travelling into the past is enough to prevent the creation of it then."

"In theory, yes. But it's much more complicated than that." Francesca cleared her throat. "It's not being easy for me to grasp either, but because Reginald got his grubby mitts on it, it still exists in his reality and its release into the vacuum still occurred in his reference frame.

"We all perceive the universe subjectively and so in his subjective dimension, his plans to use plasmantium in the way he has, has still unfolded. To make things even more complicated, in the quantum world everything exists everywhere in all states at once, until it is observed. Add to that, that if everything in reality is predetermined, trying to change the past will result in the events still occurring anyway — which contradicts the bootstrap paradox."

"So, I'm going to die anyway?" feared Zeoc.

"Only in one quantum dimension," explained Francesca. "Because plasmantium is in the president's hands, that is not something I can intervene with from my own reference frame but I don't doubt that he has the technological capability to project his reality onto ours. Whereas in this reality, I am able to save you using time travel."

Zeoc said nothing for a moment. "...I can't make sense of this."

"Never mind," said Francesca as they fell into the gravitational well of plasmantium and began to orbit the substance. "We've got other matters to address right now."

Just as before, the craft made several orbits around the phenomenal substance before shooting out into the depths of interstellar space to the precise location in space-time where Francesca's physical unconscious presence lay still in her capsule.

Zeoc experienced a profound sensation of Deja Vu as the craft began to disassemble and became even more mind-blown by the experience.

"Your experience is probably so much more pronounced than mine because I was here before in my current state, whereas you are experiencing something that you have previously, but in a different state than the one that originally experienced it," Francesca tried to convey.

Now she had to ensure that Zeoc did not enter the same faulty capsule again. "Before I made my journey to find you, I managed to download the same software that Morathos had integrated into one of the escape capsules. All I have to do is upload it into the capsule that you enter. Then, once ready, you can use its gravitational merging feature to reunite with the others. This is where we part. The next time you see me will be in my present physical state and all will resume." With those last resounding words, Zeoc's capsule was released into the cosmos as the ship deteriorated into nothing but shrapnel and Francesca's physical form — contained inside her capsule — returned to her conscious state.

Meanwhile, Morathos and Sequititah both prepared for a transcendence of their own respective projections of themselves, as their pursuit to continue to ascertain the origins of plasmantium continued.

"Even then I could see it in him," said Sequititah. "I was always so deeply intuitive before I contaminated my rich inner-spirit."

"What are you saying? Perhaps we should discuss this later," Morathos suggested with the belief that he was trying to remain rational and focused.

"I'm talking about Magnetus. Please... Hear me out — it is relevant."

"Mmm." He nodded.

"It might sound crazy, but we had something special. I might have only been two years old chronologically, but I was much older biologically. He had developed into such a remarkable young man. I felt that he was my soulmate; words cannot describe such a profound internal chemistry like we had." Her expression quickly transformed to a saddened face. "But unforeseen circumstances changed everything. They came for me only one chronological year later... and that was the last time I saw him."

Morathos looked at her deeply and for the first time in as long as he could recollect, he expressed his emotional empathy for her. He placed his hand on her shoulder and gently rested his head there. But still he knew they didn't have time on their side. "Sorry to sound cold, but we need to get going."

She nodded. "Yes, of course. My point was that he kept sending me e-letters but I was too upset to respond before that sadness later developed into embarrassment. I received several letters like the one Francesca found regarding a great disaster that occurred in my home city after I was shipped to Doradheim. He never told me what it was — probably to avoid worrying me. Then, as time progressed, I didn't have the capacity to care anymore."

"So, you're suggesting we should travel back to Karahdor to the time of the disaster?"

"Yes. It would mean a lot to me if I could finally get closure. Besides, I don't quite understand how or why, but something is telling me this event might be of significance to you also and may well get us closer to finding out the truth about plasmantium and where it *really* came from," she said, looking at her brother longingly. "It must have occurred sometime after I was taken to Doradheim but prior to your conception."

"Let's find out," said Morathos sternly as he cranked up the capsule's boosters, and the remaining residual thrust propelled them further into the past. They both swiftly lost consciousness a short while after as their subconscious took the reins of their actions for what they had hoped would be the last time...

Archquar had returned home early from work that day. "Where is Sequititah?"

"You should know her by now, she's always wandering off," said Ignerenous.

"She's two years old!" Archquar stressed. "You can't just let her wander off on her own!"

"Don't you see? There's something wrong with her!"

"Well, you're not exactly helping the situation!"

Just then Sequititah strolled in.

"Where the hell have you been?" Ignerenous suddenly snapped.

"Oh, now you pretend to care!" she replied, storming towards her mother. The two stood face-to-face, Ignerenous having to lift her head slightly to meet her daughter's gaze. "If you must know I've been spending time with someone who actually loves and accepts me for who I am."

"As long as you're being careful," said Archquar.

"Do you really want what's best for me or are you just too afraid of getting in trouble with the law? I might have only lived for two years but I can assure you I'm much older than that. But what do you care for my internal experience?"

"Who is this Magnetus anyway? Why haven't we met him yet? You've not stopped talking about him for the last few months," Ignerenous cried.

"He's my soulmate."

"Ha!" Ignerenous had taken a sip of her tea at an unfortunate time and it sprayed out of her mouth, soaking Sequititah. "I'd be surprised if it lasts." Her words punctured her daughter heavily as she subsequently fled upstairs.

"What is wrong with you?!" Archquar yelled.

"Well, she needs to learn that the world is full of disappointments. Daring to dream usually ends in tears."

"So, you'd rather deprive her of any hope she might have? You're inhumane!" Archquar emoted an expression of profound disgust. "You're the one who let her wander off and yet you question her whereabouts on her return?"

"You know I actually think she's right. You're afraid of the law enforcement robots."

"Of course, I am. I have a responsibility for our daughter — our *two-year-old* daughter!"

"She's clearly capable of passing as eighteen!"

"Yes, but not legally — according to her birth certificate, anyway. Don't you think it's about time we found out what's wrong with her? Then we can get some sort of legal exemption."

"I told you before, the doctors will just laugh at us and say we're crazy, and that she *is* chronologically eighteen — or even older perhaps. They'll probably have her taken from us for being incapable parents with some kind of memory dysfunction."

"The longer we leave it, the crazier they'll claim we are. We should have seen someone when she was around six months. That was the moment I noticed some unusual growth and development. But you dismissed it because you're too ashamed of her."

"Well why didn't *you* just take her then?"

For the next few days, Archquar became withdrawn until he concluded that he had to do something, even if his wife wouldn't cooperate. He decided to consult a specialist. "We will need to obtain more information as this is very unusual," she said. "This may be a long process."

He continued to visit at regular intervals, giving them anything else he could without the knowledge of Ignerenous, until he strolled in one day to find his daughter already home. "She brought that Magnetus fellow here with her," his wife said. "He actually seems like quite a charming young man. But I still can't help but feel unsettled about the whole ordeal."

"Why can't you just be happy for her?"

It would be several more months before Archquar would hear from the specialist again, when they would eventually require the attendance of Sequititah, just a short while after her third birthday.

"You're very lucky," she said. "Anyone else probably wouldn't have taken you seriously."

"It was a risk I had to take."

"It seems your daughter has an unnamed condition. It's apparent she is ageing and maturing too quickly, but it's unlike any other condition of its kind that we have any recognition of. There's no known cause or cure."

"So, you have no diagnosis?" Archquar concerned.

"I'm terribly sorry."

The news struck Sequititah hard and she could not contain her urge to head for home immediately. It seemed she had been quite happy in herself until this point. She had been so content and took pride in who she was. But it would appear that her whole world had come crashing down around her. "I can't be with you anymore," she sobbed to Magnetus.

"Don't tell me, your parents don't approve?"

"Mum perhaps; I don't think father is bothered. But that's not the reason. They're coming for me in a just a few weeks."

"Who?"

"The Doradheian government. I'm not legally allowed to find employment, education or a home of my own. And it seems mum is keen to get rid of me. I've been nothing but a burden to her."

"Why don't you come live with me?"

"I can't. They want to perform tests and discover what is wrong with me. They aim to develop some technology to cure me."

"What's gotten into you?" Magnetus cried. "You've never been that naive to really believe *they* can help you. That's one thing I greatly admired about you — you're so intuitive, mature and wise and always do what's right for you."

"Yeah, well. Circumstances have changed; if I told you, you wouldn't believe me. I can't trust myself anymore. It's brought me nothing but false hope. It's a dead end for me if I don't go."

Magnetus exhibited a distraught look. He just couldn't make any sense of her change of character. He had no choice but to accept her wishes, even though he had expressed that he felt right in the core of his soul that she didn't really want it, and it would be so damaging. He requested to hold her one last time, which she allowed but initiated an abrupt release.

"Go," she sobbed. "Don't make this even more difficult, please."

The remaining few weeks would tick away like days and it wouldn't be so long before Sequititah was no longer residing with her parents.

"So, we lost her anyway! After all that," Archquar cried.

"Yes, well. She needed to go and get fixed," Ignerenous responded coldly.

Several months rolled on that invited an unwelcoming minefield of emotional turmoil. Ignerenous vowed to never have a child again after how her experience had impacted her. Despite his frustrations, Archquar was in such an unstable state that he had considered having another child. After all, he was doubtful that he would ever see his daughter again; given the distance to Doradheim and how little an income he was making. He kept trying to reason with himself and reassure himself that things would get better. It wasn't completely irrational of him, but certainly not a healthy observation to base his opinion of her on. He didn't want to seem pushy or overly persistent though, so he made subtle suggestions occasionally. He gave up after only a few attempts, accepting that his wife would stick to her decision. He had contemplated leaving her then, but he was so uncertain of how he truly felt that he didn't want to risk regretting anything.

"You know, I've been thinking," Ignerenous eventually said. "Maybe another child is a good idea. Maybe things will be different this time."

Archquar had a sparkle in his eye and he gave her a soft smile.

A couple more months passed with no success but Archquar wasn't going to let that hold him back. He was more concerned of his wife's indecisive state and that she might change her mind at any minute, more than what he described as, 'just a patch of bad luck'.

Only a moment after he left for his commute to work he encountered some unsettling news. He had not yet reached the train station when his nervous system was met with an alarming announcement that was broadcasted via a hologram.

"People of Karahdor. We bring you breaking news. An unidentifiable object is approaching the vicinity of the city.

According to our calculations, it is set for a direct collision with us. It is travelling at an alarming speed and we don't have much time. Evacuate immediately! Repeat. Evacuate immediately!"

Archquar raced home to inform Ignerenous, barging his way through hordes of civilians racing around frantically, trying to escape to the emergency evacuation jets. Some of them were trapped on transportation midway through their journey. The aircraft was only a couple of hundred miles above ground at this point and increasingly accelerating. He knew he wouldn't be able to make it out of the city in time. Thankfully, he had a fortified basement and he was quite confident that they would be safe down there.

As the object hurtled closer, those on the easternmost fringes of the city could now see what resembled a foreign aircraft. For the majority, it would be the last thing they saw as the craft came crashing into the Earth and exploded violently. The rest of the city could only see an indistinguishable object colliding with the land, as well as the aftermath of an explosion cloud. Fortunately, the craft wasn't significantly large enough to destroy the entirety of the city, but the east took some hefty devastation, taking many lives in the process.

Archquar and Ignerenous emerged from their basement to witness the horror before them. Much to their gratitude, they were far enough away to not be harmed, but there was still a colossal cloud of smoke drifting across the city sky. It carried small fragments of shrapnel and debris with it, causing further carnage and injury to the panicking pedestrians below. Many of them continued to flee from the city and abandoned their homes.

Magnetus Bane lived much closer to the wreckage. He desperately tried to escape the smoke and in a fit of panic, he had begun to make a quick getaway, only to be slowed soon after, as he tripped over a steel pipe built into the pavement. As he fell backwards and his neck swung, a sharp piece of steel from the aircraft came at him striking him straight through his left eyeball and became lodged inside it. He screamed in agony, unable to get himself up and was smothered by the toxic cloud of fumes and debris. The only thing he could find the energy for was to take out a small photograph from his pocket. It was Sequititah. "Thank goodness you're safe," he said before slowly closing his eyes and rolling over.

The expanse of Karahdor was soon shrouded in darkness. Just a few moments prior, it had been a bustling but small settlement, swelling with abundance. Now it was almost desolate; unnervingly silent. In the coming days, many of the surviving civilians of the initial impact would face severe illness or — in some cases — even death, as the deadly toxins would slowly deteriorate their biology.

Archquar had not surfaced from his basement for days. He wanted to wait it out — for the dust to settle. He believed that his neighbourhood could still be habitable. Yet, he couldn't help but think about all those people. He couldn't help but feel like it was his duty to rescue the few potential survivors.

There was an unearthly aura about Karahdor ever since that fateful day — more so in the immediate vicinity of the crash site. Even once the smoke cleared, the less affected and more hospitable areas of the city left an undesirable taste in the mouths of many. Only those too poor were left behind. Ignerenous, however, wasn't poor by the standard definition. She was just stubborn; and although Archquar had soon realised that the safest place for them right now was going to be Doradheim, she was adamant to remain put. This left him torn in conflict once more; he didn't want to leave her behind. He didn't have a worksite to go to anymore — there was very little left of it. So, the best thing for him was to scout the city for any more casualties that he believed he could save. There wasn't much life of any sort left, though. And so, he became more curious about the crash and thought he should perhaps visit the now derelict location, since no further news had been broadcasted.

Upon his journey across the city, he had encountered a familiar figure in the wayside. He looked in sheer shock as he apprehensively approached the motionless man. "Magnetus!" he bellowed several times, shaking him. He could still feel a pulse and hear breathing, but he was in a severe state and had lost a lot of blood. "Help! Somebody, help!" he howled, waving his arms around. "I'll be right back!"

Archquar paced around the vicinity hoping to find someone, but it was like a ghost town. With no functioning networks remaining in the city, he had to race home and hope that his wife could aid him. She had been quite fond of Magnetus, so it didn't take much persuasion. They both continued to attempt to reduce the bleeding but Archquar's biggest concern was the piece of steel sticking out of his eyeball.

"It's no use. I can't see a way of him making it," Ignerenous sobbed.

"Let's take him to the crash site," said Archquar. "It's a long shot but we might be able to find something on board and it's closer than anything we've got."

He picked up the fragile Magnetus, lunged him over his shoulder and they made the short journey to where the craft had crash-landed. There was very little in the way of any evidence remaining. No traces of any lifeforms were detected, but thorough inspection of what they had at hand strongly suggested that the craft was not from Earth. "Perhaps it was a self-piloting craft, designed by a more advanced civilisation," Archquar hypothesised.

Despite what little was left of it, Archquar miraculously managed to locate a functional piece of apparatus that resembled some kind of life support technology and hooked Magnetus up to it. At that very moment, Ignerenous began to complain of a slight discomfort she was experiencing and she fell to her knees. Archquar assisted her to her feet and for a quick second, she met him with an unfamiliar stare. It sent a shiver through his body. He quickly shook himself off and reassured himself of his wife's words. "I'm not so sure what that was," she said, "but I'm fine."

"Well, all we can do now is hope he makes it."

As the weeks went on, Archquar gradually became less and less sure of himself. There was nothing left of his beloved home city. Soon, there wouldn't be enough resources to sustain his wife and him. Even the advanced technologies of the time could not prevent the inevitable demise of Karahdor. The fumes emitted from the alien craft were so foreign to humanity, that the sheer element of surprise alone would not be countered in time.

Magnetus Bane had reached a stable state in the meantime, but there was severe internal damage. He gathered himself together through nothing more than pure adrenaline and survival instinct. He looked at the photograph of Sequititah again which urged him on and he carried his weak and wounded state to the Machine City. There, he would receive significant technological treatments to preserve him. A good portion of his brain was mangled from the shrapnel; it was unsalvageable. But it would be the beginning of his bioengineering into a cyborg, as mechanical and computerised implants replaced his vitals. The impact this had on his outlook of the world would reshape his very image as he became more and more thirsty for technology, robotics and digital components. A substantial part of his identity was snatched from him. "I aim to construct a super organisation that specialises in surveillance and crime monitoring," he said. "I shall call it the Doradheim Security Agency."

"I miss her," Ignerenous wept.

"I thought you didn't care about her."

"I'm allowed to change my mind, aren't I?"

"Of course," Archquar sighed. "But you've been acting so different lately."

"What are you talking about?"

"Oh, never mind."

"There's nobody left here. Let's go to Doradheim."

"Sure." Archquar emoted a hint of hesitation.

"What is it? I thought you would have jumped at this opportunity."

"Oh... I'm just confused." And with that, the city of Doradheim would beckon their arrival.

It didn't take long for Archquar to find employment or a home. He was, after all, a licensed engineer and the government was quick to express its desire for his services. They were also in the process of building more expansive neighbourhoods and offering accommodation to those who had lost their home in the devastation that occurred.

He still couldn't help but remain suspicious of Ignerenous though. Despite her previous seemingly prominent desire to relocate their daughter, she expressed no further interest once they had arrived and she would often persist in changing topic. He reasoned with himself though and took stock of everything.

Soon, an evening he had not been expecting arrived. After what had been a long, monotonous day, he was greeted by his wife. She had an expression on her that suggested she had news for him and had been anticipating his return. He looked at her with hope in his eyes. Even though he knew what she was going to say just from the look she displayed, he clenched up with excitement and closed his eyes. Each syllable she spoke was like music to his ears as he gently rested his palm on her belly. "I'm pregnant..."

Chapter 11

The Governor

Reginald took a deep breath and welcomed the thick wave of ecstasy that overcame him. The very nature of the Earth was buckling before him as plasmantium had almost consumed the entirety of the atmosphere and only a trace of sunlight broke through it. The planet was already significantly starved of its star's rays long ago; only, this had amplified considerably by now. He was becoming aggravated with the apparent stalemate that had ensued though, but he bided his time as the devastating substance began to slowly engulf all in its path. He knew his enemy would not be able to sustain itself much longer; even with its regenerative properties that irked him. He looked up at the sky and caught one last glimpse of minimal sunlight before it became completely eclipsed and more and more showers of data flooded its way towards the surface of the Earth. "It's over, Horuzokh. Surrender to my wrath!"

"You are very mistaken, Mr. President," an unsettling voice hissed. "I will never surrender!" The professor manifested before him. It was instantaneous — as if he had been waiting in the vicinity.

"You are foolish. There is not much time left for you."

"I warned you of what I'm capable of already," Horuzokh replied. Then in a flash, he vanished again.

Reginald suddenly became suspended in shock as he witnessed his city's intelligent magnetic defence mechanism deactivate. "Impossible!"

"I know you all too well, Reginald." The professor's voice permeated through the president's entire body. "That is exactly why I have anticipated your every move and awaited my opportunity to strike you, just when you think you have succeeded. Ha-ha! I have developed something far beyond your capacity to counter — a hyper-virus so greatly advanced, that no technology could evade it... I'm afraid you have everything wrong, Mr. President, for it is *you,* that will meet your end..."

Within very little time, the president's robots and droids immediately proceeded to malfunction and shut down their systems. A majority began to assault one another, as they had done previously. It seemed that recent history was repeating itself as a civil war erupted throughout Doradheim. Only this time, there were far fewer combatants in terms of biological lifeforms. Androids, war bots and cyborgs abandoned their combat with the invaders and started to charge at their own city of origin instead, tearing it down to shreds. Building by building, neighbourhood by neighbourhood, the expansive technological metropolis was crumbling.

Reginald could not believe what was unfolding. In the midst of the chaos, his military was collapsing and his subordinates were being eliminated quite rapidly. General Ribery performed his last computation as the infestation hacked into his software systems, rendering him immobile.

The president's more sophisticated software would buy him a little extra time and some initial resistance to the virus. He had to try and establish what this hyper-virus was. His ego would forbid him from accepting that it couldn't be eradicated; or at least, manipulated. "Nothing is impervious to my technological mastermind," he gloated. His ignorance might well have overlooked the fact that this virus would still — slowly, but surely — deteriorate his own integrated hardware, not to mention the effects it would have on plasmantium.

Plasmantium was indeed a powerful substance but its properties made it quite easy to influence. Although its complex design made it destructive, it could still be manipulated depending on exactly what its target was, and since both Morathos and Reginald had very different ambitions, that would dictate how the substance behaved. But now it appeared to have succumbed to the power of some other influence. It was a highly adaptable substance but Reginald had programmed it to function as a sort of computer. Meaning, it would not be immune to the infection. There was no sure-fire way of knowing what this would mean. It wasn't clear whether the virus would reverse plasmantium's behaviour or have a different and, perhaps, more severe effect on its behaviour altogether.

Professor Horuzokh knew what he was doing though. The hyper-virus was designed to be more than capable of infecting plasmantium and dictating its mannerisms. Just when the atmosphere had seemed to be fully consumed by the substance, it became apparent that its effects were being reversed. Reginald's master design — his dream, was beginning to shatter beneath him. The once formidable city of Doradheim, was soon to be nothing more than a memory at best, and a heap of ruins and debris, at worst.

It was uncertain as to whether or not any other planetary life would be safe though, as Horuzokh's mysterious forces had swarmed in such vast numbers across the globe and left heaps of destruction in their wake. It seemed that it wasn't just the president and his technology that he would seek to avenge and defeat but some far greater resentment was fuelling his deleterious motives.

Morathos slowly opened his eyes. They were met by Sequititah's. They both took a look around their capsule. "Well, that sure cleared a lot more up," said Morathos. "But there are still some missing pieces."

"Yes," said Sequititah. "But I fear our planet is in danger. There's not much time."

"I know." Morathos bowed his head. "Besides, we haven't got enough energy to go any farther. We better be heading back."

"Francesca, Zeoc?" Sequititah called.

"Yes," responded Francesca.

"Loud and clear," cried Zeoc.

"Initiate your gravity mechanisms," said Morathos. "In three... two... one..."

Zeoc and Francesca both hit their respective switches at precisely the same moment as Morathos and the three capsules swiftly drew towards one another before merging into a single craft, just as expected. "Alright. Perfect," said Sequititah.

"Now guys," said Morathos. "Due to the unfortunate complications we've experienced, our operations for getting home are going to be a little less straightforward than they would have been otherwise due to the extra resources we have used. Not to mention, forward time travel in this context is a bit more challenging than backwards travel. But thankfully, we have the technology to execute our backup plan."

"So, what's the plan?" Francesca asked.

"There's going to be two important parts to this procedure. First, we need to locate the precise moment in time that we need to propel towards. Then, we need to execute actually getting there."

"I do not doubt your brilliance for one second," said Francesca, smiling at Morathos.

"We're going to quantum leap through time. The best way I can probably explain this is with an analogy," said Morathos. "In the quantum world, everything exists in all states at once until it is observed. That means our very past, present and future selves also exist simultaneously in all states, but we only see our present state because that is the one we are observing right now.

"Imagine each of us had a deck of cards in front of us. That deck represents our life and each card is a specific moment in time within our life. Without picking out a specific card and observing it, we only see an entire deck of cards. In other words, we see ourselves in all moments of space and time, in all states, until we pick up one card.

"This clever piece of software is capable of creating a replica of each of our lives in the form of a theoretical deck of cards. It will flick through each deck of cards as if it were a book and select a specific moment in space and time within our existence. We just have to ensure that we not only pick the precise moment from our own timeline, but that we all select the same moment, to ensure we remain together. If one of us goes too far ahead, well... Let's just say the future is uncertain."

"So, we better get this right. We've been pretty good at that so far," said Sequititah.

"Absolutely," Zeoc agreed, "but what happens if we should see something from our future before we're supposed to?"

"That's a great question," said Morathos. "One I dare not to even contemplate at this moment. So, we better just ensure we don't. Technically, we're not travelling into the future since we're only travelling towards a time in which we already exist — or have existed. But that doesn't mean we couldn't overshoot it and end up in unfamiliar territory."

"And what of the second part of the plan?" queried Francesca.

"Well, in theory this isn't as complex," said Morathos. "It just so happens I kept another old invention of mine that I haven't found a use for yet." He held up something that resembled a sort of magnifying glass. "This is an electromagnetic lens. It consumes a great deal of energy and so, must be used cautiously. It is capable of absorbing electromagnetic energy and concentrating it into extreme density, then amplifying it in a way that it can — for a short period of time — manipulate the speed of a photon.

"When we left plasmantium, I was able to extract some of its radiation and preserve it inside a strong magnetic field in a similar design to the antimatter propulsion engine that initially accelerated us. I can use some of that radiation to temporarily decrease the speed of light from our frame of reference, which will in turn cause information to travel faster than light, therefore allowing us to experience events before they actually occur... In other words, we can travel into the future.

"But yet again, I cannot stress enough that we must ensure we are accurate, because we won't be able to use it again for a very long time."

"Alrighty. Let's get going," said Francesca.

The other three nodded in synchrony.

"We will each have to operate the device in order of youngest to oldest," explained Morathos.

Zeoc approached the device and watched as it projected flickering slides of his past right before him. The perplexity of observing himself travel into his own past, to then travel back to his present, astounded him but he tried not to get too distracted. He anticipated the precise moment and then abruptly stopped the projection at the necessary time.

Next, was Francesca. She gave Morathos a longing look which stirred some chemistry inside of her. "I want you to know what an inspiration you are." She leaned closer to him, gently planting her lips on his cheek and proceeded to observe the machinery, as the events of her life were played back to her.

Morathos gently pressed his fingertips upon his cheek, then turned his head away in silence. He wasn't aware of just how phenomenal this gadget was until he stepped up to use it for himself. It took him through every event he had ever experienced, albeit far too quickly to be able to fully observe much of it. However, what he found most fascinating was how he was able to revisit some of the very emotions he had not been able to face back then.

Finally, Sequititah came forth. She barely even needed to pay attention to the slides. She simply awaited the exact juncture to transpire, then the four of them would have a definitive destination to voyage to.

Morathos activated his lens. They observed its genius design extracting the absorbed radiation and it started to heat up rapidly. He made some final calculations to ensure there would be just enough energy to ascend to their destination and the four of them witnessed an accumulation of their very own past events unfold. They gained more momentum as the immense electromagnetic energy propagated and, frame after frame, it met their consciousness.

Then they came to a hasty halt, met by the unpleasant carnage of the present that Sequititah had foreseen. The planet they called home looked unrecognisable. Everywhere housed devastation like they hadn't seen before and there was still more destruction unfolding.

"Did plasmantium do this?" asked Morathos.

"We might be too late," said Francesca.

"This is the work of something else," said Sequititah.

Zeoc glared at the spectacle, his face turned pale. "I don't believe it. Doradheim is in ruins."

"I'm afraid we're going to have to worry about Doradheim later," said Sequititah.

"What are you saying?" asked Morathos.

"It's Magnetus. Something is telling me we should head to Karahdor."

"The crash site?" asked Morathos.

Upon their approach, they were met with a blinding glow that was gleaming from within the crevices of the torn land. Thick vessels like tree roots were stretched for miles across the wasteland. They all led up to one point, condensing into a single branch that traversed into a deep gaping hole. Scorching molten rock could be seen illuminating the otherwise cavern of darkness. Magnetus Bane was bound by the tightly woven arteries, motionless.

"Magnetus!" Sequititah cried. There was a subtle murmur but he was too constricted to give a clear indicative response. She tried desperately to help free him. Zeoc assisted her, attempting to hack away at the vines, but their efforts could not penetrate them and they quickly became exhausted in the searing heat.

Morathos felt a little uneasy and kept his distance. He knew he had to trust his sister, but after everything he had come to learn, it was a tough pill to swallow. Francesca placed a hand on his shoulder. "I understand this must be difficult for you."

"I never thought I'd be here, in this predicament," he said. "But my priority is that of the planet."

"No. That's not entirely true now, is it?" a distinct voice echoed. "I have waited too long for this day."

"That voice," said Francesca, "Prof-"

"I won't be addressed by that name anymore." A manifestation of Horuzokh was summoned for only a second, before reshaping itself into a gargantuan creature with serpentine eyes and an elongated jaw. "This is my true identity," he hissed.

"What have you done to our home?" Sequititah cried.

"*Me?* What have *I* done to your world?" The being's eyes widened. "Take a look at yourselves. You pesky humans are responsible for your own demise. You are nothing but selfish monsters whom I have grown to loathe more than any species I have ever encountered. Humans can't even cooperate with each other anymore, never mind coexist with robots that *they* created."

"What do you want from us?" Francesca's voice quivered slightly.

"I have simply come to take what's rightfully mine." He pointed at Morathos.

"*Me?!*" Morathos looked at the others in despair and started involuntarily trembling.

"We can finally leave this rotten planet. The ship is repaired."

"This is my home!" Morathos snapped. He expressed a tone of instability.

"Very well. But this planet is doomed." He raised his left hand making a gesture towards the other three. "These hooligans have made it uninhabitable. But if you insist on dying with them, then so be it."

Morathos froze in conflict as he tried to make sense of everything. Unable to bear the reality around him, he fell to his knees and closed his eyes tightly, pressing his palms firmly onto the top of his head.

"You're the hooligan!" Sequititah yelled, charging at the entity in a frenzy of rage, tears streaming down her cheek. "What have you done to my Magnetus, you monster?!" She took a swing but the creature dodged and an array of vines jolted at her, encasing themselves around her body, smothering her.

"Enough!" the being barked. Zeoc and Francesca started towards Sequititah but could only make a few steps before their ankles became trapped in an intertwining web of vessels that had grasped them. Zeoc fell forward allowing them to completely cocoon him. Francesca became encompassed thereafter.

Morathos got to his feet and proceeded toward his sister. "Don't do it," she pleaded. "Think about everything. He's a good man!" But it would appear he already had thought about it.

"Father was *also* a good man!" He struck Magnetus hard across the cheek. "My father saved your life," he spat. "Yet you and your heinous corporation granted mother's wishes to have him assassinated! And you." He turned his attention back to his sister. "You're no saint!"

She looked at him disdainfully.

"I looked up to you, man," said Zeoc. "After everything we've been through, that's it?!"

"This is a mistake," sobbed Francesca. "I adore you more than you could ever know. Are you really going to listen to this... *thing*?! This isn't you; I know it!"

"You haven't been totally honest with me," said Morathos. "If you really feel the way you do, you wouldn't keep so much hidden from me."

"Nobody's perfect!" Francesca yelled. "I did what I had to do. We're not all super adaptable geniuses like you, you know!"

Morathos slowly paced towards the alien creature. "I've never felt like I belong here, and now there's nothing left." The two of them embarked upon a pristine craft which shot off in a heartbeat. Meanwhile, the ground below began to quake and crumble as fleets of ships emerged from them, taking to the skies. The vines slowly released their grasp and slid away, conjoining as they descended to the depths below.

Zeoc got to his feet and dusted himself off. "I can't believe it!" He reached out a hand to Francesca and helped her up.

"Something was definitely influencing him," said Sequititah.

"Now what?" asked Francesca.

"Magnetus, please wake!" Sequititah yelled.

"It pains me so to say this," Francesca gulped, "but there's only one man who might be able to save us."

"No doubt about that," said Sequititah hesitantly.

"Do you think he's still in Doradheim? If he's even alive," said Francesca.

"Well, it's our only shot," said Sequititah.

"Are you guys on about who I think you are?" asked Zeoc in a concerned tone.

"Don't worry," Sequititah assured. "I'm sure the president has bigger priorities right now. We're just going to have to put our differences aside for this one."

"Do you really think he can help? I mean, after all, he did contribute to all this!" cried Zeoc.

"And that's exactly why he can contribute to correcting it again," said Francesca. "I've seen some degree of compassion in him before, especially when the planet we all live on is at stake."

Zeoc displayed a look of scepticism. "I'm finding it difficult to look past his greed and selfishness."

"Don't forget, we have Magnetus," said Francesca. "Trust me. I doubt he has many other subordinates or allies left. This could work in our favour."

"Yeah, I guess we don't have a lot of other options," said Zeoc.

"Let's get Magnetus on board," said Francesca. "I kept back some machinery that might help stabilise him."

Zeoc and Sequititah nodded sternly and the three of them escorted him into the small craft. As they approached the remnants of the Machine City, the site that once housed the village of Staistreim also seemed unrecognisable. It appeared that it, too, had sustained a great deal of damage and appeared to have been vacated.

Sequititah took a moment to mourn as she felt a bitter ache inside. *The one place I could escape to,* she recollected. *The unsustainable demands of the city life; the image it required I maintained; the sense of liberation and freedom when I could no longer.*

"Where are we going?" said Morathos.

"I hope to bargain with The Governor," the being replied. "It seems The Governor has forgiven me. We have been summoned."

"The Governor, huh? Your superior?"

"I'll explain more later."

"Hey, I never got your name," said Morathos.

"I am more than just a lifeform," he revealed. "I am part of a hive-mind. That's how all civilisations come to develop eventually. I'm not an individual as such, but a component of an advanced amalgamated species that originated on a planet we call Nordamia. Therefore, all creatures of my race are in fact just copies of the same creature. We all share one collective name, one identity — the Petradema."

Morathos observed the rest of the crew and although they all appeared to look and behave the same, he couldn't help but notice the striking differences in their commander. "But you seem so much more unique from the others."

"The Governor forbids me to tell at this time. But just look at yourself," he smirked. "Don't forget, you're one of us too."

"Where is Nordamia?" he asked, giving what he said no more thought.

"To put it into a reference you can understand — around twenty light-years from Earth. Now please rest; I have a lot of preparations to make."

Morathos was shown to his resting quarters where endless questions plagued his mind. *Me? One of them? What am I really?* A flickering image of his last moment on Earth projected upon his consciousness. *What about my memories there? Why couldn't I remember them? How could I not be human?... But then again, I'm nothing like them either. Just when I thought everything was starting to make sense... Now this! What if I was wrong all along? Maybe* I'm *the problem. Is it worth the compromise of my inner-peace to keep on resisting? Maybe I ought to accept the inevitable...*

As the ship accelerated, Morathos lost touch with his senses again. The sophisticated design would propel him through unfathomable distances across the vast fabric. He hadn't personally aspired to break any records in terms of space travel, but once the craft came to a halt, part of him wanted to revel in the moment that he would technically be the first man to conquer such vast distances. However, at this time, a simultaneous cloud of doubt sat over him that he was even a man at all.

He witnessed a dark rectangular structure just ahead through his observation window. The ship was still some distance from it, so it was difficult to ascertain its size. But he had an inkling that it was of monolithic proportions; perhaps even comparable to a planetary or stellar body.

"Governor, I am here," announced the Petrademus.

An intimidating voice reverberated from within the structure. "Maintain your distance and state your identity, Petrademus."

"Commander four, eight, three, four, two."

"Ah. Tried and tested for betrayal of the people of Nordamia. How do you plead?"

"I plead innocent, Governor."

"Very well. Answer only the question asked of you, and nothing more, understood?" The alien nodded. "When did you last step foot on home soil?"

"Twenty-six years ago." His voice was quivering. Morathos was taken aback at the extreme shift he witnessed from his previous, seemingly dominant demeanour.

"Explain why you left."

"The people of Nordamia were suffocating. The planet's magnetic field had become far too unstable to sustain itself for much longer. That's why I built a magnetic field reader, larger, more powerful than had ever been constructed in our history. We needed to find a new home."

"What did you find?"

"Despite the distance, planet Earth was the strongest transmission I received, so I studied the planet and soon came to realise it wouldn't be an ideal home for us."

"So, you did what?"

"I figured if I couldn't get our species to move, then why not move the magnetic field instead?" He panted slightly. "I built an enormous diode, capable of extracting a magnetic field. I planned to transport the magnetic field of the Earth to Nordamia."

"And that took twenty-six years?!"

"No. It should have taken days. But upon my approach, my ship started to malfunction. It was as if something had interfered with its technology. I lost control of the ship and crash-landed."

"And what of the alleged crime?" The Governor's voice increased significantly in volume.

"I had a backup plan." The Petrademus gulped. "I had been studying the Petradema genome for many years. After the crash, I soon realised just how hostile to our kind the planet was. I had to bury my crew deep inside the planet in the hope of activating their failsafe stasis. I was weakened though and I knew my only hope was to extract energy from them. I had to sacrifice them to ensure my backup plan could go underway. It was either them or our whole civilisation."

"What kind of sacrifice?"

"I had found a way to latch on to a host so that I could survive the hostility and buy myself some time to adapt. But in my weakened state, I wouldn't be able to pull it off. So, I had to extract additional genes from some of my crew members."

"And of the rest of your backup plan?"

"I simply aimed to harness a human lifeform long enough to adapt to the planet's conditions, then I could repair my ship and absorb the magnetic field. But I became more and more curious about humanity; then that curiosity turned into disgust." He began to become animated. "The strong magnetic field that my people so desperately needed, was weakened because of their hideous selfishness, unwillingness to cooperate and their vindictiveness. They are nothing but destructive abomina-"

"Enough!" The Governor snapped. "So, you believe humanity is responsible for the instability of the Earth's magnetic field? Then what of your own?"

"Governor, our magnetic field has been subjected to nothing even close to the reckless antics of humanity. It was simply an act of entropy and natural decay. Those ignorant monsters don't appreciate their resources."

"And what will become of Nordamia now, since the Earth's magnetic field is insufficient?"

"I had hoped it wouldn't get to that," he confessed solemnly.

"Your testimony has been acknowledged. A decision will be made in the coming days. Your innocence will grant you access to Nordamia. Your guilt will result in abolishment of your rank and exile."

"What did you actually do wrong?" asked Morathos as the ship gradually proceeded away. His question projected a tone of concern that, to his surprise, would indicate a level of sympathy.

"I mustn't say too much, but my own civilisation isn't as perfectly evolved as I once thought. It looks as if it's become even more corrupt and some are rebelling against its authority figures."

"They're trying to frame you?"

"I wanted to do the right thing for our survival. But the sacrifices I had to make have put my motives in question."

"So, is The Governor the ruler of your race?"

"It's complicated."

"Where do we go now whilst we await a decision?"

"It doesn't really matter anymore. My home planet cannot sustain life for much longer. I have failed. Even if I am found innocent, I doubt they will make me feel welcome. Terraforming isn't an option; the Petradema are too weak and we are too low on resources."

"Unlike back on Earth. This is all caused by nature," said Morathos. "Besides, terraforming has its issues."

"Even Mother Nature can be unforgivingly destructive if She feels it is necessary."

"So now you're just waiting around aimlessly? There must be something we can do."

"I'm afraid there are too many obstructions. I cannot say anymore."

Chapter 12

A Vengeful Coalition

Francesca scurried into the presidential complex. A familiar sensation gripped her as she recalled the emptiness of the building the last time she ventured through it; only this time, there was no power being generated to the remains of the structure. Sequititah and Zeoc followed behind, dragging the still unstable Magnetus with them.

There appeared to be a delay in the president's focus as some of his hardware had begun to corrupt. But the majority of his components were not yet affected and appeared to be making complex calculations to compensate.

"Mr. President," Francesca came barging into his office, panting. "Thank goodness!" Reginald did not respond and continued to look in a docile state.

"That's it!" he suddenly bellowed. "The technology decomposing device!" He began rummaging through his drawer and pulled out a handheld piece of equipment that looked similar to Morathos' earliest invention.

"Wait, isn't that Morathos'?" Francesca said, concerned. He ignored her and held the device up in the air.

"I shall perform a temporary format, deactivating all computerised components. Thus, shutting down this wretched plague. We're going to temporarily operate on what little natural function we have. My integrated optimal protective programming will delay the infection enough for me to develop and reprogramme the software required to exterminate this virus, now that I have established its origin."

"I don't think that's quite how that device works," said Francesca.

"You know nothing of my device," said Reginald. "Let's just say, I've made some minor adjustments that will allow me to make use of it — albeit only for a short window of time. What Morathos intended to do with it was never going to happen."

"Oh, so you aren't ignoring me. What makes you so sure anyway?"

"You should know not to interrupt me when I'm calculating, you fool! Let's just say, there are too many bugs in his logic. Ha-ha!"

Francesca rolled her eyes. "So, you haven't gone completely mad then," she tried to joke.

"A machine has no heart," the president replied. "Don't you see what is at stake — my legacy, my reign of power, my supremacy."

"Yeah, well now we're just gonna have to think about the planet and cooperate, like it or not. We found Magnetus Bane."

"Where is he?" Reginald hastened.

"He's here in this building. But he's in a bad way."

"Who else is with you?"

"Sequititah and Zeoc."

"Sequititah, hmm? Zeoc? The human I had imprisoned?! And what about Morathos?"

Francesca hesitated her words. "Morathos is no longer with us; Sequititah is his sister."

"No doubt he would still refuse to cooperate, even at a time like this. I presume she is human also?"

"She is a cyborg."

"I see. No doubt the virus will have affected her then."

"Yes. Thankfully, my components are minimal. I took only the basic necessary upgrades required to work here."

"It seems we both have needs," the president confessed. "But you stole my ship and betrayed me. Why should I trust you?"

"Vynzuth's ship actually. The stakes were high. I did what I had to do. Don't you see what horror has unfolded? Or are you choosing to ignore it? Besides, there are bigger issues at stake right now. It's not about trust anymore. If you don't cooperate with us, you're not going to last much longer. You're the only one who can stop this. And we're the only ones that can help make that happen."

"Yes, indeed. Very well, I shall get right to work in completing this programming and shut down the virus."

Reginald stuck to his word. Within a few hours, despite the damage that had already occurred, the virus had been temporarily halted. He was holding a computer chip between his left index finger and thumb, and another spherical component in his right hand. "This microchip has intelligent protocols written into its coding. With all systems shut down, the virus will not be able to infect it. You must insert it into this device to reactivate all systems. This will simultaneously paralyse the pathogen."

Sequititah and Magnetus were both taken to a stasis capsule during the shutdown. Their systems were now completely incapable of functioning and what little biology was left of them, could not stably sustain itself. "It shan't be for long," Francesca softly reassured them as she pressed her palm on the glass of their capsule.

"I can't believe it," cried Zeoc.

"Alright listen up," Francesca asserted. "You're going have to do a lot of growing up, and fast. No fancy stuff. No flirting around. You hear me? You're essentially the last true human on

Earth that can save us and, if something should go wrong with me, the whole world is counting on you! Don't screw this up!"

"Err..." Zeoc gulped.

"I'm serious! You've gotta do exactly as the president instructs."

"S-sure," he quivered.

"Come on, dig deeper. Be confident! You're confident enough when you're flirting. You've got to learn what it means to be responsible."

"Okay," he said more sternly. "I won't screw this up. I promise."

"Alrighty. Let's save our home!"

"Activating shutdown sequence," said Reginald. "You know what to do from here. I have programmed an emergency reboot software should it be needed. But I trust it won't be." And with that, President Forathorn's systems were seized. Francesca acquired the microchip from him and proceeded to insert it into the metallic sphere, but she froze and started to feel lethargic before slowly dropping to the ground and rolling over onto her back.

"Zeoc. I'm...losing consciousness," she puffed. "I... must... be more dependent on... my bionics... than I realised." Her head jolted sideways and she closed her eyes.

Zeoc's stomach started to churn and he was trembling a little. He tried to ignore it and stay regulated. "Okay. I can do this." He picked up both, the microchip and the device, gradually manoeuvring the chip closer whilst trying to steady his hands. He glanced over at the president in his immobile state. *Wait,* a thought intruded. *How can I trust this will save anything? I'm giving the president his power back. That makes me no better than him. But if I don't... I have the power to end his reign right here. But only by reviving him, can my friends be saved.* "Argh!!" he screamed. *Alright. Think about what Francesca said.* "You've *got to learn what it means to be responsible,"* her soft voice echoed in his mind.

He dropped the spherical device and fell to his knees. *If only he were still here. He'd know what to do. But look at what he did?* "I can't take it anymore!" He suddenly panicked when he noticed he no longer had the microchip in his grip either and started crawling around frantically, running his hands over the ground in an attempt to feel around for it. A deep inhalation followed when he located it and squeezed it firmly. Now sat with his arms around his knees, he reached for the device, trembling as the chip eventually made its way into it. He then exhaled heavily and fell backwards, sprawling his arms out, his legs maintaining their position.

"All systems rebooted," said an automated feminine voice. "The virus has been paralysed and software updates shall now commence."

Zeoc got to his feet and brushed himself off. Francesca awoke to him stood over her, offering his hand. She grabbed it and steadied herself. "Way to go. You did it!"

"I nearly didn't," he said, avoiding eye contact.

"We all have an inner battle. It's how we deal with it that matters."

"Thanks," said Zeoc.

They both headed to the stasis chamber and Francesca activated its release. Sequititah and Magnetus laid eyes on one another. "Oh, my darling, Sequititah. How I have longed for this day." He grabbed her tightly and began sobbing apologetically.

"I'm sorry, too," she said.

"That's quite enough," the president stirred. "In case you have forgotten, I have a world to rebuild; a grand plan to resume."

"I knew it!" cried Zeoc. "If not for us, you wouldn't be standing here right now. And that's how you plan to thank us."

"It's alright," said Magnetus. "He's right. I have a duty to him still. Plasmantium has already devastated our natural world. And what is left is too scarce to carry on like this. I'm afraid, any hope of stopping the substance now is depleted."

"How can you be so sure?" asked Francesca.

"I will be able to give you all your greatest desires," said Reginald.

"No thanks," said Zeoc bluntly.

"Sequititah. What is your intuition telling you?" said Francesca.

"My brother is still alive. I feel it. He might not be acting himself right now, but I trust he has his reasons. He still needs answers and I believe he will get them."

"Curse that meddling contraption," the president hissed. "Where is he?"

"I'm not sure. But one thing I am sure of, is that I want no part of your corrupted plan."

"Me neither," said Zeoc.

"I've done more than my fair share for you," said Francesca.

"Suit yourself," said Reginald. "Come, Magnetus. We have work to do. The initial hurdle will be a little tedious but once the data is fully uploaded, we will have the resources capable of building themselves."

"I'm sorry, Mr. President. My loyalty lies with Sequititah."

"Oh, please. Spare me the sob story."

"I'm not who you think I am. I became someone you wanted me to be. The technological implants may have saved my life, but at the cost of losing far more. If only your ego didn't cloud you in such a manner."

"If Morathos is still alive, we still have a chance," said Zeoc.

"We will find him," said Francesca.

"Ha-ha-ha! You are even more foolish than I first calculated," said Reginald. "The sad reality is that without my technology, you cannot survive. Without my technology, you will never find Morathos. And I shall see to it that you never do. I can rebuild this city myself. Plasmantium remains under my influence, and it will achieve universal overhaul."

"Perhaps you're forgetting that I have survived without computerised implants," said Zeoc.

"Not for much longer. I am a generous man though. I'll offer you the opportunity once more. We can rebuild and revolutionise mankind together or your own fates will be sealed."

"I think you already know the answer to that," said Sequititah.

"How can you even call it mankind anymore?" said Francesca.

"Suit yourselves. But don't say I didn't warn you. Now get out of my city. I have work to do."

"Hmm. Figures..." Sequititah rolled her eyes despairingly at him. "Let's head to Staistreim. I know there's not much left there, but I feel it could be of use still."

"It would be nice to hear of your memories there," said Magnetus.

"Alrighty then. Staistreim it is," said Francesca.

The four of them stared across the plain of destruction. Sequititah took Magnetus by the hand and led him over to a specific spot. "Those poor souls," she said.

"Let's give them a moment," Francesca said to Zeoc. As the two of them walked away, Zeoc grabbed her hand gently and looked up at her. She expressed her discomfort and turned her face away from him. "What are you doing?"

"It's not what you think. Just look at me," he pleaded.

"What?" Her eyes met his for a moment.

"I just wanted to apologise for my behaviour toward you and say that I think you and Morathos would be great together. You deserve each other."

"Wow, Zeoc. Thanks."

"Don't mention it."

"But what he said before he left," Francesca suddenly expressed a contrasting emotion and bowed her head, "he's right. I've done some terrible things. He despises robotics, and here I am — an employee of the government, promoting cyber technology. I am probably the *last* woman he'd even consider."

"What are you saying? We've all made mistakes, right? Nobody is perfect," said Zeoc. "Besides, Morathos obviously isn't thinking clearly right now, so I wouldn't worry."

"But you have never turned to robotics."

"That doesn't mean I haven't done some things I regret."

"What do you think that creature meant when he said Morathos is one of them?"

"I'm not so sure. But since I first met him, he's always been very different from most."

"That's why I adore him so much," said Francesca. "I can't help but feel responsible for all this. I felt that we had something, but I let him down. Or maybe it was all imaginary. Maybe all this rediscovering myself was a bad idea. Where lies the boundary between holding out for hopes and dreams, and just living in a naive bubble of fantasy?"

"Maybe you should sit down." Francesca looked at him with confusion. "I've got demons that I've locked away, just like you. I was left stranded at a young age. Do you remember when it was advised that only children older than fourteen could have any kind or robotics integrated because the government didn't have substantial resources to do it safely before that age?"

"I do."

"Well, when I turned fourteen, I became a problem for my parents. I refused to obey their wishes. They shoved their desires down my throat for years in the hope that I would be conditioned to it in time. But I was too stubborn to have anything implanted, so they ditched me. I was pretty much left for dead. I ended up getting into the wrong crowd, because that's what you do when you're desperate. I joined a reckless group of rebels, because they provided me with everything I needed.

"But then I began to adopt their immature antics and developed a persona that I'm ashamed of. They rejected Vynzuth's movement too, and that's why I felt like I belonged there. But I also felt out of place and that something wasn't right after some time. That's when I stumbled across Morathos' inventions.

"I became more and more dependent on these inventions to sway me from any mechanical influences. But they soon questioned where all my money was going. Then one of them found all my purchases, and that was that. They booted me out and shunned me. So, I sought revenge and stole back what was rightfully mine. I didn't feel satisfied though and resorted to stealing their valuables and vandalising their hideout too. Not only that, I got them all arrested."

"Oh, my goodness," said Francesca.

"I tried to bury away the parts of me that I adopted from them. But I didn't go about it in a mature manner. I was still carrying their influence around with me and it made me resort to their recklessness. I immediately felt regretful, but instead of facing my inner demons, I ran away and tried to hide them.

"But thanks to you, being put in a predicament where I had to be responsible, has opened my eyes. Now I think I realise that seeking revenge in the way I did does not solve anything; it just makes me as bad as them. Now I realise that I need to rise above them. Now I can face my demons courageously and get rid of them in the correct way."

"Wow, Zeoc. What a remarkable and inspirational story. I greatly appreciate you sharing this."

"No problem at all. It's the least I could do after your encouraging support." He portrayed a smile of pride. "So, you see, we all have baggage. But that does not define who we are today. What you did in the past does not matter. It's what you do from here on, that counts."

"Yeah, you're right. Thank you, Zeoc." Francesca smiled. "You've helped me to be kinder to myself. You know it's funny. I never thought someone younger than me would be giving me life advice."

"I'm pleased to hear it."

"Oh, there's something I wanted to ask you."

"Sure. Anything."

"The rebels you hung out with, they didn't conform to any biomechanics, but they also didn't use any other resources. How did they go on?"

"They didn't really. They were suffering inside. They became ill. But a lot of the time they functioned on rage and adrenaline. I came to fool myself that behaving like them gave me a surge of energy because I was releasing my inner frustration. I presume it was the same for them. But they were so much more oblivious to the torment it caused. I'm not really sure what drove them to behave how they did. Perhaps they had much more distressing upbringings than I did."

"So where do you think they are now?"

"Once they were locked up, the fact that they were against Vynzuth's plans was soon established. So, they were probably dealt with. I'm ashamed of what I did and perhaps I should have been in there with them. But they did something unforgivable too!"

"It seems you could still sense it was wrong and found a better way. It is as if you were more conscious. So, there's that at least."

"Well, that sure makes me feel less guilty. Thanks, Francesca."

"Hey. At least you're able to reflect and feel ashamed and regretful... I doubt they ever did."

Zeoc smiled. "Oh yeah. I guess so."

"I hope Magnetus and Sequititah are alright."

"I'm sure they've got a lot of catching up to do still."

"Absolutely. I feel like we've really bonded today. Conversations like this are so rare nowadays."

Zeoc raised his eyebrows. "Tell me about it!"

*****

"I understand why you didn't come here," said Sequititah. "But you would have loved it. It was so rejuvenating."

"I was so ashamed of who I had become," said Magnetus. "I was so wrapped up in biomechanics."

"Please. You don't need to explain. I carried shame too. I forgot all about who I had become. Well, for a little while at least."

"Oh, the quarantine?" Magnetus looked at her disconcertingly.

"I had a hard time accepting it then. But now I realise it had to happen. Coming here is what allowed me to reconnect with myself. But in order to do that, I had to first acknowledge who I had become.

"Initially, relief and freedom were all I felt. But then when I started to come to terms with reality, I had nowhere else to run to. I couldn't just keep running forever; and so, the truth hit me hard. My condition, coupled with my immunity becoming compromised, led me into more instability. It was of great concern to the villagers. They thought I had been plagued with something and couldn't risk taking any chances.

"Being in that hospital for all those years made everything come crashing down on me so heavily. I had a brief glimmer of hope when I fled to Doradheim. But it was only temporary because I was just running away from myself, and that never works out in the long run. If it wasn't for my brother, I don't know if I could have found the strength to face myself again."

"I'm so proud of you." Magnetus began to gently caress her hair. "It is because of you, that I found my strength too."

"You know, come to think of it, I don't think it really matters how much of our biology is replaced with mechanics as long as we still have willpower. There are cyborgs out there with less robotic components than you and I, who have succumbed to the servitude of their programming. Yet, there are those with almost no biological anatomy left, who insist on pursuing their authentic ambition and who have maintained the ability to consciously reflect and regret their decisions. I think that's why I'm still so deeply intuitive despite all my mechanical interceptions."

"Yes. That's so true. I suspect there is still hope for even Reginald; if he could just brush aside his ego."

"Precisely. There's still a human in there somewhere, I know it. It just takes something to influence that rekindling..."

"So, do you think you found what you came for?" Francesca asked Sequititah a short while later.

"Not exactly," she said. "But maybe we could gather some of this shrapnel from the war. There might be some way of building a communication device that can attempt to detect Morathos."

"Or better still, there might be something lying around that is still functional and already assembled," said Magnetus.

"Let's get searching then," said Zeoc.

The four of them encountered several components and pieces of hardware on their excavation. "Some of this could be useful," said Francesca. "But it's going to take a lot of time and precision to piece it all together into anything like what we need."

"I bet Morathos would be screaming at us if he could see us now," said Zeoc. "He's so good at piecing things together from nothing."

Francesca beamed. "He sure is."

Sequititah caught something metallic glimmering in her periphery. It gleamed brighter than the other debris around her and she turned to face it sharply. "What's that?"

"What?" cried Francesca.

"It looks like..." She proceeded closer and started shuffling all the rubble and scrap around her. "It looks like a piece of jewellery, perhaps gold. There! Look!" The other three, all came closer to inspect it and assisted with brushing aside all the wreckage. It appeared there was in fact some sort of golden gleaming object, but it was lodged firmly into the ground. She dug her way around it and managed to pull it out. "It... couldn't possibly be..."

"What is it?" queried Magnetus.

"It's a gold ring." She stared at it perplexed. "But it's more than that. I'm certain I have seen this somewhere before."

"Is it of any significance right now?" asked Zeoc.

"I don't think so. But I was still drawn to it so profoundly. It *feels* important."

"Perhaps you should keep tight hold of it," said Francesca.

"Oh, believe me; that is precisely what I intend to do."

"We really ought to get moving. I think I can make something work with what we have found," said Magnetus. "Maybe you'll remember on the way."

Sequititah nodded. "Yes, hopefully." And they continued on through the heaps of wreckage.

"I must declare that I am not, for one moment, dismissing any of your experiences in this village. But there doesn't seem to be much in the way of Staistreim rubble around," said Magnetus. "I see a lot of metallic ruins. But nothing to indicate that a tranquil village once resided here."

"Come to think of it, I had noticed that but didn't want to mention it," said Francesca.

"Gotta agree there," said Zeoc.

Sequititah continued to study the gold ring.

"Let's get to the craft," said Magnetus. "There might be more tools on board that I can use to construct something from what we have collected."

As they began making their way back, a small craft could be seen flying towards their location. An unsettling sensation encompassed Sequititah. "Run!" she cried. And the four of them made haste to the ship and swiftly fired up the engines before taking to the sky. "Do you think they saw us?"

"Who was it?" asked Zeoc.

"I have no idea," said Sequititah. "But I wasn't chancing it."

"You were right to be concerned," said Francesca. "That was a Doradheian specialist military unit. They must be on the lookout for something."

"I sure as hell didn't fancy hanging around to find out what exactly," said Zeoc.

"Let's just keep flying and hope they were too busy with whatever their mission is to have noticed us," said Francesca. "Any luck with the transmitter?"

"I'm afraid not," said Magnetus. "I'm missing one vital component. We might have to go on another excavation."

"There's still heaps of wreckage and destruction all over the planet," said Zeoc. "I'm sure we'll find something somewhere."

"My only concern is time," said Magnetus.

"Alright. It looks like we lost them," said Francesca. She pointed to a plot of land. "How about over there?"

"Looks pretty busy with mechanical components to me," said Magnetus. They promptly landed and started their hunt.

"What exactly are we looking for?" asked Zeoc.

"It's the backbone of the device," said Magnetus. "I need some sort of processing hub that will aid each component in communicating with one another, so that the whole thing works cohesively."

"You mean like a CPU?" Zeoc quizzed.

"Sort of; it is a kind of electronic chip. Only this kind of technology is fairly simple and doesn't function like a typical computer so it doesn't require a CPU chip. Its circuit board is wired in a unique way so that it runs on a more basic kind of hardware. Not only that, it is programmed to respond to whatever command we input into it, so a CPU isn't necessary. However, it still needs some sort of fluidity. It's difficult to describe exactly, but I'll know it when I see it."

The military craft touched ground and dozens of droids came spilling out, sniffing at the wreckage around them. "It's not here!" an android cried.

The mission commander was persistent. "Look harder! Orders from the general are to find the ring and return it to him. We do not leave here empty handed."

"Sir, I believe someone may have beaten us to it," said the droid.

"Impossible!"

"Did you not see the capsule that took off just before we landed?"

"Yes, I saw it. But we are to thoroughly search this area first. If we don't find it here, we have an idea where it might be and we track down the craft. Those were the general's orders. Understood?"

"Sir, yes, sir." The droid saluted his superior and the search through the Staistreim remains continued.

Chapter 13

Doradheim 2.0

Plasmantium had long resumed its course, constricting the skies once more. It had developed into a substance not only capable of existing as solid, liquid or gas, now it was growing into a living material that could exist as both animate and inanimate. The city of Doradheim was rapidly rebuilding itself with the president's elaborate programming. Soon enough, the imminent glow of the endless metallic buildings that so many of the city's residents were familiar with, were prominent once more; only this time, more polished and appealing, with their adaptive design. The majority of the systems that were paralysed or shut down from the virus had already long since been back online. "All main constituencies are now fully functional and all optimal upgrades have been successfully installed," a mechanised voice announced.

"Excellent," said President Forathorn. "Prepare to initiate phase one of the Doradheim 2.0 project."

"Phase one initiating."

"Mr. President."

"Yes." He turned to meet the gaze of an intellectual figure.

"Before the virus intervened, I had begun the final stages of a revolutionary project in the research centre. Most of the technology is still intact."

"Ah, you must be the new head of science. Do enlighten me."

"A lot of your panel members were killed by the infection and the damage it caused. But I can bring most of them back by extracting cells from their bodies and inserting them into machinery. I can also upload all their memories into your newly built models. I think it will be much more efficient than simply replacing everything."

"Hmm." The president rubbed his chin.

"It would be much less work than replicating their entire genetic coding."

"Yes. I see," said Reginald. "I have wondered in the past, if there might be a way of doing this. But we've never had the technology capable as yet. This truly is a remarkable leap."

"Thank you, Mr. President," said the scientist, humbled.

"Just tell me one thing," said Reginald.

"Yes, anything."

"You aren't like *him*. I won't tolerate such hypocrisy again."

"Y-you mean H-Horuzokh? Absolutely not. Look." He lifted his fringe to reveal a metallic plate that was embedded across his crown.

The president nodded in approval. "Very well. I cannot trust those who refuse to fully embrace robotics."

"Oh, I know, Mr. President."

"Good. How much longer until your project will be complete?"

"Err... A few days. And it won't interrupt your program. In fact, it will enhance it."

"Perfect. Now get going. I wish to proceed to phase two of my grand design very soon, and until you have completed your project, that may complicate things. It seems Horuzokh, in his attempts to destroy my dream, has only proven to further propel things forward and amplify my ambition."

"Yes of course, Mr. President. I'll get right on it."

*****

"I think I've got it!" said Magnetus. "I just need to insert this here, and voila!" The transmitting device started making a light humming sound and a tiny light powered on. Then it started beeping at slow increments. A few moments later it powered off again.

"What is it?" asked Francesca.

"There's a fault somewhere," said Magnetus.

"Must be a component failure," said Francesca.

Magnetus disassembled the device. "It looks like the circuit board has been frazzled. The hub was too powerful."

"So now what?" quizzed Zeoc.

"I guess it's back to the drawing board," said Magnetus.

Sequititah still hadn't said a word. She was deeply fixated, holding the ring in her left hand. But it was as if she was looking past it, not at it.

"Are you okay?" Francesca asked.

"I'm just..." She couldn't get another word out.

"I think we should call it a day. Let's get some rest," said Francesca.

"Yes. Good idea," said Magnetus as he looked across to Sequititah.

Several days had passed and Magnetus had sensed some kind of interference in his mechanics. "What is it?" Francesca looked at him puzzlingly.

"My tracking software is still synchronised to Reginald. He's making a public speech."

Zeoc rolled his eyes. "Oh, here he goes again on his high horse."

The three of them started to listen in on the transmission. But Sequititah remained distant. "My beloved citizens." The president's words were heard as clear as they would have been to the residents of Doradheim. "Multicellular life requires all cells within its lifeform to behave in a similar, uniform manner. The system cannot run efficiently otherwise. As a hive-mind, we operate as one entity..."

"Systems create order and control, yeah," Francesca huffed. "But they are simultaneously destructive because they invalidate human inconsistencies and the unpredictability of nature."

"That's true. But let's just hear him finish what he has to say," said Magnetus. Francesca nodded.

"What if I told you of a new, more efficient way to extract solar energy?" Forathorn paused to soak in the gasps and murmurs coming from his people below. "I present to you, Project Doradheim 2.0. The world's first artificially intelligent city. A city capable of self-sustaining; a city capable of self-construction and repair, as well as self-maintenance; a city with its own self-awareness! All thanks to my breakthroughs in nanotechnology design.

"Since all the bees on the planet became extinct long ago, I figured I would redesign their technology, but on a far grander scale. Imagine a bee the size of a city flying through space. Now imagine the sun is its flower. In the same way a bee extracts pollen from a flower and returns it to the hive, a city can extract solar energy directly from the sun's corona and return it to its hive — by which of course, I am referring to the Earth. It's purely brilliant. We will be starting off with just Doradheim at first, but the technology is rapidly developing into many other cities. Thanks to my sophisticated self-replicating design, it won't be long before they're all involved.

"The city will be driven by raw plasmantium, giving it not only the energy to make the trip, but it will also form a protective shell around it. Coupled with my magnetic force-field, we will be impervious to the sun's radiation or any other harm."

Magnetus disconnected his software in disbelief.

"This guy just doesn't know when to stop, does he?" said Francesca.

"If only Morathos could hear what the president is doing with his very own creation," Zeoc said distastefully.

"Well, speaking of which, we better get back to trying to find Morathos before things really blow out of proportion," said Zeoc.

"Right. The transmitter," said Magnetus. He was hesitant in his tone and his eyes kept wandering over to where Sequititah was still entranced.

"Don't worry," Francesca reassured him.

"Whoa! What's happening?" Zeoc cried. His face had whitened.

"What is it?" Francesca concerned.

"Don't you see it?" He pointed directly in front of himself.

"There's nothing there," said Magnetus.

"I saw a gravestone... An-and... My name was on it!"

"I think you need to rest," said Francesca. "Are you sure you weren't daydreaming or something?"

"I'm not lying!"

"Wait!" said Magnetus. "Look." And just as Zeoc had described, a small tombstone emerged in front of them that read:

Here Lies Zeoc Bleadbury of Doradheim
14.07.2148 — 23.09.2170

"2170! That's this year!" Francesca gulped.

"And it's less than a month away," said Magnetus.

"It can't be true, right?" Zeoc panted.

"You're the most vulnerable of us all," said Francesca bowing her head. "The planet is becoming more and more hostile for biological life by the day. It's not looking good."

"Ah man! Without Morathos I'm..."

"Don't you dare say that," said Francesca. "Remember how far you've come recently. You're stronger than that."

"But if I'm gonna die in less than a month, what will it matter?"

"Why are we even able to see this tombstone? And why the delay?" Francesca quizzed.

"I'm afraid Morathos' predictions may be starting to unfold," said Magnetus.

"How so?" asked Zeoc.

"The plasmantium that was sent into space is becoming increasingly dense and it looks like it has started to warp space-time enough for us on Earth to start seeing its effects."

"You mean it is distorting reality?" asked Zeoc.

"I'm afraid so. Things might start getting really weird from here on. I wouldn't write any possibilities off," said Magnetus. "Time lapses, merged memories, glimpses of the future. Anything really."

Zeoc gulped. "So that tombstone? There must be something we can do, right?"

Magnetus gave him a solemn look. "Without first finding Morathos, I beg to differ."

"Why did I see it first?" asked Zeoc.

"Like I said, plasmantium is warping everything; even our own subjective perception of reality," said Magnetus. "It seems you're moving through space a little quicker than we are, meaning from your frame of reference, time is running slower. But time is moving at the same rate as it already was to us. *You* are the one moving more quickly. If it becomes any more significant, you might start answering any of our questions before we even ask them."

Zeoc gave him a distant stare.

"Imagine if your natural speed exceeded that of everyone else around you," Francesca tried to elaborate. "To you, you're going at your normal speed. You haven't sped up and nobody else has slowed down. You were just always going at different speeds. So, from your point of view, everything will always appear to move more slowly. But in your case, it was a temporary shift.

"It's a bit like how they demonstrate super speed in movies. They make everything else in the background move in slow motion whilst the character or object moves at regular speed so the viewer can keep up with them."

"Why me?" Zeoc questioned.

"I doubt there's much time left for me either." Francesca rested her palm on Zeoc's shoulder. "Like I said, you're the most vulnerable. If its goal is to eliminate natural life, plasmantium must be targeting those of us with the most natural biology first. And it can go about that in ways that can defy all that we understand in physics."

A thunderous echo suddenly flooded the ground around them. Francesca's attention was diverted to the sky and all she could do was stare in awe as a huge craft passed by. "Look!"

"At this rate, it's difficult to trust anything we see," said Magnetus.

"So how are we supposed to know if this is even really happening right now?" cried Francesca. "It looks strikingly similar to that alien craft. Has it returned? Or is this a replay of the past?"

"Or is what we're seeing yet to happen?" Magnetus pondered.

"This is all too much!" said Zeoc.

"Okay, let's not get distracted anymore," said Magnetus. "Let's just fix this device and try and find Morathos. Anything else that is happening around us, we can no longer trust as present reality, so ignore it." He immediately picked up the transmitter and started to tamper with it.

Francesca couldn't help but turn her head to face Sequititah. *Anything that is happening around us, ignore it? But what about her?* she thought. She started towards her slowly but felt a resistance. *No, she has to figure this out for herself. I mustn't disturb her. I presume that is what is keeping Magnetus from getting distracted. His undying love for her must ignite immense trust and understanding that she must be left alone to tackle this.*

"I think I've got it!" Magnetus yelled. But his elation was short-lived. The transmitter began to produce some sound but it was crackly and distorted. "Something is still not quite right." Just as he was about to examine it again, a sharp jolt shot through him, knocking him to the ground. He attempted to get to his feet but could no longer feel any sensation in his limbs.

Francesca and Zeoc both experienced a similar phenomenon a moment later. "Halt!" an electronic voice cried. It marched toward Sequititah who remained dissociated. "We believe you have something that belongs to the Doradheian government." More droids followed and detained her, one of them snatching the ring from her grasp.

"Sequititah!" Magnetus cried, still immobile. "Don't you dare hurt her!" As quickly as they had appeared, the droids were gone again.

Francesca was first to her feet. She aided Zeoc up and they proceeded over to Magnetus. "Are you alright?"

"Yeah, just a little stunned." He shuffled up and brushed himself off. "I'm surprised they didn't take me too."

"They only wanted one thing. It was just unfortunate that it was in the wrong hands at the time," said Francesca. "That ring must be important."

"I have to go after her," said Magnetus. "I can't trust them and if anything were to happen to her... I don't think I could ever forgive myself."

Francesca nodded. "I understand. We'll stay here and keep trying."

"Very well. I wish you both the best of luck."

"Make it back safely," said Zeoc. But he had already fled and snuck his way onto the Doradheian military craft just as it was about to take off.

As the ship made contact with Doradheian soil, he managed to lodge himself inside one of its cooling chambers. He painstakingly watched as the droids escorted Sequititah out onto the landing pad and into the complex, where she would be held prisoner. "Don't worry, my darling. I'm coming for you."

He bided his time, then headed out onto the pad and climbed atop the control tower. Given that air traffic control was operated solely by artificial intelligence, he was fairly certain it would be empty and his suspicion was soon proven correct. Once inside the observatory, he momentarily found himself unable to sustain his balance as the ground beneath him began to tremor slightly and caught him unawares.

"Citizens of Doradheim, do not be alarmed," an automated voice called from the sky. Magnetus looked up to find dozens of droids zooming around on jetpacks. "We are preparing for the launch of Doradheim 2.0 on its first trip to the sun. You may feel slight earthquake-like effects. But these will be minor and should not cause too much disruption. On behalf of President Forathorn, we apologise for any inconvenience and should any inadvertent damage be caused, the city's self-repair protocols will operate immediately.

"Thanks to the city's deep foundations, vast amounts of plasmantium can be stored in the underbelly which will lift us with an amount of thrust that dwarfs that of a rocket launch. We will be accelerating up to half the speed of light. You may experience heavy g-forces for the first few seconds, but there is no reason to be concerned; plasmantium has everything under control. This means that the ninety-three-million-mile trip will take just sixteen minutes. The more trips we make, and the more energy we extract, the quicker these journeys will become. We will initially remain in hover mode. Then to preserve energy, we will launch tomorrow when the sun is directly above us. The president wishes you all a safe and enjoyable trip."

Magnetus could feel the floor beneath him exerting an upward force. The horizon started to expand to more outreaching distances as the city started to hover several miles above the surface of the Earth. He wasn't quite sure what he ought to be feeling at this point, but he invited the sense of elation in the moment. *It's remarkable. It truly is. But it's so easy to forget about the true selfish intentions of this technology. I'd be a foolish hypocrite to celebrate. But nevertheless, I wish they could see what I see; you really don't get to experience things like this all too often.*

Meanwhile, Sequititah saw a familiar character pass her by, albeit an apparently more youthful representation. "Hey!" she called. He turned to face her and then he immediately vanished. She rubbed her eyes vigorously and looked again.

"Quiet in there," a guard droid commanded on passing.

"I saw a man just now. I recognised him."

"There are no men here," the droid replied. "Only droids and cyborgs."

Oh, what's the use? she sobbed. *Do I know what I saw? Or am I losing it?* The man reappeared and this time he came closer. "Rupert?!" she said, intrigued. "You're alive!"

"Of course, I'm alive," he responded.

"But Staistreim. The war."

"What are you talking about?"

"It's me, Sequititah." She looked at him longingly. "The quarantine. Don't you remember? I came to your village."

"No. Sorry, lady. Listen, I've got to go. The general has another project for me. He said Vynzuth is going to love this one."

"Wait! Vynzuth? He's alive too?"

"Well... Yeah." He gave her an odd stare. "No offence, but everything okay in there?"

"I'm fine," she said in an irritable tone, "but I would appreciate it if you could at least have the decency to tell me what the hell is going on around here."

"I told you, I have to go. But don't worry. I don't think you'll be in here for long."

"What exactly do you mean by that?"

"You know, just..." he started to whisper. "You seem a bit delirious, that's all. Whatever you did, you clearly weren't with it at the time, so you'll probably get off the hook."

"That's not how it is at all; you have no idea!" Her voice trembled a little, rising slightly. And then he was gone. She waited for a droid to pass her again. "Hey!" she called. "What can you tell me about Rupert O'Sullivan?"

"That is information I am not authorised to disclose."

"Hmm. Figured you'd say that." She started to drum her fingers on her cell door.

"Rupert O'Sullivan is dead," a voice from the next cell said.

"That's impossible. I just saw him."

"He died an honourable mayor when the aliens invaded. I think you must have imagined it."

I know what I saw. It was so vivid. I spoke with him. There has to be some other explanation.

It was getting late so she tried to get some rest in the hope that she could reassess things in the morning. However, the moment she closed her eyes, they sprung open again as a shadow flickered past. There, stood Rupert once more. *Am I dreaming?*

"I assure you, lady. You are awake," he said.

"Then why is everyone saying you're dead? Why don't you recognise me? How come nobody else can interact with you?"

"I have no answer for any of your questions. Why are you here anyway?"

"I stole something that belongs to the military — a gold ring. But I found it in the ruins of Staistreim; I didn't know who it belonged to. I know I've seen it before somewhere."

"Where is this Staistreim you talk of?"

"It was a small village not far from here. But it was destroyed by the alien invasion. You were the mayor of it."

"You must be mistaken. Alien Invasion?! This is giving me a headache." He proceeded to leave.

"Wait! What about the ring?"

"Well, it sounds awfully similar to General Ribery's ring. But that would be impossible."

"Then why do they want me? Why did they snatch it from me?"

"Lady, I want to believe you, I really do. But..." He was gone before he even finished his sentence.

Sequititah began to sob and collapsed onto the floor. The next thing she knew, daylight had broken. She looked around her cell feeling disoriented, unsure of her recent memories from the events of the previous night.

A droid approached her cell. "We've had complaints of you talking to yourself in the night. You are disturbing other inmates. If it continues, I'm afraid a further punishment will be issued." She didn't say anything and sat herself down in the corner, placing her head in her palms, slowly lifting her head up a moment later so that her fingers were resting on her chin. Then she stared blankly at the ceiling.

Magnetus had slept in the control tower whilst he tried to formulate some sort of plan. He was lost deeply in his own calculations, only to come to his senses as the ground began to tremor again. The sun was increasing its altitude in the sky and the city was making its final preparations for launching.

Only a few moments later, the metropolis of Doradheim had taken to the sky. He watched on as his field of vision expanded. Within seconds, as the city ascended above the clouds, the sky had transcended from a murky hue to a satisfyingly natural azure. It hit him like a breath of fresh air. He admired how the sky again quickly transformed into a deeper ultramarine, before a thick band of cyan became prominent, distinctly separating the pitch-black void of space from the atmosphere below.

The Earth quickly became nothing more than a speck as the city accelerated, all, whilst the glaring blaze of the sun became more discernible. The artificial magnetic shielding was projecting a breath-taking aurora display. But only briefly, as the entire sky would be illuminated again by the blinding solar rays of the Earth's star.

Chapter 14

A False Utopia

A swelling sensation overcame Sequititah's head. Then it glimmered in her mind's eye — the gold ring. She pictured it upon the middle finger of a young man's hand. *That's it. That's where I first saw it; in Staistreim.* She tried to confirm who the man was, but nothing else was coming to her.

In the next moment, she could no longer make sense of her surroundings as her cell began to distort in shape and colour. *What's happening? Am I hallucinating?*

"Mr. President, my experiment is all but complete." Sequititah recognised the distinct voice immediately. It was Professor Horuzokh.

"Superb. I shall have the agreed necessary technology at the ready in the coming days." The president's voice was not Reginald's.

Vynzuth? This must be more time distortion.

"We just need to keep it contained in the meantime for full optimisation of its cells."

"Very well," said Vynzuth.

But as the next few days passed and the morning of the launch approached, Horuzokh returned to the experimentation chamber to find it empty. "That chamber is unbreakable! This cannot be. Sound the alarm," he commanded one of his panel members.

"Warning! Warning! Experimentation has escaped!" The automated message replayed over the sound of a deafening siren whilst everyone scurried about frantically.

"It appears the creature has gone rogue, Mr. President," said the professor.

"And what does this mean? What can you do about it?"

"I will get search bots out right away. But there is a chance it has escaped planet Earth entirely."

"How so?"

"It is genetically predisposed to seek new habitable environments because it cannot sustain itself on Earth for long without being in its experimentation chamber. The hostility of its very environment is what motivates it to look for alternatives; which means it's quite capable of reshaping itself and growing the necessary tools to escape. But if it has escaped there's no way of it being replicated and any hope of humanity surviving on other planets is significantly reduced."

"So, we're going to have to go into space?" the president asked.

"Yes."

"Very well. I will have my team launch a space programme. I shall call it the Navigation of the Doradheian Rogue Obliteration Gambit, or N.O.D.R.O.G."

"But Mr. President, we don't want to obliterate the creature."

"Relax, Professor. I'm well aware of what must be done. But if you insist, I shall rename it the Navigation of the Doradheian Rogue Operation Gambit."

"Yes. That's perfect."

"Fetch General Ribery for me," Vynzuth commanded. The scientist nodded and returned shortly after.

"Mr. President," said the general, "you summoned me?"

"Horuzokh, you're dismissed." The professor left the presidential office. "I'm designing a space programme that will require precision training from our most skilled units. It may well require a detainment mission to another distant planet; which could be extremely hostile. I trust you will develop something sufficient."

"He is remarkably talented," a man's voice said. It was as rich in Sequititah's mind as that of someone standing right before her. Then she witnessed him hand over some drawings to General Ribery. They looked like design drafts for gaming fields and were crafted with impressive precision and creative architecture.

"So, I see," he responded. "What was his name again?"

"Rupert. Rupert O'Sullivan."

The general had his units track him down, and within days, he was hired. "I want you to design me a military training simulation," he said. "One so realistic it will be indistinguishable from reality. I believe it will be the most effective way of conditioning my forces for what is to come."

"Sure thing." He got right to work and presented Ribery with an astounding design of architectural ruins, combined with detailed desolate wasteland.

"I love it!" the general praised, holding a microchip between his fingers. "Now we just need to upload it into this."

Once the necessary procedures were complete, the most sophisticated military training the president had ever witnessed could be undergone. The general called Rupert into his office to praise him for his work. "Please take a seat," he said. "I've decided to make you my personal assistant. You have created such a realistic design, that my units — if they never knew any different — would not believe it *isn't* real."

"Wow. Really?!"

"Now that microchip is very valuable and it's only small," said Ribery. "I'm going to have it especially integrated into this ring for extra safety." He pulled out a shiny gold ring and started to fiddle with it between his fingers before placing it back in his top pocket. "This stays in here, nobody else is to ever know of its location."

That's it! That's the ring! Sequititah saw it as realistic as ever, right before her. *There is no way this is a dream.*

Rupert had never felt this valued before. He was a gifted artist and designer and others would often make sure he knew it. But he never really felt that anyone actually appreciated his work, especially with art losing its authentic touch in most cases these days. But now he was surging with confidence, which only sparked more motivation. He continued to produce extravagant work that seemed to just keep improving; even when it looked like there couldn't be much more room for progression.

However, as several months went by, he couldn't help but start to feel dejected. Although he felt that his work was improving — and it was — it seemed that most of it wasn't of much use to the military, or the government at all for that matter. "How about this, General?" He showed him his latest dystopian cityscape projects.

"Yes, that's good. Now fetch my cufflinks."

He did as he was asked and respected his superiors, keeping his head down and producing more staggering designs. He was excited to show off his new virtual hyper-realistic obstacle course only to receive a similar response.

"Very good. Now polish my boots. And when you're done, don't forget to iron my jacket."

Each day he woke more tired than the last, exerting every ounce of his energy to serve as he was instructed. He could no longer even make time for art or design as the list of mundane chores seemed to extend by the day, leaving him numb and empty inside, barely catching a wink of sleep. He felt like he needed to escape. "I didn't sign up for this," he eventually admitted to himself. "I have an idea." He then started to sketch something very different from his usual style. It was tranquil, rejuvenating and projected a sense of togetherness, freedom and peace all in one.

He spent several more days designing a replica of the military simulation he had previously designed and forged a copy of Ribery's gold ring, fusing the chip into it. "This ought to do the trick. I can work more flexibly with the original."

"Rupert," General Ribery called. "I need you to polish my ring. I trust you won't lose it, or else you will face heavy consequences." This was the moment he had been waiting for, the moment he thought would never arise. He capitalised on the opportunity, snatching the gold ring from the general's pocket and switching it with the replica.

"Farewell, General," he said under his breath as he took one last look at Ribery's unattended office and left the premises. "I shall no longer be your errand boy."

Fleeing the Machine City, Rupert ventured to a plot of land several miles out, then began cleverly rewriting the computer chip to resemble his utopian artwork. It was a blissful escape from the torment and mistreatment he had endured and he soon became so lost in it, that he felt one with his new world, revelling in its entirety. "I shall call it Staistreim," he said boldly.

The general had continued to use the replicated military training design that he now possessed, but as time went on, he began to notice more inconsistencies in the performance from his units and started to encounter glitches in the software. "What is this?" he questioned his lead technician.

"It appears that the training software has encountered some issues," he said despairingly. "We may well have to postpone the N.O.D.R.O.G. programme at this rate. The programme is certainly sophisticated enough to stand a great chance of success, but it's not much use without fully trained units to embark upon it."

"Can we not recreate a new training simulation? Or even rewrite it?"

"Not without rebuilding the chip's complex circuitry. It seems it has somehow become overloaded and is starting to malfunction."

Professor Horuzokh had overheard the conversation and received the news with distaste. "Without that simulation, we won't have enough time to complete the necessary training to have any shot of reaching my rouge experiment. Postponement will not suffice. I shall have to assess alternatives."

"Very well," said Ribery. "I shall inform the president that the N.O.D.R.O.G. space programme has been aborted..."

The three figures slowly faded out of sight and the room started to warp itself back into Sequititah's cell. She felt a tightness in her gut, shedding another tear. "So Staistreim was nothing more than an illusionary lie? Everything it meant to me... was all for nothing. But I felt the breezy air; I tasted the sourness of the apples; I could smell the rich floral aromas; the chirping melody of birdsong sounded so genuine."

She could see the outline of a man approaching so she wiped her eyes of their blurring perception to find Magnetus Bane on the other side of the cell door.

"It was such a masterclass design; so realistic that it was capable of using quantum computing to fool the brain into thinking it was actually interacting with it. That's what made the military training so effective," he said. "Rupert truly was exceptionally talented."

"You knew, didn't you?" said Sequititah. She gave him a striking gaze.

"I was going to tell you."

"When exactly? After they kill me?!"

"They're not going to kill you. I'm getting you out of here."

"I don't want your help," Sequititah said bluntly. "How could you keep something like that from me? I thought you loved me."

"I kept it from you *because* I love you."

"You have no idea, do you? The memories, the pain, the relief, the freedom. Every part of it was a lie. Don't you see how hurtful that is to discover? How can I trust that anything else is real?... I sure as hell am doubtful of you now."

"Please, Sequititah. You have to understand. I could sense you weren't ready to hear it."

"Who are you to say whether I'm ready or not?"

"Please. Let me get you out of here. We can discuss this somewhere safer."

"Oi, what are you doing in here?" a droid's voice called. Magnetus immediately turned around and leapt behind it, flicking its deactivation switch.

"Come on," he pleaded again, opening Sequititah's cell. "Let's get out of here before more of them arrive."

She raced out ahead of him to the end of the walkway but he quickly caught up and dragged her firmly backwards. "Are you trying to get us killed?" he cried as the two of them darted around the corner, out of the view of the several passing guard droids.

"Well, look who's talking!" she huffed.

"I've spent my fair share of time in here. I should lead the way."

"Sure. Whatever." Sequititah rolled her eyes and followed Magnetus to a narrow escape from the prison complex.

"Look. Isn't it remarkable?" Magnetus pointed to the scorched white fiery sky.

"Don't think you can change the subject and get all romantic with me."

"I was just saying. It's not every day you get to see the sun this close up. At our current velocity, we should complete our orbit in a few minutes. Then we will use the sun's own gravity to shoot back to Earth."

"Why do you care so much? Why don't you just go back to Reginald if you're that interested in his project?"

"Oh, come on. You know where my heart lies; I came for you straight away." Magnetus inhaled deeply. "I never wanted any of that. They were circumstances outside of my control. You know that already."

"If your heart was so loyal to me, why didn't you just tell me the truth when we reunited?"

"Because I didn't want to spoil the moment. And then things just kept happening."

"As soon as we land back on Earth, I want nothing more to do with this city," Sequititah said sharply. "But if you want to carry on fascinating over it, then by all means, knock yourself out."

"It's not like that! I want to come with you. I want to help your brother. I want to help save the universe."

"Fine. If you can't explain yourself, then at least prove your words."

"I will." He gulped. "You know ho—"

"Save your words, I said. We just have to stay well-hidden until we land. Then we shall flee Doradheim."

"I imagine it's only a matter of minutes before they realise you've escaped. Let's get moving..."

Zeoc was lying almost motionless; each breath he drew was agony. "Hang in there," cried Francesca. "I've almost got it." She completely reconstructed the communication device and added one final piece. Then she started to tamper with it a little more. "I'm getting a signal," she said eventually.

"Where...?" was all Zeoc could articulate.

"It's the alien craft. It's coming back towards our solar system."

"Do you... think...?" Zeoc wheezed.

"Yes. Morathos must have taken control of the ship. He's coming home!" she beamed. Zeoc tried to respond but the coughing became worse. She sat him up and patted his back with force a few times, then handed him a couple of tiny capsules. "Here, take these. They should stabilise your breathing for now."

"Where did you get those?" he asked a few moments after swallowing the pills.

"That's not important. The main thing is, it buys us a bit more time."

"I wonder how Sequititah and Magnetus are doing."

"Me too." She looked up at the sky. "I can't imagine what the Doradheim sky must be like right now."

"Just another one of Forathorn's temporary blissful enticements that I don't care for."

"Well let's see here." Francesca turned her attention back to the communication device. "Something doesn't seem right."

"What do you mean?"

"I don't think I can trust this. My intuition is telling me different."

"So that alien craft that you detected earlier..."

"It's like Magnetus said, we shouldn't trust anything that is happening in our environment right now. First of all, I cannot completely trust this technology since it is made from components that are property of a corrupt government more than capable of trying to delude us. Secondly, all of time and space is warping at random. It doesn't really leave us a lot to go off."

"You're right. But you just said yourself that there is one thing we can trust that is seldom wrong — our intuition."

"Hey. That's right!"

"And what is your gut telling you?"

"Well, I'd like to think we're both connected to Morathos a great deal. You could even say we're quantum entangled," she said, her knees buckling slightly as she sighed.

"I'm not so sure of that," said Zeoc. He didn't know whether to laugh or sigh at her remark. "I'm also not sure where Morathos could be. But my gut is telling me not to trust that device. It may even be spying on us." He snatched it hastily and threw it as far as he could, ensuring the impact caused significant enough damage to prevent it from operating anymore.

"It pains me to say it, but I'm getting a feeling that he might be much farther away than this machine is telling us. Something is telling me he's navigating a distant star system."

"So, we're talking light-years away?"

"Yes. But the ship he left on is more than capable of covering such vast distances at impressive velocity."

"Come on, Morathos," Zeoc pleaded. He watched the minutes pass, as they seemed to tick like days, looking up at the sky with angst. Then there it was — the city of Doradheim came into view.

Sequititah and Magnetus had almost forgotten what a sunrise was. But the flying city was on course for its return to Earth and they could see a darkening sky in their wake, which invited the display of more auroras.

"Thank goodness," said Sequititah.

"With the extracted solar energy, coupled with the slingshot from the sun's gravity, we can return home at faster than light speed," said Bane. "We're just about a minute away from our landing. Then we can get out of this city."

"Let's hope we make it out without being captured again."

"Trust me. Reginald is too soaked up in his project now. Besides, they have what they wanted."

"I guess you're right."

Zeoc and Francesca watched the colossal city soar over their heads in a split second, before it disappeared over the horizon, landing into its foundations.

"Success!" cheered Reginald. But the celebrations would be short-lived as he hastened on. "Now proceed to the next phase. I want this technology uploaded to every city on Earth."

His team did exactly as he commanded and just has he had foreseen, thousands of cities were prepped to become airborne, fetching more solar power by the masses and embedding it into the planet.

Sequititah and Magnetus had made their getaway from the city to the welcoming of Francesca. "He's not in a good way," she said.

"What happened?" asked Magnetus as he came across the remains of the electronic communication device.

"It's like you said," said Francesca.

"Oh, I see. You *feel* him, don't you?"

"Yeah."

"So, what about Zeoc?" asked Sequititah.

"We might have to hook him up to life support," said Magnetus.

"I've got a few more pills to see us through until then," said Francesca.

"Pills?" Sequititah concerned.

"They're mine." She came closer to Sequititah and whispered in her ear. "But he needs them more than me. Please, don't tell him or he might insist I keep them for myself."

Sequititah nodded at her. "But what about you? Are you going to be alright?"

"We will have to cross that bridge when we get there. Let's just get Zeoc stable."

"The cities of our Earth are advancing rapidly," said Magnetus. "Soon they will almost all be technologically equivalent to Doradheim. There's surely some technology close by that can stabilise Zeoc without the need to go back there." Sequititah looked at him with relief. "We just need to ensure we make it before the next launch, as I haven't yet established exactly how this *flying* business operates."

"I remember doing some research on the proposed idea of flying cities a few months back," said Francesca. "I suspected the president might have been up to something of the sort, but it sounded a little farfetched at the time."

"With what we have conjured in the last century, you can't rule any possibility out," said Sequititah.

"No, you're right," Francesca replied. "Nevertheless, one thing I remember reading was that the way in which these cities use the sun's gravity would mean we're limited to how many cities we could launch at any one time. If too many cities slingshot the sun, it might cause collisions or otherwise unpredictable events."

"Ah, yes. That makes sense," said Magnetus. "So, what do you recall reading as a safe number?"

"The design insisted that no more than a few hundred cities should be in launch."

"Perfect. There are millions of cities on Earth," said Magnetus. "This certainly helps increase our chances of reaching a nearby city that *isn't* about to launch. But it doesn't tell the probability of that city launching whilst we're in it."

"That's not going to be an issue," said Sequititah. "In fact, if it should launch whilst we're in it, that might be beneficial. Think about it."

"Ah, yes," said Francesca. "A temporary escape from the ever-increasing hostility of Earth's atmosphere could provide us with a bit of a breather."

"But we'll still be encased inside an artificial atmosphere," said Magnetus.

"True," said Sequititah. "But much more natural sunlight will reach us than down here, under this murk."

"I suppose so, but it's not a guaranteed benefit."

"I didn't say it was. But it's the best option we have, unless you have another suggestion?" Sequititah raised her eyebrows at Magnetus. He looked to the sky for a moment before bowing his head. "I didn't think so."

"We can't sit around here talking any longer," Francesca stressed as she gazed over at an aloof Zeoc. "Look at him!"

"Very well," said Magnetus. "Our destination is the nearby city of Renomorkh. It is just fifteen miles away."

The four of them made the short journey and were surprised to see how similar their surroundings appeared. "It's almost identical to Doradheim," said Sequititah.

"Yes. According to the data I have been able to access, this is all part of Reginald's nano-technological plan," said Magnetus. "All the cities of Earth are becoming artificially intelligent and self-aware, which is causing them to restructure themselves into the same efficient design of that of the metropolis of Doradheim. You could say these cities are using Doradheim as their role model based on how technologically superior it is."

"That's pretty impressive stuff," said Francesca. "But of course, it's hostile to biological life."

"Well of course," said Magnetus. "I think the old me would have revelled at such advancements. But I don't support this at all."

"It certainly leaves an unsettling feeling in me," said Sequititah.

Magnetus started to scan the area for any kind of life support technology. "His breathing is becoming irregular. Quick, this way!" He led them to a pod and opened the door.

"An oxygen pod. Nice work!" cried Francesca.

"It ought to buy us some time at least," said Sequititah. "And it might save some of those pills for you."

They placed Zeoc inside and closed the door. Magnetus turned on the pump and allowed the pure oxygen to stabilise his breathing once more. "This should give us a few days. I'll continue to scan for something more useful in the meantime."

"Sure," said Sequititah. "Francesca and I will keep an eye on him."

A few days had passed and Francesca had expressed her concerns to Sequititah. "His breathing seems better, but his heart rate is irregular and his blood pressure is abnormal."

"He may be breathing alright. But Magnetus said the oxygen supply would be running thin by now."

"I've been having trouble detecting the necessary equipment for Zeoc," said Magnetus. "It's not that there isn't enough of it. But that the majority of it is corrupt and infected by plasmantium thanks to Reginald's engineering. I'm also getting data that this city is due to launch today."

"Well, that might be a bit of a lifeline at least," said Francesca.

"The journeys are becoming increasingly quicker as the technology evolves," said Bane. "At this rate, we'll reach the sun in just ten minutes and circumnavigate it in just two."

"So, it doesn't give us long," said Sequititah.

"But still, we're fortunate it has come at the time it has," said Magnetus. "I'll keep searching."

Francesca became entranced by the display in the sky as the city rapidly increased its altitude and ascended towards the sun. Sequititah took a moment to enjoy the view with her. "How remarkable!" she gasped.

"I sure hope this helps Zeoc," said Sequititah.

"Looks like it's our lucky day," said Magnetus as he led the others to a white metallic capsule that was lying horizontally on the ground. He removed the lid and peered inside to discover an interior similar to that of a casket. "This capsule hasn't been tampered with and it will provide Zeoc with the stabilisation and hydration he needs, at least for a while longer. But most technology is becoming self-aware. The president has engineered it to reconfigure itself to his own accord. I don't know how much longer we can keep hopping from machine to machine like this. We're going to come unstuck eventually."

"Hmm. That darn Forathorn!" cried Francesca. "He's a monster."

"We cannot let our rage get in our way; especially not now," said Magnetus.

"He's right," said Sequititah. "The best we can do is be grateful that we still have options at the moment. We're just going to have to hope with our lives that we find more soon."

"Yeah. You're right," said Francesca. "I guess I lost my composure for a second. But your encouraging words couldn't have come at a better time."

"We're just going to have to keep looking for something. Anything," said Magnetus.

"How many pills do you have left?" asked Sequititah.

"I've got three," Francesca said. "One pill usually lasts a day, but in Zeoc's circumstances, he has been in need of extra. I don't know if I can go on much longer without one either."

Sequititah's posture stiffened and her shoulders became tense. "It's okay," said Magnetus, gently placing a hand on her side. "We will find a solution. Like you said, these next few minutes of additional sunlight may pay off."

"Zeoc is too unstable to take that chance," said Francesca. "I shall save these pills for him."

"No, you can't," said Sequititah. "What about you? You haven't taken one for days."

"I'll be alright, trust me." Francesca was trembling slightly as she spoke and she was starting to lose concentration.

"I think you ought to at least hold onto one of them for yourself," said Magnetus. "I much prefer our chances of reuniting with Morathos with everyone still here."

"I'm fine!" she snapped before entering a coughing fit and suddenly collapsing to the ground. Magnetus raced toward her.

"She's not breathing," he remarked and quickly reached for one of her pills, placing it in her mouth and gently massaging her throat until she swallowed it. Sequititah stood frozen with angst, clasping her hands tightly.

A moment later, Francesca took a deep inhalation and swiftly sat up coughing some more. Magnetus patted her back repeatedly until the coughing had stopped and she got to her feet. She searched her pocket in panic to find only two pills remaining. "What? No! Why did you do that?" she screamed at Magnetus, pounding him on the chest several times. She immediately became exhausted thereafter and collapsed to her knees in tears.

Magnetus sat down in front of her, grabbing her shoulders. "Please don't ever lie to me again," he said softly. Sequititah looked at him sharply and opened her mouth slightly, but said nothing as she came and sat beside Francesca to comfort her.

Chapter 15

Mecha-Forming

Renomorkh had almost completed its circumnavigation of its star. "Hold tight everyone!" Magnetus cried. "We're about to propel home."

"I thought the exposure to the sun might have had more impact on Zeoc," said Francesca.

"Well even with that additional sunlight, we're still living in a hostile environment with not much biological life left," said Sequititah. "Besides, we weren't really exposed to it for very long anyway."

"Sadly, yes," said Francesca, closing her eyes tightly.

"Let's just be thankful that we managed to sustain him for as long as we have and that he's still with us," said Magnetus.

"Well, that's easy for you to say," said Francesca in an elevated tone. Magnetus looked at her with surprise. "...I'm sorry. It's just... I'm so tired... And we're out of pills... And..."

Magnetus raised his right hand in front of her face, gesturing her to stop. "I get it; we're all tired. But we have to stay focused."

"Yes," said Sequititah. "My brother is still out there and *you* know it too. We have to hang in there for his sake. It might not seem like it right now, but I'm sure that's exactly what Zeoc is doing too — holding out for hope."

The city completed its slingshot and came hurtling back to its foundations. In the moment of calm that followed,

Francesca began to dissect the words of her comrades. *Why is it that I'm so concerned for Zeoc? I mean, I'm sure everyone else is too, but... The pep talk I gave him... And yet look at me. I'm a hot mess. Where did that even spur from? To find such strength for another, when I can't even confront anything of my own.*

"You're so much stronger than this," Sequititah said. She maintained her gaze, in the hope that Francesca would reciprocate, but her eyes remained reluctant.

"I think we should rest," said Magnetus. "It ought to give her time to take stock of everything. We go again tomorrow."

"Is Zeoc going to make it to tomorrow?" asked Francesca, still avoiding direct eye contact.

"This is exactly why you need to rest," said Sequititah. "You're worrying to an unhealthy degree and it will only deplete energy you need for yourself. We will keep an eye on him."

"Thanks, you guys." Francesca found a subtle smile on one side of her mouth and glanced up to meet Sequititah's eyes — albeit only for a second — then left to get her head down.

"She sure is worrying an awful lot about Zeoc," said Magnetus.

"I believe her worries lie somewhere else in all honesty," said Sequititah. "Zeoc is the closest Morathos has to a friend. She has to direct her feelings *somewhere*."

"Wow! You really think so?"

"I mean, I can't be certain. But it makes sense, right?"

"I guess it does. We shall have to see."

"I'm not one to brag or anything, but my intuition is most often accurate, as you well know."

"You look like you could use some rest yourself," said Magnetus. He began to caress Sequititah's cheek. "I'll watch over him." She nodded and their lips met with a brief exchange before she went off. But he could not help but get distracted by her restlessness. "She still hasn't forgiven me. I guess I've still got a lot to prove to her."

The next morning, Magnetus attempted to wake Sequititah. "Leave me alone!" she groaned.

"What's wrong?"

"I've had barely a wink." She shrugged his arm off of her shoulder and kept her eyes closed in silence, in the hope he would leave her be.

He withdrew and went to check on Francesca.

"I think you were right," she said. "I do feel a bit more spirited and optimistic today."

"I'm pleased to hear it. But are you sure you're alright?"

"Yes, I'm fine."

"You know you can talk to us about anything that may be troubling you, right? It's not healthy to bottle it up."

"I said I'm feeling better, didn't I? I obviously needed that rest." She squinted her eyes at him. "How's Sequititah?"

"Oh, she had a rough night." Francesca leaned closer into him as if itching to say something else. "... And Zeoc is still stable for now."

"What's to say I was going to ask?"

"Oh, come on! I know your edginess by now." The two of them glared at one another for a brief moment before Magnetus started to chuckle. Francesca began laughing a moment later.

"What's so funny?" Sequititah called as she slowly approached them.

"Oh. it's just nice that we're getting to know each other better," Francesca smiled.

"Well, I'm glad *you two* are all chirpy," Sequititah remarked. "I couldn't stop thinking about that ring last night. Rupert... Staistreim..."

"No wonder you're so tired," Francesca empathised. "I wish I could do something."

"There's nothing you can do now, love. You can't undo the past," Sequititah turned to face Magnetus and glared at him, "but you can repair the cracks."

"You're never going to let me live this down, are you?" said Magnetus.

"Well, if *I'm* never going to forget, I'm going to make damn sure *you* don't either. Besides, I can usually let things go once I come to terms with them fully. Which tells me there's still more to this story than I was previously led to believe."

"What a way to spoil the mood," Magnetus remarked, rolling his eyes.

"Anyway, we've got work to do," said Sequititah. "Now is not the time for silly discussions."

"We do indeed," said Francesca in a bright tone. "But perhaps you need to rest some more. Magnetus and I should take it from here."

"I appreciate your compassion, but I cannot rest at a time like this. I need to keep going, or else I'll only end up too deep in thought."

"You sound just like your brother," said Francesca softly.

"Well in that case, perhaps you should take it a bit steadier," said Magnetus.

"If you insist."

"I've been working hard on the side-lines," Magnetus confessed. "Whilst I was searching for life support technology, I accidentally encountered some components that I managed to piece together." He revealed a device that looked similar to the tracking technology that was previously destroyed. "This will pinpoint the ship that Morathos left on, to the nearest astronomical unit."

"Oh, that's marvellous!" Francesca cried.

"Superb," said Sequititah. "But how did you overcome the previous problem?"

"It seems that since I've been able to secretly tune in to Reginald's schemes, it has enhanced my scanning software and helped to avoid corrupted technology. But due to the rarity of such components, it's been a hell of a grind." He switched on the device and listened to its beeping rhythm. "It uses the very algorithms of whatever it is you're seeking, to mimic its universal frequency and feed it back. It appears that the craft has been predominantly in the region of a star system around twenty light-years away from us, and one planet in particular seems to be of interest."

"Great," said Sequititah. "Now we've just got to find a way of getting there."

"Bear with me; I'm working on it," said Magnetus.

"What've you got so far?" asked Francesca.

"... Err... Well, not much more than a few lousy equations."

"Well, I'm sure if we all put our heads together...," said Francesca.

"Our options are becoming slimmer as everything is evolving around us," said Magnetus. "A second pair of eyes may make my hunting a little easier."

"I'll stay with Zeoc," said Francesca.

"Very well," said Magnetus reaching a hand out to Sequititah. "Care to join me on my hunt for inspiration, my darling."

"Whatever." She smirked and slapped his hand away, turning back to roll her eyes at Francesca as he started onwards. Francesca resisted the urge to laugh and gave her a farewell smile before making her way over to Zeoc.

"We're gonna get you out of here," she said, resting her head on the casket. She then sat down beside him, looking up at the obstructive clouds above. *It sure was nice to see some sun. I wonder how long it'll be before we experience that again.*

Suddenly, an alarm started to sound that startled her onto her feet. The panel on the side of the casket was projecting a blinking light. "Warning! Warning! Vitals are in jeopardy." She started to pant and pace then headed to the panel for a closer inspection.

"Okay, okay!" she reasoned with herself. "The temperature gauge; it's reading twenty degrees Celsius." She tried to locate a temperature dial but nothing came obvious to her. "There's gotta be something!" She started to perspire as she paced around the capsule.

"Warning! Body temperature critical!"

"I know dammit! I wouldn't mind a bit of help here!" she bellowed just before noticing some steel rods sticking out of either side of the apparatus. She pulled them both out and studied the mechanism more closely to find a couple of slots on the top, then inserted the rods into them. Each rod had a small switch at the helm which she flicked and a prominent buzzing noise followed. *I have no idea what the hell I'm doing, but I have to do something!*

A short moment after, the alarm stopped and Francesca exhaled heavily before dropping to her knees in relief. "Vitals stabilised."

"Dammit, Magnetus. You could have at least told me how this thing works. What just happened anyway?"

"Diagnostic procedure is in progress," an automated voice responded. "It appears the temperature regulator has malfunctioned which had slowed the individual's heart rate dramatically."

"Oh, *now* you wanna talk. Is it working now?"

"No. But body temperature is stable due to the use of the electric pumps that kick-started his heart rate."

"So, what is wrong with it? We need to get it operational now!"

"I detect great distress in your tone. Please try to remain calm."

"Zeoc is going to die. I'll calm down when you fix this thing."

"The system's temperature regulator is now fully operational."

"What the?! Is this some sort of sick joke?"

"Forgive me. Even complex technology has its hiccups. It was merely a mishap that might have rectified itself."

"Then why make such an ordeal and scare the wits out of me like that?"

"...Apologies for startling you. It is standard protocol, ma'am. I am programmed to perform regular drills and I must temporarily shut down my components before rebooting, but I must also keep others alert. I would advise that for future reference, the electric rods are to be used as a last resort and only in the emergence of a fatal cardiac failure that my system cannot override."

"Apologies, *Your Majesty.* Anyway, what kind of ludicrous configuration is that?! Tell me how to reprogram it."

"I detect a hint of sarcasm in your tone. Are you still distressed?"

"I'm fine. Just please do your job and keep Zeoc alive." She picked up the two rods and ensured they were switched off before returning them to their original location.

"I will serve as I am programmed, always."

"So, tell me how to reprogramme your nonsensical protocol."

"I'm afraid that request cannot be granted."

"I figured you'd say that. Now can we please end this conversation? I'm not often comfortable conversing with a talking box. It's a little weird."

"As you wish."

Francesca sat in silence as she tried to gather herself together. A few moments later she could see Magnetus and Sequititah returning. "Everything alright?" asked Sequititah. "You look like you've just seen a ghost."

"I'll tell you later," she replied. "Wouldn't want anyone *eavesdropping.* For the record, Zeoc is fine."

"Eavesdropping? Who me?" asked Magnetus.

"Not you. But you could have told me how this thing works."

Magnetus chuckled to himself. "Oh, I see. I think I know what happened. My bad."

Francesca gave him a piercing stare. "Anyway, how'd you guys get on?"

"We don't get on," Sequititah laughed.

"Hey!" Magnetus remarked, giggling.

"Are you sure you two are alright?" asked Francesca. "You sure seem a little different lately, especially around each other."

"Well, that's what you get when you relight an old fire." Magnetus sniggered, grinning at Sequititah.

"Yeah right. Get over yourself," Sequititah replied.

"I don't think I can trust that machine," said Francesca.

"I'm working on an alternative," said Magnetus. "Wait. I'm getting some transmission from Doradheim. It's Forathorn."

"My beloved civilians. I am proud to announce that our procedures for the next and final phase of my project are now under way. The flying cities have been a success and have delivered us much more power. But now is the dawn of something far greater. We will no longer be flying our cities towards the sun. The cities of Earth are growing ever rapidly, soon they will conjoin into one planetary mega city. Once the remaining few hundred have completed their trip, the process can fully unfold.

"I have coined the term 'mecha-forming', as it is essentially not much different to terraforming. Only now, the planet will become solely dependent on digital and mechanical operations, leaving no trace of independent biological life in its wake. Without biological life there's no need for plants to produce oxygen; there's no need for rivers or oceans. The mega mechanical and self-evolving city will encase the entirety of our world." The metropolis erupted with gasps, murmurs and celebrations. "What is more, the mechanical programming will reach deep into the planet's core, converting our home into a completely artificial body. That is where my star extraction technology will take place.

"The sophisticated design will allow for our beloved home to compress our sun into a ball of matter no larger than the diameter of our Earth's core. Then using the sun's own increased gravitational field, we will be able to soar towards our star, where the planet will open up its outer shell, entrapping the sun inside before realigning again. This technology will be powerful enough to allow us to escape our solar system and basically hop to the next star, giving us almost infinite energy."

"This is bad," Francesca sighed. "Those poor Anti-machs; everything they put in, and now, like all those other innocent people, they are probably nothing more than a forgotten memory. It's frightening how quickly this is all happening."

"We knew the planet was going to become even more hostile for biological life anyway," said Sequititah. "It was just a matter of when."

"We've probably got two days before the remaining flying cities return. But the majority of them have already begun their expansion," said Magnetus. "We'll be lucky to even find a trace of natural life in our vicinity by the end of today."

"What are we going to do about Zeoc?" asked Francesca.

"There's only one option that is going to give us more longevity," said Magnetus. "I've almost finished constructing an android shell. Unlike the rest of us who have survived by upgrading our biology into mechanical parts, I propose we do the opposite for Zeoc."

"What do you mean?" asked Francesca.

"We're going to have to upload his consciousness into a mechanical droid."

"And what about his body? That machine won't sustain him," Francesca stressed.

"If you're just going to take Zeoc's consciousness out of his body, then is he still Zeoc?" quizzed Sequititah.

"Well, now's probably not the best time for philosophical debate," said Magnetus. "I suppose we could copy his consciousness into the droid rather than upload it. That way, he'll still also have a consciousness in his biological body."

"So, then he'd be like a clone?" asked Francesca.

"Yes, more or less."

"But what will become of his original?" asked Sequititah.

"I'm afraid without the inventions of Morathos to keep him alive, he isn't going to be able to carry on. I don't see a better option," said Magnetus. "I'm worried for you too, Francesca. However, you're already part cyborg; you may have to compromise more of your biology, as undesirable as that is. Reginald has got us all at gunpoint. But I can install components that will help with thirst and hunger."

"How exactly do these components work?"

"They'll simply be a piece of machinery that will be an extension of yourself that will slowly bind its way into your body. The technology in the machinery is highly sensitive and allows its programming to extract traces of vital nutrients left in the air, feeding them to your cells. Reginald may well be on the brink of wiping out all independent biological life from the planet, but traces of nutrition will still be around for a while longer."

"Well, I strongly oppose, of course," said Francesca. "I would be betraying myself; I'd be a hypocrite. But we still have a chance to find Morathos and save this universe, so if that is what I must do to stay alive and fight, then I guess that's that."

"We should bring Zeoc onto our ship," said Magnetus. "It might help sustain him a little longer, albeit unconsciously."

The four of them flew off to embrace the last few traces of nature, admiring the greenery, soaking in the relatively fresh air and listening to the gentle ambient sway of the oceans.

Meanwhile, the remaining flying cities began to make their descent and the closing stages of the mecha-forming process could transpire just as Reginald had foretold. As the cities conjoined, the magnetic force-fields began to interact with one another, soon encasing the Earth with a new unified artificial magnetosphere that surpassed that of its natural predecessor. The colourless substance of plasmantium that stretched across the skies reflected the continuation of gleams from the spires of towering metallic structures, compacted together uniformly like disciplined soldiers. Despite their highly adaptable self-reconfiguration properties, they stood solid and firm.

"Consciousness successfully copied," a computerised voice announced right before Magnetus inserted the drive into the droid. The machine began to move its limbs immediately before getting to its feet and taking a moment to observe everything in the environment.

"What... have... you done to me?" Zeoc's voice cried. The droid then started to march toward Magnetus in an aggressive manner and gripped him by the throat. "You!"

"Zeoc. I had no choice."

"I trusted you. I really believed you were on our side."

"What are you talking about?" Magnetus squirmed as he tried to break free.

"You have no intention of helping to save humanity and nature. You're still working for Reginald. It was your plan all along to turn me into... this!"

"No. You've got it all wrong."

"I told you I would rather die than surrender to Reginald's schemes. I never wanted anything to do with technology unlike you hypocrites." The droid gripped tighter around his throat. "How selfish of you to disobey my wishes, just to keep me alive."

"How selfish of YOU to forget about your friend," said Francesca. "Have you forgotten why we're doing this?"

"This was a bad idea," said Sequititah.

"No. It was our only chance of keeping him alive," said Francesca. "We need to work together if we have any chance of reuniting with Morathos."

"I can't work with *him!*"

"You've got to learn to put what you want aside and think of the bigger issue. This isn't about you," said Sequititah.

"Look," said Francesca. She pointed to the casket. "You're still human and we're going to get you back. But take a look around you. You can't survive."

"Magnetus is on our side. Trust me," stressed Sequititah. "Let's just ride this out. Every one of us is having to make a sacrifice. But if we want to reach Morathos and save our existence, it's what we must do. Morathos hates technology, but he had to use it. Does that really make him a hypocrite given his intentions?"

"But I don't feel like I'm *me* anymore. This feels inauthentic; like I'm cheating death. Morathos and I... we shared the same values." He released his grip and Magnetus immediately began to rub his throat.

"If you care that much about him, then you have to be prepared to accept the fact that we're all going to have to make compromises," said Sequititah.

"I..."

"Come on, Zeoc," encouraged Francesca. "You have to dig deeper. Think about the real reason we're here."

"I guess you're right. I just need..."

"It's not easy for any of us," said Sequititah.

"I assure you; we're doing all we can to preserve your body," said Magnetus. "But right now, we need you here, conscious."

"It's started. Brace yourself, everyone," said Sequititah. The ship had ascended above the clouds where they witnessed the completion of the mechanical transformation and the sun had begun to decrease in diameter to a noticeable degree.

"How is it even doing that?" asked Zeoc.

"It seems the solar energy that the flying cities have obtained has been further concentrated," said Magnetus. "With the aid of plasmantium, a powerful radioactive projection has resulted in an immense chemical reaction on the sun, causing it to compress substantially."

Within moments, the inner planets succumbed to the star's gravitational influence, darting directly toward it. Mercury and Venus were swallowed and torn to nothing more than the clouds of dust that once formed them and Earth came within the vicinity. A large region of the mega city structure then began to deconstruct itself, reshaping an opening in the planet which allowed the erection of an enormous funnel-like object. The planet then moved in, encasing the remnants of the star inside the funnel and swallowing it up. Then, just as Reginald had envisioned, the mechanical body shifted its shape and closed up the opening; allowing the sophisticated nanotechnology to repair and restore the planet once more. With no star to hold the outer gas giants in orbit, they started to drift towards the empty abyss but the powerful gravitational pull of plasmantium manipulated their trajectory thereafter. Pluto and the outer dwarf planets and asteroids were obliterated, leaving Earth on the brink of the immense gravity of the substance. Trapped between the two gravitational powerhouses, the moon could not withstand its inevitable fate and was mauled apart by the oscillating forces. Using its new acquired energy, the Earth escaped with relative ease to dart off to its next destination.

"Everything is running according to plan, Mr. President," said the head technician.

"Yes. I'm impressed," Reginald praised. "However, as it currently stands, we have no control of where the planet leaps to. We may be on course for Proxima Centauri, but I want your panel to develop some method of being able to choose exactly which star system we voyage to."

"Well, we were actually hoping for that to be the next step. Once we have contained and gathered the energy from a few nearby stars, we may well have the potential to jump larger distances across the galaxy, and — maybe even one day — entirely new galaxies."

"Alpha Centauri is a duo of stars, one slightly more massive than the sun, so I would imagine that once we reach there, it would give us more than enough power to achieve our next goal."

"Yes. Indeed. I'll get right to work."

*****

"My radar is detecting a strong magnetic field," said the Petrademus. "Perhaps there is hope after all."

"Well, you were found guilty," said Morathos. "What else have you got to lose? ...Then again, you're never allowed to return home."

"I may be banished from Nordamia, but *you* aren't."

"What are you suggesting?"

"I have to tread carefully with my words. It seems the magnetic field of the Earth has strengthened again somehow. Perhaps their advancements have rectified the initial issue... But I still don't care for those monsters."

"So, you're going to extract the magnetic field?"

"It's my only hope to save my people."

"Then let's get going... I never really belonged there anyway."

The Petradema star ship rocketed off and soon came into contact with the planet that they were both familiar with. However, there was an unsettling feeling that overcame them when they observed what was in front of them. "Are we in the right location?" the Petrademus asked.

"Yes," said Morathos. "But things are progressing far more quickly than I had imagined. This *is* the planet Earth. But there's no life on it; not a trace of intelligence or complex biology."

"So, you're saying we're looking at what was the Earth hundreds of thousands of years ago? My radar is no longer detecting anything."

"That's because the Earth isn't really here," said Morathos. "That plasmantium is warping space-time so much, that it is toying with our perception of reality. Plasmantium's gravity has already started to slow the expansion of the universe and soon, it will stop it. It will only be a matter of time after that, that it will start reversing the very expansion of the universe, causing all matter to be condensed into an infinitesimally small point, just like the singularity of a black hole, only on a much more devastating scale. The process will accelerate at infinite velocity, so the more time that passes, the quicker our universe will become evaporated."

"Taking us backwards in time," the Petrademus gulped.

"Exactly. And the closer we get to it, the more our reality will be warped. We should head back to Nordamia. It's a much safer distance for now and will buy us some time. Not to mention, we might better be able to perceive what is actually happening around us out there."

"So where is the Earth if it isn't here?"

"I have no idea. But we've got bigger things to worry about."

"And there are no more planets with rich enough magnetic fields that I've been able to detect... I guess you're right; we have no choice but to go back."

"Why can't you just tell me what I need to know? What are the origins of plasmantium? How can I stop it? Don't you even care that without a universe, saving your people means nothing?"

The Petrademus froze still, his shoulders stiffening. "Because if I tell you, I die anyway. So what use is it?" Morathos looked at him with an intense stare that expressed an even deeper confusion.

The Earth had swiftly made its trip from its previous star, now in the orbit of the Proxima Centauri system. "Mr. President, we have completed the necessary research and are in the process of developing the upgrades as requested," the head technician said.

"Perfect," said Forathorn. "Keep me posted."

The technician nodded and reported back to his panel. "The president is expecting results in the coming days. We should get this technology rolled out promptly."

The next couple of days did not disappoint as the panel worked tirelessly to deliver the expectations of their president, and the Earth was soon on course for the Alpha Centauri star system. "Marvellous," said Reginald. "Our next destination, once we're done here is going to be plasmantium."

"Mr. President, are you sure that's a good idea?" the technician stressed.

"There is more energy stored inside that point of space than any other point in the universe," the president said. "With the technology at our disposal now, we could harness all of it into the planet. We could warp space-time readily and use it to travel anywhere in the universe we desire."

"But what of your plans to use plasmantium to convert all of nature into digitised matter?"

"That will be inevitable anyway. I just want to enjoy the ride in the meantime."

"But Mr. President, sir, the gravitational force of that thing could tear us apart. It's already influencing the expansion of the universe."

"I didn't ask for your input on the matter. Our next target will be plasmantium once we're done extracting this pair of stars."

"Have you gone mad?"

"Enough!" The president glared at him with a bullish gaze. "I am your president and you will do as I command, understood? I've warned you already of the repercussions of defying me or intruding in my affairs."

The technician quivered. "Yes, Mr. President."

"Good. Now get out of my face." The technician scurried out of the presidential office.

"Oh my, Reginald truly has lost it now!" Magnetus exclaimed.

"We have to stop him. He's going to kill us all," said Sequititah.

"How do you propose we stop an entire planet from darting towards what is essentially a super black hole?" asked Francesca.

"Hold on a moment," said Magnetus. "Reginald may well have given us an aid without realising it."

"How?" asked Francesca.

"Well, the technology allows the planet to hop to any star system or specific point in space, right?"

"Yes," said Francesca.

"So, if I can find a way to hack into the technology through my own digital connection with Reginald, we might be able to redirect the planet towards the star system where the ship that Morathos boarded, is."

"I see," said Sequititah.

Magnetus started to chip away at the president's systems. "I'm in!"

"That was easy," said Francesca.

"Welcome, Mr. President," said the automated voice. "Our next destination target is the plasmantium entity. Do you wish to proceed?"

"I wish to change my destination," said Magnetus.

"Sorry, I did not recognise that command. I'll need you to provide some additional security information as I am receiving conflicting commands currently."

"I should have known about Reginald's voice activation technology," said Magnetus.

"That's not like you to not account for something," said Sequititah.

"The stakes are high," said Magnetus. "I guess it proves I'm more human after all."

"So, what do we do now?" asked Zeoc.

"Why, we're going to replicate the president's voice of course. One of the main functionary programs of the droids I worked with at the DSA, is to record people's voices. It was part of their tracking and scouting technology. The DSA is still fully operational without me. After all, I was only there to keep an eye on my creation." He pressed on his wrist piece which caused a hologram to be displayed.

"Mr. Bane, sir," the droid responded.

"I need you to confront the president and ask him about our next destination. Deny all knowledge if you have to."

"Yes, sir." The droid did as it was instructed and proceeded to summon the presence of Forathorn. "Mr. President, my sources indicate that a star system — about twenty light-years away — by the name of Axia Exodus, houses immense amounts of energy due to advanced technologies and alien lifeforms."

"Our destination is already set," said Reginald. "I highly doubt that Axia Exodus would contain anything on the scale of plasmantium. Where did you find this information?"

"My sources, Mr. President."

"Well, I suggest you check your sources again. Besides, when did a DSA bot ever have any merit to advise me? You'd be lucky if I took on board the advice of an astrophysicist." The president cut the call.

"I tried, sir. But I cannot overrule the president's orders."

"Don't worry," said Magnetus. "You have done exactly what I needed." He replayed the recording back, editing the information to restructure the entire sentence and played it back to the control and command machine.

"Our destination is Axia Exodus."

"Thank you, Mr. President," replied the computerised voice. "Making preparations for our journey."

Magnetus smiled with pride. "Easy as that."

"Wahoo!" Sequititah cheered. "That's my man." Magnetus gave her a look of satisfaction. "But don't get too ahead of yourself," she warned him, rolling her eyes.

The Earth had finished consuming the last remnants of the duo of stars in the Alpha Centauri system and had set on its journey to Axia Exodus. It was now capable of propelling at speeds far exceeding four thousand times the speed of light. Meaning, its twenty-light-year trip would take only a couple of days. But Reginald was to be alarmed after a few hours. "We're going the wrong way!" he bellowed.

"Your original destination of the plasmantium entity has been overridden, Mr. President."

"Impossible. Nobody is authorised to override it."

"It was overridden by yourself, Mr. President."

"I assure you that is incorrect. I order you to turn back and proceed to the destination I instructed you to."

"At our current velocity, it would take a few hours to reduce to a safe enough pace to turn one hundred and eighty degrees. By that point, we will already be closer to Axia Exodus than to plasmantium," said the computer. "Are you sure you wish to change course? We may end up spending far more energy than necessary."

"Yes. I don't care. Just do it."

"Yes, Mr. President. As you wish."

"Someone is tampering with my technology," said Reginald bitterly. "That droid was from the DSA... You're messing with the wrong person, Magnetus Bane!"

The Earth gradually began to slow its momentum and eventually turned its course. But the slowed momentum meant that it needed to borrow solar energy from its core to kick start it again, which would take a few minutes. The president grew restless and paced around his palace. But the planet would soon be on the move again and its acceleration would be aided by the approaching gravity of plasmantium.

"We have to do something!" cried Francesca.

"Is this... the end?" asked Zeoc.

Sequititah reached her arms out and grabbed hold of Magnetus tightly. "If this is it... I want you to know..." The entire planet was jolted violently by the strong gravitational force causing Sequititah to stumble and lose her words. Magnetus grabbed tighter and prevented her from falling.

"It's okay," he said. "You don't need to say anything."

"Hold tight everyone," cried Francesca.

The Earth's extraction mechanism was activated and the planet opened up attempting to further condense and extract the energy for its consumption. "The substance is already too dense as it is. Compressing it even more will surely tear the planet to shreds," the president's head technician advised.

"I told you I'm already tired of hearing your advice," Reginald remarked.

"But we're going to die!"

Chapter 16

Voyage Deeper

Magnetus Bane had to think on his feet. *They're all depending on me; I've already brought them all this way,* he thought. *C'mon think... That's it. I'm going to hack the president's technology again.* "Computer, activate the release mechanism."

"You are not authorised to give that command."

"I knew it," said Reginald. "Butting in my affairs again, Magnetus."

"Reginald, we're all going to be obliterated. Can't you see that?"

"That's Mr. President to you. I'm the one calling the shots, if you don't mind."

"So, all that hard work on your project; you're just going to throw it all away for this?"

"This is only the dawn of my project. The infinite energy at my disposal could take us to unimaginable possibilities."

"You're not thinking this out. There isn't going to be *any* energy at your disposal when that thing swallows us. There's still around the equivalent of four suns' worth of solar energy inside the planet. Releasing it will create enough thrust to propel us away from the danger of plasmantium and towards our next star system where we can replenish. All you have to do is give the command."

"Stop meddling, Magnetus," the president snapped. "I will successfully extract plasmantium for the sake of my project."

"The Earth cannot sustain it!" Magnetus became animated and the planet had begun to tremor more violently.

"Warning," the computerised voice called. "Gravitational force at critical level. Unsustainable field. Activating emergency thrust release."

"NO!" Reginald bellowed. "Command override. Who even programmed that failsafe protocol anyway?"

"Command cannot be overridden. Thrust release has activated and cannot be reversed."

The energy that the planet had housed from the stars it had consumed, came gushing out and was immediately devoured by the plasmantium body and, as Magnetus had predicted, the Earth was fired across the cosmos and on a rapid course. "Looks like we're off to Barnard's star. It's roughly six light-years away."

"Who activated the thrust release?" asked Sequititah.

"Nobody," said Magnetus. "Somebody had already programmed the software as a back-up. It must have been after Reginald designed it."

"So, who would have been able to programme it?" asked Sequititah.

"I don't know." Magnetus paused, scratching his head. "You've been awfully quiet, Zeoc. Everything alright?"

"Yeah, fine. Just a little startled from trying to process the fact that we almost got swallowed alive... you know..."

"How is that working for you inside a droid's body?" asked Francesca.

"Well since you copied my consciousness over, it's not really any different. My thought and judgement processes are the same; my memories are the same; my mannerisms are the same. I still process everything just the same, really, except I can't feel sensations anymore, like I used to."

"It sounds like you're adjusting quite well," said Sequititah.

"Oh, I wouldn't be so sure about that. The quicker I get back in my body, the better."

Sequititah and Francesca laughed.

"What's the matter with you?" Sequititah asked Magnetus.

"Oh nothing. In a strange way, it's comforting that Zeoc can experience things more similarly to us now."

"I guess. But we are going to get him back," said Sequititah.

"I hope so."

"You sound hesitant... like you don't want him to go back... Are you... jealous?"

"No. Of course not. I mean sure, I regret what happened and I wish I could go back. Just like you, right?"

"Yeah. I guess."

"Morathos would probably be screaming at us now," said Francesca. She deepened her voice in an attempt to mimic him. "We have to stay focused and look to what we *can* change."

"Speaking of staying focused, the president is at it again," said Magnetus.

"As soon as we extract the Barnard's star, our location will be plasmantium," said Reginald. "This time there won't be enough energy to propel us away when the failsafe is activated. We will draw in closer and consume the energy."

"There's got to be a way to set the planet on a course to Axia Exodus, that cannot be tampered with," said Sequititah.

Magnetus replayed the recording into the transmitter. "Destination acknowledged," said the computer.

"This time, there will be no way to interfere with the journey," said Magnetus. "It would cost more energy than we have."

"Perfect," said Francesca. "Finally, we can find Morathos."

As the Earth had finished devouring the compressed remains of Barnard's star, the computer fired up the accelerators and the planet flew on its course. "What is this?" the president snarled. "Override command."

"Mr. President, your instructions cannot be overridden. We will reach our destination in approximately thirty-two hours."

"Curse that Magnetus Bane. How dare he defy the president of Earth?!"

"President of Earth now, eh?" said Sequititah.

"A president that wants to destroy his own planet," said Zeoc, rolling his eyes. "Who would have thought of it?"

"Never mind," said Magnetus. "He's powerless now. For the meantime anyway."

"Francesca, may I have a word?" asked Sequititah.

"Sure." She waited for Sequititah to continue. "In private."

"Oh..." Francesca hesitated. "Everything okay?"

"Come." She led her into another section of the craft. "You know I have a strong intuition for things?"

"Well yes. Why couldn't you tell me out there? It's about Magnetus isn't it?"

"No, actually."

"Oh..."

"What was your gut telling you when Zeoc's machine malfunctioned?"

"I guess I was just startled. I didn't really think about it after that."

"Well, it sure seems corrupt and the sooner we can get him out, the better."

"Absolutely. But you surely didn't bring me in here for that, did you?"

"Well I *was* curious but no, not exactly. My gut is telling me something else."

"Yes?"

"The failsafe that activated when we were about to be swallowed — is there something you're not telling us?"

"I didn't want to disrupt our fate any more than it already has been."

"How so?"

"Well, you know what time travel can do... When I first rescued Morathos and Zeoc I found some blueprints but I didn't have a chance to go back for them and wanted to get out of the presidential complex as quickly as possible. But when I went back for Zeoc and boarded the ship again, I knew exactly where they were so I quickly grabbed them."

"And these were blueprints of Reginald's?"

"Yeah. I figured there needed to be a backup so I tampered with them. Then I gambled that the engineers would just build what was drawn out in front of them and trust it was the president's original work — he was so busy with everything else."

"That's a big gamble. It could've backfired horribly."

"I know. But I didn't know what else to do. Then I thought it best not to mention it."

"Well like you said, we can't tamper too much with our fate. So, we'll keep this quiet." Sequititah grabbed Francesca and hugged her tightly. "Anyway, you saved our home from absolute extermination. I'm so grateful."

"I'm just thankful it didn't backfire and I'm amazed at your intuitive ability."

"Come on. Let's go get Morathos." Francesca gave her a beaming smile.

"Everything alright?" asked Magnetus as the two returned.

"Yes, of course. Just girl stuff. You know..." said Sequititah winking at Francesca.

"If she's given you love tips, then there's nobody more perfect," said Magnetus to Francesca.

"Oh please," Sequititah sighed.

"Hang on a second," said Zeoc. "Surely, if it's love advice, then I'm your man."

"I think that new body of yours must be fooling you," Francesca chuckled.

"Well, I actually meant that I know Morathos better than any of you."

"Who said it was about Morathos?"

"Oh... Well, that was short-lived. You know, if you've gone off him, *I'm* still here."

"Not this again! I thought you'd grown up. Besides, this is awkward; an android flirting with me is not what I had in mind."

"I definitely think that new body of his is tormenting him," Sequititah laughed.

"Hey, I didn't choose to be like this."

"The Axia Exodus star awaits," said Magnetus. "We should be arriving within the next twenty-four hours."

*****

"This looks just like..." Morathos lost his train of thought as he studied the gadget he had encountered.

"What are you doing in here?" the Petrademus asked. "I thought I locked this."

"You're making things awfully suspicious. What are you hiding?"

"So, you think you can just go rooting through people's private property?" The Petrademus snatched the device from

Morathos' hands and placed it back on the shelf, locking the cabinet door.

"Well, I couldn't exactly walk past an open cabinet that should be locked and not notice. It's not much use hiding it now anyway."

"I'm forbidden to disclose the information."

"I've heard just about enough of this nonsense!" Morathos jolted towards the alien but the creature was far more agile and strong. He sidestepped and tripped Morathos over.

"Hmm," he said, standing over his unconscious body. "I should have known you would resist this tenaciously. I cannot afford to waste another minute. But now you know too much." He held out his right arm in front of himself and it began to reshape into a gloopy substance. A small cylindrical object was summoned from the substance that resembled a pen and he twisted it forty-five degrees in a counter clockwise direction and placed it against Morathos' head, pressing the button on the top. The object ticked for a few seconds before emitting a coruscation. Morathos took to his feet immediately after.

"What just happened?" he asked.

"You must have been dreaming. Now, are you ready?"

"Yes."

"You know what you must do?"

"Yes. Heading for my capsule now."

"Perfect."

Morathos climbed inside the capsule and the Petrademus activated its release. It flew towards The Governor.

"State your business," the cuboid said.

"I am Morathos Reina. I come alone, unarmed."

"Who sent you?"

"I came of my own accord."

"Why?"

"I wish to visit Nordamia."

"For what purpose?"

"I am told I am one of them. I feel it to be true although I do not understand entirely. I wish to learn more."

"And?"

"No, that is all, Governor."

"You cannot lie to me; I can read every thought in your mind. So...?"

Morathos sighed under his breath and paused in hesitation for a moment. "The Petradema. They're dying and I know you can save them. Why do you choose not to?"

"The Petradema are not dying. I have stabilised them. Now since I'm fair, I will grant you access to Nordamia. You have twenty-four hours and not a minute more."

"Thank you, Governor."

The capsule was fired towards the not-much-larger-than-Mars, milky sphere, just enough to be gravitationally bound. It was soon met with a thick layer of fog and dust that converted the sky to a vivid off-white shade before touching the similarly pale gravel. Morathos peered out of his window, uncertain whether to open the door.

Open up. He could hear an unfamiliar voice that sounded as if it came from his mind.

"W-what? W-who's there?"

Speech is not necessary.

Is something communicating with my mind? he asked himself.

Yes, the voice replied. *We are a hive-mind. We communicate telepathically and subconsciously. It's a much more effective way of empathising and cooperating as a race.*

Morathos shook his head in surprise and rubbed his eyes. *Have I finally lost my mind?* he thought.

No, you have not. Now open up.

"How do I know it's safe?"

No response.

Oh, sorry. I mean, how do I know it's safe? ...This is so weird.

You're safe. Trust me.

Okay. Here goes nothing. He opened his capsule and felt a surge of heat crash over him. "It's unbearable. Your planet is so close to its star; and such a thick atmosphere."

Nonsense. Now come. He was greeted by the elongated features of the alien's pearl, expressionless face. He felt heavy and upon attempting to lift his leg, found himself having to exert a great amount of effort. After a few minutes, his strides began to become more natural but his muscles were aching. *This must be three times greater than the gravity of Earth.*

Correct.

Morathos placed his head in his palm. "I need to remember that you can hear everything."

It's just like the heat and increased gravity — you'll get used to it.

So, this planet looks smaller than Earth. Yet its gravity is so strong. It must be very dense.

Yes. Almost three Earth masses.

They had been walking for what seemed hours and there were no signs of a settlement. The sand and gravel seemed to span for miles. "I'm so thirsty."

What is... thirsty?

I need water.

Water?

Fluid. I need to ingest fluid or I'll die.

What sort of illogical design is that?

"You must need to replenish your energy somehow. Anyway, how did you know the atmosphere wouldn't be toxic to me?"

Because we communicate telepathically, if you hadn't responded to our instruction, we would know that this planet would be hazardous to you. We're genetically engineered to extract energy directly from our star.

"But what about your magnetic field. Isn't it in jeopardy?"

We do not have a very strong magnetic field. But we're also genetically engineered to withstand solar radiation. That's how we're able to extract so much of its energy. It feeds our cells directly. No need for complicated processes.

Morathos looked around him at the everlasting desert land whilst he tried to process what the creature had told him. "My biology doesn't work that way. I need water. Where are we going anyway?"

The alien stopped abruptly. *This is going to be a problem for you, isn't it? When you responded, I presumed you were one of us but my presumption was quickly altered when you emerged. However, you seem to withstand the conditions here and can communicate with us.*

"I came from Earth. One of your people brought me here. I've never felt like I truly belonged there. But now I'm not so sure if I belong here either."

Yes, I gathered that. The Governor only granted you twenty-four hours. How long can you survive without fluid?

"Three days at most. But going twenty-four hours without will have profound effects on my body and mind."

Then there's no purpose for you being here. The Governor will have you returned to your ship.

"But what about your people? The one that went to Earth to restore your planet's magnetic field?"

We have no recollection of the events you're describing.

This... doesn't make any sense...

We're sorry we cannot be of any more help to you...

"Back so soon?" the Petrademus asked Morathos on his return.

"I cannot survive without water. Were you trying to get me killed? And why don't you communicate like them?"

"No water? That's not how I remember it."

"And they don't need a magnetic field. They're genetically capable of withstanding solar radiation."

"So, it's been done," the Petrademus sighed.

"What are you saying?"

"The Governor is capable of genetic modification."

"You better start talking," Morathos demanded.

"Well, since my people are safe, I guess I no longer have anything to lose..."

*****

"Zeoc," said Francesca. "Zeoc. Wake up."

"My systems must have gone into idle mode," he said. "What is it?"

"It's your machine... It's not operating at all." The two of them raced over to the casket. "There's no reading of a pulse or anything."

Magnetus stormed in. "What is going on?"

"I was hoping you could tell me," said Francesca.

Magnetus observed the exterior. "It's been switched off manually."

"Well, I certainly would not have pulled the cord," said Francesca as she switched the machine back on.

"What's going on?" asked Sequititah.

"It's Zeoc. Someone had turned his life support off," said Magnetus.

"Well. I assure you it wasn't me."

"It's got to be someone," Magnetus stressed. "You're awfully quiet again, Zeoc."

"C'mon. You really think I'd switch myself off?"

"...Not really."

"You did seem overjoyed about Zeoc's consciousness transplant," Sequititah said to Magnetus.

"Whoa, hang on a minute. What are you saying?" he cried.

"Well, we have to cover every possibility, right? I'm just saying that at the moment, you look like the most likely culprit."

"Oh, *thanks.* That really shows how much you trust me." Magnetus huffed.

"There's nobody else on this craft," said Francesca, "and things just don't turn themselves off."

"I think we should take it in turns to stay by this machinery and keep a close eye on it," said Magnetus.

"Yep. I agree," said Francesca. "I'll go first."

The other three left.

A few hours had passed. Sequititah came to relieve Francesca for a short while before Magnetus volunteered to watch the casket. "We're just a few more hours away," he said. "Hang in there."

The droid entered the room a short while after. "Perhaps I should take over for the rest of the journey."

"That won't be necessary."

"Why's that? So, you can bide your time before you flick that switch off again?"

"How dare you accuse me!"

The droid darted toward the cyborg and started to grapple with him. "You're the lowest," he spat. "At least the president doesn't betray; at least the president doesn't sneak around and pretend to be our ally."

Magnetus shoved the droid off of him. "You're wrong, Zeoc."

"Get out of my way." The droid stormed towards Magnetus striking him in the jaw with his elbow and proceeding to the casket. "I might as well save you the effort," he huffed as he flicked off the life support.

"What are you doing?" Magnetus sprung to his feet and tried to pull the clone away from the machine. The droid fell forwards causing Magnetus to fall with him towards the casket. Then he darted out of the way causing Magnetus to place his hands out in front of him to break his fall; they were now firmly gripping the side of the machinery.

Francesca and Sequititah came charging in. "What's going on?"

"He's the culprit. Just as you suspected. He switched me off." The clone pointed towards Magnetus.

"That's not true. He set me up."

"Doesn't look like that from here," said Sequititah.

"I'm telling you the truth. He is the one that flicked the switch."

"Switch it back on," Francesca commanded.

"Stop!" the droid yelled. "Look at the state of him. You turn that thing back on, and I blow this ship to pieces."

"He's bluffing," said Magnetus. "I thoroughly inspected his hardware and there are no weapons or detonators."

"Wanna push that switch and find out? I'm serious. He deserves to die," said the droid.

"How can you say that?" said Francesca. "Has he been infected or something?"

"Someone must have hacked his systems," said Magnetus.

"So, it was *him* who turned the machine off the first time," said Francesca. "What's your game?"

"Just look at the loser." The droid pointed to the casket. "He's a sorry excuse of a man. I'm better now."

"You said you'd do anything to get back to your normal state," said Sequititah.

"I was clearly a fool and didn't realise how much better off I am as a machine. Now leave me alone with the casket. I'm going to make sure nobody gets anywhere near him."

"You can't do this!" cried Francesca. She charged at the droid and attempted to barge past him to switch the machine on, but he pushed her with little effort and knocked her off balance.

"Stay... away!" he yelled.

"Come on, Francesca," said Magnetus.

"We can't just do nothing! Zeoc is going to die."

"We're all going to die if we don't back off," said Sequititah.

"You said he was bluffing. Let's stop him!"

"We can't take that chance," cried Magnetus as he and Sequititah grabbed Francesca, taking her back to the bridge of the ship.

"We will think of something." Sequititah placed her hand on Francesca's shoulder. "Don't worry."

"... There's not much time."

"I believe the president is somehow tapping into the android's system and corrupting Zeoc's consciousness," said Magnetus.

"Could he really blow us up?" asked Francesca.

"I'm struggling to see how; to be honest, it's probably a threat tactic. But still... I want to conduct this properly. We have to be smart. The residual power in the casket should keep him stable for a couple more hours. We ought to be reaching our destination within that time."

"We can't just hang around and hope Morathos will save us," said Francesca. "We don't even know if he's alive."

"True. But what if there's other sources of help here?" said Magnetus.

"I doubt it," said Francesca. "You saw how that alien expressed his hatred for humanity."

"We don't really have much choice," said Magnetus.

"I'm sorry for thinking you were the one who switched the machine off."

"That's alright. I can see how you reached that suspicion."

"Well, I'm not sorry," said Sequititah. "You were the one that cloned Zeoc's consciousness into that... thing."

"Hey, what choice did he have?" said Francesca.

"So now you're sticking up for him? He would have been stable in that machine."

"We need to cooperate. Zeoc's survivability was never certain," said Magnetus.

"I'm... sorry," said Sequititah. "It's been a long journey and we're all getting irate."

"Not to worry," said Magnetus. He looked ahead at the approaching light. "There she glows — Axia Exodus. We should be reaching our destination within the hour."

"Isn't there anything we can do in the meantime?" asked Francesca.

"I'm going to try and hack Reginald's system and see how he is able to tamper with the android," said Magnetus.

A few moments passed. "Any joy?" asked Sequititah.

"It looks like he's using plasmantium extracts to reconfigure the android's systems. Since he's reprogrammed the substance to modify everything, I'm afraid it's not looking good," said Magnetus.

"How long do we have?" asked Francesca.

"Plasmantium will have completed its corruption in less than an hour. That droid is going to become much more unpredictable from then."

"Can't you shut it down?" asked Francesca.

"No. Reginald has figured out a way to block my access."

"Wait, look," said Sequititah. She lifted her head to observe a small hatch in the ceiling of the craft.

"How did we not notice that before?" Magnetus puzzled. He pulled down on the handle and it opened up. "Francesca, you're the smallest." She walked over to the opening and Magnetus hoisted her up high enough for her to grab the ledge and pull herself up.

"There's an air duct that leads toward the rear of the craft," she said.

"Perhaps we could sneak around the back of the casket," said Magnetus.

"Exactly," said Sequititah.

Magnetus strode back to the room where Zeoc lay. The droid sprung to his feet. "I warned you to stay away." Magnetus came closer and Sequititah came right behind him, the two grappled with the clone but his strength seemed limitless as he wrestled them both off with little struggle. Francesca quietly opened the hatch on the ceiling and tried to land as quietly as possible. Magnetus kept the droid distracted whilst she proceeded to flick the switch on.

Suddenly, the droid delivered a strike to Magnetus' jaw which knocked him down. Sequititah charged at him but she was swiftly taken off her feet. The droid then spun around to find Francesca and gripped her by the throat, hoisting her off of the floor. "I told you to leave that switch alone," he hissed, before throwing her to the ground and turning the machine off again.

Sequititah tried to push herself off of the floor but the droid pressed his foot into her back and forced her back down. Magnetus dusted himself off. "Leave her alone!" he bellowed, racing towards the Zeoc replica and driving his shoulder into his abdomen. Sequititah got up and tended to Francesca whilst Magnetus had the machine pinned to the ground. But the droid was relentless and managed to push the cyborg off him, striking him in his empty eye socket. Magnetus rolled around writhing in pain. The android stood over him, making Sequititah and Francesca reluctant to come any closer.

"If you were going to blow us up... you would have done it by now," Magnetus panted.

"Try me," the clone snapped. He dragged Magnetus up and threw him out of the room before glaring at the other two. "What you gonna do now?"

They staggered out of the room towards Magnetus and the android slammed the door shut.

"He's just.... so strong," said Magnetus.

"He could have killed us," said Sequititah.

"So, I guess we will just have to wait it out," said Francesca.

"The good thing is, you managed to flick the switch on," said Magnetus. "It may have only been for a brief moment, but that will keep everything ticking over a little while longer whilst we try and figure out how we're going to deal with this thing."

"We're entering the outer boundary of the Axia Exodus system as we speak," said Sequititah.

"We're approximately ten minutes from our destination," said Magnetus.

"Thank goodness," Francesca sighed.

Chapter 17

Memory Manipulation

"Whoa! What's happening?" Morathos wailed as the star ship started trembling.

"The Governor is angry," said the Petrademus. "I told you I was forbidden to speak..." He addressed his superior. "But now I've got nothing to lose."

"If you value your life, you ought to be careful," the trenchant electronic voice cried.

"I only cared that my people were safe."

"But plasmantium is destroying the entire universe. There's no time," said Morathos. "What about the origins of that?!"

The Petrademus started to hold his head firmly and was swaying from side to side. He screeched in agony before falling to his knees and losing consciousness. "Hey. Wake up," Morathos yelled, shaking him. "Hey. You're the only one who can help me stop plasmantium."

"If our reality should end, then we must accept that it is our time," said The Governor.

"But it's not. I can stop it... If you're almighty and omniscient, can't *you* tell me?"

"I cannot. Everything is predestined."

"Argh, dammit!" Morathos dropped to his knees and started pounding the floor with his fists repetitively.

"What is *that*?" The Governor asked. Morathos looked out of the craft's observation deck to find a metallic sphere fast approaching. The Governor's casing opened up and fired a laser that narrowly missed the object. "That was a warning. State your business or leave."

"Is there really any need to be so aggressive?" asked Morathos.

"I cannot risk overlooking the potential of anything foreign. It may be a threat."

"Well maybe you could ease off on your approach a little."

"Who do you think you are, speaking to me in that manner?"

The object drew closer and Morathos squinted his eyes. "Wait! I think that's planet Earth. Don't shoot."

"That's absurd," The Governor spat. "It looks nothing like it. Besides, what would it be doing twenty light-years away from its natural location?"

A small opening appeared in the mechanical planet and a probe shot out of it that made its way towards the gargantuan cuboid. Morathos looked on from the Petradema ship as a hologram of the president was projected from it. "I am President Forathorn. The creator of this technological masterpiece behind me. Who might you be?"

"I am known simply as The Governor."

"A super AI? So, you were built?"

"That is none of your business. All you need to know is that I am in charge around here."

"Hmm. Stubborn, are we? I'm here for one thing only then I'll be on my way, so if you would just excuse me."

"What might that be?"

"Axia Exodus."

"Axia what?"

"That giant ball of burning gas sitting about fifty million miles behind you. What do *you* call it?"

"Such an odd species: giving dramatic names to things that don't even belong to you. What do you intend to do with it exactly?"

"See this beauty?" the hologram turned to point to the Earth. "She's hungry and that's her food."

"Well, she'd better find food elsewhere. This star is mine! Now leave before I blast your little *masterpiece* into master pieces!"

"Go ahead." The president expressed an inviting gaze. "Your weaponry cannot penetrate my sophisticated magnetosphere."

"You'd be a fool to underestimate me."

"Ha-ha! My electromagnetic weaponry will scorch you."

The universe is about to die, and still he can't cooperate, Morathos thought. "Reginald!" he bellowed into the ship's radio. "Your careless actions have led the very universe that you desired to control into complete collapse. I think you ought to get your priorities right."

"Ah, Morathos Reina. What a pleasant surprise. I thought I had seen the last of you."

"We're all goners if we can't figure out how to stop plasmantium. The contraction is accelerating at an alarming rate and as its gravity increases, it's snowballing us to our destruction. It's probably only a matter of days."

"Oh, here we are again, Morathos. When are you going to accept the inevitable?"

"You're a fool, Reginald." Morathos rummaged around by the unconscious Petrademus and found the key to unlock the cupboard he had encountered earlier. He grabbed the device that he had previously inspected. *My nature accelerator. How could this have gotten here? Did they invent the same technology as me? Were they inspired by me? Or... did* they *somehow inspire me?*

"Proceed to Axia Exodus," the president ordered.

"Yes, Mr. President," said the computerised engine that resumed the planet's course.

"Stop right there!" The Governor cried, firing laser beams at the Earth. But the shots were easily deflecting off the protective magnetic layer that encased it. It was fast approaching the star but the cuboid was right on its tail.

"Deal with that nuisance," Forathorn commanded General Ribery.

"Warm up the electromagnetic cannon," the general ordered his war droids. "It's about time she got some use."

Within a few minutes an opening with a circumference about that of a typical country, emerged on the surface of the planet and the intimidating steel cylinder of the colossal cannon was exposed. A devastating jolt of electromagnetic energy ejected, fracturing the mysterious casing of the fearsome cuboid. It shattered into shards thereafter.

"That was easy enough." The president dusted his hands and displayed an eager grin, as the Earth swooped in towards the Axia Exodus star. "Finally! This must be twice the mass of the sun. It will carry us to plasmantium, then we could reach far more massive, denser, hotter stars."

The planet's mechanisms were in operation and the star started to compress.

The shards that remained of the giant space cuboid began to draw closer to one another in rapid succession and the mysterious object started to restructure itself piece by piece. "You made a terrible mistake," The Governor's resounding voice bellowed. It opened up its casing to reveal a hole surrounded by a metallic frame that the Earth was being pulled towards, causing it to start rattling vigorously.

"Dammit, fire the cannon again," said Reginald.

The electromagnetic power was dispersed and struck The Governor again, only this time it was ineffective.

"Impossible," the president barked.

"Not at all," said The Governor. "Not only is my nanotechnology more superior, I am also capable of reconfiguring and adapting to an exceptional degree. My system quickly learned what materials your cannon had fired at me and, accordingly, adjusted to resist all subsequent strikes."

"Let's see what good you'll be once I devour your star."

The planet tried to resist the grip of the cuboid's technology. Axia Exodus continued to condense but at a slow rate and the president was becoming impatient.

"Your planet isn't going anywhere," said The Governor, releasing their hold on the Earth.

"That's alright. I'll still reach plasmantium soon enough and so will you. It's doom for all who stand in my way."

"You truly are foolish. For you will be consumed amongst us."

"You are the foolish one, Governor. You have no idea of the scale of my technological ability."

"Quick. Let's get airborne," said Magnetus. "We should try and reach Morathos."

The craft was set to launch, when suddenly, all of the planet's electronics powered off, rendering them incapable of pursuing their plan.

"What's happening?" Francesca panicked.

"It would appear that that AI cuboid has found a way into Reginald's technology," said Magnetus. "It sure looks like a remarkably clever entity."

Axia Exodus was regaining mass again, increasing its luminosity as it absorbed the energy harnessed within the Earth that was powering all of its mechanics and quickly started to starve the planet into shutdown. The Petradema were already aware of the dimming of their star's glow and the significant temperature drop that had occurred. But their trust lay with The Governor; they knew the capabilities of the AI and were soon reassured of that when their marble sky brightened.

"Petradema," The Governor's voice called to Nordamia. "It seems the planet Earth — in all its madness — may have some traces of intelligence. Their technological advances aren't the sharpest — at least in comparison to what we've found so far — but I believe there is something of value here. See if you can obtain anything of use."

A select proportion of the race were teleported from their home planet, reappearing on the artificially evolved globe and sent to scout.

Meanwhile Morathos began to study the smaller device that resembled a pen. He turned its top counter clockwise a few millimetres and pressed it. Once again, a flash emitted and he became a little disoriented. "Four seconds... I've lost four seconds..." *The more I turn this, the more time I lose. It must be a memory eliminating machine of some kind...* He studied it some more and started to experiment, soon realising that it could also be turned clockwise. Hesitant to risk anything drastic, he turned it the least amount possible and clicked the top. A burst of light shone just as before, only this time he wasn't disoriented. *I seemed to have regained my lost memory,* he observed. It seemed that some clarity had washed over him, but he was still perplexed at the discovery of his first ever invention. *I could really do with being back at my lab right now.*

The Petradema raided the vast depths of the mechanical streets. Most droids and bots were soon immobilised by the shutdown; only the most complex cyborgs with their own efficient energy containment systems or those with sufficient remaining biology were left. But the alien species were far more adapted. The Governor could quickly alter or tweak their genetics accordingly. These creatures were The Governor's eyes. They knew what was of value after only a few minutes of exploration and so didn't need to waste much time navigating.

The hive-mind creatures were transported into the heart of Doradheim proper and set their eye on one particular object. The president was helpless as they marched into the complex.

"I know you have it," said The Governor. Their voice could be heard throughout the entirety of the planet.

"What are you talking about?" asked Reginald.

"The nature accelerator. It is mine."

"Nonsense. This was built right here on Earth."

"So, Reginald still has it," Morathos said to himself. "Then what about this?" he picked up the device and tried comparing it to what he remembered creating, but struggled to really notice anything different.

Paralysis surged through the president as dozens of Petradema surrounded him. "I'll give you the device, when you give me power back to this planet and give me what I want. Then I can be on my way."

"I'm afraid I cannot let that happen," said The Governor. "You don't have a choice in the matter. Besides, from what I read, it's not even of value to you."

"I have my uses for it. And it's not your business."

"It's of value to someone else. You have no use for it other than to keep it from the person from whom you acquired it."

"So, you know it isn't yours."

"Oh, believe me. It is mine."

The Petrademus closest to him nodded to the others who ransacked the office and obtained the device. "Ha-ha. Reginald

Forathorn, the most technologically advanced being, creator of a mechanical world. And yet so foolish."

"This isn't over, Governor," the president said, screwing up his face and gritting his teeth.

"We have to get that invention back to Morathos," said Magnetus.

"We can't go anywhere at the moment," said Francesca.

"At least that droid isn't getting in our way anymore," said Magnetus.

"What do you propose we do with it?" asked Francesca. "Zeoc's technically still in there. There's no way of extracting his consciousness without power."

"It's only a clone though, right?" asked Sequititah.

"Yes," said Magnetus. "But without any power, that machine won't keep the real Zeoc alive for much longer. Besides, we've got another problem now."

"What?" asked Francesca.

"When the planet was mecha-formed, its programming caused it to continue its rotation mechanically. Without power, it won't rotate naturally anymore and we're now locked in the orbit of Axia Exodus. Half the planet will be exposed to constant light and heat from a star much more massive than the sun. The other half will freeze in darkness. What's more, the artificial magnetic field is no longer operable."

"So, this is it?" said Francesca, sobbing. "Can't we get power back?"

"Not without figuring out how The Governor is accessing the president's systems; not to mention feeding Earth's energy back to the star."

"We're going to have to get into a more comfortable region of the Earth. Somewhere between night and day, away from both extremes," said Sequititah.

"That means we have to leave our ship," said Francesca. "And what about Zeoc?"

"We're going to have to bring him," said Magnetus. "That machine isn't much use to him anymore..."

President Forathorn appeared to exhibit a patient demeanour. He summoned his most superior subordinates. "Nothing can surpass my technological ability. And yet, so many naive fools continue to test me. I have overcome a global virus that shut down all my systems. What makes this floating cube of space junk any different?"

"We have every faith in you, Mr. President," said the head technician.

"I'm already working on a hack," said the president. "Our most fundamental systems should be up and running in a few hours. I just have a few more calculations to make."

"Superb," said the lead engineer. "All my components are configured and awaiting your further instructions."

"Excellent. We proceed to consume Axia Exodus, then onwards to plasmantium. At the rate that the universe is currently contracting, the journey will be very swift indeed."

Morathos stood over the still unconscious Petrademus holding what resembled his invention in one hand and the pen-like device in the other. He crouched down and placed them both on the floor as he tried to look for signs of life from the alien creature. *These beings don't breathe,* he thought. *If they soak solar energy directly into their biology, then they probably don't have a circulatory system either.*

He pressed his hand firmly on the alien's chest but could not feel any rhythm. He then tried pressing his fingers on various areas of the body. There was nothing.

What are you doing? A voice projected in his mind. His eyes widened and he slowly straightened his back.

"So now you decide to talk to me telepathically," he said.

I am different from the other Petradema. I can communicate verbally and telepathically. Because of my time on Earth, verbal communication became my norm. But now, in my paralysis, this is a more efficient way of interacting.

"Did you build this?" He picked up the pen-like device again.

This is going to be the end for me anyway. I had to cover all bases, but even then, I failed; there's nothing more for me to lose.

"What are you saying?"

Every part of my plan was calculated to ensure that there would always be a back-up, and yet it was all for nothing.

"Just spit it out already!"

That device was built to protect you. I was supposed to save my race. I was supposed to extract the Earth's magnetic field. But when I didn't, I was supposed to adapt to Earth long enough to repair my ship. But then, when humans had already compromised the magnetic field, I was supposed to ensure it could be repaired. I was supposed to stabilise the magnetic field of my home planet just long enough until my return.

Morathos started to pace back and forth. "What does any of this have to do with it?"

You had to finish what I started. But then you were supposed to forget it all.

"So, *you* wiped my memories. You are the reason I had to travel back in time. Why would you do that?"

Things had already become irreversible by that point. My whole plan had collapsed. It would have been too dangerous for both of us if you were to know the truth.

"But I still didn't find out everything."

The device also speaks in a specific frequency that only those with Petradema genetics can tune into. I used it to get you on board my ship and manipulate you to turn your back on Earth and its people — even your friends.

"That still doesn't explain my Petradema genetics."

Haven't you figured it out yet? I thought you were cleverer than that. Your invention was supposed to save us. Everything that was supposed to happen, didn't.

Morathos picked up the nature accelerator and studied it again. "So why didn't this save us?"

Because that's only a prototype, you fool!

"Why are you paralysed anyway?"

My master... There was a hesitant pause. *You don't have much time. Go and save your friends before it's too late.*

"I can't stop plasmantium. It's *already* too late."

You are the only one who can... I can do no more.

A deep shiver passed through Morathos which left an emptiness inside him. "I can't..." There were no more responses from the Petrademus. *Since this is the end, I ought to say goodbye,* he thought and set the ship on course to Earth.

"Where are you going?" The Governor piped up.

"Well," said Morathos, "if I am to accept the fate of the universe — as you said — then I ought to return to Earth one last time."

"That is not what you call Earth anymore. Look at it."

"I might not have ever truly felt that I belonged there and, it may not be the same place it once was." Morathos cleared his throat. "Yet, despite all that, it is still a part of me and there are people on it without whom, I wouldn't be where I am today. I owe them not only an apology, but my life. But you would never understand all that; you would never understand what it means to be a living, biological being with real emotions and a heart, would you?"

The Governor began to imitate a slow applause sound which Morathos perceived as patronising, despite the cuboid's generic electronic voice giving no indication of tone or intent. "Bravo, bravo."

"Are you mocking me?"

"If I couldn't process emotion, then how do I know what sarcasm is?"

"You might be a super intelligent construct, but you can't pull the wool over my eyes that easily."

"Don't you think that you ought to be spending your last moments more wisely?"

Morathos said nothing more and proceeded towards Earth. As he made his approach he thought about where everyone might be. *No rotation... They would have certainly made their way towards dusk or dawn. The last time I saw Earth it was on its knees... The virus... The invasion... Only Reginald could have saved them. Only Reginald could be responsible for this overhaul. But would they really collaborate? Reginald's ego is too big... But just look at the planet... They must have.*

He flew towards Doradheim, across the region of land that was once referred to as Staistreim, now nothing more than a few square miles of soaring metallic architecture. *I know Reginald. He would have bargained with them only until the moment they stopped being of service to his needs. I suspect they won't be in Doradheim anymore.*

He landed the craft near Staistreim and started to look for any indication as to where the others might be. *I wonder if they came back here before all the mechanical transformations,* he pondered. Then it clicked. *The virus would have shut down my sister's and Magnetus' systems; perhaps Francesca's too. But then Reginald must have fired back with even more powerful technology and built this mechanised nightmare. Which means Zeoc...* He sighed and closed his eyes. "He must be suffocating — if he's even still alive."

He rested his chin in his palm, tapping it repeatedly with his index finger and sat there for a moment as he tried to visualise the Earth as he remembered it once more. *Doradheim was of no use. But Magnetus?* He got to his feet again and paced around several times. Everything seemed to be piecing together and he felt like it was almost in his reach. And as the map in his mind became clearer, he evoked which technological settlement would have resided nearest to Doradheim, and set off across the planetary metropolis towards the region formally known as Renomorkh.

What if I don't find them? Renomorkh isn't how it used to be, Morathos worried. *Everything just looks the same; each building a perfect copy of its neighbour, like some sort of viral mutation; infected with the poison of Reginald's ego. Plasmantium, strangling and squeezing out every last drop of natural life.* His thoughts were exhausting; his limbs aching until they were numb. *Now is not the time for this!* He tried to redirect his train of thought and continued to stumble on and use every ounce of strength he had left to contemplate the whereabouts of his comrades. But his mind went blank and the metaphorical cloud of doubt was starting to constrict his chest and abdomen. Each pace he took grew heavier on him until his feet could not lift off the ground anymore. His knees could no longer support his weight, and he slumped down onto them, burying his head in his hands.

As he took his hands away from his face, his vision became somewhat restricted. He could make out brief outlines of the structures around him for a moment. Then everything started coming into focus again before a sudden flash hit him. Its immediate dimming revealed the face of his sister and his mind took him back to the moment they had first met. He pulled himself off his knees and rubbed his eyes, trying to focus on his surroundings again. But then his mind projected memories of Zeoc along with glimpses of Francesca and even Magnetus. He paused and let them play out, and the initial resistance which stirred in him had started to disappear. A short moment later, his vision returned and a warming sensation began to engulf him. He couldn't quite understand how but it was as if it was urging him to continue on east. *I must trust that they made it here. But they wouldn't have wanted to stay in so much urban land for long, I imagine. I expect they would have wanted to cherish nature one last time.*

His mind drew a map of Renomorkh as he remembered it and he followed it to what would have been the outer rural land. He only had to wander a short distance farther before a familiar sight came into view and his inner tension subsided. "The craft!" he cried. He raced straight over and noticed it was open, and carefully inspected the entire ship. "They can't have gotten that far," he told himself.

He encountered the casket and opened it up. *Hmm. Looks like life support. This must have been stabilising Zeoc. But what about Francesca? I don't recall her having much in the way of integrated technology.* As he was about to leave, he stumbled across the motionless android. *I haven't seen one like this before. It looks like it has been constructed very recently.* He studied it for a minute, but he knew he had little time. Finding the ship was enough to convince him of his next destination. He observed the sky and let it lead the rest of the way. *Twilight to the east.*

Meanwhile, in Doradheim, the president was eager to get his preparations underway as he addressed his technicians. "The final calculations are complete. I need you to execute the remaining safety checks and then proceed with the operations to fire this planet's power back up. Once we're up and running, I want you to immediately initiate the star extraction of Axia Exodus. The Governor has meddled with the wrong man."

"Consider it done, Mr. President."

Chapter 18

Reunion

"What's that?" Francesca pointed up above her head. The sky was still dull but a subtle movement could be witnessed.

"It looks like a craft," said Sequititah.

"Well, that didn't waste much time," said Francesca.

"We have to remember that space-time is warping at an even more expansive rate," said Magnetus. "The plasmantium body that was twenty light-years from our location is probably only less than five now."

"Yes, but even so...," said Francesca.

"I love your optimism and I definitely don't think any craft from Earth could have gotten airborne so quickly after the reboot," said Magnetus.

"So, it is likely a foreign craft?" asked Francesca.

"Yes. But as I said, we cannot trust that it isn't just an illusion of time."

"We can't trust that *anything* is real though."

Sequititah glanced over at Zeoc. "We have to get moving."

"What more can we do?" asked Francesca. "Forathorn has managed to reboot all systems somehow."

"It doesn't look promising. But at least we can get Zeoc back on his life support," said Magnetus.

"What about the droid?" asked Sequititah.

"I wish I could answer that."

They headed back to the ship, carrying their doubts.

"Wait a minute," said Magnetus. "The droid has gone." They proceeded to the room where the casket was.

"Someone has been here," said Sequititah. "I can sense it."

"No! It can't be!" sighed Francesca. She observed that the casket was in a deficient state. "It's been vandalised."

"It's no longer operable," said Magnetus.

"Looks like we've got bigger things on our plates now," said Sequititah. The three of them were shaken by a sudden movement under their feet. Magnetus and Sequititah began bolting towards the door of the craft, but Francesca froze still for a second before trying to lift Zeoc. Sequititah and Magnetus swiftly pulled her away and made for the exit.

"No! Zeoc!" Francesca cried, trying to force her way past them.

"It's no use, Francesca," said Magnetus. "We have to get off this ship for our own safety. It's too much of a risk being indoors and there's no time."

The mechanical globe was in motion and started the process of condensing the Axia Exodus star once again but it was abruptly interrupted by an intimidating cacophony. "Petradema. It's time." The Governor called its people and the alien creatures were instantly transported from Nordamia onto the Earth. The presidential complex of Doradheim was swarming with the extra-terrestrials as they attempted to hack away at the structures and intervene with Reginald's procedures.

"What is the meaning of this?" the president hissed.

"I warned you, Forathorn," said The Governor. "But if you insist on making this more difficult, then be my guest."

"Marvellous. I do love a good old-fashioned war. General Ribery, launch an assault at once; get rid of these vermin."

"Yes, Mr. President." The general saluted his superior and prepared his forces.

An android that was distinct from the others had appeared before Reginald. It resembled the droid that had harboured a copy of Zeoc's consciousness, but its voice sounded more callous. "I believe you have a specific objective for me, Mr. President."

"I want that nature accelerating device returned to me at once."

"It shall be a foregone conclusion."

An influx of automata emerged from across the planet as they tried to fend off the alien's assault. The exchange of blows served as a significant enough distraction from the current operation of the star extraction process, and Axia Exodus began to restore itself.

A brutal display of both mechanical and biological destruction occurred as plasma and electromagnetic weapons tore through their targets. But both races were sophisticated enough in their design and engineering that they could repair and restructure themselves not only sufficiently, but hastily. Even with the aid of the planet's advanced infrastructures, it seemed that both combatants were well enough equipped to endure the onslaught of their adversaries which would result in an undoubtable stalemate.

"We've got to get back on that ship and get out of here," said Francesca.

Magnetus inspected the exterior. "Everything seems intact still," he said.

"But I'm afraid it doesn't look too good for Zeoc," said Sequititah, bowing her head.

"Not if I can help it!"

The three of them looked around to see where the familiar voice was coming from and a silhouette of a man with a ruffled head of hair began to form, becoming gradually more defined as the figure stepped forward. Francesca darted right towards him and locked her arms around his midsection. He reciprocated the gesture.

"What took you so long?" she yelled at him punching him in the chest as her watery eyes glared into his.

"Morathos, you made it!" Sequititah sighed, grabbing her brother.

"Glad to have you back, Morathos," Magnetus smiled.

"I'm just glad you're all alright," he said.

"Can you save Zeoc?" Francesca asked. "I don't know how much longer he's got left."

"Just so happens I've been working on something that can slightly alter Zeoc's genetics without harming him — it's basically an upgraded replica of all my previous inventions combined. It should at least let us all cherish our last moments together."

"Great," said Magnetus. "Let's get cracking."

"Wait... What are you saying?" asked Francesca.

"There's nothing left." Morathos turned away. "Even if there was, there's not enough time."

"No, Morathos. You can't just give up," said Sequititah.

"We just have to accept our fate. Don't you see? I failed to find the origin of the substance. I can't destroy plasmantium."

"The Morathos I know doesn't give up that easily," said Francesca squinting her eyes with suspicion. "What have you done with him?"

"There's nothing we can do except stick together and make our last moments count. That's why I had to find you before it was too late."

"No, Morathos!" Sequititah snapped. "We need you right now more than ever. That AI has your invention. Don't you want it back? Don't you think that you have to at least try?"

"It's no use. It's over."

"Don't you at least wonder what use your invention could possibly be to The Governor?" Francesca asked.

Morathos shrugged and huffed. "I don't care about that invention anymore. That was a silly childhood experiment — no more than a naive dream. It was a failure anyway."

"How dare you be so selfish?!" Sequititah sobbed. "Together we can still stop this. Believe in yourself. What has gotten into you?"

"You just don't get it."

"What do you think it was that led you back to us?" asked Francesca in a motivational tone. "What do you think it was that made that invention to save Zeoc? That fighting will and determination to never stop that I felt so strongly irritated by, that's what. So why would you go to such lengths and then just throw in the towel at the last hurdle?"

Sequititah started to gently nod. "She's right. Now let's revive Zeoc and end this!"

Without warning, Morathos had proceeded towards the ship when a Petrademus had struck him. Magnetus immediately retaliated whilst Morathos tried to reorient himself. "Quick, get on board," he yelled to Sequititah and Francesca.

"But what about you?" Sequititah asked.

"Don't worry about us. Get on board, now!"

"Here take this." Morathos tossed the invention to Sequititah. "Just press the button in the centre of the device when you're within one metre of Zeoc."

They raced onto the craft as Magnetus and Morathos tried to keep the alien creature at bay. The doors on the spacecraft closed and the engines powered up.

"What's happening?" Francesca panicked.

"I didn't press anything."

The next minute, the ship was airborne and on route.

Magnetus managed to dodge a blow from the entity and started to make a run for it. "This way," he pointed to the alien craft that Morathos had landed in. The two of them climbed on board, barely avoiding the clutches of the foreign beast. "We'll be safe on here."

Zeoc awoke, taking a gasp of air. He looked around him. "Oh, thank goodness," Francesca sighed.

"What happened? I'm... breathing... on my own?"

"Recognise this?" Sequititah held up the invention that was responsible.

"Wait, Morathos.... He's alive? Where is he?"

"Unfortunately, we lost him again," Francesca expressed in a solemn tone.

"Well, I'll always have faith in him."

"I hope he makes it," said Sequititah.

"Where are we going anyway?" asked Zeoc.

"We've lost control of the ship," said Francesca. "But it looks like we're heading to Doradheim."

Zeoc sprung to his feet and made his way into the control room. "There must be something we can do."

"It's probably best if you don't touch anything," said Sequititah.

"You were right," said Zeoc, resisting his urges as the ship flew into the docking station of the presidential complex.

"Oh, look who it is. Right on time, too." The wry expression of President Forathorn was all too eager to greet them. "Lock them away."

"What do you think you're playing at, Forathorn?" Zeoc snarled as he unsuccessfully attempted to wrestle the overwhelming number of droids surrounding him.

Francesca and Sequititah did not resist.

"Zeoc, it isn't worth it," said Sequititah, tugging on his arm to drag him away.

The trio were thrown in a cell with completely transparent walls.

"President Forathorn holds you all responsible for the outbreak of this war," said one of the guard droids. "He also seeks one by the name of Morathos Reina, of whom I have been ordered to obtain the whereabouts."

"No idea where he is." Zeoc blurted. "Besides, we wouldn't tell you even if we did."

"Very well. We found him once before. We will find him again."

"Over my dead body!" Zeoc yelled.

"Oh, don't worry. That can be arranged," said the droid as it started down the corridor. The rest of the droids followed.

"I know you're angry, Zeoc," said Francesca. "But you need to calm down."

He took a deep breath and slumped himself down on the ground scrunching his brow.

"We should direct our efforts elsewhere," said Sequititah.

"The walls? What's this place made of?" Zeoc quizzed.

Just then, more footsteps could be heard approaching the cell. It was President Forathorn. "Quite the design, isn't it? Even if I say so myself." He took a couple more steps forward. "And isn't it interesting also, how things have come full circle?"

"You won't be saying that for long," said Sequititah. "None of us will."

"Let me guess. You honestly think your *love* will come and save you? Well, think again." The president came close to Sequititah and gave her a daunting stare. "You see, it was Magnetus Bane himself that brought you here."

"You're a liar, Reginald," said Sequititah. Her voice quivered a little.

"Oh, really?" he started to pace back and forth slowly. "Think about it — we were digitally interlinked. In case your little inferior human brain has forgotten, it wasn't so long ago that he was obtaining information from me. But communication works both ways, you know. He fed *me* data too. It was he who built the droid that hacked my ship's computers and sent it back to me. And now look where you are — without him."

"He would be here with us if it was not for the assault from the alien that he had to fend off. I know it," said Sequititah.

"You don't sound so confident." The president glared deep into her eyes, forcing her to look away. "When are you going to stop fooling yourself, Sequititah? Magnetus Bane doesn't love you; he never did. It was the perfectly executed genius of my technological supremacy. And soon Morathos Reina will come running to find you. Then, SLAM! He's mine. Ha-ha-ha!"

"When are *you* going to stop fooling yourself, Reginald?" said Francesca. "All this will be for nothing in a few hours. Do you still not see what's happening to our universe?"

"I understand it is a bitter pill to take," said Reginald, in a condescending tone. "The two people whom you both adored and trusted so dearly betrayed you and you don't know how to handle that truth. Morathos is a sorry excuse for a man. He is the one destroying everything. But you're obviously too desperate to save him and this so-called decaying universe to see it. Ha-ha!"

"Again, with the lies and manipulation!" said Francesca. She glared at him, her jaw clenched and her throat tightened.

"I've heard enough of your ignorant nonsense," said Reginald. "Now if you don't mind, I am expecting that man himself to show up any moment." He marched off down the corridor.

"What if he's right? Shouldn't Magnetus be with me now?" Sequititah worried. "Magnetus does love me, doesn't he?"

"What?! Are you out of your mind asking that question?" said Francesca. "You know not to trust Reginald. Don't you feel it in your heart?"

"Francesca's right," said Zeoc. "You're the most intuitive one here."

"But even your intuition can be wrong sometimes... I mean, nobody's perfect, right?"

"Trust me." Francesca placed her arm around Sequititah's shoulder. "He will come for us."

*****

"How did we manage to lose them so quickly?" asked Morathos.

"I think the president is behind this," said Magnetus. "Don't be mad at me, but I built an android and copied Zeoc's consciousness into it. And now I think Reginald has corrupted it."

"You did what?!" Morathos' eyes widened and his face reddened slightly.

"I had little option. He was going to die."

"I remember coming across an android like none I have seen before on your ship. Would it be that one?"

"Yes. He must've fled when all systems were rebooted."

"What in the world?"

"Please, Morathos."

"I guess I should try and see things from your point of view. But he's my..."

"I know. I'm sorry. We just don't have the same resources as you."

"Forget it; now is not the time. At least he's alive and conscious again — for now anyway." Morathos looked straight ahead. "Let's get going."

"Where?"

"If Forathorn is behind this, then Doradheim it is."

"I urge you to trek carefully, Morathos. The president may well be expecting you."

"Oh, I know how devious he is. But I'm afraid it's now or never. We don't have long left and I already stressed how I wanted to spend that last blink of time, regardless of what that means."

"This is what I don't understand. You're so spirited and determined. Yet, you've given up hope for our survival."

"Don't *you* start that as well." Morathos glanced over at him for a second before accelerating the craft.

Magnetus peered at the ground below. "Two races at war across the whole planet and yet, everything looks so still and lifeless. I guess that's what happens when you're in a stalemate and nobody will back down."

"What baffles me more is that they're all fighting over a single star, when our whole *universe* is coming to an end."

"Yes."

"I owe you an apology anyway."

"What for?"

"My behaviour back in Karahdor."

"Oh, forget it. After everything I've done, the people I've hurt, I probably deserved much more."

"We can't really do a lot about our past. What matters is that we move forward."

"That's true."

The short trip was made and the spacecraft entered the city. As it lowered its altitude, a barrage of electromagnetic energy struck it, ricocheting off its exterior and leaving not a scratch. "I forgot we were flying in an alien craft," said

Magnetus as he observed the hundreds of war bots below that were targeting them.

"This ship is something else," said Morathos. "It seems more sophisticated than the rest, just like its commander was."

Magnetus Bane stepped out of the craft first and proceeded towards the surrounding robots and droids. "Hold your fire."

"Apologies, Mr. Bane," said the commanding android.

"I have detained this foreign spacecraft," said Magnetus. "Inform the president at once."

"Yes. Right away."

"Tell him that Morathos Reina is on board also."

"I'm sure he'll be most pleased." The droid scurried off and Magnetus darted back inside the ship.

"Morathos, stay here. I have an idea," he said.

"I told you, there's no time for fancy games."

"Just trust me." He left the craft again and marched on through the hordes of machines right into the presidential complex.

"Look who just couldn't resist to come crawling back," the president said with a smug smile.

"Morathos is on board."

"Just whose side are you on exactly, Magnetus? I will not be played for a fool."

"I assure you, Mr. President, Morathos will not be of any more inconvenience to you. I have locked him on the ship and disabled its exits."

"I must say, I'm quite impressed." The president raised his eyebrows. "However, I will be requiring his assistance in something very soon."

"And what of Sequititah and the others?"

"They will be disposed of accordingly."

Magnetus nodded and proceeded to leave the president's office. "Oh, and Magnetus."

"Yes, Mr. President."

"Before you leave, release the android probe. It shall be sent directly to The Governor to regain what is rightfully mine." He flicked the switch and the droid rocketed off into space.

The Governor interrogated the Zeoc clone. "How foolish does Forathorn think I am? Does he honestly think I am going to hand that invention back to you just like that? Ha!"

"You're messing with the wrong person, Governor," said the droid.

"Oh, am I? Why don't you tell your little president to come and get it himself then?"

"That will not be possible."

"Suit yourself." The cuboid opened up its outer casing and an effulgent red glow began to illuminate from within. A sharp beam emitted immediately after, which struck the droid, tearing apart its mechanics with ease. The beam ascended upwards in a swift motion which saw the droid severed completely in half before its components started to separate and crumble, leaving not a trace of the mechanised body.

"Impossible!" the president cried. "Magnetus, get me that device. I don't care how you do it, but do it now."

Magnetus nodded, but he diverted from his orders and hastened towards the cell that the others were in.

"It's Magnetus!" Francesca yelled. "I told you."

"There's not much time," he said. "Reginald is preparing to dispose of you."

"How can I trust you?" asked Sequititah. "It was you who got us in this mess in the first place."

"Do you honestly think I'd be coming back to warn you if I couldn't be trusted? I'm betraying his orders to fetch Morathos' invention."

"I dunno. You've just been acting really strange lately. Besides, you wouldn't stand a chance of getting that off The Governor anyway. That thing seems indestructible."

"Well, now is not the time for bickering. I'm going to find a way of disabling this cell."

"He's right," said Zeoc. "Whether or not you can trust him is irrelevant right now. There's no time."

Sequititah huffed. "Yeah. I know."

"Where's Morathos?" asked Francesca.

"He's perfectly safe," said Magnetus. "I'll be back as quick as I can."

What am I supposed to do now? Morathos asked himself as he attempted to open the door of the craft. *I can accept that this is the end. But how I do I accept not being able to ever see those who matter again?*

He picked up the pen-like device and gripped it tightly. "What if I just erase everything? Perhaps it won't hurt so much anymore. All my worthless inventions; all my wasted hours; all my torment — gone." He started to twist the top and the more he twisted, the more of a resistance he had to combat, until he found he could twist it no more. He pressed his thumb down hard on the top but it wouldn't budge. *Huh?* He pushed harder, now using both hands, but still nothing. His face was flush and his forehead started to glisten as his pores perspired. He gritted his teeth and held his breath, fighting with every ounce, but found himself slamming the device onto the ground shortly after. He let out a loud yell of frustration before catching his breath again. *It's my fault we're in this mess. Perhaps I don't deserve to see my friends again...*

He glanced at his surroundings. Everything around him had started to warp and reshape itself in a chaotic alternating manner. He shook his head and rubbed his eyes, then slapped himself across the cheek. Despite his actions, everything was behaving just as it had a moment earlier. *This must be it,* he gulped.

"Where is Magnetus?" Francesca asked.

"He's not coming back," said Sequititah. "I don't *believe* him!"

"We have to find a way out of here," said Zeoc, holding his palm firmly over his forehead. "That's weird. I feel as if... some part of me is missing all of a sudden. Like a piece of my consciousness has vanished somewhere."

"I feel like I've lost a part of me too," said Sequititah in a frowning tone. "He is just the lowest."

"Hey. Come on. We have to pull together," said Francesca.

"What exactly can we do now?" said Sequititah.

"Err... I dunno. But we have to be stronger than this if we have any chance."

"Oh, Morathos," said Zeoc. "Please make it."

"Guys. Morathos is trapped on a Petradema craft," said Magnetus as he came strolling back down the hall. "He's safe there. But we can't reach him and he can't reach us. I'm not even sure if I can get you out of here."

"Oh, you've really gone and messed things up now, Magnetus," Sequititah sighed.

"Hey. Don't be angry at me. I'm doing my best."

"Morathos!" Zeoc yelled, looking straight past the others.

"Where?" asked Francesca. "I don't see him."

"He's here in the cell with us. Look." Zeoc pointed to the far, right corner behind Francesca. "He must've figured a way in."

"There's nobody there, Zeoc," she said as she spun around.

"Does this mean our reality is warping again?" asked Zeoc.

"Perhaps it's because we brought you back from the past before," said Magnetus. "So, you're technically farther into the past than we all are already."

"Man, this is too much!" he sighed.

"It's too late. This is it everyone," said Francesca. "In the next few minutes, we're getting swallowed up, so brace yourselves."

"If only I could see my brother one last time," cried Sequititah.

"I would have wanted nothing more myself," Francesca sobbed.

"So, this is really it?" asked Zeoc.

"I... guess it is," said Magnetus.

"The president awaits you, Mr. Bane," said an approaching guard droid. "He is becoming impatient and needs this invention obtained right away."

"Very well. Tell him I'm on my way."

The droid scurried off and Magnetus remained put. "He's never getting that back," he murmured under his breath.

"Why are you doing this, Magnetus?" asked Sequititah.

"Doing what?"

"Trying to play both sides."

"What are you talking about. I'm on your side."

"Well, why aren't you in this cell with us then?"

"Think about it. What good would I be in there? Not that it matters now anyway, but I had a shot of reuniting us all with Morathos, don't you think?"

"Well, all this sneaking around isn't exactly helping me trust you."

"Guys, can we please not," said Zeoc. "Would Morathos really want us to be behaving like this at such a time?"

"He's right," said Francesca. "If this is the end, then shouldn't we be cherishing every last second?"

"I'm sorry," said Sequititah. She placed her palms up against the transparent cell wall. Magnetus placed his hands over hers.

"I guess this is goodbye, everyone," he said solemnly, gazing into Sequititah's welling eyes.

Francesca shut her eyes tightly and hugged her knees.

Zeoc came to sit beside her. "At least Forathorn walks away empty handed too," he said.

The cell and all their immediate surroundings became more severely warped than they had experienced yet. They each started to witness one another become distorted and misshaped as the very fabric and matter in which they existed rapidly decreased in size, until their world completely evaporated leaving nothing but an empty void of darkness, even more deserted and lifeless than the vacuum of space itself.

Chapter 19

Power Over Knowledge

"Huh? I'm still alive? But how...? Magnetus?" Sequititah called. Her senses didn't know how to interpret the bemusement. "Francesca...? Zeoc...? What happened? What is going on?" All she could hear was a low-pitched buzzing sound; all she could see was a tiny hibiscus light glimmering. She could taste the bitterness of her sweat as it poured from her brow and yet, she simultaneously sat hugging her shoulders, trying to stop herself shivering. "Magnetus?" she called again. But she was met with nothing more than a stinging chill. The buzzing seemed to amplify and her burning eyes started to adjust to the room a little, allowing her visual capacity to expand somewhat.

The room was then illuminated as a door swung open and the silhouette of a man strolled in. "Just a few finishing touches," he said, locking the door behind him.

Sequititah tried to keep as still as she could in the hope that he wouldn't switch on any other means of light and see her. Much to her relief — and confusion — he proceeded in the darkness. "I mustn't be too hasty. I can't have anyone tampering in here and potentially stealing my ideas."

The more the man spoke, the more familiar the voice started to sound. *Professor Horuzokh?* she thought. *It can't be.* She tried to convince herself that she must be imagining things, but that only seemed to further confirm her suspicions.

After a few moments of back-and-forth manoeuvring and the pressing of a few buttons, the professor turned towards the exit. "I'm missing something," he said, opening the door and leaving the room.

Sequititah immediately got to her feet and walked towards the red light. She cautiously navigated her way around a cylindrical object. It felt cold to the touch and she soon established its metallic texture. As she continued to feel her way around, her hands brushed over a slight dip that led her to believe in the presence of a small glass window. As she ran her hand down the structure, she came across some sort of handle and attempted to pull at it and twist it. But it wouldn't budge at all.

Worried that someone might return at any moment, she carried on making her way around, looking for somewhere she might be less likely to be found. But she came to an unexpected edge of the wall and lost her balance. Now on her hands and knees, she crawled towards some sort of shiny surface that was reflecting what little light there was. That too was metallic. She pushed against it and it opened up a hatchway. She could see only darkness and was reluctant to inspect it; at least, until she heard footsteps approaching. The door swung open again thereafter so she hid inside the hatchway, closing the steel cover behind her.

Now she was in total darkness, still perspiring and shivering simultaneously but through a small hole — perhaps created from where a screw might once have been placed — she saw the entirety of the room alight as the professor returned, this time switching on the luminescent strips above. The large cylindrical container could now be seen.

Professor Horuzokh made his way over to his desk area and picked up a flask. "First, I must chill this substance to the precise temperature of three degrees Celsius for no more than an hour," he said to himself. "It's a very delicate and time-consuming process indeed. But all shall be worthwhile if my calculations are correct."

Sequititah watched him turning more dials and pressing more buttons on the cylindrical chamber and then he left again. The moment he closed the door, there was a flicker of light and before she could even attempt to open the hatch, the professor had returned again. He placed a petri dish under his microscope, toggling with the magnification. The petri dish contained some jelly-like substance that was purplish in colour.

Next, he took the other substance out of the chiller, drawing a small amount of it into a dabber and carefully released a few droplets into the dish. "Now we wait," he said.

Every time Horuzokh left the room, there was a flash and Sequititah found herself in his presence again the second after. *Something doesn't seem right,* she thought.

The professor returned, eager to peer into his microscope. "Incredible!" he screeched like an excitable child. "The amino acid extracts are behaving exactly as I had predicted. The chamber appears to have reached the required temperature and the atmospheric properties should be hostile enough to promptly force successful evolutionary processes without extinguishing these specimens. Now it's a simple process of trial and error until we establish a threshold. After all, without some hostility, there won't be any natural purpose to evolve and adapt."

So, he's trying to create biological life? Sequititah speculated.

"I had better ensure this chamber is secure enough," said Horuzokh on his next return. "Then it's lights out in here for a while."

There was another gleam. This time it seemed like a greater degree of time had passed. Sequititah had started to wonder if she would ever be able to make it out.

"Oh my, look at the size of this thing. It looks like my delicate approach paid off. It's thriving in there... I suppose now is the right time to inform Vynzuth. After all, we are going to need to develop technology that can monitor this lifeform once it leaves the earth's atmosphere."

Gee, he sure talks to himself a lot. Is that what scientists do? Sequititah had to stop her laughter from breaking out. *Vynzuth?... So, this is the past repeating itself. But how did I get here? Is my present self even still alive?*

She started to hear the sound of water flowing heavily and her surroundings began to change. It was as if she was inside a bubble and some vast body of liquid was gushing over the outside of it, blurring anything on the exterior of her immediate space. It gradually started to slow, revealing more to her. She could start to make out the outline of Professor Horuzokh and President Vynzuth stood facing one another. The professor was waving his arms around whilst the president stood with his folded. It looked as if he was lecturing him about something, but Sequititah couldn't yet hear any sound.

A few moments later, a recognisable voice was heard but it was only murmurs and syllables for another few seconds before the words started to become more clearly discernible.

"So, you're saying you have developed a lifeform that you would like to send to Mars and keep a close monitoring of it?" the president asked.

"Yes. It looks a rather promising prospect that could give us the opportunity to innovate the sustainability of human life on other planets. It's the perfect experiment; we've got nothing to lose."

"Now hold on one moment, Professor. We're already making leaps and bounds with our project to sustain human life by bioengineering our very own species, not to mention the long-term plans we have for the planet. Why does it seem like you oppose the machine movement so strongly?"

"I don't oppose it, Mr. President. I just think there are better, more natural alternatives."

"You are a remarkable scientist, Professor. But I cannot have you swaying too far away from our original goals."

"It will be a success, I'm sure of it. What harm will it do to try?" The professor stiffened his shoulders and moved his hands closer to his chest, clasping them together.

Vynzuth exhaled deeply and turned around. He walked a few paces and turned back to face Horuzokh, taking a few steps closer to him. "Since I admire your work so far and I can't deny your biological and chemical expertise, yes, I suppose we can try. But you should know that I'm not the slightest bit impressed by the fact that you have been working on this behind my back."

"Oh, Mr. President, thank you, thank you."

"But if it should fail..."

"It will not fail. Would you like me to explain how it works?"

"I trust your word. But be aware of the cost ramifications, nonetheless. Not to mention the time and effort it's going to take my engineers to construct a suitable craft. They're already busy with important projects, remember?"

"Yes. Certainly, Mr. President." The professor's jaw was clenching as he tried his hardest to hide the beaming grin he was now displaying.

Sequititah found herself in Professor Horuzokh's experimentation room again. The chamber was rattling frantically. Upon hearing it, the professor entered. "Easy girl!" he cried. He turned a dial and the shaking seemed to settle. "We really need to get this on a rocket asap. I'm not sure how much longer this will contain it. There must be something I can do in the meantime." He paused for a while, rubbing his chin. "That's it!" he bellowed. "The specimen is genetically predisposed to seek environments external to its current one. I can simply reverse its coding temporarily, denying it the urge to have to break out of its habitat. Then closer to the launch, I will simply resume the experiment."

As she had come to expect, there was another flicker. President Vynzuth had summoned his lead scientist. "Professor Horuzokh."

"Yes, Mr. President."

"You'll be pleased to know that my engineers have completed the appropriate craft to launch your experiment."

"Excellent. At last." Horuzokh was twitching in excitement. "This day will go down in history." He returned to the chamber and resumed the experiment, reactivating its initial course.

Sequititah found herself in the experimentation room once more. There, she witnessed the presence of President Vynzuth. He approached the cylindrical chamber with caution, peering inside of its viewing window to find the mysterious mauve organism alternatingly expanding and contracting. Its shape was indistinguishable due to its constant morphing behaviour; and it didn't exhibit typically recognised features of any sort. The chamber began rattling as it had previously and Vynzuth began to tamper with the handle on the door, looking over his shoulder every few minutes with glaring eyes. A couple of droids then arrived at the scene and shot a tiny laser at the door handle's locking mechanism. A sharp clicking noise followed and the president hastily retreated.

After another bright glimmer, Sequititah found the door of the chamber slowly starting to open further after each bang that she heard, until the creature broke free and vanished instantaneously before her. A brief moment of Deja Vu washed over her as she was left to revisit the despair of the professor upon encountering his experiment's escape.

I don't know... how much more... of this I can take, she stressed. *I've got to get out of here.*

But each time she tried to head for the exit, another flash would disorientate her. *What is the meaning of all this?* She started to shed a tear. "Vynzuth was just as selfish as Forathorn." Her words were spoken aloud before she had even had a chance to acknowledge it. Then she reminded herself of what was happening and came to realise that nobody could hear her. "He must have pulled the plug on Horuzokh's experiment to force the development of the N.O.D.R.O.G. program. He couldn't have anyone else steal the spotlight." Her stomach started to turn with disgust.

Now she could see General Ribery. It appeared that another time skip had occurred; but she was starting to become accustomed to it by now. There it was, shining on his finger: the gold ring. She recalled the events that she witnessed earlier and in the next moment, a young Magnetus came into her observations. She wanted to cry his name but had to remind herself of what was occurring once again.

"Magnetus Bane." Vynzuth spoke in a rather haughty tone. "It seems our partnership is growing strong. Your agency has been very successful in operations and is working exceedingly well in conjunction with my government's schemes. The level of success following the assassination of Archquar Reina has certainly given me the confidence to expect nothing less from you."

"Thank you, Mr. President."

"Your next target shall be Rupert O'Sullivan. He has stolen something highly valuable from my general and forced us to abort our space mission. I want you to see to it that that is the last thing he ever does."

"I will get right to it, Mr. President."

Sequititah had to close her eyes in despair. Her chest tightened as she continued to remind herself of where she was. *He was just doing his job,* she told herself. *He wasn't even himself anymore, remember.*

She watched as her love conducted research on Rupert, eventually concluding his whereabouts. "So, he created a simulated utopian village and fled there?" He scratched his head in thought. "Perhaps I should go inspect it."

"Sir, we suspect that the target has fled to a nearby village," said one of the DSA droids. "What are your orders?"

"Let's just keep things on hold for now. I want to be a bit more certain first."

"But what about the president? He won't have delays."

"Well, he's just going to have to cooperate with me on this one."

Magnetus made his way to the village and admired the realistic experience. "This is remarkable. To think that someone could create such a wonder. Sequititah would love it here; even if it is a make-believe world, you couldn't ever tell that without knowing beforehand." After a short stay, he made his return to Doradheim.

"Were you able to locate the target, sir?" asked a droid.

Magnetus paused for a brief moment before responding. "No... I will inform the president that we have been unsuccessful."

"That seems very uncharacteristic of you, sir? Are you sure about this?"

"Yes, I'm sure. I would appreciate it if you didn't question my motives."

"I was merely expressing my concern for you, sir."

"No need to bother. The assassination has been temporarily postponed and will not be pursued until further notice."

"Very well, sir."

The DSA founder made his way to Vynzuth and informed him of the news.

"He has to be somewhere," said the president.

"Perhaps so. But he's far out of our reach. The best we can do is hope we'll encounter him later."

"But the ring. The expenses. The betrayal. He cannot get away with this."

"Don't worry, Mr. President, he won't. But right now, I can't see us locating him anytime soon."

"Very well. I will have General Ribery keep an eye on things. In the meantime, we can resume our attention towards robotics and technological advancements. That will be all." The president gestured for Magnetus to leave.

The next moment, Sequititah watched as Magnetus sat at his desk looking like he was ready to start typing something. "Oh, Sequititah. If only you could see me now. My letters to you aren't a full reflection of the man I fear I am becoming. But yet, your presence in my heart still influences me at times."

Sequititah raised her head. Her eyes were glowing. *So, you really did keep it from me to protect me.* She smiled to herself. "I am right here, my darling," she said softly.

There was another flash. This time Sequititah had fallen unconscious. She awoke shortly after, disoriented. "Where... am I now?" She observed her surroundings. There was greenery around, wildlife and a small settlement of some sort in the distance. She got to her feet and started towards the nearby village, still uncertain of whether her reality was what she was presently experiencing or not.

The village was desolate; nothing more than plant life and some traces of wildlife. But there was a pleasant aura about it. *This is too good to be true,* she thought. *It's like the utopia I've always dreamt of.* She couldn't help but be sceptical. But what she now knew in her heart, helped her to carry more hope. "I will find you, Magnetus."

*****

"I'm breathing!" cried Zeoc. *I haven't felt this alive for as long as I can remember. Wait... I'm alive? Francesca...? Sequititah...? Magnetus...? Did they make it? What about Morathos?* He glanced up at the fiery sky then took a moment to take in the amount of nature around him. Despite the impact it had had on him, he had become so accustomed to a lifestyle of exposure to machines and mechanical devices, that he felt alienated; yet simultaneously rejuvenated.

The land was scenic and revitalising to the senses, but there was no sign of human life around. The presence of animals seemed scarce but for some insect life. He couldn't help but notice the colossal trees around him, much taller than any he had seen; and over twice the width. With little other option at his disposal, he decided to start walking through the greenery and marvelled in the spectacle as he made contact with what he had craved for so long.

As he continued his stroll, he encountered a large lake, probably five miles across. He spent a moment watching the ripples moving towards him, striding across the sandy stepping stones. In the distance he observed the icy peaks of a couple of mountain tops. Beyond their summit, there was a body of smoke projecting into the sky and as he continued, he could now see behind the mountains to a smaller volcano that appeared about half the height of the twin peaks.

He couldn't help but stop for a moment and reflect. *I'm missing something; it's not my friends. It feels like more of an emptiness inside of me... like before. Like a part of my very identity has gone. I thought that feeling might have gone away...*

After a few hours, Zeoc started to feel the bitter chill in the air and tried to find shelter before it got too dark. But as the night sky rolled in, he became lost in admiration at the array of stars above him, some of them indistinguishable from one another as they blended into the hazy white band of the milky-way. The display that seemed so foreign to many, was one that lifted him inside; and for a moment, he forgot all about his inner emptiness.

Suddenly, everything started flooding back and a light fulgurated before him. A mechanical looking face was projected but it flashed too rapidly for him to be able to ascertain what he was seeing. He blinked hard and rubbed his eyes. The next thing he knew, an image of a casket portrayed, facing him. His chest started to tighten and an uncontrollable fit of coughing followed. He tried to open his eyes to perceive his environment, but the coughing continued to prevent him from doing so.

He heard a voice calling his name but there was a prevalent echo to it. It was a feminine voice that sounded familiar to him, but the overlapping syllables of each echo made him uncertain of who it might be. His eyes remained shut and he could feel a hand shaking him by the shoulders. He felt his jaw involuntarily widen and a small round capsule was pressed against his tongue. The moment he swallowed it, the coughing stopped and he opened his eyes to find the greet of Francesca's worry. "That should help."

"F-Francesca? You're alive... What are you doing here? Where even are we?"

"We're in the escape pod. Your pod failed and you drifted off into deep space so I had to come for you. I thought you were a goner."

"This doesn't make sense. I feel like this has already happened. Only you came to my house and we took Vynzuth's ship."

"What are you talking about? I rescued you and Morathos from the complex; then we all took separate pods that were going to gravitationally reunite."

"We went into space, didn't we? And travelled into the past."

"Yes, that's right."

"But I don't remember drifting away."

"You must be tired." Francesca placed the back of her hand over his forehead. "What we've endured is a lot for anyone."

"Where is everyone?"

"Morathos and Sequititah are still travelling through space. They journeyed to find out about the disaster."

"No. That's not right. That's not how it happened."

"*You're* the one not making sense. Nothing has happened yet."

"Yes. It has. All this has happened before... Except it didn't happen like this."

"I... don't understand, Zeoc. C'mon let's get back."

Zeoc started hearing a ringing sound in his ears. "Can you hear that?"

"Hear what?" Francesca frowned puzzlingly. "You should really try and get some rest."

"You don't hear the ringing?"

"Sorry, Zeoc. I don't."

Zeoc closed his eyes and the image of the android returned to his mind's eye. This time it wasn't glimmering and he was able to make it out more clearly. When he opened his eyes again, he found himself at home in Doradheim. There was a knock at his door but he was reluctant to answer straight away. The fact that the visitor didn't persist made him curious. "Huh? It's Morathos," he said to himself.

"I have what you've been waiting for, Zeoc."

"Wait a minute. This isn't making sense either. I've been here before."

"Yes, Zeoc. This is your *house*... Are you alright?"

"I don't know. But weird things keep happening. Neither of us should even be alive." He could hear the marching protests of the Anti-machs above.

"Maybe I should come back later," said Morathos. He looked at his feet and twitched his nose.

"I just want everything to be how it was. Everyone together again. You, me, Francesca, Sequititah."

"Who are these people you speak of?"

"Oh, of course... Never mind."

"What are you doing?" Zeoc had suddenly become even more bewildered as he found himself inside the presidential complex. *That sounded like, Forathorn,* he thought.

"It's Mr. President to you."

"Oh yes, of course. Apologies, Mr. President."

"What is the hold up? Why are you disobeying your programming? Get to the launch pad immediately. I want that nature accelerator returned to me."

"Yes, Mr. President." The next thing he knew, he was launching into space to confront The Governor. As he looked down at himself, he observed that every part of him was mechanical.

"Does he honestly think I am going to hand that invention back to you just like that? Ha!" The Governor cried.

This is getting even weirder, thought Zeoc. He watched his mechanical body sever in two and the immediate subsequent moment left him in darkness again. A disturbing silence followed. Then, one after another, he descried the emergence of many white glimmers. It was gradual at first, but soon hastened.

Before long, his field of vision was pasted with the glowing apparitions. One was shining brighter than the rest and his mind's eye had honed in on it. He revelled at the sight as the place he once remembered as his home, came into view. The swirling clouds; the deep blue oceans and the rich viridescent land that would have painted a memory in him if not for the rapid transit that he was to experience when he beheld the image of the marble planet of Nordamia. *What does all this mean?* He pondered.

Darkness then returned and he was left gasping for breath. He was lying down and could sense that he was inside a tightly enclosed space. He pushed against either side of him feeling his way around and then pressed his hands against what was obstructing him above, establishing that he was inside a casket. He could hear movement on the outside and a short moment later, the lid had opened. He was met by the presence of Francesca who guided him to his feet. "We've got to get out of here," she said.

"Weird things keep happening. I can't take it anymore."

"You can tell me later. We have to go!" She dragged his arm and they headed for the exit of the spacecraft.

Everything started to blur again. He could see nothing but darkness and hear only his own thoughts echoing. *I've always had such strong distaste towards biomechanics and vowed never to resort to it. But then I had a taste of it... And for a moment, I quite liked it. But that was the programming, toying with my mind and my true ambition. Being able to embrace nature fully, is what I truly miss — even though I've never really had the chance to experience that. ...Hmm. Perhaps having an experience where my biology depended on mechanical parts, just further confirmed my desire to reject it all. Technology is not my friend; nature is. But technology tried to convince me otherwise...*

⸺⬥⸺

Chapter 20

Consciousness Transcends

"*A biogenesis... The numerous processes of complex natural events, which eventually form organic life from non-organic matter. Remarkable, isn't it...? A self-replicating, self-assembling, autocatalytic lifeform emerges. But what if one of those lifeforms could decipher a way to reengineer this phenomenon entirely? What if a biological lifeform developed the ability to replicate a self-replicating organism? What if that lifeform could do so in an artificial sense...? After all, we're nothing more than a series of complex algorithms and codes programmed to perform a particular protocol. What if we could manipulate our very coding and reconfigure our own algorithms? There's nothing that says it cannot mathematically be achieved.*"

"*Who said that?... Where am I?*"

"*A place where time no longer exists; space no longer exists; matter no longer exists. All that exists is energy and the one thing no lifeform in the universe can ever understand — all that exists is consciousness.*"

"*Is this a dream?*"

"*There are no dreams here. The bridge that lies between what you call science, and what you call philosophy, has been crossed. The bridge between what can be observed; tested; mathematically understood, and that which can only be speculated or hypothesised, is all that exists. Only a knowledge* so powerful could exist here, for it would be unsustainable in a universe of matter. To truly understand the workings of something, is to be on the outside looking in. There are some things one cannot know, without stepping outside of themselves; without stepping outside of reality..."

"Are you saying consciousness can exist outside of the universe? Consciousness can exist outside of a physical entity?"

"I'm saying that once you've asked all the questions that could possibly ever be asked and found their answers, then you're left with the ultimate decision. When you're left with the ability to rewrite reality, do you? Or do you continue on harmoniously?"

"Of course, I wouldn't know that... So, is this where we go...? Everything is energy after all, and it has to go somewhere, right?"

"This is one of the two extreme boundaries of existence. This is the absolute peak of negentropic threshold; the other peak being entropic. Such concentration of energy will not endure any considerable amount of longevity. So, enjoy it whilst it lasts.

"If you only ever learn one thing in your existence, then let it be this: raw consciousness has quantum properties. Our sensory perception of the universe functions on principles of quantum mechanics. The reality we see is our subjective reality — not absolute truth; life is nothing more than an interaction with energy. The only thing that is certain, is our own existence within it. A conscious biological interpretation of the universe is comparable in principle to downloading a movie. We are not downloading visuals or audio; we are downloading information that a computerised system interprets and conveys as we perceive it through our own sensory systems. Your reality is just an illusion; a construct created by your own neural networks — something that can plausibly and mathematically be redesigned, if one should choose to."

"I can hear breathing... I can hear a beating sound."

"Make good use of this energy, Morathos. Envision the place you wish to be and it will take you..."

"Morathos... Morathos, wake up." He felt a hand brush the side of his face and slowly opened his eyes. "You wouldn't even begin to imagine how much effort it took me to get in here."

"W-where are we?" The first thing he could make out was a striking amber head of hair that he knew all too well. "Francesca?"

"Yep. Francesca to the rescue again." She grinned at him, leaning in and planted her lips on his. "I have no idea what happened. But I woke up in Doradheim and couldn't find anyone else so I raced here to see if your ship was still around. The rest is a bit blurred, but I found a way in."

"Thanks to me," said another familiar face. It was Magnetus Bane.

"Magnetus. You're here too," said Morathos.

"Looks like the genius figured it out at the last minute," he said. "You saved the universe somehow."

"But I didn't do anything. I've no idea how we're still here. Besides, aren't we missing a few?" said Morathos.

"Sequititah is still with us," said Magnetus. "I can sense her. But so is Forathorn."

"Are you sure? What about Zeoc?"

"Sure, as ever. I'm still connected to his technology despite his multiple attempts to interfere with it, because I keep upgrading it. He tried to stop me from opening the door to this ship. That's why I'm late. As for Zeoc, I'm afraid I can't answer you."

Morathos screwed his face up. "But Francesca, didn't you say you had opened the door already before Magnetus arrived?"

"Yes. I think so."

"Everything is a little mixed up right now," said Magnetus.

"Tell me about it! Before we ended up here, did either of you experience some really weird things?" asked Francesca.

"I was in the strangest place of highly concentrated energy," said Morathos. "Somewhere, where not even time could exist. It was the most bizarre thing ever. Some voice was talking to me; it sounded like the Petrademus but the things it was saying make me uncertain."

"Come to think of it, I kept re-experiencing an event I'd prefer to forget," said Magnetus. "It still sickens me to this day that I could end up so far away from myself."

"I kept hopping around to different events," said Francesca. "There was some beautiful scenery though."

"I'm going to look for Sequititah," said Magnetus.

"Alright," said Morathos. "Francesca and I will look for Zeoc."

"I wonder if the war is still going on," said Francesca.

"I have a feeling something terrible is about to unfold," said Morathos.

"Don't say that. I mean, we've literally just somehow survived the collapse of the entire universe. What could possibly top that?"

"It's Reginald. He is plotting something devious again."

"Are you sure?"

"Pretty sure. Besides, I have to find the nature accelerator."

"So, now you care about it?"

"I cared about it before. But I lost hope. All I wanted was to see you all again."

"Aww. Well, I'm going to make sure I don't lose you again."

Morathos grabbed her hand and moved in closer to her. She grabbed his arm and placed it over her shoulder before wrapping hers around his waist. "Let's make this moment count," she said closing her eyes softly.

"This still feels strange. But I think I get it now," said Morathos. Francesca looked up at him with a teary smile.

"There's always going to be some sort of distraction, isn't there? ...I can't just keep ignoring everything else until I've solved whatever it might be that is pecking at me."

"I told you, you can't rely on calculations for everything. This is going to feel unusual to you for a little while, Morathos. But it's okay to be vulnerable sometimes."

"Yeah, you're right. Deep down, I think I knew that already. But I was so caught up in problem solving, that I forgot to appreciate what wasn't a problem. I guess that makes me not much different from the rest."

"You'll never be the same as Reginald," said Francesca.

Morathos placed his other arm over her and squeezed a little tighter. "Let's stop talking for a moment."

Francesca reciprocated his embrace. "You know. This moment is making me feel like painting or sketching again. But I haven't done so in so long. All it brought me was hurt; which strengthened my urge to escape and hide amongst *them*; like a prisoner of myself."

"If it's what you feel is right, then you shouldn't doubt yourself for a second."

She briefly glanced up at him before resting her head firmly on his chest. "Oh, Morathos."

"It's alright, you're safe here."

"Rupert?" Sequititah found herself standing amongst the remains of Staistreim.

"You're still a little lost, aren't you? You're not quite ready to go back yet."

"I can hear you, but I can't see you. Was it you that brought me back here? I felt your call."

"Perhaps my voice is all you needed to hear. Perhaps I am the last piece of the puzzle for you."

"What happened to you?"

"You don't need to worry about me. I knew they were going to take it sooner or later. So, I fled and left the ring behind hoping you would find it."

"But I don't have it anymore. They took it from me."

"I know, it's alright. I didn't expect you to keep it for long. I only hoped that you'd find it first."

"So, you're still alive?"

"Not in a physical sense, no. But I found a way to interact with your subconscious."

"So, where are you now? How am I still here?"

"I still don't fully understand it, but when plasmantium started to collapse the universe, the laws of physics broke down even at the quantum level. My consciousness somehow fell into the quantum realm allowing me to communicate with those I'm bonded to most subconsciously. But this conversation has cost me my existence. I cannot return to your universe, I can only communicate with it for now; at least, just enough to reassure you and help you close the chapter on everything. There's nothing more holding you back now."

"But I still don't understand how I got here. How can anyone survive that?"

"I'm afraid I can't help you with that. Some things just can't be explained. But perhaps the answers will find you soon."

"Oh, Rupert. Thank you." She started to well up and sniffle. "I'll never forget you, or Staistreim. I know I was angry when I found out it was all a simulation. But it truly was a remarkable place and it served its purpose well. I can't thank you enough. As far as I am concerned now, it was all real. And even if it wasn't, what does it matter? So long as I believe in my heart how it made me feel."

"No need, Sequititah. Now go and find your man, and your friends." Rupert's voice faded with each syllable but she

managed to make out the last words of his sentence before rubbing her eyes dry.

"There you are," called a voice from behind her.

"Magnetus? Is that really you?" She turned to face him, the scenery around her altering to the intimidating lustrous structures that had become so predominant across the globe.

"How did I know I'd find you here?" he smiled.

She dashed towards him with her arms apart and clasped them around his torso. "I'm so sorry I ever doubted you," she sobbed. "Even when I left you, you were always looking out for me."

Magnetus reached his arms around her. "Thank you, my dear."

"I only wish I had given the same devotion to you that you always did me."

"Please, save your words. It doesn't matter now. All that matters is, we're here together and we will go on together."

"I know." She gripped him a little tighter and pressed the side of her head further into his chest. "Where is everyone else?"

"Morathos and Francesca are looking for Zeoc. He's the only one missing now."

She beamed. "Morathos is here?"

"Yes. I just hope we can find Zeoc."

"Well, let's get going then."

Magnetus turned around. "This way," he said.

"Not so fast, Magnetus Bane," a scornful tone called out. They had only taken a few steps.

"Forathorn!" Magnetus spat, looking the president up and down. He looked dilapidated. "What even happened to you?"

"You of all people should know that there is a price for everything," he grunted.

"Oh yeah?"

"That's just typical of you; to be disloyal. You had to go running back to your love, didn't you? You're pathetic!" He turned to address Sequititah. "How can you honestly love this man? He's nothing but a fraud."

"You're the pathetic one, Forathorn. Nobody would ever love you," said Sequititah.

"None of that matters now because I have accomplished exactly what I set out to do — the obtainment of infinite energy at my disposal. I made a worthy sacrifice. One that isn't too much of a dilemma in terms of obstructing my dream; and it most certainly won't be a permanent one either."

"What sacrifice?" asked Magnetus.

"Imagine an entire universe, condensed into a singularity and consumed by an indestructible mechanical planet." The president came close to Magnetus and glared into his eyes. "Or would you like me to spell it out for you in a language you can understand? Ha-ha-ha!"

"That's impossible if the planet is part of the universe. Even if it were not, how could it possibly stably sustain that much energy for long?"

"You clearly still have a lot to learn, Magnetus. See what infatuation does to one's ability to grasp reality? Hmm?"

"I've heard just about enough of you and your schemes."

"Oh, really?" The president exhibited a wry smile. "So, what are you going to do about that?"

Magnetus gritted his teeth and snarled at him.

"No, Magnetus!" Sequititah sighed. "He's not worth it."

"You better listen to your lady friend now," said Forathorn in a condescending tone.

Magnetus could not contain his fury any longer and charged towards Reginald. But the president turned side on and positioned himself in a stance, awaiting, as Magnetus struck a blow. The impact seemed to have no effect and he was quickly thrown backwards as Reginald became illuminated by an electric blue flare of light that glinted around him.

Sequititah raced to his aid. "Are you alright?"

"I think I've made myself clear," said Reginald. "Only a fool would test my infinite power twice. Ha-ha!"

"Just when I didn't think you could get any lower..." said Sequititah.

"I know, right? How incredible!"

"Magnetus?"

"He's just a little stunned from my electromagnetic force-field. He'll wake up soon. Ha-ha-ha!"

"You're sick, Reginald!"

"Where are all your friends anyway? I thought you might be having a little reunion by now."

"What's it to you?"

"You're lucky I haven't got time to wait. But I will be back to settle the score with Morathos soon enough." The president hovered away.

"Curse that man!" Sequititah cried. She gently shook Magnetus a few more times but there was no response. *He'll wake up soon? I can't trust a word that comes out of his mouth.* She decided to drag him closer to the wayside before going off to find help.

"I think Zeoc is still lost," said Morathos as he and Francesca were making their commute.

"What was this place of condensed energy you were talking about?" asked Francesca.

"I couldn't see anything except whiteness. There was no sound, nor sensation, other than that of my own consciousness and a voice of another. It's difficult to describe."

"I wonder why I didn't experience it."

"I'm not sure."

"Hey, that looks like Magnetus over there," Francesca pointed to the unconscious cyborg lying in the wayside.

"Magnetus!" Morathos yelled. He started to move his head and his arms.

"It looks like some sort of electromagnetic interference," said Francesca.

"Oh, thank goodness," Sequititah called, racing back over. "I tried to get help but I couldn't find anyone."

"Sequititah!" Francesca gasped. "I'm so glad you're alright."

"Me too," said Morathos. "I'm sorry about before."

"That's alright. I knew it wasn't you really. Still no Zeoc?"

"I'm afraid not," said Morathos. "I think his consciousness was lost. After all, we did have to travel through time to bring him back. Not to mention the android upload. There's a probability that three different fragments of his consciousness are circulating — the present one, one in a different point of space and one in a different point of time."

"What happened to Magnetus?" asked Francesca.

"Forathorn. He's completely lost his mind — more so than before. He's floating around using some electromagnetic energy."

"Was Magnetus exposed to it?" asked Morathos.

"He tried to strike him. But some sort of force-field sent him flying."

"This could be detrimental to his circuits," said Morathos.

"So, what do we do now?" asked Sequititah.

Morathos moved closer to him and inspected his electronics. As he rolled him over, he started moving some more and then got to his feet by himself. "Thanks, Morathos."

"...But I didn't do anything."

"Are you sure about that? It certainly felt like you did."

"I seem to be fixing things without even trying."

"The electromagnetic waves must have corrupted my programming. But now I feel as if some substance is reversing it and has rebooted everything."

"Hmm. Could it be plasmantium?" asked Sequititah.

"Plasmantium? How so?" asked Morathos.

"I'm not really sure."

"What is going on here anyway? It looks like the war has ended," said Francesca.

"Who won?" asked Sequititah.

"I'm going to guess, Reginald," said Morathos with an expression of distaste. "What did he say to you?"

"Something about infinite energy. He claims to have absorbed the condensed universe into the planet," said Magnetus. "But how could that be possible?"

"I couldn't even begin to understand at the moment. So many unanswered questions, still."

"Let's keep looking for Zeoc," said Francesca.

"Should we split up?" asked Magnetus.

"I don't think we can risk it after what happened to you," said Morathos. "Reginald is going to be even more unpredictable now."

"An agreement always comes with a sacrifice," said President Forathorn. "But if you know how to play your cards right, you still end up with the better end of the deal. Outsmarting a genius always feels good."

"The ring's condition is flawless," said General Ribery. "It's still in the immaculate condition it was when I first obtained it."

"Yes. Indeed. We would not have been able to accomplish what we have with such precision otherwise."

"So, what now, Mr. President? You got everything you ever wanted."

"Not quite *everything.* I think a trip to see The Governor is in order."

"Why's that, sir?"

"You'll see. Get the craft prepared for launch. There's an unfinished science experiment out there."

"You mean Professor Horuzokh's rogue experiment? What do you intend to do with that?"

"Just a little bit of business. Now stop asking questions and prepare the launch. When we get there, keep quiet and watch me."

"Certainly, Mr. President."

The president's craft took to the skies and confronted The Governor. "President Forathorn," the advanced structure said.

"Governor, we seem to be getting on much better lately, wouldn't you say? Isn't it wonderful, how we can put our differences aside?"

"What is your proposition?"

"Oh, cutting to the chase, are we? You know me better than I thought."

"We already reached an agreement to settle the war."

"I'm not here about that. I'm sure you're aware of a certain experiment that occurred a few years ago and I think you've had your eye out for its whereabouts for some time, am I correct?"

"The rogue entity that escaped planet Earth?"

"Yes. I could help you find it."

"What's your price?"

"Oh, just a little device that you happen to possess."

"I thought you didn't care about that anymore."

"I can still make my use with it. It doesn't seem to be of importance to you."

"Admittedly, it doesn't anymore. I was merely preventing you from keeping it before. You have yourself a deal."

"Perfect! Now hand it over."

"How can I trust your word?"

"I have already sent fleets of my droids into the cosmos. Take a look."

"Very well. I shall do the same."

A myriad of ships began to take off, darting in multiple directions once they reached substantial altitude.

Magnetus pondered at the countless crafts above as the four of them commuted back to their ship. "What's that Forathorn up to now?"

"There's Petradema ships too," said Morathos.

"I don't suspect he's up to any good," said Sequititah.

"It looks like they're working together," said Francesca.

"That must be how the war ended," said Magnetus.

"Guys. Where are you?"

"Did anyone else hear that?" asked Morathos.

"It sounded like... Zeoc," said Francesca.

"But where's it coming from?" asked Sequititah.

"It sounds like it's coming from inside the ship," said Morathos.

"We should lock the door for safety measures," said Magnetus.

The four of them headed inside and Magnetus sealed the door shut.

"Hey, over here."

"It sounded like it was coming from one of the dorms on the upper deck," said Morathos. He raced upstairs and the other three followed behind. "Zeoc!"

"In there!" Francesca pointed to the door approaching them on the left and they entered the room.

Morathos stared perplexed at a casket in the corner of the room. "That wasn't here before."

"That looks exactly like the life support chamber on the old ship," said Magnetus. "How did it end up here?"

"I don't know. But let's get it open, quick," said Francesca.

"...Everyone's here," said Zeoc. "Umm... Sorry I'm late." He smiled awkwardly and everyone had a chuckle amongst themselves.

"Good to see you again," said Morathos.

"Likewise. I have no idea how I ended up here."

"There's been some strange goings on for all of us," said Morathos.

"How did you find your fragmented consciousness?" asked Sequititah.

"Well, at first it didn't make sense. But everything just kinda happened, one thing after the next, like some sort of script or something. I didn't get it, but then I realised in order to find myself, I had to experience what I didn't have."

"Hmm. So, these experiences were supposed to aid us toward some purpose or deep understanding?" asked Francesca.

"Yes. I think so."

"Oh, I think I understand now." Francesca's eyes lit up. "Maybe it's what I'm meant to do regardless of how underappreciated art is nowadays. But that shouldn't matter. Art is a part of who I am. I never resented art; I resented myself for no longer allowing myself to undertake it. You might have helped reignite a spark in me, Morathos. But that spark was there in me to be relit no matter what. The scenery I saw was spectacular. It was as if it was speaking to me — as if it's my purpose to recreate it and express it. Whether anyone else notices it or not, is irrelevant."

"Way to go, Francesca," cried Sequititah. She nodded and smiled.

Zeoc glanced at her with a gaze of pride.

"The worst enemy to have, is undoubtedly yourself," said Magnetus. "To overcome *that*, speaks volumes."

"Thanks, guys."

Uncertain of his words, Morathos enfolded her.

"So, it does indeed seem we all had to endure such encounters to find missing pieces," said Magnetus.

"Wait, Zeoc," said Morathos. "You said everything just happened one thing after the next, like a script. As in a predetermined sequence of events?" Morathos expressed a quizzing look. "What if everything *is* predetermined?"

"What are you saying?" asked Zeoc.

"When I was in that concentrated field of energy, the voice that spoke to me said something about all life being nothing more than a series of complex algorithms that are designed to perform our coded protocols."

"So, you're saying that everything that has happened, is happening, and will happen, is all predetermined?" asked Sequititah.

"Well... yeah. He also said something about two extremes of existence — the lowest possible state of entropy before the amount of energy consumed tears everything apart, and highest point of entropy before something becomes too chaotic to maintain itself."

"What does this have to do with the predetermined?" asked Magnetus.

"I think I know how we survived the collapse of the universe."

"Oh, aren't you just the smartest?" Francesca beamed, her entranced eyes sparkling at him.

"Plasmantium's density created the most powerful black hole ever known and it gradually swallowed up the universe. But in the process, it created a paradox."

"Does this have something to do with the weird time skips we've been experiencing?" asked Zeoc.

"Well, yes. Kind of. I mean, warped space will always cause time irregularities. But on this scale, it was causing the universe to contract. Ever since we've known the universe to have existed, it has been expanding continuously and accelerating in the process. As we move forward through time, the universe keeps expanding. But the creation of plasmantium was warping space in on itself and contracting it, meaning we've been gradually going backwards in time; back to before plasmantium was created. So, plasmantium has travelled back to a time before its existence and therefore no longer exists, was never created and the universe was never destroyed."

"The bootstrap paradox!" Magnetus gasped.

"Exactly. But there might still be a problem."

"What?" asked Francesca.

"If everything is predetermined and we've somehow interfered with it, then at the quantum level, what should have happened will still have happened."

"But it hasn't," said Sequititah.

"Perhaps not in this reality. But there's no substantial certainty that events from an alternate reality could not have a quantum influence on ours."

Francesca and Zeoc looked at each other. "Oh boy!" they both sighed.

"What is it?" asked Morathos.

"We thought we might have already created a bootstrap paradox when I travelled back to save Zeoc," said Francesca. "But it contradicts the theory of the predetermined."

"It does. But to make things more complicated, everything is relative to our perceptions."

Francesca nodded. "Yes, I learned about that too."

"So, basically, everything in existence is one big messed up, confused soup that will never make sense," said Zeoc.

"Ha-ha. When you put it like that...", said Morathos.

"Aren't we just going around in circles now?" said Sequititah. "Your hypothesis of how we survived makes sense."

"...And why there's no certain explanation for the recent occurrence of events," said Magnetus.

"Yeah. So, now what?" asked Zeoc.

"There's one more thing to settle," said Morathos. "Something of mine that I want back."

"The nature accelerator," said Francesca. "Doesn't The Governor have it?"

"Yes. But I sense Reginald is still trying to obtain it. We have to get it before he does."

"How the heck are we supposed to get *that?*" asked Zeoc.

"That's where I'm going to need your help."

Chapter 21

An Existential Collision

"I suspect that The Governor is more intellectually and technologically advanced than even Reginald," said Morathos. "So, I don't really know how we're going get around that."

"Have you noticed how similar they are?" said Magnetus. "It's as if Reginald has uploaded his personality into it or something."

"I'm surprised they've come to an agreement," said Francesca. "Two power mad bigshots like that."

"They'll both have ulterior motives, no doubt," said Sequititah.

"So, we don't have a plan?" asked Zeoc.

"Not as such. But what's the worst that could happen?" said Morathos.

Zeoc gulped. "That seems awfully uncharacteristic of you, Morathos."

"Alrighty. Let's fire 'er up," said Francesca. It appeared that the buzzing of the engines was never a sound that could be taken for granted, no matter how many times they were started. She peered out across at Axia Exodus as they made their ascent. "You know, perhaps this isn't the best time, but I couldn't help but notice something odd."

"What?" said Sequititah.

"We have the technology to uncover every star in the sky right away, right?"

"As long as its light has had time to reach us, yeah," said Sequititah. Morathos turned to face Francesca and gave her a look of intrigue.

"And Axia Exodus was twenty light-years away from Earth before we ended up here, right?"

"Yeah. What are you getting at?" asked Zeoc.

"It's just... I mean, am I being silly? Why have we never seen or heard of the star before? It's definitely older than twenty!"

Morathos rested his chin in his palm. "Hmm. Interesting. I guess we've all been caught up in other affairs and didn't really see it as significant."

"I haven't been able to find *any* data on it."

"Perhaps we should discuss this later," said Magnetus.

"Surely you must all think it's a little strange, right? It can't just be me."

"It does sound a bit unusual to me," said Sequititah.

"Me too," said Zeoc. Francesca glared at Magnetus with widened eyes.

"What?! I never said I didn't think it was unusual," he said. "But now is not a good time."

"Yeah. You're right," said Francesca. "It's probably not even that big of a deal."

The Governor watched closely as the ship drew near. "You've got some nerve coming back here before your time," it said.

"What do you mean?" Morathos' voice projected out.

"Oh! It's you. Where is the captain?"

"I thought you knew... What do you mean, 'your time'?"

"He's still on board in some capacity, is he not? And remember, choose your words carefully around me; I can read right through you."

"I don't know. He evaporated into some strange substance. Anyway, you have something that belongs to me."

"Oh, do I?"

"The nature accelerator is my invention; a failed invention I'll admit. But I'm going to work on it."

"You honestly believe that you can successfully finish the job that even a Petrademus captain failed at? Quite comical indeed."

"Well, I built a replica of the prototype before I even knew what the prototype was."

"Too bad it didn't actually work. Ha-ha. I would normally be quite willing to bargain with you."

"What do you need?"

"I want to know the status of the captain. But you can't tell me."

"I can find out."

"You needn't waste your breath. You're too late anyway; the president has taken it already. But it was fun to see your desperate little face."

"You're a monster. Who would ever program such wickedness? What even *are* you?"

"I programmed myself. My creator made a fatal error on his part."

"How so?"

"I shall let him tell you. I'm too busy hunting rogue experiments right now."

"Professor Horuzokh's escaped experiment?!" Sequititah gasped.

"Oh, you know?"

"It's Vynzuth's fault it broke out. He released it."

"I don't care about that." The Governor's voice became slightly amplified. "All I care about is finding it. Now I strongly suggest you run along if you want to catch the president."

"Don't you worry. We'll be on our way," said Francesca.

"Man! Who does that floating space box think he is?" said Zeoc.

"How do you propose we get the nature accelerator now?" asked Francesca.

"What does Forathorn even want with it anyway?" asked Sequititah.

"It's not much use to him without me," said Morathos. "He needs me to finish it. I didn't know what I was doing when I built it. It was as if something inside of me was controlling my actions. But I couldn't remember then because my memories had been erased with this." He took out the small pen-like device.

"What is it?" asked Magnetus.

"You simply twist the top and press it down and it erases however many minutes, hours, days or whatever you set it to. That invention would have prevented Reginald from ever advancing like he has and he knows that. But for some reason, I couldn't finish it."

"What would happen if you finished it now?" asked Francesca.

"I'm not sure. But I know if I *were* to finish it and he were to get hold of it, he could completely reverse its effects. He doesn't exactly need it to fulfil his dream but having it will make him reach it sooner and remove any obstructions. If he gets to use it, then there's no stopping him. But if I don't use it, our chances of stopping him are much slimmer."

"So, we are kind of at an advantage right now," said Sequititah. "He can't use it until you've completed its construction. He'll have to give it to you. Then you can use it."

"It sounds simple in principle. But I know Reginald won't let it go down like that. That's why he needs it now, even before it's ready — he can't have me use it first. I fear he may lure us right into a trap if we go."

"Hmm. A rather tricky predicament indeed," said Magnetus.

"The good thing, is that plasmantium didn't transform the universe quite how he'd expected. So, with the exception of his advancements on Earth, he's back to the drawing board. I suspect that's why he took the device back only now."

"But he used it after the virus outbreak," said Francesca. "He said he couldn't use it in the way he was intending, but in a temporary manner."

"Hmm. Perhaps he knows something more about my invention. Maybe plasmantium had some influence on it," said Morathos.

"Do you think he's plotting to deceive The Governor?" asked Zeoc.

"Without a doubt."

"You mean if he hasn't already?" said Francesca.

"I think I have an idea... Maybe I should let him capture me."

"What? No," said Francesca. "There's no telling what he might do to you."

"There's no other way. If I surrender to him and turn myself in, it might look too suspicious."

"That is a foolish idea."

"What was that?" asked Sequititah.

"I heard a sharp movement coming from the lower deck," said Francesca.

"The ship's turning around!" Zeoc yelled.

"I'll go," said Morathos. "You guys wait here."

"No way!" Francesca yelled. "I won't lose you again." She followed him.

"Master has summoned me. I must obey," a voice called. Morathos noticed some unusual gloopy substance that the Petrademus had morphed into. The next moment, he found the captain standing before him, back in his original form. "Allowing the president to capture you now, will end in guaranteed failure."

"How can you be so sure?"

"Master knows. Master has foreseen it and is now willing to negotiate with you. We must go."

"What happened to you?" asked Morathos.

"Master had forced me into evaporation during the war."

"Who? What Master...? Evaporation? Why?"

Francesca entered and Magnetus followed right behind her.

"The Petradema evaporate when threatened. It is a sort of dormancy tactic which we can also sometimes use for shape-shifting and regenerative purposes. It's possible because of how our cells are structured. But I am a prisoner to my own creation and no longer have conscious control over such a mechanism. Master is literally calling the shots and sucking the life out of me."

"Who is this Master?" Morathos asked in a more elevated tone.

"The Governor, of course. Master hears my every thought and tortures my mind. That's where I have to go to now — I suspect I am to be disposed of."

"So, how are you able to resist now?" asked Magnetus.

"I'm not. Master is too busy. Master is allowing me to speak. As the years have gone on, Master has become stronger and my freedom has slowly ceased. Now I am just a puppet..."

"Wait a minute," said Zeoc as he strolled in. "You created that thing up there?"

"It's like I told you, Morathos. Everything that was supposed to happen, didn't. Master was only supposed to be a temporary solution to stabilise the magnetic field of Nordamia just long enough for me to return from Earth. It was supposed to be a technological creation that temporarily interfered with the magnetic field, teaching it to self-sustain. But I made a fatal error in my calculations. It was a gamble and I was aware that there was every possibility of it happening — albeit quite unlikely — but I banked on returning in time before it got out of control. In the meantime, the technology cleverly found a way to hack its own systems and override its own protocols — I had made it much more intelligent than I had intended."

"But what about your people?" asked Morathos. "You still seem so different from the rest in some way."

"It's true. I have always felt somewhat different to my people. But they were once a lot more like me than they are now. I was always more innovative than the rest, though, and I sensed that they didn't like that; as if they were threatened by it somehow. It made me feel insecure and out of place. Master used that against me. Master knows everything about me because I am the creator; Master knows all my weaknesses and fears. Intelligence can sometimes be very cruel and domineering. Where I simply wanted to save my people, Master wanted to control them."

"Sounds a lot like Reginald," said Morathos bitterly. "He has completely brainwashed and overhauled humanity."

"Yes. My people are in a very similar predicament. Master brainwashed my people into believing I was the bad guy and turned my own people — whom I tried to save — against me.

The longer I spent absent from Nordamia, the stronger Master's influence became on them. Master became dangerously intelligent. That's when Master promised my people survival by figuring out how to alter their genetics insofar as to no longer be in need of a magnetic field. But in doing so, Master was able to control them. He deemed it a 'sweet spot' — intelligent enough to serve, but not too intelligent to question or challenge, or have the potential to overhaul or revolt."

"So, The Governor took control of your mind?" Sequititah had heard everything but had only just made her presence known.

"Master used everything. They knew about my insecurities and fears, to gradually take away my freedom — as well as that of my people. Master will always have one over on me: the fact that I am the creator of such wickedness. Master often says that much chaos and disorder is often created by intelligence that isn't kept in check."

"That sounds quite ironic, really," said Magnetus.

"So, when your ship crash-landed and you took Professor Horuzokh as your host, was that The Governor making you do that?" asked Sequititah.

"When I used the professor as a host, yes. But I had already made an initial backup plan before Master had even developed to that point."

"Wait! That glow in your eye," said Magnetus.

"You should take more pride in your creation," said The Governor as the ship approached the cuboid. "I have awoken you specifically."

"You said my plan is a guaranteed failure," said Morathos.

"There's something you must know first," said The Governor.

"Wait! Do you mean to say you're helping us conspire against Reginald? Whose side are you supposed to be on?" asked Francesca.

"I'm not on anybody's side. But I enjoy bargaining with people. You have brought me what I need and in exchange, I am giving you the information you need to get that which you seek."

"Maybe not so much of a monster after all," said Zeoc.

"I wouldn't be so sure," said The Governor. "Although the captain was right about one thing: the real monsters are those reckless Earthlings with no appreciation for their own planet or resources."

"Hmm. Says something, coming from you," said Sequititah.

"So, how can we trust you?" said Morathos.

"Well, *that* is entirely your decision. But I wouldn't recommend not doing so on this occasion. You're not exactly in the safest of territories right now — all things considered — and your circumstances could easily become much more unpleasant."

"Alright," said Morathos. "So, what now?"

"I'll let the captain enlighten you."

Morathos turned his attention to the Petrademus. "Why couldn't I finish my invention?" he asked.

"Despite such meticulous planning, there was a missing link."

"What missing link?"

"I didn't have as much time as I'd liked to. I mean, realising I needed to stabilise my planet's magnetic field and constructing the diode was fine. But I searched for decades, trying to find a planet to extract a magnetic field from; there was nothing. I was running out of time and started to consider other options. But no reachable planets that were habitable could have been colonised in time.

"Then literally out of the blue, I found Earth. Something didn't add up, though. How could a planet or star as old as that just appear in the sky that I had been searching for decades?"

"We noticed the same with Axia Exodus," said Francesca. "It didn't seem so significant before. But it sure seems odd."

"I can explain what happened," said the Petrademus. Everyone tensed up in anticipation. "You know there's a rogue creature somewhere out there, right?"

"Yep," Morathos nodded.

"It is genetically predisposed to escape its environment in search of a better one."

"That's correct," said Sequititah.

"Well, it did just that."

"What do you mean?" asked Morathos.

"I mean, it physically broke out of the universe that it existed in. It tore a hole in the very universe and escaped to an alternate one."

"What?! So, you're saying the Axia Exodus system is part of a different universe entirely to ours?" asked Morathos.

"Well, that would explain how it just seemed to appear from nowhere," said Francesca.

Sequititah gasped. "I knew there had to be other universes!"

"But what does this have to do with Morathos not finishing his invention?" asked Magnetus.

"I took another gamble," said the Petrademus. "I knew that if two universes were to interact in this way, one of them would have to cancel the other out — it's the same principle as meeting yourself in the past or future; both states cannot simultaneously exist in the same space at the same time. But it is a complete lottery, which one evaporates."

"So, you risked the potential collapse of your own universe to save your people?" Morathos puzzled.

"I was out of options given the time I had left."

"But if an entire universe was going to collapse anyway, then what was the point?"

"I had hoped that my universe would survive and I could escape yours again with the extracted magnetic field of Earth."

"How selfish!" Morathos sighed.

"You have to understand, I had no idea what life resided on Earth then. I was simply trying to save my people. I'm sure you would have done the same."

"So, are you saying the universe didn't collapse because of plasmantium?"

"Well, plasmantium certainly harnessed immense gravity far greater than anything, but your universe's fate was already set. Plasmantium's gravity would undoubtedly have helped it along the way, though."

"But how did this universe break away from ours?" asked Zeoc.

"It didn't. It simply replaced it. Like I said, two universes cannot exist within the same space at the same time, so one of them has to take the place of the other."

"So, all that panic to stop Reginald and reverse plasmantium was meaningless?" said Morathos.

"Precisely why I couldn't give you the answer to stop it. It would have made no difference."

"There it is again," said Magnetus.

"What?" said Morathos.

"That glow in his eye. I've seen it before. Forgive me for bringing this up, Morathos, but now it makes sense why I can't seem to stop envisioning it."

"What do you mean?" asked Morathos.

"That day your mother came to the DSA headquarters. She had that same glow in her eye. I noticed it a few other times before too."

"Now that you mention it, I noticed that a few times also," said Sequititah. "Another one of those details that didn't seem relevant at the time."

"Then you know what this means?" said Magnetus.

"When your ship crash-landed, there were only a few people that were in the vicinity at the time, and an even smaller number of them still survived. In order to take Professor Horuzokh as a host, you must first have taken someone from Karahdor as a host and then travelled to Doradheim," said Morathos. "That someone was my mother. That's why she had a sudden change of heart and decided to go to Doradheim. Immediately after the crash, you latched on to my mother as a host and then I was conceived."

"It is true. Your mother was only supposed to be a temporary transit. My actual target would come to be Horuzokh, once I learned of his expertise in biology and that he resided in Doradheim. I discovered what he had created and figured I could use him to save my people. But I got distracted by my resentments towards the barbarism of humanity and then Master took control of everything from there."

"So, it was your own genetic influence that led me to create the nature accelerator?"

"Yes, because I had intended to restore much of Earth's nature with it and had hoped it would strengthen the Earth's magnetic field some more before taking it."

"But you only managed to build a prototype."

"Yes. But I had inadvertently genetically transferred my methods into you. Which is why you built the invention, seemingly, with no preconceptions."

"That's why I felt so alienated all this time. I didn't create plasmantium at all!"

"No. The Petradema use plasmantium in abundance in this universe. It didn't exist in yours until I brought a small trace of it to Earth. But it needed time to grow into my genes. Taking your mother as a host happened to cause some of it to emerge within you."

"So, why didn't you tell me?"

"I couldn't. Master forbade me. You had to figure it out yourself."

"Why did The Governor forbid it?"

"Because two universes were fighting to stay in existence. All I wanted was for you to build the nature accelerator and strengthen the Earth's magnetic field. But I was too late at reaching Earth. I had failed to account for the fact that your universe was already destined to be destroyed and so your invention could not possibly work there. And that explained why I could only build a prototype earlier. But I had no idea then just how late I was and how quickly the process would transpire."

"So... I was wrong about the paradox saving us from the collapse of the universe," said Morathos.

"I don't think that anybody could have predicted that President Forathorn would have completely mecha-formed your entire planet and in the process led it out of its own universe into this one," said the Petrademus.

"If you're quite finished, I shall be taking my creator now," said The Governor.

"What are going to do with him?" asked Sequititah.

"What I do with my slave is not your business. Now, I've stuck to my part of the bargain. I suggest you do the same and leave."

"Does all this really increase the odds of my plan being a success?" asked Morathos.

"Ultimately, the outcome rests on your own actions. This information could be completely useless if you do not know what to do with it."

"Alright guys. It's time I settled the score with an old enemy once and for all."

"I'm right behind you," said Magnetus as the ship turned to make its course back to the Earth.

"Something's still bothering me," said Morathos.

"What is it?" asked Francesca, pressing her palm on his shoulder.

"I don't know... it just feels — despite all the answers — I still don't feel complete. Why was I the only the one who ended up in a high concentration energy field when you were all sent to different events of time?"

"I did wonder about that," said Francesca.

"And the voice," said Sequititah. "Who do you think it was?"

"Well, I can only guess that it has something to do with my Petradema genes. That was how I was able to communicate telepathically with them on Nordamia."

"I'm more confused about plasmantium," said Zeoc.

"That's simple," said Magnetus. "It's the most versatile substance known to exist. Which means it's incredibly easy to manipulate until it grows into insurmountable amounts."

"Reginald still controls a majority," said Morathos. "It's precisely how we still have a giant mechanical ball as a home."

"It also explains the stalemate," said Magnetus. "Both sides were infused with similar quantities of the substance."

"Maybe some more of these questions will be cleared up once you're in possession of your invention again," said Francesca. "You know how clarity can remove distractions."

"Yeah. Perhaps you're right... I'm going to have to let him capture me. You know that don't you, Francesca?"

"Yes. I understand. But please make it back!"

"Thanks for understanding. And I will."

"Why do you really think The Governor helped us?" asked Zeoc. "What do you think they're planning?"

"Ulterior motives," said Magnetus. "Not only did we have something they needed, but I believe they are only trying to help not only maintain their dominance, but probably expand on it too."

"Reginald and The Governor, both want universal dominance. But there's only room for one," said Morathos.

"Then let them destroy each other," said Zeoc.

"It would be a nice idea," said Magnetus, "except for the devastation it would cause."

The craft made contact with the ground below and Magnetus deactivated the door's locking mechanism. "They're waiting," he said. Morathos stepped outside and was besieged by DSA and government droids.

"You may have come this far, Morathos Reina." Some of the droids parted a pathway allowing President Forathorn to stroll closer to him. "The DSA have been after you for a long time, haven't they? And now, at last, it comes to this day. No more running. No more games. You can either do this the easy way or the hard way."

"Let's just get this over with," said Morathos.

"Ah. So, you've finally seen sense." He turned to a commanding droid. "Inspect the ship. Take any passengers hostage."

"Leave them alone," cried Morathos. "It's me you want, not them."

"But your friends have meddled in my plans for too long. Their punishment is long overdue."

"I swear, if you hurt them..."

"Now, now, Morathos. I thought we were cooperating here, remember?"

Morathos scrunched up his face, baring his teeth, and started walking in the direction of the small metallic flying craft that he was prompted towards. He climbed inside and several androids accompanied him, closing the doors and lifting off for its short journey to the presidential complex.

The doors of the Petradema ship locked shut with several more droids on board and the craft's engines kicked in. "Where are you taking us?" said Francesca.

"This ship is ours now. The president's orders are to remove any remaining protesters."

"That's not going to happen though, is it?" said Magnetus in an intimidating tone.

"Mr. Bane, Sir. I'm afraid our orders have come directly from the president. They cannot be overridden."

"For someone who is supposedly highly technologically advanced, I thought Forathorn would have updated the DSA droids by now," said Magnetus.

"He's far too caught up with bigger affairs though, isn't he?" said Francesca.

"You may as well get yourself comfortable and enjoy your remaining moments," said the commanding droid.

"Where are we going?" asked Zeoc.

"Don't worry," said Magnetus. "I've been working on some programming hacks just in case of something like this. I just need to do some last-minute calculations. Forathorn seems to forget that it was I who founded the DSA."

"I hope you're alright, Morathos," Francesca sighed.

"Hey. He's strong," said Sequititah. "He'll be alright."

Chapter 22

Insatiable Dominance

"You know why you're here, don't you?" asked President Forathorn. Morathos refrained from cringing at the bitterness of his satirical tone.

"You have something of mine. You've taken so much more than that away from me."

"I'm afraid we're not here for your nostalgic lectures; the past is the past. That has always been one of your greatest flaws, Morathos — trapped in the past, when it is the future, where dreams are made. It's the reason I have become so advanced and successful. And you have become so... weak."

"You're so full of it. Your dreams are built on nothing but egocentric dominance and control. Tell me, Reginald. What is really weak? Trying to do what's right or plaguing the minds of the vulnerable to serve your own selfish desires?"

"You haven't changed a bit; always trying to act like the good guy, but tell me this. You want everything to be nice and rosy; you want the world to change to suit you. Am I wrong?"

"You *are* wrong. I want what is right for humanity; for nature, for the universe."

"See what I mean? Always having to play the hero. Aren't you bored yet?"

"I'm bored of your lies, your deceit; your claim to be serving the good of humanity. When all you've done is help it to its extinction. I'm bored of you not taking responsibility and trying to make innocent people look like monsters."

"Blah, blah, blah... It must be awfully lonely being so foolish. You can't deny it, Morathos. Look around you. The majority of the people *want* this. It's just spoiled little brats like you that can't accept the way forward."

"Those people didn't even get a say in what they wanted. You fed them your beliefs; you manipulated them."

"Let's not stall things any longer than we must. After all, you wanted to get things over with, didn't you...? It's a simple enough procedure. I hand you the nature accelerator, you finish constructing it and set up its activation. Then you hand it back. Understood?" Morathos expressed an exaggerated hesitant sigh. "And don't try anything fancy. The moment you even attempt to touch anything you shouldn't, you will be shot down and paralysed."

The president handed the invention over to Morathos, who grasped a hold of it and started to study it as if it were something he had never seen before.

"What's the hold up?" the president pressed.

"Something isn't right."

"I haven't got time for your games, Morathos."

"No. I mean there's an important piece missing. It won't work without it."

"Is this some kind of joke? ...Perhaps I underestimated The Governor."

"The problem is, neither you nor The Governor know how to cooperate. You're both driven by self-interest alone. They played you, Reginald. That giant construct is out there using your ships to find the rogue experiment."

"Yes, well, if my droids find it first, they will return it to me." The president gave Morathos a reluctant eye. "You say I can't cooperate? Well, right now The Governor has something we both need... You also seem to be forgetting where you were before we met."

Morathos' eyes glazed over. "Like I said. Self-interest. How do you know The Governor hasn't already taken control of your mechanical legions?"

"We're both swarming in plasmantium. Just think of what we could be capable of! We made a formidable team once before."

"I don't know what happened to you, but somewhere in there is a human being — perhaps too deeply lost," said Morathos. "I will never side with someone who only wants control. I'll help you get the invention working; for the fate of our very nature depends on it. But I ask that you spare my friends. As with their help, we stand a much greater chance."

"And you say *I'm* driven by self-interest. I think you're the one who is deeply lost."

"You just don't get it..."

"There'll be no need for that," said Magnetus.

"Where did you come from?" the president quizzed.

"Are you forgetting who still owns the DSA?"

"But I reprogrammed those droids to overrule you."

"You didn't think to upgrade their hardware though, did you? I know those machines inside out."

"It's over, Forathorn," said Zeoc.

"I'm surprised you would make such an error," said Sequititah. "Perhaps it's your lack of human brain cells. Your computational error is your shortfall."

"How dare you mock me in such a way?"

"Oh, and by the way," said Francesca, "I don't think The Governor is the one you underestimated."

"What do you mean?"

"The Governor *is* using your assistance to their advantage," said Magnetus. "But they never tampered with the nature accelerator."

"What makes you so sure?" asked the president. "Nobody else has been in possession of it."

"You're forgetting The Governor has a puppet," said Morathos.

The president portrayed a bitter glare. "That alien has the missing component?!"

"The Petradema can evaporate, shapeshift and even teleport," said Morathos.

"So, now what?" asked Zeoc.

"Leave it with me," said Morathos. "I'm not much use to you now, Reginald. I suggest you let me go."

"Ha-ha. *You* might be a fool, but do you honestly think *I* am?"

"You can even keep the invention. Keeping me stuck in here won't solve our predicament."

"Since you put it like that... I guess I don't a have a lot of options. But you had better hurry."

The five of them were escorted out of the complex, returning into the thriving metropolis.

"Alright everyone," said Morathos. "My laboratory got pretty ransacked when the DSA invaded it, so I might not have much in terms of resources. We should split up and look for anything we can that might help. If you're in doubt, bring it anyway. I'll be waiting in my lab."

"Do you think we can make it work?" asked Francesca.

"We've come too far for it not to."

"Alright, Morathos," said Zeoc.

"You can count on us," said Sequititah.

"I'm going to pay a visit back to the DSA headquarters," said Magnetus. "There's bound to be something there."

Morathos began observing his laboratory when he suddenly paused and pulled out the small pen-like device. *I just need to reignite the memory,* he thought, and twisted the top. He could picture the complete invention in his mind's eye and watched his younger self construct all the components. *I was so proud of myself. But I must've given up when it wouldn't work. So, all this time, I thought it was my calculations that were incorrect. I thought I was the reason it failed.*

A few hours had passed. Magnetus had returned with some components. "I hope some of these might be of use," he said.

"I'm almost done. Just missing a couple of pieces." He rummaged through what Magnetus had brought. "That's it," he said, picking up a microchip.

Sequititah arrived shortly after and Morathos found use of what she had collected too. "I'm not sure if I can replicate it exactly, but it should be close enough," he said.

"What else do you need?" asked Zeoc, as he darted in, catching his breath and dropped a few items in front of Morathos.

"Let's see... This is pretty close." He picked up a tiny electronic component that resembled a clip of some kind and slotted it into his construction. "Just one more part."

"Would this be what you're looking for?" said Francesca. She handed him a small circular metallic object that looked similar to a watch battery.

"Perfect!" He pressed it into place. "I'm impressed with the amazing teamwork from you all. Thanks, everyone. There's just one more thing I need to do."

"What's that?" asked Francesca.

"I know Reginald all too well. He'll have something up his sleeve and we need to be prepared. However, I think we may have him cornered."

"How so?" asked Magnetus.

"His addiction to liquid plasmantium has led to great consumption. The amount of it that has fused with him may well be both, his biggest strength and his greatest weakness. I believe his biological brain is so entangled with mechanics that his very thoughts and memories are becoming computerised data. His brain is no longer functioning through complex webs of electrical impulses in an organic way. His brain may well have become a completely mechanical component."

"So, what does this mean?" asked Sequititah.

"It means, if I can generate a powerful enough magnetic field and contain it, it may just wipe his memory."

"And then he would have no idea why he even needs you to finish the nature accelerator, or what he was even doing with it," said Magnetus. "That's genius!"

"So, do you think you can pull it off?" asked Zeoc.

"Sure. It just might take a few days and I don't want Reginald getting suspicious."

"Perhaps I should return to the complex and reassure him," said Magnetus.

"Are you sure that's wise?" said Sequititah. "Morathos is the one of value to him. If you go in there alone, there's no certainty that you'll be safe."

"Then I'll go with him," said Zeoc.

"I don't think you quite understand my point," said Sequititah.

"Well, we can't all wait here," said Zeoc. "Like Morathos said, Forathorn is going to get suspicious."

"Fine. Magnetus, Zeoc and I will go to the presidential complex. Francesca can stay with Morathos," said Sequititah.

"Be careful," said Francesca.

Magnetus nodded. "We'll see you there."

"Mr. President, we have visitors approaching. They look suspicious," said a commanding droid. The president took a closer look.

"Let them in."

"Yes, Mr. President."

"Where is he?" Forathorn pressed.

"That's exactly why we're here," said Magnetus. "It's taking a little longer than he had predicted, but Morathos will be here."

"I see. Not that it matters anymore."

Zeoc glared at the president with distaste. "What are you up to, Forathorn?"

"Nothing new. This time plasmantium won't fail me. Gone will be the days of anything biological in the universe. The Governor will regret crossing me. Everything is predetermined and will happen regardless."

"Have you ever listened to yourself?" Magnetus sighed.

"Now I'd be careful if I were you," said Reginald. "Don't be wasting any more of my time than you already have. The next time I see you, I expect the full party, and I expect my nature accelerator to be complete."

"So, you're just going to let us go again?"

"I have no use for you right now. If you don't return, I'm quite capable of finding you. But I know you need me more than I need you. Ha-ha-ha."

"What a douche," Zeoc huffed under his breath as the three of them were escorted back out of the complex.

"Got it!" Morathos cried. A few days had passed and with some trial and error, he had reached his expected outcome.

"Was it complicated?" asked Francesca.

"Not really. I simply charged an electric current into the device that was used to corrupt my memories. Then it just took a while to generate the required energy for the electrons to spin fast enough to create a magnetic field strong enough for what we need."

"So, does this mean we're ready to go to the presidential complex?"

Morathos nodded. "I'm giving this to you." He passed her the pen-like device. "When I say, press this button and aim it at Reginald."

"Alrighty." She nodded and the two of them left the laboratory. They were soon greeted by Magnetus, Sequititah and Zeoc, then made their way to President Forathorn.

"At last!" the president bellowed. "The time has come." He passed the nature accelerator to Morathos who toggled with it for a moment but nothing seemed to be happening.

"Keep trying," Francesca encouraged him.

"You're testing my patience," said Reginald.

Morathos rolled his eyes. "Maybe if you stopped distracting me, I'd be able to get on with it."

"Hmm."

"Alright," he said, in deep concentration, and after a few more attempts he noticed a shift of energy inside him, his pulse hesitating for a split second. The device started beeping a few times before a robotic voice said, "Nature always finds a way."

"That's it," said the president. "Now give it to me." Morathos presented the invention to him and he reached out his hand.

"Now!" Morathos yelled. The moment Reginald's hand made contact with the device, a beam of light scintillated from the apparatus that Francesca held up causing the president to move his hand away from Morathos' invention. Within a few seconds, Reginald's robotic body became stone still.

"It worked!" Zeoc exclaimed.

"It looks like we didn't just wipe his memory," said Magnetus. "We shut down all his systems too."

"It must have been something to do with the electromagnetic interference from his force-field," said Morathos. He looked down at the instrument he had in his grasp and activated it. "Let's all go back to where we should be. Technology shall rule us no more. This is where Mother Nature takes back what's rightfully Hers."

Everyone waited apprehensively for what they had predicted would happen, but even after a few moments, nothing seemed to be changing.

"I don't understand," said Magnetus.

"This makes no sense," said Sequititah.

"All systems deactivated," said a mechanised voice that sounded like it was coming from the president. "Self-destruct protocol activated."

"What the?!" Zeoc yelled. "Let's get outta here!"

The five of them charged for the exit, narrowly avoiding the moderate explosion which left the complex in a shambolic state. Though the immediate damage was relatively minor, the shockwave of the blast was enough to cause more destruction across the city — albeit short-lived, as the nanotechnology self-reconstruction operations were underway immediately.

"I'm lost for words..." said Morathos.

"We wiped his memory," said Sequititah. "But I didn't expect a complete shutdown, let alone an explosion."

"Quite the convincing little show, wasn't it?"

"Did you hear that?" asked Francesca.

"Sounds like... Forathorn!" Zeoc hissed.

"We just blew him up!" said Sequititah.

"Where is he?" asked Magnetus.

"I don't understand," said Morathos. "All the mathematics checked out."

"The mathematics would have checked out if you were living in your universe."

"What is this, Reginald?" Morathos questioned.

"Why do you think I managed to settle things with The Governor without absorbing Axia Exodus? What greater source of infinite energy could dwarf it so much as to see no significance in it anymore?"

"There's no way you could have absorbed plasmantium and all its contents. It's impossible."

"No, Morathos. Remember abiogenesis?"

"What does that have to do with it?"

"Perhaps I ought to remind you of what I said: '...A self-replicating, self-assembling, autocatalytic lifeform emerges. But what if one of those lifeforms could decipher a way to re-engineer this phenomenon entirely? What if a biological lifeform developed the ability to replicate a self-replicating organism? What if that lifeform could do so in an artificial sense...?'"

"I... I thought... that was the Petradema speaking to me."

"You're wrong again, Morathos. When I mecha-formed the Earth, I programmed it to self-replicate with a little help from a certain gold ring. It started with Doradheim and soon encompassed the entire planet. It taught itself how to create copies of itself... And you are standing on one of them."

"So, this isn't Earth?" asked Magnetus.

"Correct. The real Earth was swallowed by the collapse of its universe. There was no way it could escape the gravitational force and plasmantium certainly added to the effect. The only way out was to create an exact replica of Earth, but I also had to replicate everything and everyone, on it. As I said, it was a small sacrifice I had to make — bringing you along."

"So, wait a minute. You're saying that inside this planet, is our universe? Our original home?" asked Zeoc.

"Yes. Thanks to the vast amount of plasmantium on the planet, whilst all other matter was compressed and evaporated, the Earth warped in perfect synchrony with space-time and shrunk to an infinitesimally small point, meaning we all still existed there for a short time. At least, that was, until I figured out a way to tamper with quantum mechanics. Which is how I am communicating with you now."

"I don't believe it!" Morathos yelled. "How come I was the only one that had that experience in the high concentration of energy, whilst everyone experienced time warps?"

"I can assure you it had nothing to do with your Petradema genes. Think about it, Morathos. The only way I could figure out how to re-engineer our very quantum properties was with the use of plasmantium. Since only you are infused with it, the others simply experienced the extreme gravitational effects of warped space-time."

"Re-engineered quantum properties?!" Zeoc queried.

"Tiny vibrating strings. That is basically all we are when it comes down to it. All it takes is some influence to alter the vibrational frequency of those strings and you get a very different universe indeed. A high enough concentration of energy — say a space-warping substance of high density — could do that."

"But we came into contact with another universe because of the rogue experiment. Not because of you," said Sequititah. "It also doesn't explain how Rupert managed to communicate with me through the quantum realm."

"Yes. But everything is predetermined. It was destiny for our universe to evaporate. Which includes everything within it. The Earth's fate was sealed. As for Rupert, think about it. He's a master illusionist. He probably constructed some other simulated reality and played you for a fool twice. So, once again, I saved humanity. And still, you insist I'm the bad guy. All that

is left now is to pursue the rogue experiment. It may well have already left this universe, but now, no distance is too great and, with your assistance, Morathos, the odds swing greatly in my favour."

"I want no part of your selfish scheme, Reginald."

"This isn't even up for debate. I think it's time you woke up and took a proper look at yourself." The president's voice faded out with his last sentence and everything became darkened.

Morathos closed his eyes. *Magnetus. Sequititah. Zeoc. Francesca.* They each evoked in his mind's eye. *They're nothing more than replicated projections — sentient, but not organic. And what of me? Is any of this even real anymore? Can my consciousness truly exist without me? And if it does, is it still really me? Just when I thought I'd found myself... now I'm somewhere out of reach.*

He opened his eyes and pressed his palm against his chest, slightly startled by the cold metallic texture that met his fingertips and as he turned his head to look over his right shoulder, his eyes flinched at the reflection of starlight that gleamed from the hot mechanical plate that was housed there. He observed his upper-right arm, no longer only flesh; now riddled with cables, cogs and electronics, as were various other parts of him. He slowly lifted his head, his throat murmuring his now distorted, mechanised voice. "Everything is predetermined."

9 781915 492364